Louis James is at present Senior Lecturer in English and American Literature at the University of Kent at Canterbury. Born in 1933, he was educated in Africa and England, and in 1952 went as Open Scholar to Jesus College, Oxford, where he later received a doctorate for his work in nineteenth-century popular literature. Since then he has taught at various universities in England, in the United States, in the Caribbean, and in Africa. Besides more conventional academic interests, he has written and broadcast on Commonwealth literature and various aspects of nineteenth-century culture, in particular that of the working class. He is editor of *The Islands in Between* (1968), a collection of studies in West Indian literature. He lives in a house near Canterbury, which only just contains four young and noisy children.

Louis James

FICTION FOR THE WORKING MAN
1830–50

*A study of the literature produced
for the working classes in early
Victorian urban England*

PENGUIN UNIVERSITY BOOKS

Penguin Books Ltd, Harmondsworth, Middlesex, England
Penguin Books Inc., 7110 Ambassador Road, Baltimore, Maryland 21207, U.S.A.
Penguin Books Australia Ltd, Ringwood, Victoria, Australia

First published by Oxford University Press 1963
Published in Penguin University Books 1974

Copyright © Louis James, 1973

Made and printed in Great Britain by
Richard Clay (The Chaucer Press) Ltd, Bungay, Suffolk
Set in Monotype Garamond

To

JILL

With my love

Contents

1. The Emergence of a New Lower-class Culture in the Towns   1

2. From Politics to Fiction, 1830–40   14

3. Currents in Popular Publishing, 1840–50   32

4. The Beginnings of a New Type of Popular Fiction: Plagiarisms of Dickens   51

5. Further Literary Influences: the Tale of Terror and the Historical Novel   83

6. The Paradox of the Domestic Story   114

7. The Contribution of the Upper Classes: Religious, Moral, and Instructive   135

8. Fiction from America and France   151

9. The Impact of the Towns   170

Appendices

I Some Minor Poets and Poetry   201

II London Publishers of Penny-issue Fiction, 1830–50   212

III Check-list of Penny-issue Novels Partially Listed in or Omitted from Montague Summers's *Gothic Bibliography*   216

Supplementary Notes   228

Bibliographies

1. Libraries and Private Collections   232

2. Manuscripts and Typescripts   232

3. Parliamentary Papers   233

4. Primary Sources   234

5. Secondary Sources   246

Index   255

List of Illustrations

1. Contemporary picture of a lower-class library (1848)

2. *Comic Observations of Life* (*Grant's Illustrations*)

(a) Mr Pickwick is robbed
(b) A dance in the slums

3. *Dickens and His Imitators*

(a) Pickwick Club: 'Boz'
(b) Cadgers' Club: Anon.
(c) Pickwick Club: 'Bos'
(d) Wonderful Discovery Club: 'Poz'

4. *The Gothic Novel*

(a) The female Wizard presenting the Magic Helmet to Hieronymo
(b) 'A flight of stairs was immediately revealed'
(c) 'Heaven,' said Caroline, 'will not desert the innocent'
(d) 'I am here, then,' sobbed Flora, 'in the lair of the tiger'

5. *The Historical Novel*

(a) 'The black waters of the Fleet-ditch were clearly visible'
(b) 'The conflict that now ensued was terrific'
(c) 'My liege,' cried Isaac, 'you see before you a broken-hearted father'

6. *Decorative Effect in Illustration*

'He hurried with all the precipitation in his power towards the main road'

7. *The Domestic Story*

(a) 'There was a charm about the mellow glorious voice of Adeline, which tempted him to linger'
(b) 'Emily trimmed the lamp, and then taking the manuscripts from her bosom, read the contents aloud to Patty'
(c) 'Beauteous damsel, banish your fears'
(d) 'The tall and majestic form of a woman rushed precipitately in between them'

8. Ela (*1839–41*)

9. *The Fortunes of Ada*

(a) 'A deed of blood!'
(b) 'The child of the dead – save her!'
(c) 'To the wicked can there be a more terrible apparition than youth, beauty, and innocence?'

10. *The Theatre and the Novel*

(a) Madame Celeste as the Dumb Arab Boy
(b) 'Shock not mine ears with thine odious vows, in every one of which is pollution'

11. *Nautical Novel and Criminal Romance*

(a) 'Nothing but death surrounded us on every side'
(b) Marian is seized by Clarrington

12. *The Rich and the Poor*: The Mysteries of London

(a) Richard Markham becomes Regent of Castelicicala
(b) Woman in a workhouse, refused permission to see her dying husband
(c) The public executioner initiates his deformed son into his trade
(d) Two luxurious beauties talk of love as they disrobe

Abbreviations Used

B.M.	British Museum
D.N.B.	*Dictionary of National Biography*
I.L.N.	*Illustrated London News*
L.J.	*London Journal*
N. & Q.	*Notes and Queries*
P.M.L.A.	*Publications of the Modern Language Association of America*
P.P.	*Parliamentary Papers, Select Committee Reports, &c.*
P.P.L.	*Parliamentary Papers, Public Libraries* (1849)
PLACE ADD. MSS.	F. Place, collection of MSS., British Museum
Q.R.	*Quarterly Review*
R.N.L.	*Romancist and Novelist's Library*
S.H.	Somerset House, London
S.S.L.	*Journal of the Royal Statistical Society of London*
W.R.	*Westminster Review*

Acknowledgements

With the exception of nos. 2(b) and 2(d), which appear by courtesy of the British Museum, and no. 2(c), which appears by courtesy of the Bodleian Library, Oxford, the illustrations are all reproduced from photographs by A. Marshall, Esq., of Hull University Library Photographic Department.

METHODS OF REFERENCES

All books are published in London, unless it is otherwise stated. The date given for books published in parts is that of the work's completion; title-pages were issued with the last number. Where no pagination exists in a book I have made my own, in small roman numerals, starting from the title-page. The penny-issue novels discussed have erratic spelling, grammar, and pagination; do not blame the author or printer for curiosities in quotations. Titles and names of characters sometimes vary during the course of a book – I have given the most common name and, wherever possible, the title appearing on the title-page.

Supplementary notes to certain features in the text will be found on pages 228–31.

Introduction

THIS is primarily the study of a *literature*; the literature published for the working classes in the towns of England from about 1830 – when the delayed effects of the paper-making machine and the rotary press drastically reduced the cost of publication and thus made possible a new phase of mass literature – to 1850, when the 'popular press' had begun to find its feet in the new field. It has been based on a wider range of cheap fiction than has ever before, I believe, been available to a single researcher in this subject. Its aims are therefore different from those of Professor Richard Altick, Mr R. K. Webb and Mr Raymond Williams, who have been pre-occupied primarily with the working-class reader. Nor does it attempt to be a sociological study in the manner of Professor Richard Hoggart's *The Uses of Literacy*. However, it has been written with the social, economic, and historical background always in mind, and with a strict attention to chronology, since this period, often treated as a unity, saw the situations changing even from year to year. This I believe also differentiates the work from previous literary studies in this field.

While the works examined are generally of too low a quality to be usefully judged except by their own limited standards, this study is of importance to the literary student. For by revealing the extent and nature of the field, it throws new light on the lower levels of literature that inevitably shifts the perspective of the total scene. This is particularly so with Dickens, who is finally divested of the myth of a universal readership; but the contemporary significance of the Romantics, Scott, Ainsworth, and other upper-class writers is also clarified. The study should turn scholars to reconsider certain aspects of upper-class Victorian literature – in particular the importance of French and American fiction, and domestic romance.

While concerned with literature, the study has wider implications. The sociologist, for example, while he will not surmise from the analysis of *Ada the Betrayed* that orphans, seized from the flames of burning smithies and kept by the murderers of their fathers, are a common part of the Victorian scene, will find much to interest him concerning the imaginations, moral attitudes, and sensibilities of the readers who made it one of the bestsellers of the century. Moreover, since the period covered is crucial to the emergence of mass literature in the modern industrial context, it poses a number of contemporary questions. Can popular culture survive? Did working-class cultural aspirations of the 1830s fail because of commercial exploitation, from misdirection, through a natural inertia of the popular mind, or because those attaining genuine cultural standards inevitably cut themselves off from the masses?

The pursuit of this research has involved a number of problems. There was first the question of limits. It was with regret that the work was confined mainly to the reading of the urban areas, since past studies have neglected the country in favour of the towns, for which there is the most material available. However, I doubt if the country areas can be adequately dealt with in a single work: the situation varied so widely in various parts that it is best left to local historians close to the ground in their own areas. Moreover, I wished to concentrate on the towns as centres from which the publications came, and whose developing cultural life was the deciding factor in the evolution of cheap publications.

More difficult was the decision on how to limit the literature to that for the working classes, an important point because of the very mass of material involved. Also, since it would have been unreal to consider it by upper-class standards, certain literary values, based on the popular traditions in which it appeared, had to be formulated, again demanding a known background. But what *were* 'the working classes'? The factory hand and the miner certainly, but where should one place the small tradesman, or educated and generally respected 'lower-class' men like William Lovett and S. T. Hall? There was a large and growing intermediary class. What was 'the reading of the lower classes'? Starting with *The Poor Man's Guardian* and *Cleave's Penny Gazette* we move up the range until with *Chambers's Edinburgh Journal* and *The Family Herald* one realizes that some periodicals span two fields. Then, the young Rossetti read *Ada the Betrayed*, while workmen in coffee houses read *Blackwood's*. There is no neat definition. Fortunately, the problem is less acute here than it would be even ten years later, for the working classes were closely unified by political and class feeling, and poverty meant that the price of literature largely determined the class of the reader, the poor buying the penny part, the middle classes feeling cheap literature had a social stigma. We are therefore reasonably safe to take as 'lower class', literature published at a penny, and some at three half-pence, largely omitting *Chambers's Journal* after 1840, and *The Family Herald*.

Only a moiety of this literature has survived. It was printed on easily torn paper, and the quality of illustration and repetitive story left no encouragement to readers to preserve the weekly instalments once they had been read. There were too many uses for paper. The British Museum, although Panizzi appeared on the scene in 1837, had no interest in these works, especially as they were not copyright, and today their scarcity gives the few surviving copies inflated value. In spite of constant acquisitions by libraries here and in America, the researcher needs patience, willingness to travel, and a modicum of good fortune.

My good fortune began with the great kindness shown me in the North Library of the British Museum when, following up a hint in *The Times Literary Supplement*, I was allowed to catalogue the then unlisted case of books in the library stack left to the Museum by a music-hall artist, 'Barry Ono'. This proved a mine of interesting penny-issue novels and juvenile fiction. Then another helper, Mr E. S. Turner, put me on a trail which led to a number of private collections.

I first knocked on the scratched and grimy door of a condemned house in an East End square. Here Mr A. W. Lawson, although now wealthy, remained in the squalor of his earlier days as an East End waste-paper collector. A magnificent collection of Victorian periodical literature was piled, dusty and damp, around the walls. Although I do not think he ever grasped who I was, he showed me the greatest kindness, and I worked many days in his dark sitting-room, examining unique book after unique book, dreading the day when I would not be admitted. At last the end came – the collection was sold by a visiting bookseller to the University of California, and soon afterwards Mr Lawson was killed in a car accident. Not even the memory of a maggot, intercepted crawling up a grimy cup of flat orangeade I was offered, dims my gratitude to the recluse who so kindly allowed an intruder into his strange world.

Another person who gave me help was Mr Frank Algar. Mr

Algar shut himself in even more completely, living in a world of books which he would not allow to be disturbed by wireless or newspapers. He taught me much about research. He would sit back in front of the fire, demolishing point after point of other people's scholarship, fixing me with a dark eye, and interjecting a fierce 'Oh, yes!' Alas, he died recently of cancer, and his immense bibliography of eighteenth-century books will probably never see publication. His fine collection is being dispersed.

Those who have given help are too many for me to hope to record. I give my thanks to Mr R. A. Brimmell; Mr F. Jones, and the long-suffering staff of the British Museum North Library; Mrs Joy Jones, who did the typing; Professor G. E. T. Mayfield and the Hull University Adult Education Department for giving me time for research; Mr A. Reynolds; Mr R. E. J. Rouse; Mr Wilbur J. Smith; Mr J. I. M. Stewart; Mr Graham Storey; Dr J. M. S. Tompkins; the Rev. E. J. Tongue; Mr E. S. Turner; Professor R. K. Webb; Dr Bryan Wilson; Mr R. C. Russell; and the many others I have not mentioned. In particular I am grateful to Mr Frank Pettingell and Mr J. V. B. Stewart Hunter who opened their houses to me, giving me the run of their fine collections. Last and first must come Professor Kathleen Tillotson and Mr John Jones. Both have given encouragement and expert help however pressed they were with other commitments. Without them this book could not have been written.

No one will be more aware than myself of its inadequacies, its omissions, the wrongly placed emphases. But in literary criticism there is no absolute truth, and the time comes when one must entrust the work to the indulgence of the readers.

Hall Cottage, South Kelsey
22 June 1962

SECOND IMPRESSION

This edition includes extensive corrections. I would like to thank the many correspondents who have given information and advice.

University of South Carolina
3 December 1969

I

The Emergence of a New
Lower-class Culture in the Towns

In the descriptions of life and society, as we read them in these papers, the manners of the lower classes in the *country* are not, of course, represented. We can judge only here of the people of the great towns – a tremendous society moving around us, and unknown to us – a vast mass of active, stirring life, in which the upper and the lower classes form an insignificant speck, and of which we (taking for granted that WE applies to both writer and reader) are quite ignorant and uninformed. An English gentleman knows as much about the people of Lapland or California as he does of the aborigines of The Seven Dials or the natives of Wapping. . .[1]

So wrote Thackeray in 1838, holding up for the readers of *Fraser's Magazine* the lower-class periodicals he had bought for half-a-crown. What surprised Thackeray was not the existence of the immense working-class communities in the towns – these must have been evident to anyone moving outside his own front door – but the fact that they had their own distinct culture and literature. Moreover, it was not just a continuation of the old popular cultures which expressed themselves in broadsheets, chapbooks, and popular drama – it was new, and had formed itself in the past decade. It was quite cut off from the middle and upper classes.

This culture had been formed by the Enclosure Acts and by the Industrial Revolution. The enclosure of the open fields and the coming of small land-owners had begun first, breaking up the integrated village communities and driving dispossessed labourers to swell the new industrial townships. But even in the towns, at the turn of the century, there had been a certain unity, for many factory owners were those who had risen by their industry from lower-class origins. It was in the 1820s that a second generation of employers were taking over, men who had no contact with the

1. 'Half-a-crown's worth of Cheap Knowledge'. *Fraser's Magazine*, XVII, March 1838, p. 280.

social life of their employees. There was an increasing number of workers, too, who knew nothing but the towns, and from the chaos and squalor of the mushroom townships were finding their own new ways of life. These were also becoming aware of their own position and unity, and were reaching out for their share of the new prosperity industry was bringing. About this time they ceased being called 'the poor' and were referred to as 'the working classes'. 'It is *leze majestie* now to speak of the lower orders',[1] grumbled Christopher North in *Blackwood's*, and the *Examiner* noted with amazement that whereas in the past the lower-class men who had won distinction 'have only rejoiced in escaping from their order', Detroisier, an educated and talented labourer, was proud of his status.[2]

A most important part in the coming of the new urban working classes was played by the increase of popular literacy. It has been generally accepted that a significant working-class reading public came into being only with Forster's Education Act of 1870, but major popular educational movements were taking place as early as the beginning of the eighteenth century. The greatest single influence on this was Locke's teaching about the nature of personality. In his *Essay Concerning Human Understanding* (1690–1706), and *Some Thoughts concerning Education* (1699), he propounded the widely accepted theory that the child was born without any innate ideas, with his mind a 'clean sheet' waiting to be made or marred under the hand of the teacher. While Rousseau with *Emile* (1762), reacted against the imposition of ideas on the growing child, he formulated his very protest into a scheme of education, and again placed great importance on the growing mind. The major philosophers after Locke, whether economic philosophers like Adam Smith (*Wealth of Nations*, 1776), and Malthus (*Essay on Population*, 1798), social reformers like Robert Owen, or Utilitarians like Bentham and Mill, all saw popular education as an important part of their schemes for an improved State.

Education therefore was of crucial importance to anyone concerned with philanthropy or religious work, and the eighteenth century has been described as the 'Age of Benevolence' for such activities. Those in the Evangelical movement, from the Anglican layman Robert Nelson (active 1699–1715) to Hannah More (d.

---

1. 'Noctes Ambrosianae', XXXII, 1832, p. 848.
2. 1220, 1831, p. 385.

1833), set up hundreds of Charity Schools throughout England and Wales. By 1750 these had some 30,000 children in their care. The Methodist movement had a powerful means of popular education in the class meeting, groups formed for communal devotion but which often also met for reading and discussion. From the time of Wesley, the Methodists provided a wide range of cheap literature, and they were active in the Sunday School movement when it began. The latter started in 1780, when Robert Raikes and Thomas Stokes started teaching the children they found wandering aimlessly about the streets of Gloucester on Sundays. Sunday Schools could draw upon both pupils and teachers who were employed during the week, they could use temporary accommodation, and the estimated cost of teaching a pupil for one year was two shillings. By 1830 they were educating numbers variously estimated at between 800,000 and 1,500,000.

Sunday Schools opened new possibilities for popular education. Another development of immense importance was the introduction of the monitorial system, where the teacher taught senior scholars, who in turn educated those less advanced. By the means of using 'monitors' a small staff could teach and keep in order an immense number of pupils, low as the standard was. Anglican educationalists hailed Andrew Bell, a clergyman, as the inventor of this system, and founded The National Society (1811), while the nonconformists, following the Quaker Joseph Lancaster, founded The British and Foreign School Society (1813). In the mid-1830s they were educating about 1,000,000 and 70,000 respectively.[1] It was to these two societies that the government looked for a basis for national education when making its first grant in 1833. There were also a large number of other societies engaged in lower-class education, including the adventurous Ragged Schools, which provided for the unwashed and ragged urchins of the city streets.

These societies were organized by the middle and upper classes, and received considerable notice – many working-class parents, however, preferred to pay about a pound a year and have their children taught in an independent private school. These were of greatly varying type and quality, and included dame schools for infants and evening schools for those working in the day. Many teachers would not be as well qualified as Thomas Cooper, who, largely self-taught, at the age of twenty-one ended his apprentice-

1. *P.P., State of Education*, 1834 (572), IX, sec. 1876.

ship as a shoemaker to open his own school in Lincoln.[1] But if the standards in these schools were often appallingly low, they taught rudiments that could be built upon later. A government survey of Manchester education was found to have noted only two thirds of the private education actually in progress, and its extent was almost certainly underestimated elsewhere.

Finally, we may notice adult education which, from obscure beginnings in Bala, Merionethshire, in 1811, by the mid-century was teaching an estimated 3,500 adult poor to read – the number who attended without being judged to learn anything was much larger. Reading and discussion groups also grew out of Methodist class meetings, as has already been mentioned, from Societies of Odd-fellows, Mutual Aid Societies, and from the spontaneous interest which formed lower-class gatherings such as those discovered by William Lovett and George Henry Lewes when they came to London. Some of these branched out into larger ventures. From the formation of the first Mechanics Institutes in 1823, Athenaeums, Polytechnics, People's Instruction Societies and similar institutions proliferated. Some of them were large and well organized. Many were small, rather pompous village affairs like John Poole's satirized 'Little-Peddlington Universal-Knowledge Society', whose crest, Minerva with an owl, had been designed from a penny-piece Britannia and a cockatoo, the only bird available as a model. The secretary told Poole:

We have meetings—*conversyshonys*—twice a-week; a library, too: Murray's 'Grammar', Entick's 'Dictionary', Guthrie's 'Geography', and, (besides other useful works) we have the 'Penny Magazine', complete *from—the—very—first*.[2]

The great power behind the Mechanics Institutes was the Utilitarian movement, as the title of the society publishing *The Penny Magazine* – The Society for the Diffusion of Useful Knowledge – would suggest. Information was more than interesting, it was *useful*, indeed essential to the man or woman advancing into the era of enlightenment and progress, and we find Christopher North grumbling that 'now-a-days, reading is placed on the list of necessaries before eating'.[3] While this Utilitarian concept of

1. T. Cooper, *Life of Thomas Cooper*, 1872, p. 72.
2. J. Poole, *Little Peddlington*, 1839, I, p. 99.
3. *Blackwood's*, XXXII, 1832, p. 848.

knowledge permeated the attitudes of many working-class readers towards literature, however, it went hand in hand with personal experience. For many men and women the discovery of the world of books was intensely exciting. William Lovett, on first going to a literary study group, declared that his 'mind seemed to be awakened to a new mental existence; new feelings, hopes and aspirations sprang up within me'.[1] As literacy spread, it thus brought the working classes hopes of a new and better life to come, both physically and mentally. Many comments can be found in lower-class literature about this time similar to Christopher Thompson's: 'A new era was opening to us; the prejudice mists, amongst which we had been groping for ages, were gathering, and as the blessed morning broke, the rusty bolts of ignorance fell down.'[2]

It is only against this background that we can understand how, at a time when the working day was often fourteen hours, when overcrowding, lack of lighting, overwork, and jeers from fellow-workers provided active discouragement, the reading habit could spread dramatically among the labouring classes.

By 1830, therefore, there was a large potential working-class reading public – what was there for them to read? There were, first, libraries. There was not even a rudimentary public library system before Ewart's Public Library Bill of 1850, and the formation of libraries appears to have been the first thought of working men when they came together in any form of educational group, large or small. Sometimes the larger institutions threw open their libraries to the public for a small charge. Much of the stock was 'junk' given by those who had no further use for it, but they served some purpose, for the 1849 Parliamentary Report on libraries shows they were extensively used. Most of these libraries stocked fiction, and even the Sheffield Mechanics Institute, which barred it, allowed in the novels of Bulwer Lytton, Washington Irving, Thackeray, and Samuel Warren.[3] Libraries also appear in the most unlikely places – in factories, particularly after lower-class interest was aroused by 'a tale of factory life' in Manchester (perhaps Mrs Gaskell's *Mary Barton*),[4] in army barracks, police-stations, and linen drapers.[5] Almost all Sunday, Ragged, and Factory Schools kept libraries, and sometimes used them as a means of

1. W. Lovett, *Life and Struggles*, 1876, p. 35.
2. C. Thompson, *Autobiography*, 1847, p. 20.
3. Hudson, p. 160.   4. *P.P.L.*, sec. 1366.   5. Hudson, p. 212.

keeping in touch with scholars when these had left. Libraries were also to be found in many churches and chapels. St Martin's-in-the-Fields stopped stocking fiction when parishioners were found staying away from Sunday services to read Scott, but few contained even the religious novels Alexander Somerville found in Innerwick church library – readers had to be satisfied with religious tracts and other devotional works. The S.P.C.K., the Kildare Place, and similar societies sent out libraries designed for such places – the Religious Tract Society alone issued 5,411 *libraries* between 1832 and 1849. The trouble and expense taken in providing them indicates that they were used, and they must have helped to create the tastes of the working-class public.

As with the educational movements, however, a large amount was done by comparatively unnoticed private enterprise. Middle-class libraries charged about one and a half guineas a year, and a heavy entrance fee, but there were lower-class ones, charging between a penny and threepence a volume. These go back at least as far as 1778, when we find Fanny Burney writing that they were open to 'every butcher and baker, cobler, and tinker, throughout the three kingdoms'.[1] Christopher Thompson, a tailor, found his fellow-workers in the early nineteenth century reading 'the obscene trash raked up from the pest holes that are unfortunately to be found in every town',[2] and reference to these libraries can be discovered scattered throughout the literature and autobiographies of the lower classes at this time. In 1838 a survey of three London parishes found thirty-eight of them in existence there alone.[3]

They were generally to be found attached to tobacco and stationery shops. Their wares varied with the tastes of the time. In the early nineteenth century they contained 'trashy romance[s] of the Minerva Press, or Radcliffe, or Monk Lewis School';[4] later the taste moved towards historical and 'silver fork' romances.[5] From about 1838, penny-issue fiction was published, and this was offered for loan, bound into as many volumes as possible in order to extort the maximum from the borrower. Surviving volumes of these romances occasionally have the addresses of the library,

1. F. Burney, *Early Diary*, 1889, I, p. 215.
2. Thompson, p. 72.   3. *S.S.L.*, 1, 1838, p. 485.
4. 'Working Man', *Scenes from my Life*, 1858, p. 41.
5. *S.S.L.*, 1, 1838, p. 485.

1. Contemporary picture of a lower-class library (1848)

written in ink on the inside of the cover. Albert Smith amusingly describes Smedlar's Library, found by Christopher Tadpole in a dingy London square. The dusty interior of the shop had piles of novels alongside the items of a tobacconist's trade, and against the windows, 'Well-thumbed novels were opened enticingly at exciting pages, and displayed flat up against the panes, with the intelligence that they were "Lent to read" on top of them . . .'[1] Their titles included *Mabel the Mildewed*, *The Light of Other Days*; *or the Heart that Never Felt Renewing*, and *The Brigand of Bagshot*. As in

1. Albert Smith, *Christopher Tadpole*, 1849, pp. 178–83.

7

other lower-class libraries, these works could be bought as well as borrowed.

Right up to 1850, newspapers and even books could often be borrowed from another unexpected source, the public house. From about 1800, however, particularly in London, their place as suppliers of literature was taken over by coffee houses. The popularity of coffee houses increased dramatically in the metropolis because the price of coffee was gradually reduced from a shilling to between threepence and a penny a cup, and as the city grew, workmen found it convenient to eat meals there instead of going long distances home. They were allowed to bring their own food. During the political agitation of the 1830s they became centres for radical discussion, and both John Cleave and William Lovett ran coffee houses for just this purpose. By 1840, London had between 1,600 and 1,800 coffee houses.

All these provided periodicals; in 1849 at least 500 also had libraries attached. 'They are schools of instruction,' wrote Angus B. Reach, 'where instruction is meted out, as well as coffee sold.' One went in through a façade of playbills to find oneself in 'an air of stillness and repose, yet perhaps a hundred people are seated in different boxes, conning over books and newspapers, and sipping their coffee at the same time. You can see at a glance that the majority of the guests are working men.'[1] In J. M. Rymer's *The White Slave* (1844), Tom, wishing to read the latest news about a murder hunt, went naturally into a coffee house to read about it over a cup of coffee.

The periodicals to be found covered a wide range. *Pickwick* was read there, also *Bentley's Miscellany*, but there were greater numbers of *Chambers's Edinburgh Journal* and Limbird's cheap magazine, *The Mirror*. They also took lower-class fiction such as *The Penny Storyteller* and *The Calendar of Horrors*.[2] It is not likely that many took scurrilous or pornographic works, although the Baptist pastor, G. W. Macree, spent a harrowing afternoon reading through the books he found in a coffee house near Seven Dials, a very rough quarter. 'There are a vast number of immoral books, the worst in our language, and from their appearance much read', he noted in his diary.[3]

1. Angus B. Reach, 'The Coffee Houses of London', *New Parley Library*, II, 1845, pp. 293 ff.

2. *S.S.L.*, I, 1838, p. 486.   3. C. W. Macree, *G. W. Macree*, 1893, p. 30.

The coffee houses offered literature to many who would have not gone out of their way to obtain it, and Reach declared they were 'rapidly effecting a change in the conditions and tastes of the working men'. They also had a good effect on the quality of cheap periodicals, for the coffee house proprietors were discriminating purchasers.

In the north there was no such popularity for coffee houses, perhaps because the northerners kept to beer. Their place was taken by penny reading rooms, which were particularly successful during the political agitation of the 1830s. One of those in Manchester was run by Abel Heywood, who opened at six in the morning and closed at ten at night for the benefit of those who worked throughout the day.

There was therefore a considerable range of sources for those who wished to read. Beside these we must place the public readings of newspapers, and accounts such as that given by an anonymous working man whom his fellow workers paid to read to them while they worked.[1] The workers wished to read and would find means to do so.

Workers were also able to buy literature. About 1830, Francis Place 'found that between Temple-Bar and Fleet-market there were many houses, in each of which there were more books than all the tradesmen's houses in the street contained when I was a youth'.[2] In 1848, a survey of a lower-class parish in London revealed that each family possessed on an aggregate eleven books each, and this figure did not include the perishable penny-issue fiction most likely to be bought. For the backbone of the cheap literature industry was serial publications. The immense popularity of Dickens's novels in part issue has tended to obscure the fact that literature in this form does in fact go back to the seventeenth century. By 1677 'number books, independently issued in weekly and monthly parts, wrapped in a blue cover, had become a popular commodity in publishing business', as R. M. Wiles has shown in his study of these works.[3] These number books ranged from immense Biblical commentaries to criminal biographies and standard novels. Serial publication in fact opened up a range of new possibilities for the small printer. The eight pages could be printed as

1. Anon., *Memoirs of a Working Man*, 1845, p. 90.
2. P.P., *Education in England and Wales*, 1835, (465) vii, sec. 796.
3. *Serial Publication in England*, Cambridge, 1957, esp. pp. 110 ff.

one sheet on a hand-press, and lengthy volumes could be printed with almost no capital, since the income of the one issue paid for the printing of the next. Unsold weekly parts could be stitched together to be offered as monthly parts, then bound and sold as a normal volume. All pockets were appealed to and the public combed three times. By printing works on which the copyright had lapsed, writer's fees were evaded. The publisher John Harrison, with his marathon series containing most of the fiction currently popular, *The Novelist's Magazine* (1780–88), discovered the additional appeal of a woodcut on the front of each issue. These were by artists of the standing of Corbould, Stothard, and Heath. These illustrations 'sold' the issue to the uncritical reader, much as the cover sells the modern paperback. It also bridged the gap between the broadsheet and the novel for the lower-class reader.

In the early years of the nineteenth century the number trade found its staple in serious works such as *Fox's Book of Martyrs* and *The History of England*; between 1815 and 1820 Thomas Cooper in Gainsborough was buying Kelly's *Geography* and Barclay's quarto *Dictionary*, while his mother took numbers of *Dialogues between a Pilgrim*, *Adam*, *Noah and Cleopas*.[1] The giant among the serious number publishers was Thomas Kelly, who in 1809 opened his shop in Paternoster Row. He invested in the then new invention of stereotypes in order to print huge editions of elaborately illustrated works such as his first venture, a folio family Bible which weighed twenty pounds complete. He organized an elaborate sales network throughout the country and sold 40,000 copies of this, largely to servants and better-paid artisans, who, Kelly declared, found them 'highly appreciated in after-life' as 'heirlooms' for their children. In all, Kelly sold some 230,000 Bibles in various editions, besides many other ventures. Close behind him in this field came James Cooke and George Virtue. Their success indicates that a serious if sometimes naïve lower-class readership was being formed by the new educational movements.

Publishers of serial fiction were smaller, but the circulation of number novels was still considerable. Here the main figures were William Emans and George MacGowan, with George Virtue active in both fields. These novels present an interesting point for collectors and librarians. Very few of the actual parts have sur-

1. T. Cooper, *Life of Thomas Cooper*, 1872, pp. 33 ff.

vived, but bound into volumes they are catalogued as ordinary editions. They can be distinguished, however, by small numbers, distinct from the binder's symbols, in the bottom left-hand corner of the right-hand page, at sixteen-page intervals. Original works, for example several of the works of Hannah Maria Jones, as well as reprints, were issued in this way.

The parts were sold direct through the publisher's canvasser who called on town subscribers weekly, monthly on those in more remote areas. As their profit was on the numbers sold, they were active propagators of literature among many who would never have visited a bookshop. Charles Knight, remembering the salesman who called at their kitchen door when he was a child, declared that 'no refusal can prevent him in the end leaving his number for inspection'.[1] Sometimes their commission was as high as sixty per cent, and Knight and J. O. Robinson said they were well paid.[2] J. D. Burn, however, who had been one, declared that the trade was 'the last resort of fallen gentility',[3] and Renton Nicholson describes his Mr Cheekey as having to sleep on a deserted barge in a tunnel under the Strand.[4]

Books were also sold by auction. In the 1820s we find Thomas Nelson tramping with a pack of cheap standard works through towns and villages, hiring an empty shop, and when the labourers had finished work for the day, auctioning his books to them. This was evidently a profitable business. It laid the foundations of the future business of Thomas Tegg, and when he had established a business in Cheapside he still continued his book auctions. Other booksellers were holding them too.

Many of the books auctioned and issued serially were remainders that had failed when they first came out; as Thomas Baines of Leeds discovered with *The History of the Wars of the French Revolution*, a work which had not survived its first edition could make a large profit when sold in parts.[5] Lackington, Thomas Tegg, and others, however, found it possible to buy volumes sold originally at half-a-guinea as remainders, perhaps add a new title-page, and resell them at as low a cost as one shilling and sixpence. They

---

1. C. Knight, *Old Printer and Modern Press*, 1864, pp. 216 ff.
2. T. Constable, *Archibald Constable*, 1873, III, p. 364.
3. *Autobiography of a Beggar Boy*, 1855, p. 174.
4. *Dombey and Daughter*, 1850, p. 24.
5. Constable, op. cit., III, p. 364.

would make only a small profit but, as Lackington had painted on the carriage he was able eventually to drive about in, 'Small Profits do Great Things'. Several publishers who were to rise to importance in this way began selling remainders. In the 1830s the leader in this field was Henry Bohn, challenged by the young George Routledge.

About 1820, however, two new inventions radically altered the whole publishing scene. During the Napoleonic wars, the publishing trade had been crippled by the high price and uncertain supplies of paper. The cost of books soared, and Charles Cooke told a Parliamentary Commission that he was unable to complete serial publications because the cost of the later issues would have left him at a loss.[1] Paper cost as much as thirty-four shillings a ream, with threepence a pound tax, and a high wastage because of imperfect sheets. The paper-making machine was patented in England by John Gamble as early as 1801, but opposition from the trade held back its use until about 1820. When the factories began production, however, the cost of paper was halved. Not only that, but the paper produced was better in quality and larger in size than hand-produced material, making possible the rotary steam press. The combination of cheap paper and mechanical printing was the greatest step forward in book production since Caxton. It was also to have profound social and political effects. Looking up at the roaring mass of machinery in a new steam press, Frederick von Raumer declared that 'it's might' should 'convince censors and the secret police of their impotency'.[2]

The immediate result was a wave of cheap publications; a small wave compared with the flood that came ten years later, but considerable nevertheless. These periodicals sold at the unprecedented price of twopence. The pioneer was John Limbird, a seller of cheap reprints, school, and juvenile books in the Strand. On 22 November 1822 he brought out number one of *The Mirror of Literature, Amusement and Instruction*, a miniature lower-class equivalent of periodicals like *Blackwood's*, from which it gleaned most of its matter. It was an octavo gathering with a sensational woodcut of Brixton treadmill. The first issue sold in all 150,000 copies, and the magazine called out a host of imitators. The subsequent issues were kept up to a high standard by its editor, Thomas

1. P.P., *Mr Koop's Invention*, 1801 (55), iii, sec. 132.
2. F. von Raumer, *England in 1841*, 1842, p. 317.

Byerly, and beside articles of general interest and some poetry, early issues included prose by Galt, Theodore Hook, and Washington Irving. Brougham declared paternally that 'its circulation must prove highly beneficial to the bulk of the people'.[1] The regular booksellers, however, refused to handle it, so Limbird toured the country, gaining agents in all walks of life; in Manchester, a shoemaker, in Coventry, a tinman. It therefore helped to create the new working-class reading public, and had a regular circulation of 80,000 a week. In 1837 it was still a major periodical.

While *The Mirror* remained staid and respectable, rivals soon began to exploit the possibilities of more sensational matter. *The Portfolio* (1823–9), *The Tell-Tale* (1823–4), *Endless Entertainments* (1825), and *Legends of Horror* (1825–6), to name but a few, contained plenty of items for the seeker of passion or excitement. For the moment *The Mirror*, backed by the serious-minded readers produced by Sunday and Monitorial schools, held undoubted supremacy. But *The Olio* (1828), with its 'racy stories', was wrong when it said it was 'the last in the field'.[2] It was on the edge of one much more extensive.

1. *Practical Observations on the Education of the People,* 1825, p. 1.
2. I, 1828, p. iii.

2

From Politics to Fiction,
1830—40

THE decade that followed 1830 is of great interest to anyone concerned with the problems of class and culture, for it opened with the masses seeking, in an unprecedented way, serious political and cultural reading matter; and in the failure of their aspirations we see a blueprint of many cultural problems that face modern society.

The situation was largely the product of the historical background. We have already seen the causes that were creating a new self-aware working class from the diverse elements the industrial revolution had brought to the towns. The final coalescence came about 1830. The popular mood was inflamed by industrial distress (freely blamed on the government), and by news of revolutions in France and Belgium. Great hopes were focused on the Whig government returned to Parliament at the beginning of the year and pledged to reform the electoral system. Then the House of Commons threw out the Reform Bill. An excited nation went to the polls, a new Parliament was elected, and a Reform Bill passed. When this was defeated in the House of Lords, angry meetings were held throughout the country, serious rioting broke out in Bristol, Nottingham, and Derby, and only a policy of restraint by radical leaders prevented wider disorders. At last in June 1832, after months of intense excitement, the House of Lords passed the first Reform Bill.

This political agitation had features distinct from any that had preceded it. In the first place, it must be linked with the wider cultural aspirations, already mentioned, that brought working-class educational movements, discussion groups, and libraries. Secondly, in an unprecedented way, it was connected with the printed word. As a contemporary commentator told a committee of the S.P.C.K., 'The population of this country [was] for the first time becoming a *reading* population, actuated by tastes and habits unknown to preceding generations, and particularly susceptible to such an influence as that of the press.'[1] With cheap paper and mechanical printing, great opportunities for directing the radical movement with low-priced periodicals lay open. The government was acutely aware of this, and turned to the Seditious Publications Act of 1819 which levied a tax of fourpence on any periodicals containing anything that could be remotely construed as news. With this they hoped to price cheap radical publications out of existence, as they had Cobbett's twopenny Register.

The tax in fact had precisely the opposite effect to that intended. If the Whigs feared cheap literature, it was something for which to strive. The issue was seen as more than one of political organization: all reading and self-improvement was seen as part of the class struggle. Illegal radical publications frequently displayed the mystic Utilitarian slogan 'Knowledge is Power', and the Whig tax was referred to as 'the Tax on Knowledge'. Politics and culture were interknit.

It is significant of this that Hetherington, the first rebel against the tax, also had been a worker with Birkbeck in the formation of Mechanics Institutes, and a founder-member of the newly formed National Union of the Working Classes. In October 1830 he published a series of unstamped pamphlets, *Penny Papers for the People*, which in June of 1831 he changed to *The Poor Man's Guardian*, 'A Weekly Newspaper for the People, Established Contrary to Law to try the Power of Might against Right'. Over five hundred sellers of the paper were imprisoned for three and a half years, and Hetherington, as publisher, for six months. National funds were set up to help 'the victims of Whig tyranny', and Hetherington openly advertised for men willing to go to prison, where at least one was fed. Copies were circulated in boxes of shoes, in cabs, even, it was said, in a coffin. The working classes, and some middle class sympathizers, combined to ensure *The Poor Man's Guardian* came out weekly. A whole new sales organization was built up, using cellars, tradesmen's shops, and private houses. By these means between 12,000 and 15,000 copies an issue were circulated throughout England each week, and most copies found many readers.

As early as October 1830, William Carpenter had begun publishing his *Political Letters*. Once he and Hetherington showed that the

1. *S.P.C.K. Minutes*, 21 May 1832, pp. 284–5.

law could be defied, others were quick to follow: *The Radical* (1831) and *The Reformer* (1833–4) were two of many. The radical press was joined by the free-thinking and atheist publications with which, in many upper-class minds, it was synonymous. Richard Carlile began *The Prompter* in November 1830; it had a small circulation until prosecution for libel gave it publicity and a nationwide sale.[1] James Watson reprinted Hone's *Parodies* of the Lord's Prayer and the Creed, Paine's *Works*, and other proscribed books. Free-thinking literature had in fact only a limited appeal; attacks on the Established Church with its rich stipends and its tithes, on the other hand, received wide support. Caricatured bishops with carbuncled noses and monstrous bellies, weighing down on the starving poor, were stock figures in such periodicals as George Cruikshank's *A Slap at the Church* (1832), which claimed a circulation of 7,000. Richard Carlile had a stuffed figure of a bishop in his shop window, arm in arm with a distraining officer and the devil.

Hard on the heels of the lower-class publishers came certain of the middle classes. The first was Leigh Hunt, who started *The Tatler* in September 1830, declaring, with a glance at the Stamp Office that had stopped his magazine *Chat of the Week*, that it was a 'companion' to the daily newspapers. It was even printed in the form of a newspaper folio, although its content of essays, scraps of information, reviews and dramatic criticism tried to follow its eighteenth-century namesake. Neither this nor *Leigh Hunt's London Journal* (1834), though containing essays of merit, hit the tone required for the lower-class readers; the former ran daily for a year and six months (1830–31), the latter for only sixty-seven numbers.

Three upper-class periodicals did, however, gain considerable popularity among the new mass public, if only for a short period. On 4 February 1831 the Chambers brothers published the first number of *Chambers's Edinburgh Journal*. They were well fitted to produce such a periodical, for they had been booksellers in a poor quarter of Edinburgh, and closely watched the reaction of their customers to their various wares. In their intentions they were high-minded, comprehensive, and methodical. They wished to

1. F. Place, *B.M.Add. Mss.* 27,789; for a bibliography of the various types of unstamped literature, see Joel H. Weiner, *Unstamped British Periodicals 1830–1836,* 1970.

supply 'a meal of healthful, useful and agreeable mental instruction' for readers of every age and profession, and in particular for
the working-class man or woman who was beginning to discover
literary culture. There were essays, poetry, and articles of information. Fiction was only admitted to attract those who would not
take the solid food without sugar. There was a good deal of
borrowed material; on just one page of an early number we find
extracts from *The Library of Entertaining Knowledge*, *The Keepsake*,
The Working Man's Companion, and *The Foreign Quarterly Review*. But
as its success grew, it became increasingly original, employing
writers of the quality of Mary Howitt and Hugh Miller. This success came quickly. At the third number, with sales in England
through W. S. Orr, circulation reached 50,000 per issue, and a few
years later it was 80,000. In Galloway the shepherds passed their
copies around the mountains, leaving them under stones to be
collected by the next reader,[1] and it remained a steady favourite in
lower-class London coffee houses. The Chambers brothers were
ostracized by polite society, and called the 'three half-penny
people'. However, prosperity changed this, and the nature of the
magazine, which became increasingly middle class, until in 1841
The People's Police Gazette accused William Chambers of having
'prostituted himself to the crop-sick monopolists and to the
bloated mill-owning proprietors of the factory slaves'.[2]

A close rival of *Chambers's Edinburgh Journal* was *The Penny
Magazine* of the Society for the Diffusion of Useful Knowledge,
which had a similar career. The Society had been formed in 1827
as an upper-class offshoot of the Mechanics Institutes. Their early
publications failed to reach the public they sought, but the *Penny
Magazine*, first issued in March 1832, sold 50,000 in the first week,
and by the end of the year had a circulation of 200,000, with a
readership estimated at five times this number. Critics then and
since have denied that this donnish compilation of historical and
scientific knowledge, with a little classical poetry, was bought by
the lower classes, but the circulation alone suggests that it exactly
caught the taste of those packing the Athenaeums and similar institutions, which audiences at this time did include a significant proportion of the working classes. Labourers like Christopher Thompson were willing to go without food to buy it, enthusiastic letters

1. W. Chambers, *Memoir of Robert Chambers*, Edinburgh, 1872, p. 237.
2. Q., M. Dalziel, *Popular Fiction a Hundred Years Ago*, 1957, p. 13.

from worker readers can still be read in the Society archives,[1] and as late as 1842 a brick-burner in the potteries wrote on behalf of his fellow-workers to protest against the reduction in the amount of poetry in the magazine.[2] A number of working-class publishers flattered it with imitation, producing such works as *The True Half-penny Magazine of a Society for the Diffusion of Useful Knowledge* (1832), and *The Weekly Visitor, conducted by a Society for the Diffusion of Useful Knowledge* (1832). *The Fool's Cap* (13 October 1832) thought it worth a virulent attack as 'Penny Wise and Pound Foolish'.

A great measure of its appeal undoubtedly came from the wood-cut that was presented on the front of each issue. The Society engaged such artists as William Harvey, G. Bonner, and Charles and Thomas Landseer, regardless of expense, and after the stylized illustrations of previous works, their photographic realism and expert finish caused a sensation. G. J. Holyoake tells how when he found himself in a country inn without money, he thought of producing copies of *The Penny Magazine*, and found them 'as valu-able as glass beads in dealing with Indians' when settling with the astonished hosteller.[3] Their success reached beyond England. Stereotyped copies, often accompanied with translated script, were circulated as part of educational movements in France, Ger-many, Holland, Lithuania, Bohemia (Slavonic), Italy, the Ionian Islands, Sweden, Norway, Spanish America, the Brazils, and the United States. 'The Penny Magazine', boasted Charles Knight, the printer, 'produced a revolution in popular art throughout the world.'[4] Although *The Penny Magazine* lost most of its lower-class readers after the first years, when it closed in 1845 its circulation was still over 25,000 a week.

The third upper-class success of the early 1830s was the Society for the Propagation of Christian Knowledge's *Saturday Magazine*, first published 7 July 1832. This was aimed at counteracting the infidel publications already mentioned; indeed, the S.P.C.K. was already issuing half a million 'anti-infidel' tracts a year as a moral disinfectant to this offensive. But it also expressed the determi-nation of the Anglican Church not to leave the initiative for popu-lar periodicals in the hands of the secular S.D.U.K. *The Saturday*

1. In the library of University College, London.
2. M. Grobel, *S.D.U.K.*, Univ. of London M.A. Thesis, 1933, II, pp. 144 ff.
3. G. J. Holyoake, *Sixty Years of an Agitator's Life*, 1892, p. 70.
4. Knight, *Old Printer*, p. 258.

Magazine resembles *The Penny Magazine* in providing scientific and historical information, although wherever possible it is given from a Christian viewpoint. The woodcuts were poorer, but the less academic approach also made it easier to read, and it was not afraid to use the sensational appeal of such topics as the mass human sacrifices of the Druids. The delighted committee announced that it had sold 450,000 issues in the first four months, after which its circulation settled down to 80,000 copies a week. Although its circulation later declined, it was still a major periodical in 1837.[1]

The most important immediate effect of these three magazines was to make a mockery of any further prosecutions of publishers and sellers of unstamped periodicals. With figures such as the Bishop of Chichester and the Attorney General sponsoring unstamped magazines, what could the government do? Moreover, their success and that even of the prosecuted *Poor Man's Guardian*, which was making the fortunes of men such as Abel Heywood of Manchester, showed the immense commercial possibilities of cheap publications. Furthermore, after a severe depression in the printing trade, which had driven men such as C. M. Smith overseas, printers were returning to London, often taking up cramped quarters in disused residential buildings. A correspondent in *The Westminster Review* declared, no doubt with exaggeration, that they could be found in 'every street'.[2] These were willing to undertake printing a periodical for very small sums, in many cases not demanding a premium. Gilbert A'Beckett and Henry Mayhew started a magazine with three pounds; Henry Downes Miles ran a sporting magazine with a capital of ten.

A flood of periodicals ensued. 'At every corner of the streets', said a correspondent in *The Bee*, '[one] meets with some vendor of food for the mind, anxiously displaying the various treasures, which its brown paper wrapper protects from the too rough grasp of a hand not always devoted to so lofty an employment', for the readers were 'people who, some years ago, would never have thought of opening a book of any description'.[3]

The majority were political or instructive, or general literary magazines containing snippets of general knowledge, dramatic criticism, and references to current affairs. The most useful apparatus of the editor was generally a pair of scissors. In 'How to make

1. N. Whittock, *The Complete Book of Trades*, 1837, p. 41.
2. XXIV, 1830, p. 70.   3. II, 16 March 1833, p. 9.

a Paper,' the writer describes the process of running through other periodicals for suitable material.[1] *The Thief* (1832–3) brazenly admitted its technique, and outlived all the others, incidentally pirating the first work of Dickens to come into print, 'A Dinner at Poplar Walk', without, of course, offering payment. The best of this type of magazine was *The National Omnibus* (1831–3), which outcantered *The Lancashire Omnibus* (Liverpool 1832), and the half-size, half-penny *The Cab* (1832).

The only lasting element in this mass of ephemeral journalism was the comic literature, which had an important part to play in the Victorian comic tradition which produced Jerrold, Thackeray, and Dickens, besides *Punch* (1841–), which grew directly out of it. *Figaro in London* (1831–9), the most successful venture, was written first by Gilbert A'Beckett, then by Henry Mayhew, with Robert Seymour doing most of the illustrations. Modelled on the French *Figaro*, it offered satire on public figures, punning jokes – A'Beckett's speciality – and dramatic criticism. Circulation rose to 70,000,[2] and *Figaro in Sheffield* (1832–7), *Figaro in Birmingham* (1832), and *Figaro in Liverpool* (1833) appeared in their respective cities. It was 'Figaro here! Figaro there! Figaro everywhere,' boasted A'Beckett. A number of similar periodicals also sprang up with other names, such as *Punchinello* (1832), illustrated by George Cruikshank.

It is interesting to note how directly these periodicals were the expression of the new life of the towns. Their existence relies on interest in events and people in a particular urban society – the suffix 'in London', 'in Liverpool', and so on, is important. Most of these periodicals were neither scandal sheets, nor general gossip magazines drawing on the appeal of glamour in the fashion of modern 'society' columnists. They tried to reveal the organism of town life, claiming omniscience. Below a woodcut of Satan brooding over the city the editorial to *The Devil in London* runs:

London, our darling London, so characteristically called *our* drawing room, now lay at our feet ... One whisk of our tail, and, *hey presto*, away went the roofs of the houses, and with them too, the artificial covering of every human breast.[3]

1. *Sharpe's London Magazine*, I, August 1829, pp. 64–72.
2. F. Boase, *Modern English Biography*, 1892–1921, III, p. 789.
3. I, 1832, p. 1.

Such an interest had been expressed by such eighteenth-century writers as Pope and Swift: what is new is the shift in class and tone. Instead of satire that claims to support a certain code of values, the nineteenth-century version pries into life out of curiosity. The stance is that of knowing intimacy, the wag with a sly grin and first finger rubbing against the side of the nose that appears at the head of *The Odd Fellow* magazine. A few papers did in fact carry scandal of an objectionable type; *The Hoxton Sausage* (*c.* 1834), or *The Penny Punch* (1849), which nearly gained Thomas Frost a well-deserved ducking from his neighbours.[1] One or two were even used for blackmail, such as *The Satirist* (1831–45): Gregory Barnard, however, the editor of this, was ostracized by other journalists.[2]

Less than one-tenth of the flood of periodicals paid their way, and in 1834 only a few of the better ones survived. As early as 1832 the projector of *The Thief* reported that the publisher cried, 'What, sir, *another* penny paper? I have already burnt my fingers'.[3] While they disappeared almost as quickly as they had sprung up, however, together with the political journals they set up a number of publishers and a network of newsagents who turned to other literature.

The new lower-class publishers were centred on London, although all provincial towns of any size had also their own political and social magazines, often modelled on the metropolitan ones. Various reasons have been given for this overwhelming predominance of London. A contributor to *The Westminster Review*[4] said it was due to the comparative lack of printers in the provinces, but a more important factor was circulation. A penny paper needed to sell about 2,000 copies a week to be profitable, although this varied widely depending on the size and type of the periodical. While a local provincial paper had to find this number of readers locally, the London publishers sent out issues with parcels of books throughout the country. The new railroads made the cost of transport negligible: stamped periodicals went free.

The most important London publisher to emerge from the early 1830s was William Strange, who in Paternoster Row had begun handling better-class periodicals such as *The Olio*. His attention

1. T. Frost, *Reminiscences of a Country Journalist*, 1886, p. 59.
2. Wilson, p. 98.   3. I, 1832, p. 1.
4. XXIV, 1830, p. 70.

was probably turned to penny magazines by the success of his publication *Figaro in London*. Together with B. Steill he was the only purveyor of cheap literature in the traditional distribution centre of Paternoster Row – most of the other publishers by-passed the traditional channels. Second to Strange was G. Berger, a journeyman compositor who published a number of small periodicals from Holywell Street before his gains enabled him, in 1838, to set up a shop in the Strand. From here he grew to be the biggest newsagent in London until the coming of W. H. Smith. G. Purkess of Soho, a seller of *The Poor Man's Guardian*, was sometimes associated with Berger; in the 1840s he dealt largely in cheap fiction. James Watson, primarily a publisher of political and antireligious works, sold comic and literary works alongside his own productions.[1] Less important publishers and newsagents included J. Crisp, W. Howden, J. Viar, and Charles Smith.

Although there were few major publishers in the provinces, each town did have its minor printers and publishers. Here we need only mention J. S. Pratt of Stokesley, who in 1846 had ninety-seven full-length novels in his catalogue – about this time, however, he also opened an office in London. Besides middle-class booksellers, there was also a network of lower-class newsagents throughout the country that had been organized largely to circulate illegal political periodicals which the conventional channels would not receive, such as *The Poor Man's Guardian*. Of those who emerged in the later 1830s, such as J. Guest and J. Watts in Birmingham, J. G. Smith and Shepherd in Liverpool, J. Hobson and J. Mann in Leeds, many had been imprisoned for their earlier work. It is probable that many others remained in obscurity, diffusing cheap literature unknown to the 'respectable' public. A newsagent, Mr S. G. Bucknell of Stroud, told an 1851 Parliamentary Commission that in his town at least one man was so engaged 'below my own observation', and declared there were similar sellers throughout the country.[2]

A figure who did emerge before the public, however, was Abel Heywood of Manchester. Born in Prestwich in 1810, by the age of nine he was working in a Manchester warehouse. He educated himself in a Mechanics Institute, and opened a successful reading room in Manchester. He tramped the streets as an agent for *The*

1. W. J. Linton, *James Watson*, 1879, p. 48.
2. P.P., *Stamp Duties*, 1851 (558), xvii, sec. 1212.

Poor Man's Guardian, then opened his own shop in Oldham in 1832: in March of that year he was imprisoned for selling Hetherington's paper. His business was nevertheless continued in a neighbouring cellar, a different salesman being employed each night to lessen the risk of arrest. Far from being ruined, by 1840 he was the largest dealer in cheap periodicals outside London, with the possible exception of the Londoner Henry Robinson, who, from his shop in the Canongate, Edinburgh, was distributing them throughout Scotland.

The number of periodicals sold by provincial agents was considerable. In 1836 James Guest estimated that nearly 75,000 periodicals costing twopence or less were circulating in Birmingham every month.[1] A cautious and incomplete survey made in Manchester[2] gave an estimate for that city of about 57,000 a month, excluding cheap editions of such works as Paine's *Age of Reason*. Here by 1851 Heywood was handling over 75,000 copies *a week* of fifteen penny-issue novels alone.[3]

It is not easy to say definitely what social classes bought these works; there is probably no precise answer. In London and Edinburgh the social prejudice against them was stronger than in the provinces. The Chambers brothers were snubbed by society, and publishers like Hetherington and Watson, although men of high intelligence and integrity, were completely outside the pale of 'respectable' society. 'Of course we are not blind to the fact that there is still so much aristocratic feeling among us,' said the editor of *The Half-penny Magazine*, 'as to make our modest charge an obstacle to some.'[4] Yet in Manchester, Heywood, by the age of twenty-six, was serving on Manchester City Council, and he rose to become Mayor in 1863. Although Queen Victoria's refusal to attend the opening of the Town Hall was said to be due to his presence, he was highly respected by the Mancunians. Even in London, however, the division was not rigid. In *The National Omnibus* a London firm advertised both caps at two-and-six and beaver hats at a guinea, and this magazine reviewed *Poor Richard's Journal for Poor People* alongside periodicals like *Blackwood's* and *Tait's*. Much of the humour in *Figaro in London* and *Punchinello* is

1. *Birmingham*, 1835, p. 290.
2. Ashton, *Economic and Social Investigations*, p. 18.
3. A. Heywood, *Papers of the Manchester Literary Club*, II, 1876, p. 49.
4. I, 1840, p. 1.

essentially middle class, and their contributors moved naturally into *Punch* when it started in 1841.

The humorous press is a particular case. With the help of John Doyle and Thomas Hood, it developed its middle-class humour in a particular genre, and separated from the lower-class elements which assimilated rather the traditions of the broadsheets it was superseding. An early example of this is *Bell's Life in London*, which was circulating 22,000 copies every Sunday among 'the very lowest part of the population'.[1] This issued sheets of cartoons concerned with the comic aspects of low life in general, accompanied by explanatory text. One print of these cartoons, published in 1831, claims '128,000 copies sold'.[2]

John Cleave fused the traditions of the broadsheet with the new unstamped periodical press in 1835 when he published the first number of *Cleave's Weekly Gazette*, which ran under various titles until 1841. It gained a circulation of 40,000 a week.[3] Cleave correctly described it as 'a broadsheet as big as a newspaper'. He gave it the imprint of his own personality. He was an impulsive, rough-and-ready sailor who had little use for the more intellectual radicalism of men like Place, Linton, or even Watson and Hetherington. His periodical is full of crude lampoons and coarse caricatures that would never have found a place in *The Poor Man's Guardian*. Most of its woodcuts were after designs by C. J. Grant. Thackeray said of Grant's works, 'they are outrageous caricatures; squinting eyes, wooden legs, and pimpled noses forming the chief points of fun'.[4] Much as they irritated Thackeray, Grant's drawings under the hand of a good cutter show a unique style and distinct, vigorous humour. They present the comedy of the old broadsheets, robbed of its naïve charm by the self-consciousness of the new metropolitan society, yet more individual than the modern press cartoons towards which they point.

After *Cleave's Gazette* had been appearing for a year, a marked change came over the whole radical press. The Whigs repealed the confusion of past newspaper acts and lowered the tax per copy to a penny, enforcing this, however, with such vigour that even Hetherington found himself forced to give in, and abandon

1. *W.R.*, X, 1829, pp. 470, 479.
2. *Gallery of Comicalities*, 24 June 1831, p. 1.
3. F. Place, *Place Add. MSS.* 27, 791, p. 67.
4. *Fraser's Magazine*, XVII, 1838, p. 287.

Hetherington's Twopenny Dispatch (1834–6) for his stamped *London Dispatch* (1836–7). The indignity of the red stamp, on periodicals that once so defiantly resisted it, was a much greater blow than the extra penny in cost, and the radical press never fully recovered. 'Since the change in the stamp duty,' wrote Thackeray, 'the penny gazettes, which flooded the town with treason, have disappeared altogether.'[1]

But there were other changes at work too. The Mechanics' Institutes and the educative periodicals were also losing their appeal to the main body of the working classes, and the whole wave of enthusiasm for learning and political self-betterment subsided. It is true that the Chartist movement rose to its climax about 1842, and popular disorders occurred in 1848: working men continued to educate themselves, and periodicals such as Cassell's *Working Man's Friend* catered for a still considerable body of lower-class readers. But the tone was muted, and lower-class education tended to be focused on a number of exceptional men and women. The masses who read the early numbers of *The Penny Magazine* turned mainly to the growing number of sensational periodicals.

It is tempting to see in the upsurge of interest in reading, linked as it was in a unique way to social and political factors and the first impact of cheap paper and printing, a possible turning point in the emergence of the English working classes. If lower-class aspirations had not been exploited by publishers offering titillating but worthless fiction, if upper-class publishers had been more in sympathy with the needs of the emerging new reader, would habits of thought and appreciation have been built up that would have changed the picture of English democracy? This view, however, does not fit into the historical scene, for cheap fiction began to appear *after* the working classes had largely abandoned their earlier aspirations. In fact, the latter hopes were based on a glowing discovery of new worlds of the mind: they had no hope of fulfilment without changing conditions in work and living conditions, without more informed social attitudes, and without a real understanding of the roots of art and knowledge. If there is a relevance of this situation to that of today, it is the futility of superficial, immediately exciting culture, and the importance of a prolonged education into the principles behind cultural values.

As it was, the working classes were open to literature of the

1. art. cit., pp. 280 ff.

lowest taste. The best-known semi-pornographic publication of this time was probably Renton Nicholson's *The Town* (1837–40), with its scandal about theatrical people and descriptions of public houses, music halls, brothels, and ladies of pleasure. (Some of the pieces appearing in this periodical, however, such as those reprinted in *Cockney Adventures* (1846), have vigour and genuine feeling for the flavour of cockney life.) But, as a correspondent to *Blackwood's* in 1834 warned darkly, *The Town* was not alone.

It is not generally known to our readers out of the metropolis, what immense manufactories of infidelity and exciting sensuality there exist, and to what extent they are diffused in the cheapest form throughout the great towns of the empire ... great part of these publications profess to detail the intrigues and devices of the aristocracy, illustrated, of course, by appropriate cuts and innuendoes ... The most popular licentious works of the age of Charles II, from Rochester's Poems downwards, are reprinted, and regularly issued in penny numbers, for a class never reached by the profligacy of the Cavaliers; and memoirs, narrating, with appropriate engravings, the sixty-eight intrigues of one of the most licentious of valets with his mistresses and their ladies' maids, are regularly issued in weekly numbers for the edification of the footmen and the *femmes de chambre* of London, and the numerous class which the Schoolmaster has trained to mental activity in the metropolis[1]

The main offender was William Dugdale, who spent half his life in prison for his dedication to peddling indecent publications. I have seen a penny or sixpenny issue edition from his press of *The Memoirs of Harriet Wilson ... the Whole forming the most astonishing Picture of Voluptuousness and Sensuality* (1838). Collectors of erotica mention surviving Dugdale editions of John Cleland's *Life of Fanny Hill*, a woman of the easiest virtue, and pornographic serials running under such names as *Anonyma* and *The Rambler*. William Benbow was frequently his associate; similar publishers include John Joseph Stockdale and J. Hucklebridge (pseud. ?). There is no doubt there was a certain amount of pornography being published, and some of it was aimed at the lower classes. *Fanny Hill's New Friskey Chanter and Amorous Toast Master* (c. 1836) was a small, wretchedly printed booklet that could not have cost more than sixpence. Contents included 'The Human Needle', 'Two Penno' worth of SHAG', 'My Little Brown Thing', 'William's Silent

1. 'The Schoolmaster', XXV, p. 242.

Flute', and 'The Thing that's in his Breeches'. In 'The Queen of the Wrigglewell Islands', Jack Junk finds himself in that archetypal position, the only man on the island.

> The Queen the game so pleasant found,
> Of being mounted on the ground,
> That she made him take her women round,
> Did the Queen of the Wrigglewell Islands.
> Poor Jack, at this, looked mighty blue,
> It was a work for a whole ship's crew;
> But what, poor devil, could he do?
> So, like a man, he the work went through.
> He did it once, he did it twice,
> The ladies found the sport so nice,
> That they installed him, in a trice,
> The King of the Wrigglewell Islands.
> Hokey, pokey, &c.

It is doubtful, however, whether the picture was as bad as the *Blackwood's* correspondent suggested. It is significant that most of this pornography was only reprinted from a previous age, and Francis Place, who made a thorough study of this, declared that in comparison with the eighteenth century, the early nineteenth century showed a virtual disappearance of this literature among the lower classes. *The Town* appealed mainly to the young 'bucks' of the city, and Thomas Frost, who had worked for Dugdale, declared that most of his works were too expensive for the workers. Prosecutions made by the Society for the Suppression of Vice suggest they were mostly peddled around to army barracks and boarding schools.

The lower-class publishers turned to the eighteenth century not only for erotica but for historical series and criminal biographies. The seminal work of 'true confessions', *The Ordinary of Newgate* by Paul Lorraine, issued in numbers in the early eighteenth century, was paralleled by numerous 'Newgate Calendars' based on earlier series, and we can compare *A General and True History of the Most Famous Highwaymen, Murderers, Street-robbers, etc.* (W. Walker 1742) with the title of J. Duncombe's publication *Adventures of Famous Highwaymen and other Public Robbers . . . New Edition* (c. 1834). Next in popularity were naval and military series; one issue of *Cleave's Penny Gazette* alone advertised three *Tales of the Wars* from different publishers.[1] Thackeray, reviewing one 'by a distinguished Officer of the Blues', declared 'nobly indeed, does this "distinguished officer" write. But, stay, have we not read something of this in a book called *The History of the Peninsular War*, by one Napier?' But, he went on, 'these stories are taken from good books, are written in good language, and tell of things it does one good to hear.'[2]

The publishers also went back to the eighteenth century to supply the growing desire for fiction. Previous series of standard novels in numbers such as Harrison's *Novelist's Magazine* had continued into this period through Limbird's *British Novelist* (1823–46), which linked the two eras. In the spate of periodicals at the beginning of the 1830s we find such series as *The Standard Works of Fiction of all Countries* (1831–2?), and *Pattie's Pocket Library* (1836–?), offering a wide range of fiction, mainly from old sources. Modern novels appeared in Foster and Hextall's *The Novelist* (1838–?), good value at eight folio sheets densely printed, with a woodcut, for twopence. *The Novel Newspaper* gave no woodcut, but concentrated on giving as much reading matter as possible in thirty-two pages of double-columned small print. Appearing variously under the imprints of Thomas Lyttleton Holt, J. Cunningham, and N. Bruce, it evidently prospered, to the jeopardy of the readers' eyes. Between 1838 and 1846 it published over eighty novels ranging from Dr Johnson's *Rasselas* to *The Last of the Mohicans*. *The Romancist and Novelist's Library*, edited by William Hazlitt, probably found a better-class readership, for after two years of twopenny issues (1839–40), it was continued in volume form only.

From reprinted fiction the popular press was to move on to fiction written specifically for the new working-class public. The central figure in this change is Edward Lloyd. Lloyd was the son of a Surrey farmer who left school at an early age to become a bookseller. He came to London and took a small shop adjoining Wych Street, among the many printing and publishing offices that were springing up in the area of Drury Lane. He had been 'strongly imbued with liberal opinions' from the age of fourteen, and in the war of the unstamped press made two attempts to start cheap periodicals; but both were quickly stopped by threats from the stamp office. He was no Hetherington. He studied at the Mechanics' Institute in Chancery Lane and showed his interest in the

1. I, 27 January 1838, p. 2.
2. *Fraser's Magazine*, XVII, 1838, p. 284.

methods of journalism by bringing out, at the age of nineteen, a booklet explaining his own system of stenography. His money, however, came from his trade in comic valentines, penny story books, and the theatrical portraits published by such men as Park, Dyer, and Hodson. In 1835 he began to feel his way as a publisher with *The History of Pirates, Smugglers, &c. of All Nations*, then with *The History of and Lives of the Most Notorious Highwaymen, Footpads . . . and Robbers of Every Description* (1836–7). In *The Calendar of Horrors* (1835, no imprint), he may have begun his association with Thomas Peckett Prest, a young song-writer and general literary hack who was to establish his publisher's fortune before being left aside to die in poverty.

In 1836 *Pickwick Papers* appeared. This serial publication began in the tradition of Seymour's early *Humorous Sketches* (1833–6) which had been issued by the lower-class publisher Carlile, and it was written by one who was then a practically unknown penny-a-line reporter. Its success revealed the immense prospects of cheap serial literature. Edward Lloyd, who had moved into new premises in Broad Street, immediately issued a plagiarism of *Sketches by 'Boz'*, which had just come out in a collected edition, called *The Sketch Book, by 'Bos'* (1836). After this, plagiarisms of other works by Dickens, Ainsworth, Henry Cockton and Mrs Crowe followed.

This will be studied in a later chapter. Here it may be noted that, once established by the success of works based on upper-class writers, publishers turned, with the experience they had gained in catering for lower-class readers, to producing new types of fiction. Tastes were changing, and the old romances which had done good service in the reprint libraries began to appear archaic to the new town readers. Their language was uncongenial to the worker accustomed to the idiom of the broadsheet and melodrama, and the life they portrayed strange. 'The chief value of this work,' said the *Odd Fellow* reviewer of a cheap reprint of *Pamela*, 'lies in its being a faithful transcript of the manners of a century ago.'[1] In 1839 Edward Lloyd began publishing three works in a more contemporary idiom. Two of them, *Victoria: or the Mysterious Stranger*, and *Mary, the Maid of the Inn*, failed; *Ela, the Outcast: or, the Gipsy of Rosemary Dell* by Thomas Peckett Prest, was one of Lloyd's best-selling novels, which was still reprinting in 1856. The road for the new fiction was open.

1. III, 1841, p. 86.

While new publishers like Edward Lloyd, T. Paine, and W. M. Clarke rose into prominence, the radical press was redirecting its energies, also towards fiction. There had never been a sharp division between political and literary publications. W. Strange published both *Carpenter's Political Magazine*, and *Figaro in London*, and James Watson sold the latter periodical next to Roebuck's pamphlets and Volney's *Ruins of Empires*.[1] John Cleave became an agent for *The Novel Newspaper* (1837?–48?): in 1845 he was publishing a large series of his own, *The Penny Novelist and Library of Romance*, besides original novels such as *The Gipsy Sibyl; or, the Riddle of Destiny* (1841).

Henry Hetherington also turned to the sale and publication of non-political literature. In 1838 he was advertising to country agents that he could supply 'all London Newspapers at the most advantageous terms, with punctuality, for CASH'.[2] In this year his political journal, *The London Dispatch*, which had known a circulation of 25,000 a week, failed for lack of support. At this time he published the theatrical *Actors by Gaslight; or, 'Boz' in the Boxes* (1838) and *The Odd Fellow* (1839–41), edited in succession by the dramatist James Cooke and W. J. Linton.[3] Although this claimed to be concerned with the Society of Odd Fellows, it was entirely a literary magazine. From this he turned to publishing fiction, such as the edition of *Pamela* already mentioned, and a good prose version of Southey's *Thalaba the Destroyer* (1842), made by one Thomas Moore. As he was becoming prosperous, in 1841 he moved into more extensive offices off Fleet Street.[4] His radical zeal was unabated. In 1840 he was imprisoned for selling Haslam's *Letters to the Clergy*, and to his death in 1849 he was a courageous supporter of free speech and reform. Nevertheless his publications ranged over a wider field than in his *Poor Man's Guardian* days.

At the beginning of 1840 two independent surveys were made of the literature circulating among the lower classes in London. One was by C. R. Weld for the Royal Statistical Society,[5] the other fell into the hands of a contributor to *The British and Foreign Review*.[6]

1. W. J. Linton, *James Watson*, 1879, p. 48.
2. *Cleave's Penny Gazette*, II, 24 March 1838, p. 4.
3. Linton, *Memories*, p. 37.
4. 'To my Friends', *Odd Fellow*, III, 1841, p. 54.
5. 'Fourth Ordinary Meeting', *S.S.L.*, III, 1840, p. 106; *Athenaeum*, no. 643, 1840, p. 157.
6. 'Popular Literature', X, 1840, p. 242.

By combining them we can see the picture of the cheap periodical trade at this time.

There were approximately eighty cheap periodicals circulating in London. Two thirds of this number cost a penny, none cost more than twopence. Nine were scientific – the vestiges of *The Penny Magazine* and its followers. Only four were political. Five were considered licentious. Four were devoted to drama, and sixteen to biographies and memoirs. Twenty-two contained nothing but romances or stories. Large as this proportion of fiction was, it was to increase rapidly in the ensuing decade.

3

Currents in Popular Publishing,
1840—50

THE industrial township, the American sociologist Louis Wirth has written, has a distinct impact on the culture of the men and women drawn into it. The urban worker is brought 'within the range of stimulation by a great number of diverse individuals, and subjects himself to fluctuating states in the differentiated social groups that compose the social structure of the city'. This leads to the disintegration of old traditions, and the coming of a new cosmopolitan outlook.[1]

Here Mr Wirth's account of the modern situation reflects that of England in the 1830s. The essentially rural lower-class culture which expressed itself in ballads, broadsheets, and chapbooks, was fragmented when the worker moved into the towns. A multifarious range of interests was opened up, expressing itself in the short-lived enthusiasm for Mechanics' Institutes, reading circles, and periodicals packed with items of information taken from every field and period of learning – even works such as *The Percy Anecdotes* and Shakespeare's *Plays* were sold in twopenny numbers.

We have seen how these seeds, without roots in a genuine culture, shot up and withered, and the periodicals that remained tended towards a new, disillusioned cosmopolitan outlook. But what was to be the basis of the new urban culture? J. D. Burn saw no way forward. 'The highly poetical, and in any case harmless, superstitions of the last century, with their train of supernatural events, have been substituted by the vilest trash imaginable.'[2] The destruction of old poetic traditions was not the only disaster to popular literature. Shoddy and poor as much of it had been in the past, it was expensive and rare enough to be written to keep; the mass literature in penny numbers was meant to please for a few

1. 'Urbanism as a Way of Life', *American Journal of Sociology*, XLIV, 1938, pp. 1–24.
2. *The Language of the Walls*, 1855, p. 211.

hours, and the less demands it made on the comprehension of the tired workman the better. The need for a constant stream of material also meant a lowering in quality. Fiction has always been written for money, but a massive commercial enterprise catering for the transient stimulation of bored minds meant something new. 'Upon the narrow isthmus on which we stand,' wrote John Wilson Ross, 'on one hand rolls the literature of the past, and on the other, the ocean of literature of the future. [We] hail . . . a new coming epoch in the world of letters – ECONOMIC LITERATURE.'[1] The era of mass popular fiction had arrived.

'Economic Literature' drew upon the drive and ingenuity shown by commercial enterprise in all fields at this period. In the ten years following 1840, some fifty publishers sought to exploit the new prospects.[2] One of Edward Lloyd's first rivals was T. Paine, of 22 Bride Lane, Fleet Street. In 1840 Paine began issuing *Angela the Orphan: or, the Bandit Monk of Italy*. It grafted melodrama on to a story reminiscent of *The Mysteries of Udolpho*, and was declared to be 'The most successful Romance ever published' with a weekly sale of 14,000.[3] This figure, well under half the circulation of Cleave's *Penny Gazette*, is not impossible. Reprinting was announced at the third number. In 1841 George Vickers, a newsagent, published the *Mysteries of Old St Paul's*, a travesty of Ainsworth's romance which was running concurrently in *The Sunday Times*.

Some of these penny-issue publishers were newcomers, others were those already noticed as rising in the period of political journalism with paste-and-scissors magazines. Almost all were concerned exclusively with publishing for the lower classes. The one exception was W. M. Clarke, of Warwick Lane, Paternoster Row, who published a range of works from the middle-class *Man in the Moon* (1847–9) and many educational books, to penny-issue series such as *Tales of Shipwrecks, and Adventures at Sea* (1846–7), or *Will Watch* (1848).

Some of those publishers, like Clarke, were also printers. The names of five of them appeared as printers in *The Typographical Gazette* for 1846, and this list was not complete.[4] Anyone who

1. 'The Influence of Cheap Literature', *L.J.*, I, 1845, p. 115.
2. v. Appendix II.
3. (Advert.), *Odd Fellow*, II, 1840, p. 204.
4. 'London Printing Offices', no. 4, 1846, pp. 62–4.

wished could publish, however, as did William Sinnett, who gave French tuition in rooms in Oxford Street, and who published his own translation of Frédéric Soulié's *The She-Tiger of Paris* (*c.* 1850). Some publishers, like the person responsible for *Nell Gwynne: or, the Court of Charles II* (1849), preferred to remain anonymous. The *Odd Fellow* complained of 'novel, small and licentious publications' some of which 'bear also fabricated names of printers and publishers'.[1] 'J. Hucklebridge' may have been a fabricated name which covered the publisher of *The Dodger* (later, *The Sunday Chronicle* [1841]). Each number was claimed to contain 'Tales of the most Absorbing Interest, and which absolutely rivet the attention of the reader with a species of galvanic force. These Tales are replete with MYSTERY, HORROR, LOVE & SEDUCTION!'[2] One such story was 'A True and Faithful Account of an Amour of His Royal Highness Prince Albert.'[3]

Edward Lloyd may himself have wished on certain occasions to withhold his imprint. Thomas Frost took two novels to him, and had them accepted. No surviving novel by Frost bears Lloyd's imprint, but *Paul the Poacher* (1848) bears that of G. Purkess, who often collaborated with Lloyd. Although Frost later became a writer for the Religious Tract Society, *Paul the Poacher* contains scenes, particularly one of rape in a subterranean chamber, which Lloyd would have preferred not to own. It is therefore possible that he came to an arrangement with his less nice fellow-publisher. Both of Lloyd's Dickens plagiarisms *The Penny Pickwick* and *Oliver Twiss* appeared, simultaneously and for the same number of weeks, under the imprint of W. Haydon and then of J. Graves: again, Lloyd may well have been avoiding indignation against the plagiarisms.[4]

This does not exhaust the complications of publishers' imprints. Thomas Lyttleton Holt, part-proprietor of *Figaro in London*, 'obtained credit for starting more newspapers and publications than any other man'. But his name does not appear usually on the title-page. He would write a piece, then 'get it nominally published by Berger or Vickers (both well-known newsagents in Holywell Street), but would take copies round to the wholesale dealers

1. 'The Taste of the Public', I, 12 January 1839, p. 6.
2. (Advert.), *Sunday Chronicle*, I, 25 July 1841, p. 2; but see infra, p. 188.
3. I, 18 April 1841, p. 1.
4. *Penny Pickwick*, nos. 91–9, 100–105; *Twiss*, 57–65, 66–9.

and sell them himself'.[1] Joseph Last was another indefatigable promoter of cheap periodicals, but his name does not appear on the works themselves: when Renton Nicholson wished to find employment from the publisher of *The Tales of the Wars* (*c.* 1837) he applied at the office of A. Forrester, 310 Strand, but was referred to the real proprietor, Last, who was living off the Hampstead Road.[2]

Although this little-explored corner of Victorian publishing is full of interest, it is important not to overestimate its extent. Many of these publishers were small, and in financial straits. Those in the vicinity of Drury Lane used to patronize a small public house run by a 'Mother Trimby'. Frequently they could not afford to pay for their drinks, and the landlady would chalk up their debts, in units of a penny, on a board above the counter.[3] Although B. D. Cousins was able to publish *The Farthing Journal* for a farthing for four pages 8⅞ in. × 5⅜ in., and at the end of sixty-six numbers claim it had 'paid its expenses',[4] these publications were not lucrative.

Charles Knight gave an interesting estimate of the cost of publishing a cheap sheet, which he called *The Sewer*.[5] This was in 1850, but prices had not changed much in the preceding decade.

	£	s.	d.
Contributors to *The Sewer*	5	0	0
Composition by Parish Apprentices – no Corrections, no Reader	3	0	0
Stereotyping (*nil*) no back demand – Advertising – a placard on a cart	2	0	0
Fixed cost	10	0	0
40,000 copies (with duty)			
80 reams whitey-brown paper – 24 lbs @ 6d	48	0	0
Machined in the worst way, 3s.	12	0	0
(Total cost)	70	0	0
By 40,000 wholesale	110	0	0
Profit	40	0	0

1. Wilson, p. 45.
2. R. Nicholson, *Autobiography*, 1860, pp. 229 ff.
3. Wilson, p. 34.
4. *Farthing Journal*, I, 1841, p. 260.
5. *Struggles of a Book* . . ., 1850, pp. 14 ff.

These items can be examined more closely. First, paper. By Knight's estimate the paper used was nine shillings a ream, or, with duty of 1½d per pound, twelve shillings. This is only half the cost of the paper normally used, which cost seventeen shillings a ream, twenty-four shillings taxed. Periodicals did not normally use this cheapest paper because the ink came through it, ruining any illustrations. When Edward Lloyd tried to use a cheaper paper for *The People's Periodical*, he had to leave the page on the obverse of the woodcut unused. Secondly, composition. On the normal scale this would have cost £8. Knight's accusation that lower-class printers used child labour 'at the wages of scavengers' must be taken with the realization that the printing trade had the most powerful union of the time, and as early as 1804 this had laid down standard wages for compositors. Hetherington, Watson, White, and W. M. Clarke were recognized Master Printers. Besides, anyone who has worked in a printing office will recognize that all these cheap publications have passed through correction (6d per hour, standard rate). Thirdly, advertising. Knight's jibe 'a placard on a cart' was misplaced. Even if advertisements which appeared in periodicals of a similar class were arranged by a gentleman's agreement, there were still handbills to be distributed and displayed on shop doors. One observer declared he met them 'at every step'.[1] Fourthly, sales. Knight counts on a sale of 40,000. For this, he has taken the ream at its extended number of 500 sheets, but he has not made allowance for the average wastage of about twenty per ream. More important, he has calculated on the upper-class rates of wholesale, 7½d to 8d per dozen. Lower-class publications were in fact sold at the rate of the broadsheet, i.e. 6d–6½d per dozen, which brings receipts, allowing for no wastage, to £89 at the most. Unsold numbers were exchanged, too, for current numbers, and in the case of penny-issue novels the second number was given away with the first. If, after all this, there still remained a profit, this was only when sales were high – and few of the lesser penny periodicals can have had a circulation as high as 40,000.

The penny-issue novel also had the expense of stitching, of printing a coloured cover for each number, of more machining, and of making one or possibly two woodcuts at ten shillings each; this was in part offset by its being a little smaller than Knight's *Sewer*: although they were both made from one sheet, Knight's estimate, if accurate, makes it about $\frac{3}{4}$ oz. per number, whereas a 'penny dreadful' (which may have been further trimmed) was found to be about $\frac{1}{2}$ oz.

The fees paid to contributors were therefore meagre, or, if possible, evaded. Thomas Frost made an inquiry after a contribution he had sent to one editor: the editor denied having received it, but later published it, without notifying Frost.[1] The Editor of *Lloyd's Penny Weekly Miscellany* was more open. In a note to 'G.A.' he declared, 'We do not pay for any contributions.'[2] No publisher was going to pay if the pride of seeing oneself in print was sufficient recompense. 'G.A.' however, may have been puzzled by the preface to volume three, which declared that Lloyd's stories 'are really written by established authors, and liberally paid for'.[3] This referred to experienced writers, who often would submit only ten or twelve chapters, which if satisfactory would be accepted with the understanding that the story would be prolonged if it were successful.

The fees paid for this varied. George Mansell gave E. L. L. Blanchard who, in the 1830s was a struggling playwright, penny-a-liner, and literary hack, five shillings a page to write a life of Jack Sheppard. Blanchard was paid ten shillings a number by John Cleave to abbreviate classics for his *Popular Library*.[4] Edward Lloyd paid twelve shillings a column for correspondence-column writing. These, following the example of *The Family Herald*, were generally a feature of lower-class literary magazines. They provided information on everything from the choice of a career to the way to make ink. When there were not enough letters, the writer also had the task of composing inquiries.[5]

Edward Lloyd showed early the practical ingenuity which accounted for much of his success. When a writer was established as a reliable contributor, Lloyd issued him with specially lined paper, which, covered with average-sized writing, would constitute one penny issue. Payment was strictly on delivery, ten shillings a number. Small as this amount was (and ten years later it was only 5s. 9d.) it enabled a rapid writer such as E. P. Hingston to make

1. Frost, *Reminiscences*, pp. 192 ff.
2. I, 1843, p. 640.   3. 'Preface', III, p. iii.
4. E. L. L. Blanchard, *Life and Reminiscences*, ed. C. Scott and G. Howard, 1891, pp. 31, 49 f.
5. J. Bertram, *Glimpses of Real Life*, Edinburgh, 1864, p. 157.

enough money in a week to spend the next two or three weeks in France; and it helped James Malcolm Rymer, who was said to have written ten serials simultaneously, to retire later on a fortune. At death his estate was £8,000. The pace, however, was inexorable, and a writer such as Thomas Peckett Prest, author of *Ela the Outcast*, who suffered from lung trouble, died a pauper in a cheap lodging house.

The method of payment naturally influenced the style of these romances. When E. P. Hingston had been writing for Lloyd for some time, 'He saw that his brother authors wrote as much conversation as possible, and made their lines very short; whereas [he] had filled in all solid matter, and by so doing was giving half as much work again for the money as any of the authors. "I did not do it again," said Hingston.' It is therefore interesting to note that Hingston's early novel *Helen Porter: or the Mysteries of the Sewers of London* is in a style relatively dense for this literature, while the later *Amy: or, Love and Madness*, which claims the same author, is particularly diffuse. I quote a passage:

'I need no assistance, dear father. But where is Archy gone?'
'He has followed your brother Frank.'
'And Frank, you said——'
'Has gone in pursuit of Ernest.'
Amy looked at her father inquiringly, and demanded, –
'Are you sure that Archy has gone in company with Frank?'
'It is my belief that he has,' returned Mr Heyton.
A smile of satisfaction passed over the face of the maiden, as she ejaculated –
'I am glad of that – very glad of that!'
'Of what Amy – of what are you glad?'
'That Archy has accompanied Frank; said you not so, dear father?'
'He has, child.'
'And they have gone to seek Ernest?'
'They have.'
'That is fortunate; oh! that is very fortunate.'[1]

. . . And so on. The very repetition, however, was not altogether without its appeal to the reader who could only pick out the few words he could recognize. The limited vocabulary and range of plot in these novels catered for a partially educated mentality.

The diffuse style required its own peculiar techniques. One

1. pp. 58–9.

writer, a Mr Watkins, used to write the first twenty lines of his chapter with large spaces in between the lines. He then interpolated others until he had matter for about half a page, and copied this on to a clean sheet, 'the stuff', as he called it, being expanded to double or treble the length. By constant rewriting he produced the tale which he transferred to the lined paper, which was taken to the publisher.[1] Charles Manby Smith described a 'popular author' who did the same thing, only he wrote in the publishing office itself, expecting each re-issue to be set up for him by a printer who then had to work all night. Even then the final copy often had to be filled out by means of interpolations such as 'Ha!' 'Ugh!' 'Indeed!' 'You don't say so!' 'The Devil', 'ejaculations which were kept standing on a galley in separate lines, to be had recourse to in a case of last emergency'.[2] There do not seem to be other contemporary references to text being expanded while in the press, although J. F. Smith used to write in the printing office. He would arrive, look over the end of the last instalment, then lock himself in a room with a bottle of port until he had composed the next number.[3]

Penny-issue novels were only part of the new commercial literature that was being published week by week. Cheap magazines provided even easier reading, and grew in importance as the 1840s progressed. Credit for starting the first illustrated story magazine at a penny has been given to William Strange, who had brought out *The Penny Story-Teller* in 1832. In 1837 it was still running and was favourably mentioned by Thackeray.[4]

In 1840 periodical fiction received a new impetus when *The Sunday Times* began to serialize William Blanchard Rede's novel *The History of a Royal Rake*. Its apology for this 'Novelty' was symptomatic of the new reading habits – 'In these stirring times men scarcely find leisure for the perusal of volumes.'[5] *The Sunday Times* was sevenpence: a few months after this serial began, Edward Lloyd, whose plagiarisms over this period make a reliable index of what was most popular, began *The Penny Sunday Times and People's Police Gazette* (1840–49?). In order to avoid the stamp

1. Bertram, pp. 154 ff.
2. C. M. Smith, *A Working Man's Way in the World*, 1857, p. 215.
3. H. Vizetelly, *Glances Back through Seventy Years*, 1893, p. 12.
4. art. cit., *Fraser's Magazine*, XVII, March 1838, p. 140.
5. 'Introduction', *The Sunday Times*, 5 January 1840, p. 2.

duty on newspapers, it consisted entirely of fiction and fabricated police reports. In 1843 a survey of reading in a representative lower-class part of London placed it sixth out of twelve papers in popularity;[1] in 1848 a similar survey placed it above all other papers either Sunday or weekly.[2] From 1841 a similar sheet was published entitled *The Companion to Lloyd's Penny Sunday Times*.

Sunday papers, as a contemporary observer declared, were 'essentially the papers of the poor'.[3] They were increasing in popularity over this period among the large number of comparatively uncritical readers in the new towns who had neither time nor money to read a newspaper daily. Sunday, moreover, was traditionally a day for trade in working-class literature, not only papers, but broadsheets and what Charles Manby Smith called 'blood-and-murder, ghost-and-goblin journals'[4] – the penny serial novels.

Other publishers were quick to follow Lloyd in providing cheap imitations of established London papers. *Bell's Weekly Dispatch*, whose respectable appearance belied the content of crime reports, was at this time the most popular paper among the working classes. It inspired *The Penny Weekly Dispatch* (1840), *Clarke's Weekly Dispatch* (1841–2) and *Bell's Penny Dispatch, Sporting and Police Gazette and Newspaper of Romance* (1841).

These papers were decorated with lurid woodcuts and, as the last-mentioned title suggests, tried to cover as many fields as possible; but the vigilant stamp office prevented them from giving any news. Herbert Ingram, an American, who had been a journeyman-printer in London in the early 1830s and was at this time a newsagent in Nottingham, was struck by the increase in sales in the papers which provided illustrations. He had acquired the formula of a famous aperient, Parr's Life Pills, and partly with the profits from this, in order to exploit the attraction of lavish illustrations, started *The Illustrated London News* in 1842. His first editor was F. W. N. Bayley, and he aimed the paper at the working classes. 'Our business will be with the household gods of the English people, and, above all, of the English Poor.'[5] After two years the circulation exceeded 25,000 copies weekly.

1. 'Conditions of the Working Classes . . .', *S.S.L.*, VI, February 1843, p. 21.
2. 'Report . . .', *S.S.L.*, XI, August 1848, p. 216.
3. A. Andrewes, *A History of English Journalism*, 1838, II, p. 340.
4. C. M. Smith, *Curiosities of London Life*, 1853, pp. 256–7.
5. 'Preface', I, 1842, p. 1.

Edward Lloyd promptly issued *Lloyd's Illustrated London Newspaper*. This was unstamped. After seven numbers the stamp office
threatened prosecution over a report of an escaped lion, and Lloyd
stamped his paper, which at first sold for twopence, then twopence
halfpenny, for eight pages. It carried news in full. The regular
newsagents boycotted it on account of its low price, but Lloyd
built up his own sales organization. He placed his advertisements
on walls, trees, and fences throughout the country, and even
stamped them on pennies paid to his workmen, until stopped by
Act of Parliament.

The early success of this paper and of *The Penny Sunday Times*
(which claimed a circulation of over 95,000),[1] led Lloyd in 1843 to
move from Shoreditch to larger premises off Fleet Street in Salisbury Square, where, as he was fond of informing readers, Samuel
Richardson had been a printer. Here he installed two power presses
of a new design, which could handle over 5,000 copies an hour.
He could therefore expand his trade. During the same year he
began publishing *Lloyd's Penny Weekly Miscellany* (1843–6), using a
woodcut of one of his new presses as his heading. The editor was
James Malcolm Rymer, a mechanic whom Lloyd may have met
while attending the Mechanics' Institute in Chancery Lane.

Works by Rymer appeared under at least seven names, of which
the most common was M. J. Errym. Even such authorities as *The
Library of Congress Catalogue* and A. Fergusson, in *A Bibliography of
Australia*, believe he was Prest, and there has been a good deal of
confusion. This was cleared up when the late Mr Frank Algar
bought a collection of his books and papers, including a proof
copy of one of his novels. Perhaps most interesting were two
volumes of cuttings from various periodicals with a signed note in
Rymer's hand saying they are all by him, and would borrowers be
careful since they are the only copy he had kept. These scrapbooks
are now in my possession.

Rymer was born in 1804 in a middle-class home, probably in the
Scottish highlands. Between 1838 and 1860 his name appears in
the London Directories, where he is described first as a civil
engineer, surveyor, and mechanical draughtsman. In 1846 his
name appears in the Patent Register. Writing was in the family – a
copy of *The Spaniard* (1806) by Ellen Rymer appeared among his
collection of books – and the entries in the Directories show him

1. (Advert.), *Lloyd's Weekly London Newspaper*, I, 19 March 1843, p. 4.

forsaking his other pursuits as he turned to literary work. His ambition was to be a middle-class writer. Many scrapbook entries show him a competent essayist in the style of Leigh Hunt. In the respectable *The Queen's Magazine* he writes disparagingly about popular fiction, and even his own popular works, such as *Varney the Vampyre* (1847), contain passages where the mass of the workers are castigated as fickle and unintelligent, criticism which, to paraphrase Swift, they no doubt transferred to the shoulders of the world, as well broad enough to bear it. His middle-class ventures, however, such as *The Queen's Magazine*, failed, whereas *Ada the Betrayed* was in current demand fifteen years after its first publication. He therefore turned his contempt to good advantage, following his own advice to the writer who would become popular, to 'study the animals for whom he has to cater'.[1] Future chapters will show the way in which he did this, and also why Robert Louis Stevenson said if anyone gave him a copy of *The Mystery in Scarlet*, his 'gratitude (the Muse consenting) will even drop into poetry'.[2]

Rymer began the *Miscellany* auspiciously with *Ada, the Betrayed* and followed it with another success, *Jane Brightwell*. In spite of what these titles may suggest, the magazine did not appeal mainly to female or juvenile readers. It had an adult viewpoint, and claimed to offer to the poor pleasures of reading that were hitherto reserved for the wealthy. The Editor had found that 'correct tastes, glowing fancies, and an admirable perception of the poetical and beautiful ... are to be found by the humblest firesides' as the workers perused his periodicals.[3] A workman from the Staffordshire potteries wrote to say that the *Miscellany* was particularly appreciated by those

... who have no time for profound research, immersed in trading speculations, or their whole time engrossed by manual operations, so that they may only catch an occasional glimpse of the world of letters. To these individuals the 'Miscellany' presents itself in smiles and dimples – it invites them to pastimes without a laborious renewal of those laborious efforts, to which the faculties have already been stretched to their utmost degree of tension, and offers a refreshing treat

1. 'Popular Writing', *The Queen's Magazine*, 1, 1842, p. 99.
2. 'Popular Authors', *Works*, Tusitala Ed., 1923, pp. 27–8.
3. 'Preface', I, 1843, p. 1.

to the mental and moral constitution, so well adapted to our wants, that it must be duly appreciated.[1]

These readers were invited to laugh at the illiterate artisan in the person of Squashtottle, who wrote this kind of poetry:

> Jewlia, – Jewlia, luk at Squashtottle
> & turne is hart too blazes
> While this ere bit of pottery
> Greanplushes sole amazes![2]

(Greenplush is his rival for the hand of Julia.) The Squashtottle contributions are the most readable verses in the volume. The 'serious' verse is trite and sentimental in content, and is written with little regard for style or syntax. The following example illustrates this, and is also given because it shows the earnest way in which some readers evidently took the romances. There appear a number of poems on *Ada, the Betrayed*, all apparently written by men.

> Sonnet Addressed to the Author
> of 'Ada' by the author of 'Emily
> Anson'. (R.B.)

> A dream of beauty and of passionate love
> Hath visited thy spirit – such a dream
> As some sweet fairy gliding down a stream
> Glassing the stars, that shine sublime above –
> Might love to fold unto her heart! Oh thou
> Unknown, yet not uncherished – if to be
> The wizard of the fancy's starry glow –
> A glow empearling immortality! . . .
> If a deep worship of the beautiful
> Display a soul of love – a pious heart, –
> Then thou a true and gentle poet art.[3]

Apart from poetry, the Editor soon had so much material offered him that he sometimes brought out two numbers in one week 'to less the stock of tales by us'.[4] Lloyd also resorted to publishing an

1. 'Miscellany in 1843', ibid., p. 599.
2. I, 1843, p. 44.   3. ibid., p. 649.   4. ibid., p. 640.

almost identical periodical, *Lloyd's Penny Atlas, and Weekly Register of Novel Entertainment* (1843–5). Then, in its third year, the Editor of *The Miscellany*, while exulting in the 'melancholy suicide' of Knight's *Penny Magazine* in the face of 'the talent, the learning, and the profound experience' of his own writers, had to announce that his own magazine would henceforth be incorporated with *Lloyd's Entertaining Journal*.[1]

This was in part perhaps to give Lloyd more space to publish his penny-issue novels, which rose to their peak of about thirty-eight new works in 1847. But Lloyd's publications were being ousted by the rise of a more sophisticated type of popular periodical. The first of these was *The Family Herald* which was started by George Biggs in December 1842 to use the first composing machine to be invented, in which he had an investment.[2] The machine was a failure, but the magazine made Biggs's fortune. It met the requirements of the self-respecting family for a magazine which not only could be left about where the children might read it – an important factor as morality began to get stricter and more self-conscious – but it could be read aloud at family gatherings, a diversion pictured in the woodcut heading Edwin Dipple's *Family Journal* (1846). This public became increasingly important to the periodical trade, and occasioned such magazines as *The Home Circle* (1849–54), *The Family Friend* (1849–1921), and *Household Words* (1850–59). These need not be studied in detail, as they generally appealed more to the middle classes, and had somewhat higher prices – it must be remembered that the difference of a halfpenny meant the equivalent of more than fivepence today, and this to people who had to count every penny. Overcrowding – sometimes three or four families had to share a room in the worst slums – and the whole family going out to work, hardly encouraged family reading among the lower classes. Cheap periodicals like Edward Lloyd's *The Family Portfolio* (n.d.), *The People's Periodical and Family Library* (1846–7), and Edwin Dipple's *Family Journal* (1846) were none of them very successful.

An exception was *The Family Economist . . . Devoted to the Moral, Physical, and Domestic Improvement of the Industrious Classes*, a work produced by an upper-class concern, which ran from 1848 to 1860. This good monthly magazine contained articles such as practical cheap recipes, and hints on housekeeping on a small budget. Each

1. 'Preface', VI, 1846, p. vi.   2. Wilson, p. 21.

issue contained two stories, which rarely showed the condescension of an article 'How to endure Poverty'.[1] More usual sentiments were those of encouragement. 'How to get on in the World'[2] shows how sending a boy to school, and having to keep him neat, transforms the family's slovenly habits. This leads to the son changing over from being a nailmaker's apprentice to training as a draughtsman. The story is remarkably free from the sententiousness of many didactic tales at this time: for instance, there is a spark of observed humanity in the picture of the father, the centre of ridicule from the villagers because he has given up drink. He becomes violently angry, and keeps to his resolution not with a glow of self-righteousness, but in stubborn independence.

The Family Herald found and kept a distinct audience, for although it never resorted to illustrations, special features, or prizes its sales remained steady whatever the fluctuations of other periodicals.[3] This audience can be gauged by the homely mottoes that appear below the heading in early numbers. *The London Journal* (1845–1912), however, appealed to stronger tastes. It was started by George Stiff, an engraver who had risen to a position of importance for his work on *The Illustrated London News*, although he had been sacked later for incompetence. To start his new venture he found a paper-making firm to back him, then got involved in such heavy debt that his financiers were obliged to forward a much larger sum to avoid a total loss. (This procedure was later used by Ralph Rollington to start another periodical.)[4] With greater capital, the magazine proved a success. Its profits rose to between £10,000 and £12,000 a year – an exceptional figure for this period – with a circulation of 500,000 copies per issue. It established for George Vickers, its first publisher, a business which is still running today.

Its first editor was George W. M. Reynolds. Reynolds gave *The London Journal* a tone quite different from that of Lloyd's *Miscellany*, or of *The Family Herald*. He was a middle-class man of some interest in the development of cheap fiction, and deserves a brief study here. He was the son of Captain Sir George Reynolds who sent him, at the age of fourteen, to Sandhurst to train for an army

1. I, 1848, p. 24.
2. ibid., pp. 3, 30, 48, 83, 97.
3. Bertram, p. 140.
4. R. Rollington, *A History of Boys' Periodicals*, Leicester, 1913, p. 75.

career. His independent and sensitive feelings made him dislike army life, and at twenty-one when his father died and he inherited £12,000, he at once left Sandhurst for Paris. There he set up in the Rue-Neuve, St Augustin, investing his money in an Anglo-French newspaper called *The London and Paris Courier*, opening 'The French, English, and American Library', and trying his hand at fiction with *The Youthful Impostor* (1835). He gained experience at the cost of his fortune, and in 1836 returned to England in straitened circumstances. Here he continued as a writer for the middle classes, producing a novel, *Grace Darling* (1836), contributions to *Bentley's Miscellany*, and editing *The Monthly Magazine*. However, the opportunities offered by the new mass audience evidently appealed to him. He had a somewhat paternal attitude to this semi-literate public, as is seen in his articles 'Etiquette for the Millions'. Here there is instruction of the level of 'Never convey the knife to your mouth; nor put bread into the gravy. Eat slowly, and never let anything drop from your mouth on your plate.'[1] There are also articles which discuss the procedure of helping your partner to wine and similar rituals, which can only have been read for the interest of a 'silver fork' story.

In 1845 Reynolds quarrelled with Stiff, left *The London Journal*, and began *Reynolds's Miscellany of Romance, General Interest, Science and Art*. The first number carried a half-page engraving of the proprietor, and the first number of his novel *Wagner: the Wehrwolf*. In the preface Reynolds avowed his intention of steering between the periodicals devoted exclusively to fiction (e.g. *The London Journal*), and those concerned exclusively with instruction. It included articles on physiology, on the provincial press, and a weekly address to 'the industrial classes', in which Reynolds was able to expound his Chartist views. There was the usual column of 'Notices to Correspondents' which Reynolds used as a means of advertising and of giving publicity about himself and other writers. From these columns we learn that the *Miscellany* was selling 30,000 current numbers a week, and 10,000 back numbers.[2]

There is also the information that Reynolds's *Mysteries of London* was selling nearly 40,000 copies a week.[3] This work also was stereotyped, and so back numbers were always in stock. The content of Reynolds's writing will be considered later, but it is in place to mention the extent of his work. Between 1841 and 1856 over

1. *L.J.*, 1845, p. 119. 2. I, 1847, p. 303. 3. ibid., p. 175.

thirty full-length novels appear under his name, besides a large number of smaller pieces. One of these alone, *The Mysteries of the Court of London*, has been estimated to contain just under 4,500,000 words, or forty-eight average modern novels. It is possible that Reynolds did not write all this himself: J. J. Wilson stated[1] that he trained several 'ghost' writers.

His publisher for the first volume of *The Mysteries of London* was George Vickers. In 1846 Vickers died, and although his business was carried on capably by his widow Mary Ann Vickers, and by his sons,[2] Reynolds transferred the *Miscellany* and the rest of his publications to John Dicks, at this time a small publisher issuing works from Warwick Square.[3] Reynolds's works made the fortune of Dicks, who rose in the 1850s to be one of the largest publishers in London. When he became 'respectable', he changed the title *Reynolds's Miscellany* to *Bow Bells*, perhaps to conceal the way by which he had come to his wealth.

After Reynolds left *The London Journal*, it continued under the editorship of John Wilson Ross. Its circulation was increased by the woodcuts of the young John Gilbert. In 1849 J. F. Smith, a Bohemian figure, who had spent his life adventuring in France and Italy, returned to England. He turned from drama to writing fiction, contributed to *The London Journal* first *Marianne, a Tale of the Temple*, then *Stanfield Hall*. This novel, which will be examined in due course, brought the *Journal*'s circulation up to 100,000 copies a week in 1849. His next novel, *Minnigrey*, brought it up to half a million. Smith used to increase the tension of his stories until the work-girls of the northern towns, one of his biggest class of readers, bought a copy each instead of waiting to borrow one, and the circulation would soar. When a story in *The London Journal*, or its rival *Reynolds's Miscellany*, moved towards its climax, James Bertram, at this time a small newsagent in Edinburgh, had to hire a special waggon to bring his copies from the station.[4]

The success of these two major periodicals brought the usual crop of imitations. *Chambers's London Journal* (1844–5), published by Strange, Clements, and Berger behind the name of a fictional 'H. H. Chambers', tried to draw on the popularity of the publica-

1. *Bootle Times*, 28 January 1916, p. 2.
2. *Home Office Reports* (P.R.O.), Pressmark 107, 1512/1/6.
3. 'John Dicks', *Bookseller*, March 1881, p. 231.
4. Bertram, p. 140.

tions both of Stiff and of the Chambers brothers. Probably more popular, *The London Pioneer* (1846–7, becoming *The London Literary Pioneer*, 1848), was modelled on *The London Journal*, with a distinct lowering in tone. It led off with 'The Unwedded One' by Mrs Smerdon that gave everything its title promised, and followed it up with translations from Eugene Sue and Dumas. The first volume contained *The Outcasts of London*, running beside one of Sue's less tasteful works, *Martin the Foundling*. Nevertheless, *The London Pioneer* was brought out by B. D. Cousins as the direct successor to the indecent broadsheet periodical *The Penny Satirist*. This indicates the fact that the readers who used to buy the latter or *Cleave's Penny Gazette* were turning to works of the type of *The London Journal* – a less crude form of journalism.

Similar changes are noticeable in political and free-thinking literature at this time. The Reform Act agitation, with its simple faith in extended suffrage, had been followed by disillusionment when its aim had been partially achieved; and the Chartist movement, although its 'physical force' wing aroused fears of revolution in 1848, was more intellectually informed, working towards its programme of 'six points'. Even Feargus O'Connor's aggressive *Northern Star* was stamped and had a more respectable image than Hetherington's *Poor Man's Guardian*. When *The Morning Chronicle* investigated a popular rationalist periodical *The Lancashire Beacon*, it could find nothing more inflammatory than an attack on the Bishop of Manchester.[1] Working-class radicalism was not declining, but it became more theoretically aware and controlled.

On the working-class side, some of the frustrations were channelled into the development of trades unionism, and through acceptance of the respectability of labour. On that of the middle classes, writers like Carlyle were urging that notice be taken of the working-class situation. In 1832 Carlyle gave Ebenezer Elliott a rousing notice in *The Edinburgh Review*.[2] Elliott was in fact the middle-class owner of a small iron-foundry business in Sheffield, but his associations with the north and with industry gave him a working-class image. He was respectfully noticed by *The London Review* in an article 'The Poetry of the Poor'.[3] Thomas Cooper, the Chartist poet and editor of *The Chartist Rushlight* (1841), became a

1. 'Labour and the Poor. Manchester', 5 November 1849, 5.
2. 'Ebenezer Elliott', LV, 1832, pp. 338 ff.
3. I, 1838, p. 187.

contributor to *Jerrold's Shilling Magazine*. Ebenezer Enoch, writer of the radical *Songs of Universal Brotherhood* (1849), gained connections with *The Pall Mall Gazette*, and Thomas Miller, once a basket-maker, became lionized in Lady Blessington's circle. Kingsley made Cooper his model for Alton Locke in his novel of that name (1850), and Gerald Massey, once a silk-weaver, was to lie behind George Eliot's *Felix Holt* (1866). The very recognition of 'the two nations' by Disraeli in *Sybil* (1845) indicated that the barrier between them was to a limited extent becoming bridged.

J. Hepworth Dixon's articles in *The Daily News* on 'The Literature of the Lower Orders' were part of a wide notice of lower-class reading habits.[1] Concern was reflected in Parliamentary Reports, social surveys, and in the increasing number of magazines concerned with social conditions, such as *The Ragged School Magazine* and *The Englishwoman's Magazine*. *Household Words* (1850–59) was launched as Dickens's contribution to lower-class reading.

Whatever their effect on the upper classes – these will be looked at later – these investigations provide us with a good deal of information. Between 1840 and 1850 the number of cheap publications in London had grown approximately from eighty to a hundred, and whereas before twenty-two had been exclusively concerned with fiction, now the number was sixty. There are no statistics that reliably cover the whole cheap periodical trade, but in Manchester in 1850, Heywood was selling about 80,000 periodicals costing twopence or under,[2] and Shepherd in Liverpool was selling about 9,900.[3] G. W. Macree, without stating sources, declared that apart from religious publications, cheap periodicals in the whole of England had at this time a circulation of 2,900,000.[4]

The decade had seen the rise and fall of many small publishers, and the establishment of a few successful ones. A correspondent in *The Morning Chronicle* declared that six men who had begun in poverty had now risen through publishing cheap fiction to being able to run both town and country houses.[5] The men were un-named, but they were perhaps Edward Lloyd, the younger George Vickers, John Dicks, George Stiff, W. M. Clarke, and G. W. M.

1. 29 October, 7 November, 9 November 1847.
2. *Morning Chronicle*, 5 November 1849, p. 5.
3. ibid., 5 September 1850, p. 5.
4. Q., T. C. Worsley, *Juvenile Depravity*, 1850, p. 113.
5. Q., F. Mayne, *Perilous Nature of Penny Press*, 1850, p. 8.

Reynolds. On the other hand, Thomas Frost declared that only three or four publishers remained at this time who would accept penny-issue fiction for publication.[1] Lower-class 'penny dreadfuls' had begun to develop in 1830, and by the 1850s they were beginning to share the fate of much out-of-date fiction, and became juvenile literature. Yet they had played their part in the development of an urban adult culture; in what way, the following chapters attempt to show.

1. Frost, *Reminiscences*, p. 75.

4

The Beginnings of a New Type of Popular Fiction: Plagiarisms of Dickens

THE urban working-class reading public of the early nineteenth century was not only a new market for literature, it had its own tastes. Publishers felt their way into the field by trial and error, or sometimes with primitive forms of market research. Even Edward Lloyd, who had grown up in the slums of Drury Lane, educating himself in a Mechanics' Institute, did not trust his own judgement in these matters. His manager explained to Thomas Frost:

> Our publications circulate among a class so different in education and social position from the readers of three-volume novels, that we sometimes distrust our judgement and place the manuscript in the hands of an illiterate person – a servant, or machine boy, for instance. If they pronounce favourably upon it, we think it will do.[1]

Lloyd began by publishing plagiarisms, which are particularly interesting in that we can compare the altered version with the middle-class work. Plagiarisms were first made in order to avoid prosecution. By the 1814 Copyright Act, an author's works were protected for twenty-eight years. Lower-class periodicals such as *Cleave's Penny Gazette* carried long quotations, in particular from Dickens and Ainsworth, but in this they followed the practice of upper-class magazines; it was even encouraged by the publishers as a means of advertisement. When Henry Hetherington published thirty-two complete 'Sketches by "Boz"', in *The Odd Fellow*, he was stopped from further piracy by the threat of legal action, and had to publish an apology.[2]

The author, however, had little redress against plagiarism. In June 1838 Vice-Chancellor Knight Bruce refused to give Chapman and Hall an injunction restraining Lloyd's *Penny Pickwick*, although he

1. Frost, *Forty Years' Recollections*, 1880, p. 90.
2. *Odd Fellow*, I, 1839, p. 204.

admitted the cheaper work's origin in Dickens's novel, on the grounds that no one would have confused the two books. 'A Christmas Ghost Story', an adaptation of *A Christmas Carol* in *Parley's Penny Library* (6 January 1844), was much closer to Dickens's work, and Knight Bruce issued an injunction restraining the second issue from being published. Dickens was awarded costs and, jubilant, proceeded to file five chancery suits against the publishers and booksellers. Egan Lee and John Haddock, publishers, pressed for costs and £1,000 damages, declared themselves insolvent and dissolved their partnership; this was little consolation to Dickens, who had to pay some £500 costs. The booksellers, William Strange, George Berger, W. M. Clarke, and John Cleave tried every evasion, and even threatened Dickens with a beating; finally they paid their costs, no more. Refusing to prosecute another plagiarism in 1846, Dickens wrote to Forster, 'I shall not easily forget the expense, and anxiety and horrible injustice of the Carol case, wherein, in asserting the plainest right upon earth, I was really treated as the robber instead of the robbed.'[1]

Dickens's *The Pickwick Papers* (1836–7) suffered more plagiarizing than any other book of its time. This novel started off with the poor circulation of only 400 copies; then, with the appearance of Sam Weller in the fifth number, caught the public imagination. By the fifteenth number it was selling 40,000 copies an issue. One met *Pickwick* everywhere – one rode in 'Boz' cabs, wore Pickwick coats and hats and smoked Pickwick cigars.

Even the common people, both in town and country, are equally intense in their admiration [wrote G. H. Lewes in *The National Magazine*] Frequently, have we seen the butcher-boy, with his tray on his shoulder, reading with the greatest avidity the last 'Pickwick'; the footman, (whose fopperies are so inimitably laid bare,) the maidservant, the chimney sweep, all classes, in fact, read 'Boz'.[2]

The Pickwick Papers, however, was something more to the lower-class mind than a particularly popular serial. The cultivated reader sees a character within the framework of a particular story, and is suspicious, generally rightly, of a further regeneration; the return of Pickwick and the Wellers in *Master Humphrey's Clock* was

1. *Letters of Charles Dickens*, Nonesuch, 1938, I, p. 780.
2. I, December 1837, pp. 445 ff.; attributed to Lewes by Professor Kathleen Tillotson.

not successful. The popular imagination, however, is interested in character conceived on a simple, well-defined plane, which exists independent of a complex literary form. All the popular heroes have been subjects of prolonged story-cycles, whether Odysseus, King Arthur, Sexton Blake, or 'Coronation Street', the long-running English television serial. *The Pickwick Papers* created a set of characters that became common property.

Dickens's greatest characters can exist independently of the novels partly because of their pictorial conception in the tradition of portraying comic *types*. This tradition which arrived from the eighteenth century through the work of the Cruikshanks and Seymour's *Humorous Sketches* (1843–6) – the direct antecedent of *Pickwick* – has been defined by William West in his 'Rules for Drawing Caricaturas'.[1] He gives a gallery of 'normal' faces, which are to be studied, then the artist is to portray a character by that which departs from the norm. James Cooke, who had himself used this technique in the series 'The world we live in',[2] called Dickens 'an accurate copier of eccentric physiognomies'.[3] *The London and Westminster Review* noted he had 'delighted to employ these powers [of character drawing] mostly in describing and commenting on the comic peculiarities of the lower orders of Englishmen', and notes his ability to portray 'the striking outlines of character, – the peculiarities of manner'.[4] The early pages of *Pickwick* at once give a visual picture:

What a study for an artist did that exciting scene present! The eloquent Pickwick, with one hand gracefully concealed behind his coat tails, and the other waving in air, to assist his glowing declamation; his elevated position revealing those tights and gaiters. . .

The tights, gaiters, round face, and green spectacles are essential to the conception of Pickwick, and made plagiarization possible by writers incapable of seeing how, particularly through his relation to Sam Weller, Dickens raised him above mere comic peculiarity. 'I hope you aren't arter changing that broad-brimmed tile . . .

---

1. In West's *Fifty Years' Recollections*, 1837.
2. *Odd Fellow*, I, 1839, p. 93 et seqq.
3. ibid., III, 1841, p. 107.
4. V and XXVII, 1837, pp. 196, 200.

celebrated black gaiters, or . . . them yaller tights', exclaims Weller in a plagiarism of 1840.[1]

As *The Pickwick Papers* grew to a certain extent out of the traditions of pictorial comic types, the popular press brought it back into the world of illustration. J. Fairburn published a gallery of *Pickwick Characters* (*c.* 1837), and 'W.C.W.' made forty woodcuts of 'all the Pickwick characters' (of course by no means all: Dickens portrays some three hundred). These appeared in *Sam Weller's Scrap Sheet* (J. Cleave, *c.* 1837), and, selected, in *Portraits of the Pickwick Characters* (1837) and in *The Casket* (1837–8). This treatment was not confined to *Pickwick*. Cleave issued *The Twist and Nickleby Scrapsheet* (*c.* 1839), with twenty-four woodcuts, and the 'principal Characters' of Dickens's work appeared in *Sketches of Character, from Master Humphrey's Clock* (W. Brittain, 1840), by 'Brush'.

While the world of the Pickwickians was extended by woodcuts, it was also recreated in music hall and theatre. Dickens was soaked in the world of the theatre, and its influence is a major one on his writing, particularly up to and including *Nicholas Nickleby*. Sam Weller's cockney humour and bizarre comparisons were preceded, in a paler image, in Captain Beaufort's servant, Simon Spatterdash, of Sam Beazley Jun.'s popular farce *The Boarding House*. Jingle's staccato speech would have been familiar to those who had enjoyed Charles Mathew's entertainments 'At Home', or Goldfinch in T. Holcroft's *The Road to Ruin*: it is significant that when Pierce Egan Sen. introduces his Jingle-type character, Tim Bronze,[2] just *after* the publication of *Pickwick*, he says that his staccato sentences were given with 'the rapidity of a *Goldfinch*'. One might note that both Jingle and his counterpart in *The Penny Pickwick* are travelling players.

One could go on citing similar comparisons. The relevant point here, however, is that the dramatic element in Dickens's characters as well as the pictorial, attracted the dramatists, who in any case preyed upon popular literary successes. William Leman Rede composed *The Peregrinations of Pickwick* after the appearance of the eighth number, and by October 1836 it was being played at the Adelphi theatre. It is hard to discover just how many other dramatic versions came out – at least three reached the permanence of

1. 'Noctes Pickwickianae', q. *Dickensian*, XIII, 1917, p. 187.
2. *Pilgrims of the Thames*, 1838, p. 20.

print. These printed plays make very little attempt to follow Dickens's plot; their interest was almost entirely in the characters, and these characterizations became real to many who could not have appreciated the literary creations of Dickens. *Mr Pickwick's Collection of Songs* (*c.* 1838), for instance, has on the frontispiece a picture of Weller, not as portrayed by Hablôt K. Browne, but as impersonated by Edmund Yates.

As the above work would suggest, the Pickwickians invaded music hall and public house as well as the theatre. At 'Manders' (probably the Sun Tavern, a lower-class pub in Long Acre), members formed 'The Pickwick Club', where they could listen to songs such as 'Sam Weller's Adventures', sung by a Mr J. Thomas.[1] Here, however, names of the Pickwickians were used often merely as a selling tag. *The Pickwick Songster* (1839), or *Lloyd's Pickwickian Songster* (*c.* 1837), have little Dickensian in them other than the title. The name was used to denote something amusing, just as that of Joe Miller had been used previously – in fact, we find *The Pickwickian Treasury of Wit, or Joe Miller's Jest Book* (1846). This was especially true of Sam Weller, under whose name appear such works as *Sam Weller, a Journal of Wit and Humour* (1837), and *Sam Weller's Pickwick Jest Book* (1837).

From music hall and theatre it was not far to popular fiction. In April or early May of 1837, when the popularity of *The Pickwick Papers* was at its height, Edward Lloyd published the first number of *The Posthumous Notes of the Pickwick Club*, 'edited by "Bos" '. The title on the yellow cover of the weekly parts was *The Penny Pickwick*, executed in a 'wood' motif similar to that used by Seymour in his design. In the preface it claimed a sale of 50,000 copies a week, which is quite possible: a much less noticed penny-issue plagiarism of *The Old Curiosity Shop* was said in court to have sold between 50,000 and 70,000.[2] Sala said of *The Penny Pickwick*, 'this disgraceful fabrication had an enormous sale'.[3] It ran for over two years, making two plump volumes of 112 numbers in all.

The identity of 'Bos' is not certain, but the evidence – which I have listed at the back – points to Thomas Peckett Prest. The style is very like that of Prest in his comic recitations.[4]

1. *London Singer's Magazine*, II, *c.* 1839, pp. 9 ff.
2. E. T. Jaques, *Dickens in Chancery*, 1914, p. 71.
3. G. A. Sala, *Charles Dickens*, 1870, p. 74.
4. E.g. 'The Sensible Family', *London Singer's Magazine*, I, 1839, p. 97.

'Bos' aimed directly at the lower classes.

Upon the appearance of those Shilling Publications which have been productive of so much mirth and amusement, it occurred to us that while the wealthier classes had their Momus, the poor man should not be debarred from possessing to himself as lively a source of entertainment and at a price consistent with his means...

The story opens with the formation of the Pickwick Club, consisting of Christopher Pickwick, Percy Tupnall, Arthur Snodgreen, Matthew Winkletop, Jeremiah Smuggins, and Captain Julius Caesar [*sic*] Fitzflash. The following day they set out on their explorations, not in a cab, but in a boat on the Thames in London. Pickwick falls into the river, and is finally saved, when stuck in the mud, by one Shirk (Jingle). Returning to the shore, they find themselves in the middle of a working-class holiday celebration, in which they join. Tupnall and Fitzflash climb a greasy pole along with a filthy sweep. The next day Pickwick takes part in a donkey race. They leave London, and there is an episode in which Shirk goes to a dance in Snodgreen's clothes, leaving his own rags in their place. The episode of the runaway coach is introduced, after which they all arrive at 'Mushroom Hall, Violet Vale, near Uxbridge' (Dingley Dell). There Pickwick pursues a widow (Dupps), in competition with Tupnall. Pickwick is successful, and the loving couple are surprised by the fat boy and by a new figure, John White, a negro servant. They go to the theatre, and recognize one of the actors as Shirk. Determined to recover Snodgreen's clothes, they bring the show to a close amid confusion. Pickwick pursues Shirk and the actors to a public house, but he is no match for them. They all escape, leaving the publican to understand that Pickwick will pay for their drinks. When Pickwick, somewhat poorer, returns to the Hall, he finds his widow is missing – she has eloped with Shirk. (This is a rehandling of the Rachel Wardle incident.) Pickwick follows the pair – on the way he is robbed by highwaymen – and eventually finds them at an inn. The popular desire to see virtue triumphant did not allow 'Bos' to show Shirk escaping; or perhaps 'Bos' did not feel capable of rewriting Dickens's masterly picture of Jingle's insolence: in any case, Shirk is bundled off to gaol for debt. At this point Samuel Weller appears for the first time.

The long story continues with the same mixture of rearranged Dickens and crude innovation. Sam Weller reappears in response to Pickwick's advertisement for 'a companion of virtuous principles' – a reference similar to marital advertisements that can be found in lower-class papers. There is an election, not at 'Eatanswill' but at 'Guzzelton'. It is Pickwick who stands for Parliament, although he is defeated. The Reverent Smirkins makes love to Mrs Weller, and is well trounced by both Mr Weller and Sam.

The whole story is carefully adapted for the working-class reader. An example of this is seen in the way the archaeological discovery is made. The readers of 'Bos' would not have understood Dickens's satire on the newly formed British Association. Instead, 'Bos' inserts a comic episode in Dreary Castle, with Weller masquerading in armour as a ghost, and Pickwick attacked by rats. (This, incidentally, is the first time I have found a lower-class author laughing at Gothic novels of the Minerva Press type.) In this castle a coin is found bearing the inscription:

GI
LE   SSNIP
EMA NC
HEST
ER

The readers would have understood the joke of a Manchester-made antique. There must have been several Giles Snipes among their number.

The whole level of the comedy is altered. In the breach of promise case, all legal subtlety is removed, and Pickwick is tried for assault. For comic restraint physical slapstick is substituted wherever possible. Physical chastisement is inflicted on Shirk, and on Quizzgig and Fidge (Dodgson and Fogg). Pickwick was seen as he would have actually appeared to a working-class person, not as a high-intentioned innocent, a Quixote to Weller's Sancho Panza, but as an odd, comically pompous old gentleman. He is treated as this audience would have treated him. In the course of the first volume alone, he is ducked eight times, generally in filthy water, and once, in a duel with Squib, the editor of *The Guzzelton Mercury*, he is shot in the buttocks.

As might be expected, Samuel Weller is the true hero. Dickens

had balanced this character, so that while his native resourceful-
ness and wit endeared him to the lower-class reader, his devoted
service to his master made him approved by those who had servants themselves. With 'Bos' this balance is lost. On one occasion,
Pickwick finds Sam on the stage during a play and demands his
immediate withdrawal; Sam insists on finishing his part – he is in
command, and he must have his glory. The Society of Flunkeys, it
is interesting to note, grows into a Trades Union, 'The Society of
Grand United and Independent Flunkeys', which receives Sam as
its respected leader. Weller had become the idol of the lower
classes: one article in *Cleave's London Satirist* is called *Sam Weller's
Sentiments on the Poor Law*.

For all his false facetiousness however, 'Bos' was a competent
adaptor. He never tries to go beyond his brash, unsubtle range of
characters. Moments of pathos, like 'A Madman's Manuscript',
are omitted, and the stories he inserts in their stead are straight-
forward narratives such as may be found in *The Penny Story-Teller*.
His faults – a blithe ignorance of grammar and vocabulary, and a
weak facetiousness – and his virtue of vigour, are seen in his
description of Shirk.

The straight-haired man was the master of a face of immense longi-
tude; eyes of sedate, tub-thumping expression; a nose of truly puggy-
fied quality and quantity; a figure extremely small, and legs extremely
bandy. His head was surmounted by a hat, the period of the creation of
which no doubt would be very difficult to elicit; his neck was bound
round several times with a cravat, which probably might once have
been white . . . his person was enveloped in a shocking bad coat, which
had long been in a declining state from its exposure to thorough
draughts; added to which, it had evidently been, in its pristine state,
manufactured for the huge person of a second Daniel Lambert, and
consequently, fitted its present owner with about the same grace that
the skin of an elephant would fit the body of a Jerusalem poney. . .

A reviewer had criticized the use of latinate words and peri-
phrases in Dickens as 'the little tasteless artifices of the Cockney
school'.[1] They were very congenial to the lower-class writer. Another quality of 'Boz' which the plagiarist tried to imitate was
intimacy of style. Dickens took his readers into his confidence, and
communicated his feelings and attitudes in his personal tone. The

1. *Eclectic Review*, 1837, p. 355.

plagiarists only became 'cocky', for they did not have Dickens's delicacy of touch. 'The Obtuse Smoker', a tale in *The Penny Story-Teller* of which Thackeray said, 'The imitation of Boz is very happy . . . worth a dozen pennies',[1] may have been an exception, but the British Museum copy was destroyed in the last war. *The Sketch Book by 'Bos'* (1837) carried a number of parallel stories, but only six of them derived from the original 'Sketches'. Of these, 'The Election of the Sexton' is the crudest comedy; 'Field Lane, a Graphic Sketch', makes fun of urban squalor rather than conveys atmosphere.

This is reflected in the work of C. J. Grant, who provided many of the illustrations for *The Penny Pickwick*, *The Sketch Book by 'Bos'*, *Oliver Twiss*, and *Nickelas Nicklebery*. Grant has already been mentioned as showing, in spite of the appalling cutting his designs usually received, the most vigorous and essentially lower-class qualities of the cartoonists of his time. Many of his drawings are well proportioned and full of character, honest in their boisterous portrayal of comic ugliness in people and setting. Although their comedy is based on physical deformity, violence and sordid surroundings, they are too objective to be morbid. Their modern counterparts in such periodicals as *Reveille* or the *Weekend Mail* may appear more 'respectable', with their stereotyped characters and council-house backgrounds, but in comparison they range over their limited field of stock situations; the 'sex' relationship of the engaged couple, the mother-in-law joke, the 'magic' television set with the bullets coming out of the screen, and so on. Grant's cartoons are concerned with the variety of people, though it may be with their ugliness, and with their relationship to the dirt and squalor around them.

Grant appears to have stopped work about 1842. About this time a less healthy type of humour was appearing from France. It can be seen colouring the Pickwick plagiarism of G. W. M. Reynolds, *Pickwick Abroad: or the Tour in France*. At first serialized in *The Monthly Magazine*,[2] it was considered successful enough to be issued in twenty parts by Sherwood and Co., illustrated by 'Crowquill', Bonner, and John Phillips. It claimed a weekly sale of 12,000, and was reissued by Willoughby and Co. in seventy-nine penny parts about 1840 (not dated): however, similar editions

---

1. art. cit., *Fraser's Magazine*, XVII, 1838, p. 284.
2. XXIV, December 1837 – XXV, June 1838.

2. Comic Observations of Life (Grant's Illustrations)

(a) Mr Pickwick is robbed

(b) A dance in the slums

appearing under at least five different imprints suggests a good number were remaindered. It achieved fair popularity, and a good press, from lower-middle and lower-class sections of the community. *Cleave's Penny Gazette* thought it was 'the best of the bad [Dickensian] imitations'; the *Age* warned 'Boz' to look to his laurels'[1].

Reynolds was frank about his source of inspiration.

If the talented 'Boz' has not chosen to enact the part of Mr Pickwick's biographer in his continental tour, it is not my fault; . . . it is now my duty to compile and put in order the notes taken by him abroad.[2]

In this story the Pickwickians, who all retain their proper names, decide to tour France, and in this way make a study of life and manners in that country. During their stay they are continually involved with a gang of criminals which works through a girl of aristocratic pretentions, Anastasie de Volage, and an English 'Jingle' character called Mr Sugden Jun., alias Adolphus Crashem.

The Pilot invited readers to find in Reynolds's work the qualities of 'the identical Cid Hamet Benegilli, who introduced us to the immortal club':[3] the modern reader, at least, is disappointed. Reynolds musters all the Pickwickians' idiosyncrasies, but cannot go beyond them. His inadequacies are particularly evident in his additions to the group. These include Mr Septimus Chitty, a poet whose mannerism is to add tags of dog Latin to whatever he says (in Reynolds's plagiarism of *Master Humphrey's Clock*, *Master Timothy's Book-Case*, it is Snodgrass who uses Latin). Other innovations are Mr Hook Walker, a general sponge, whose fad is to resolve everything to a 'system', and Mr Scuttle, who went to such extremes of absent-mindedness as wiping his mouth with the morning paper and reading his serviette.

The original Pickwickians, on the other hand, are very subdued in characterization. Sam Weller is merely an efficient servant – the only one of the party not outwitted by the criminals – and Pickwick becomes a sane shepherd extricating Tupman and Snodgrass from the sensualities of the Paris underworld. This work gave Reynolds preliminary exercise in depicting the vice that was going

1. *Cleave's*, I, 7 April 1838, p. 2; *Age*, 4 March 1838, p. 67.
2. *Pickwick Abroad*, Sherwood, 1839, p. 2.
3. X, 4 April 1838, p. 3.

to form the basis for *The Mysteries of London*, and the description of this unsavoury world was no doubt one reason for the book's success.

Reynolds's interest in France, however, went beyond this theme, and his affectionate reminiscences of his stay in Paris two years before led the critic of *Sherwood's Monthly Miscellany*[1] to call it 'one of the most faithful pictures of French manners, peculiarities and customs ever presented to the English reader'. Bonner's woodcuts are purely of French landmarks and scenes. Even the French underworld has an element of the factual; Douglas Jerrold and George Hodder, when visiting Paris, were induced by a Mr Harold Parkes to enter 'a gorgeously decorated apartment au quatrième, occupied by a lady who was (fraudulently) described as a person of high birth and distinguished manners', who asks them to play cards.[2] This is very like what happens to Reynolds's Pickwickians. The French background is also used by Reynolds to air his republican views.

'Vot indeed?' replied the beauteous Loveminski, 'De poor mans is but the shuttlecock which the aristocrat strike wid his bat for his pleasure'.[3]

It is a careful work, lacking the abandon that is one delight of Dickens's novel. Stories and songs are methodically inserted and indexed at the back. Apart from the characters and a few echoes from Dickens (there is a description of insanity, a law-suit, and an episode in which Pickwick becomes involved with a widow), it is original. From the literary point of view, it is the best of all the Dickens plagiarisms, although few readers today would wish to follow it to the last page.

The success of Reynolds's work led 'Bos', who was coming to the end of the first volume of *The Penny Pickwick*, to take the hero abroad also. The preface given away with number fifty-four of the latter novel announced 'we have had the honour conferred upon us to be deputed the detailers of the extraordinary adventures of *Mr Pickwick in America*'. In this serial[4] Mr Christopher Pickwick has a large estate in America, and he has to cross the Atlantic to investigate its mismanagement. All the Pickwickians, including

1. 1, 1838, p. 85.
2. G. Hodder, *Memories of My Time*, 1870, p. 397.   3. p. 337.
4. *Pickwick in America* . . . Edited by 'Bos' (E. Lloyd), 44 nos.

Sam Weller, insist on accompanying him. Even the fat boy and the older Weller eventually appear in the States. Mr Jingle, however, is replaced by an American, Mr Jonathon Junket, who tells tales in the current vein of American humour. In this one a cat is blown from a cannon.

Killed! – pooh! stuff! – No such thing; it was blown more than five hundred yards – passed slick through the bodies of two niggers who happened to be in the way at the time; had not a hair singed, and went in five minutes afterwards and killed six American rats, and they're as big as young buffaloes – I reckon! – Fact! Very remarkable, – eh?

The 'I reckon' and 'slick through' are attempts to imitate the yankee idiom as it was being popularized by 'Sam Slick'. Interest in America and Americans is further exploited by a travelogue of New York and a visit to the 'Shakers'. (Pickwick's plantation is never brought in.) There are moments when 'Bos' promises more serious things. The American militia are crudely satirized as ragged, conceited, and incompetent, and Pickwick is visited by a deputation of negroes from 'th' Nigger Associashun o' th' Mancipated Blacks' who bring a list of petitions including 'Dat no nigger shall be flog more dan twite a day, namely, vonce in de mornin' an vonce at night'. Pickwick promises to give his support to full emancipation, but then the topic is quickly dropped. In all the whole work is even more careless and dull than the second volume of *The Penny Pickwick*.

Current American Notes, by 'Buz' (*c.* 1842), which may be conveniently mentioned here, again exploits the interest aroused by America in England. Occasionally, there is direct transcription from Dickens's *American Notes* (1842), but in general the account of a journey through America has been exchanged for a series of tales in an American setting. Sometimes these are expansions of observations made by Dickens. For example, his criticism of the American worship of 'smartness' prompts the story of Theodore Mina. Theodore, a young immigrant, forms an adulterous relationship with the wife of a farmer, and then poisons the husband so that this will not be interrupted. The crime is discovered, and Theodore is hanged, but the widow sets up a school which is much patronized, for 'everyone must admit that she was an uncommon smart woman'. This ending is forced, but the stories are told with reasonable competence, and there is a delightful (apparently original) account of the laconic buying of a farm which unfortunately is too long to be quoted here. The author follows Dickens in criticizing such things as American spitting, and always being in a hurry, but the whole edge of Dickens's commentary has gone. It is more a collection of stories.

Pickwick in India was published in India and therefore comes outside this story. Pickwick reappears also in 'Noctes Pickwickianae' which G. W. M. Reynolds contributed to his temperance magazine *The Teetotaller*.[1] Reynolds clearly fancied himself as a Dickensian writer. Here the Wellers and Mr Pickwick one by one become teetotallers, and hurry off to the 'Aldersgate Street Chapel' to sign the pledge book of 'The London United Temperance Association'. Later, in this periodical, Reynolds ran *Pickwick Married*.[2] Here, Mr Pickwick saves Miss Teresina Hyppolyta Sago, a beautiful girl, from the undesirable attentions of a policeman. He then begins a senile courtship, which includes his falling into a barrel of treacle, an idea which had somehow escaped 'Bos'. He wins her hand, and there is a double wedding, for Mr Weller enters to make what he announces to be his third marriage. All the Pickwickians arrive for the ceremony, including Jingle, fresh from America, where he has been saved from Red Indians by a beautiful princess. He cheats the Dulwich populace into financing a Great Self-Regulating Steam-Balloon project, and leaves for new fields, pursued by an angry mob.

The story would be very unpleasant had not Reynolds failed so completely to recreate the Pickwickians of Dickens. As it is, the marriage is in keeping with the sleazy moral world which Reynolds draws. There is some radical satire – Pickwick, for instance, reads an account of a workman starving, placed in a paragraph between court announcements of the Queen's extravagance – but there is little to justify its place in *The Teetotaller* apart from Mr Weller's complaint that his past intemperance has brought on a 'delirian trimmings'.

This story reappears in Reynolds's plagiarism of *Master Humphrey's Clock* – *Master Timothy's Book-Case* (1842). Here it is shortened, Mr Jingle's speculations omitted, and the story of a barber inserted at the end. In a late reprint of *Timothy's Book-Case* (J. Dicks, 1886), 'Pickwick Married' is omitted altogether. It had been left to

1. I, 27 June–8 August 1840.   2. II, 23 January–19 June 1841.

Edward Viles to 'kill off' Mr Pickwick. In *Marmaduke Midge, the Pickwickian Legatee* (*c.* 1852), the hero, a cousin of Pickwick, is in financial difficulties, and his relative bequeathes him his whole fortune on condition that he keeps his good name until he is twenty-two. Before reaching this age, he murders a man, and becomes involved with a gang of resurrectionists. Nevertheless he escapes the consequences, is penitent, and his guardian, who has been observing his adventures, makes the surprising decision that he shows enough promise to be given the money. Pickwick, of course, never appears, but even at this distance of time from the publication of *The Pickwick Papers*, his name was considered sufficient to raise the sales of a work.

If there were a number of works plagiarizing the characters of Dickens's work, there were yet more who adopted the idea of a club holding together a group of varied characters on travelling adventures. When the Pickwickians 'were busily engaged in spreading wide that universal spirit of adventure and philosophic discovery, which has since so greatly contributed to the enlightenment and the delight of mankind', declared the anonymous author of *The Posthumous Papers of the Cadgers' Club* (1838), 'the public seized upon the glorious idea with avidity, and it was truly remarkable to see the extraordinary effect it had upon all classes of society; clubs sprang up in every direction; the dustmen formed themselves into a society, the principal object of which was, to mature their knowledge in the *belles lettres*; the chummies combined together . . . The scavengers also united . . .'[1] The Cadgers' Club, went on the writer, was the lowest of them all, 'a union of all those respectable individuals who obtained a living by duping the public and those who were the most expert rogues were considered the most effective members'.[1] The first illustration, by C. J. Grant, shows a gathering of hideous rogues in a filthy room, 'The Cadgers' Snuggery, Black Slums, St Giles'.' The counterpart of Pickwick is Jeremiah Jumper Esq., S.G.C. & M.C.C., portrayed with two wooden legs. Other members include Jack the Scraper (blind musician), Billy Bimper (mechanic out of work, gammoner) and Black-Berry (a wooden-legged negro). The opening parts, contain a zestful and vivid description of brutality, filth, and crime, and they are well supported by the woodcuts; the author, however, lost his distinctive bite when he continued with the

1. I, 7 April 1838, p. 2.

(a) Pickwick Club: 'Boz'

(b) Cadgers' Club: Anon.

POSTHUMOUS PAPERS

OF THE

CADGERS' CLUB.

(c) Pickwick Club: 'Bos'

(d) Wonderful Discovery Club: 'Poz'

biographies of two of his criminals, Scapegrace Jack and Dick the Vagrant, where the narrative falls to the level of any Newgate Calendar account. Although it hoped for 'an interest which will even eclipse, it is expected, the most distinguished history of the transactions of the "Pickwick Club"', it failed after twelve numbers, on 22 March.

Major Rudbank at Home and Abroad, which a reviewer in *Cleave's Penny Gazette* called 'another imitation of *The Pickwick Papers*, and, as might be expected, another failure',[1] probably collapsed even quicker – no other reference to it can be found. Another Pickwickian Society appears in 'The Dutchy Club', which ran in *Lloyd's Penny Weekly Miscellany*.[1] James Cooke's lively 'The Bachelor Club' was serialized in *The Odd Fellow*.[2] *The Cadgers' Club* had been a satire on life in St Giles', *The Posthumous Papers of the Wonderful Discovery Club, Edited by 'Poz'*, was one of life in Camden Town. 'Poz' aimed at those in the Mechanics' Institutes, and in particular at the pretentions to culture of tradesmen who had risen in the world. The story tells how Peter Patron has been knighted for making a court lady a saddle, and so retires from business. He gathers around himself a small group of tradesmen and artisans to form a club for their common advancement of learning. To begin with, their researches are patently ridiculous; Mr Lacteal the milkman gives suck to a child, the beekeeper observes a bee playing a trumpet. There is slapstick comedy when Peter Patron, intent on hearing the trumpet, is attacked by a swarm of bees. The writer, however, was himself too much of a pedant to continue in this strain too long, and the accounts begin to become credible, until we have authentic information, sometimes even documented, on hypnotism, the migration of eels, and the habits of the ant. By the twelfth number the author announced that he was compelled to end because of 'more important claims on his time'.

This section on the influence of Pickwick may well conclude with *The Pilgrims of the Thames in Search of the National*, by Pierce Egan, Sen. Egan's earlier work had itself helped to create the literary world out of which *The Pickwick Papers* grew. He had produced *Life in London* in 1821, which came out, as the work of Dickens did, in weekly parts accompanied by etchings (from Isaac Robert and George Cruikshank). It had an immense popularity –

1. II, 1844, pp. 55–371.
2. II, 1840, pp. 13–77.

some sixty-seven derivative publications have been recorded.[1] Although the sporting life it portrayed was very different from the world of Samuel Pickwick, or even of Sam Weller, it did introduce London low life and its idioms into fiction. The *'Finish' to the Adventures of Tom and Jerry* and *Logic* (1828) had an even closer link with *Pickwick*, in particular through the introduction of Sir John Blubber, a retired wealthy businessman and the soul of benevolence, whom Tom and Jerry meet up with on the way to a little Somerset town called Pickwick. Other resemblances include Hawthorne Hall, a kind of Dingley Dell, and an introduction to community life within a debtors' prison. After following this work with studies of life in Bristol, Liverpool, Birmingham, and Dublin, Pierce Egan in 1837 turned, under the influence of Dickens, to show the spirit of England, or 'The National', by sending a small group of inquirers on a journey together. He uses the same techniques here as in *Life in London*. There he made his revelations by the novice, Jerry, being instructed by the cosmopolitan Corinthian Tom. Here the man-of-the-world, Frank Flourish, initiates the inexperienced James Sprightly. The work has a certain if undeveloped symbolism: the chief character, Peter Makemoney, is a retired tradesman personalizing the prosperity of England which is one of the book's themes. The trio decide to tour the Thames since it is linked with England's fame in commerce, history, and literature. Their main adventures, however, serve to discover the English character, with its rogues, philanthropists, actors, sportsmen, and other types. This is a quaint, high-spirited book, eighteenth century in thought and idiom, and on the twelfth number Egan ends with a flourish untypical of its time: it is a dedication to Queen Victoria, wishing that 'Your Majesty will long reign over a brave and free people, the mistress of their HEARTS, as you are of your kingdom, which is MISTRESS of the WORLD'. Apart from the 'Jingle' character, Tim Bronze, the work is very different from that of Dickens, but the journey in search of the 'National' was undoubtedly prompted by the travels of the Pickwick Club.

If *The Pickwick Papers* drew on one tradition of popular literature, *Oliver Twist* (*Bentley's Miscellany* from February 1838), was

1. J. Franklyn, *The Cockney*, 1953, p. 17; J. C. Reid, *Bucks and Bruisers*, 1971, pp. 59–92; P. J. Keating, *The Working Classes in Victorian Fiction*, 1971, pp. 13–16.

following themes to be found in the popular domestic romance, and such criminal literature as *The Newgate Calendar*, and *Dick Turpin*. (*Hue and Cry*, which Oliver found in Fagin's house, was not one of these, but the official police gazette – Dickens avoided all chance of perverting his readers.) *Oliver Twist*, however, attracted very little interest from the lower-class press, probably in part because the theme of a small boy of respectable parentage being victimized by the London underworld was too middle class to appeal to its readers, especially when they could draw on so much more germane criminal literature.

Nothing, however, could deter Edward Lloyd's 'Bos', whose *Oliver Twiss* (1838–9) ran to more than twice the length of Dickens's novel. As might be expected with a story more organically constructed, the plagiarism followed the original more closely than did *The Penny Pickwick*. All the main characters reappear: Fagin (called Solomons), Nancy (Polly), Bumble (Theophilus Mumble), and the others. They are overdrawn with melodramatic crudity. Poll not only sacrifices herself for Oliver, she goes to gaol in order to save Jem Blount (Sykes). Solomons is a common villain, and commits a murder. Yet because the story is told from the view-point of the lower classes, he also has a cause to plead:

If the wealthy of our land choose to lay claim to those things that are intended as much for the use of the poor man as for the rich one, we cannot be much surprised that men are to be found who will resist the laws that have been made for the purpose of depriving them of their share in the gifts of heaven. The poor man feels his wrongs, and boldly asserts his rights.

This eloquent appeal from Fagin is inconceivable. Oliver, who could not be made too sympathetically middle class, has very little character, but is simply the pretext for the action.

The best character is Beeswing, the butler to Mr Perkins (Beaumont in *Twiss*), and an innovation. He is the distinct descendant of the other efficient servant, Sam Weller, but he is under a constant threat of dismissal by his irascible master, to whom he is really indispensable. On two occasions he outwits Solomons and recovers Oliver. Around Beeswing revolves much crude, below-stairs comedy with Tom Trot, Molly Duster, and a milkmaid; this takes up a fair proportion of the book. Slapstick also comes into Solomons's school. In one scene, curiously like that in the early chapters of Marryatt's *Percival Keene*, young thief Jack White fires explosives under the Knowing Cove (Artful Dodger). All this is crude, and is introduced purely for cheap laughs; nevertheless, the Artful Dodger would probably have laughed over it, and these Cockney high spirits were probably more true to life than the young thieves' humour in *Oliver Twist*, which Dickens makes as sinister as the accompanying etchings of Cruikshank. 'Bos' in fact went to some pains to give a more detailed description of this underworld than did his original. I give an excerpt from one of Solomons's accounts of young thieves.

'Well, these lads all live upon what is called the *cross*, and each has his own peculiar way of going to work. They, however, mostly begin by sneaking in the markets, stealing from the stalls and carts fruit and vegetables which they sell to the old women who have standings in the streets. Children under six years of age, my dear, will in this way start in the world on their own account, and never after pursue any other calling.'

'And that, in the end, brings them of course to the gallows!' said Oliver.

'Oh, no,' answered the Jew, 'they must get a good deal worse before they come to that. Their next step is to attack the cheesemongers', the butchers' and the bakers' shops, hanging about and watching for an opportunity to snatch and mizzle; these are called *sawney hunters* and *grubbers*. The old women on the streets are still their *fences*, that is to say, my child, they buy the things they have stolen.'

'And how old are they when they begin this?' asked Oliver.

'Perhaps about ten or so,' answered the old man.

This study of the criminal's career continues, forestalling Mayhew by several years. Dickens is carefully selective in his description of the underworld, but 'Bos' does not hesitate to portray prostitutes and call them by their right name. For all this, the book does not give an unduly sordid impression.

There are other deviations from the story of Dickens besides the introduction of adventure 'below stairs'. Oliver is discharged from the workhouse at Mudanslush (where 'Christopher Pickwick' in *The Penny Pickwick* stood for Parliament), not for asking for more gruel but convicted for trouble-making when defending the idiot-girl Mary from her persecutors. He becomes involved with gypsies and arson, is wrongfully imprisoned, and escapes with Gypsy Ned, who takes him to Solomons. Gypsies reappear later, for one of them, Barbara, knows the secret of Oliver, and prophesies his future good fortune. She does not live to see it, for Solomons murders her. The love story of Harry Maylie and Rose Fleming is expanded in the romance of Beaumont's daughter Lilian with Frederick Masterton. Jem murders Poll, strangling her clumsily throughout the course of a fair-sized chapter. Dickens's restraint over Sykes's crime evidently seemed to be a waste of a good opportunity. One of the greatest expansions, however, comes at the end of the story as told by Dickens. Sales of *Twiss* were evidently high, so 'Bos' does not let Blount die: instead, Blount rescues Solomons from the condemned cell, and the two go through various adventures, including an attempt on Oliver's life. A maniac father stands beneath the body of his son which is rotting on a gibbet, and tells a story quite unrelated to Oliver or anyone else. Finally all the criminals, including the pupils of Solomons, are killed, hung, or imprisoned and, as a gesture to the middle-class origins of the story, Oliver gains his B.A. at Oxford.

A rival *Oliver Twiss*, by 'Poz', was brought out by James Pattie and James Turner at the Starr Press. It bore the impudent imprint 'Copyright secured by Act of Parliament'. It singles out and intensifies the reformist zeal of Dickens's work. Oliver's father is committed to prison for vagrancy, and starved to death. Social injustice drives his mother to commit suicide. Oliver, left on a doorstep, is brought up in a workhouse amid horrors even exceeding those portrayed by Dickens. He is transferred to the undertaker Merryberry (Sowerberry), then to a lawyer, Clincher. This master ends up, with Oliver, in a workhouse. During this narrative, 'Poz' has let fly at upper-class education for the poor, speculative inventors, the law, the Royal Humane Society, and fire insurance companies. By the end of the fourth weekly number he appears exhausted, and when the only known surviving copy breaks off with Oliver back in the workhouse, it is probably the end of all that was published. It is an inferior affair, but it is unique among these works for its appreciation of Dickens's radicalism. Cleave headed an extract from *Oliver Twist* 'A Scene in a Workhouse',[1] and Solomons justifies the underprivileged, but 'Bos' and his fellows generally watered out the social issues in Dickens.

1. *Cleave's London Satirist*, I, 10 February 1838, p. 3.

One penny periodical even attacked Dickens and Jerrold for their reformist attitudes:

> ... what satisfaction can it give the mechanic, to hear the upper classes of society attacked in language however eloquent? Does it make their labour lighter or the earth happier? And to what end ought the labours of the philanthropist to tend?[1]

A leading school of writing today lays down as one of its maxims that no fiction should be tragic or too much in earnest as the public have enough seriousness in real life. 'Bos' and his fellow-writers would approve this enervating rule.

After the fruitless attempt to stop *The Penny Pickwick* in June 1837 Knight, Chapman and Hall's lawyer, declared he would prosecute again, but no further action followed.[2] At the beginning of March 1838 Dickens, in the hope of saving his coming *Nicholas Nickleby* from the hands of pirates, had published in the press and on handbills a notice against 'some dishonest dullards resident in the by-streets and cellars of this town', who 'impose upon the unwary and credulous, by producing cheap and wretched imitations of our delectable Works'. This was placed pointedly next to Lloyd's advertisement for *Oliver Twiss* in *Cleave's London Satirist*.[3] Even by the contemporary standards of journalism this notice, which among other insults compares his imitators with 'kennel vermin' it is not worth shooting, is a little puerile, although Dickens probably felt these literary hacks should be spoken to in their own language. 'Bos' was delighted. *Cleave's London Satirist* for 31 March bore a proclamation from 'Bos', a very fair parody of Dickens's notice set up in identical type. He complained of those who 'are ambitious to rob us of a share of that fame and patronage, which we hope and trust for these our humble exertions ... to merit and receive', and he declared he would regard all such 'offenders, delinquents, aggressors and criminals, in the light of those contemptible insects, whom it would be the height of barbarity to tread upon'.

This insolence was to be carried further. Chapman and Hall had been advertising *The Life and Adventures of Nicholas Nickleby, containing the Fortunes, Misfortunes, Uprising, Downfallings and complete*

1. *Family Journal* (E. Dipple), I, 5 December 1846, p. 1.
2. art. cit., *The Times*, 9 June 1837, p. 7.
3. I, 3 March 1838, p. 4.

career of the Nickleby Family, and on 17 March Lloyd was advertising *Nickolberry Nikollas, containing the Adventures, Mis-Adventures, Chances, Mis-Chances, Fortunes, Mis-Fortunes, Mys-teries and Miscellanious Manoeuvres of the Family of Nikollas. By 'Bos'.*[1] From this advertisement it appears that on 31 March, when Dickens published the first number of *Nickleby*, Lloyd issued *Nickelas Nicklebery*.

This is borne out by the plagiarism. 'Bos' clearly did not know what he was imitating, and he was in some straits to conceal what he denied in the opening paragraph – 'we are not . . . in want of a hero'. He reproduced his proclamation against dishonest plagiarists, and filled two pages with an extraordinary description of Nickelbery Hall, which he placed near Harrogate in Yorkshire.

. . . it may perhaps be as well known to our readers as to ourselves, that most houses are constructed, built and appropriated, for the purpose of being inhabited; so was Nickelbery Hall; it is also generally known that houses so constructed, built and appropriated, have windows and doors; of such indispensables boasted Nickelbery Hall.

And so on. Finally he launched out into a music-hall story of a man who abhorred children and was presented by his wife with twins. Only at the end of the second number did he begin to bring the story round to his original with the appearance of 'The New London Limited Hot-Baked Flourry Potatoe [*sic*] Conveyance and Delivery Company!!!'

Once the unfortunate husband's twins have been identified as Nickelas and Flora Nickelbery, the story continues as the closest of the Dickens plagiarisms up to this date, with even an interlude called 'The Wonderful Legend of Stoffenhausen von Stuffenblock' (cf. Dickens's 'The Baron of Groswig'). The weekly parts can be read in sections of four or five alongside the monthly issues of Dickens to reveal generally a mere expansion of the original, and occasionally verbatim transcription. The names were changed but, apart from the startling picture of Newton Nobbs (Noggs), who 'was worthy of being preserved in the British Museum as a natural curiosity . . . His large red nose, shone like a red-hot cinder in the centre of a snowball upon his ghastly face,' 'Bos' attempts to follow the characterization of the original. The plagiarism was in

1. *Cleave's Penny Gazette*, p. 4.

fact an uncongenial task to him, and he confessed himself to be 'out of [his] element among subjects of grave description'. The Crummles episode came as a godsend, and he curtailed other themes in order to expand the account of the theatrical world he knew well; but at the end of the tenth issue of *Nicholas Nickleby*, where Nicholas said good-bye to the company to return to his sister's aid, 'Bos' decided to bring his story to an end. He showed that Roger Nickelbery had been concealing a will which gave Snike (Smike) £20,000: Nobbs finds it, confronts Roger with his crime, and the book concludes with Snike entering into his fortune.

Master Humphries' [sic] Clock, by 'Bos', published by Lloyd in 1840 as a 'Miscellany of Striking Interest', reads as if by another hand. The new writer did not attempt to reproduce the jocular style of *Pickwick* in works which render it quite unsuitable, as his predecessor had done. His writing is comparatively sober and literary. The framework of the story of the clock and the group of friends follows Dickens. The giants Gog and Magog are introduced, although the story of Magog varies from the original. The story Mr Pickwick tells during his visit with Sam Weller, on the other hand, only differs in the language and the names of the characters. The serial was evidently doing badly, and it ended directly after this, at the twelfth number. A *Barnaby Fudge* by 'Bos' (E. Lloyd, nine numbers, 1841), and a *Life and Adventures of Martin Puzzlewhit*, also by 'Bos' (*Lloyds Penny Sunday Times* [1843], pp. 246 et seqq.), have been recorded,[1] but I have never seen copies.

Lloyd's interest in plagiarism was in any case passing. Dickens plagiarisms had given him experience in penny-issue publishing, and his writers, a chance to experiment in finding lower-class literary tastes. Prest now turned to develop the domestic themes he had portrayed in *Oliver Twiss* with Barbara the gypsy, and Lilian Beaumont and Frederick Masterton, writing his first and greatest original success *Ela the Outcast* (1839–40). With *Ela*, a lower-class type of novel had arrived which could stand on its own feet.

Dickens's later works were also less suited to lower-class tastes. There are two sides to this. Some critics in lower-class periodicals were enthusiastic about them. The *Odd Fellow* reviewer, probably W. J. Linton, declared that 'among literary people, Nicholas Nickleby, like SAUL among the Israelites, has stood head and

1. W. Miller, *Dickens Student*, 1946, pp. 246 ff.

shoulders above the rest'.[1] He was even more eloquent about *Master Humphrey's Clock*.

[*The Old Curiosity Shop*] is a higher work than *The Pickwick Papers* . . . Dickens is a poet . . . he is a hearer and echoer of the still small voice that cometh from the human heart; a looker into the depths of the human soul; a seer and revealer of the wonderous affinities and deep harmonies of all nature. His comedy, or rather, his broad farce, is by no means the best thing about him. In this department, his 'Pickwick Papers' was certainly his best productions [*sic*], for the laughable portions of 'Master Humphrey's Clock' want the ease of his first essay . . .

His 'Nell' is one of the most wonderful creations of modern literature . . . she is an emblem and a portion of the Universal Beauty, an incarnation of gentlest heroism.[2]

Readers of like mind bought between 50,000 and 70,000 copies a week of *The Old Curiosity Shop* and *Barnaby Rudge*, in the versions abridged by H. Hewitt, which appeared in *Parley's Penny Library; or, Treasury of Knowledge, Entertainment and Delight* during 1841.[3] The use of the pseudonym of the American children's writer Samuel Goodrich does not mean it was intended exclusively for children: it was reviewed by such publications as *The Sun* and *The Weekly Dispatch* as being a periodical of interest for adults as well. (A later publication, *The New Parley Library* [1844], was entirely an adult magazine.) A great proportion of the issues of Hewitt's successful abridgement, which was published by Cleave, will have gone to working-class readers who probably read it not only because of the great difference in price, but also because the simplified version was easier for them to read than the original.

On the other hand, many who had been delighted with *Pickwick* found Dickens was moving into a type of novel foreign to their tastes. The reviewer in *Actors by Daylight* declared of *Nicholas Nickleby* (part XI), 'the incidents are ill contrived, and the new characters introduced are much overcharged'. He goes on to criticize Dickens for introducing unconvincing and stock characters. Mantalini and his wife are found to be 'commonplace', 'they are to be found in a hundred modern farces, and are again lugged

1. 'Old Year', I, 1839, p. 2.
2. 'Review', III, 1841, p. 107.
3. R. Lee, G. Mudie, *Chancery Affidavits*, January 1844, P.R.O., C. 33/666, pt 2; C. 31/666, pt 2.

into the present number, without either aim or object'.[1] The same line of attack is taken by James Cooke in *The Actor's Note Book*, where he reviews *Barnaby Rudge*.

A few passages of beauty were mixed up with a quantity of matter utterly worthless, and not only a disgrace to Charles Dickens, but what, issuing from the pen of a third-rate author, would have been the same. ... The language is common-place, and there is, throughout, a mingling of iron-like humour and oft-repeated mannerisms. The writer's mind revolves only in one circle, and that is a narrow one.[2]

Cooke declares that Dickens uses stereotyped characters, and introduces them again and again. He quotes as an example Miggs in *Barnaby Rudge*, whom he claims to be a reincarnation of the Marchioness in *The Old Curiosity Shop*. The reiteration of the term 'commonplace' in both the above criticisms is significant. The lower classes did not generally appreciate the more restrained mode of style and characterization in Dickens's serious works, and they felt uneasy with his sentiment. 'If the dear public would be candid,' declared Rymer, whose success in writing for them demands respect for his judgement, they would admit that 'the pathos of Dickens ... fairly bothered them'.[3] His tragic scenes were comic.

As, therefore, the lower-class plagiarists turned more to writing their own type of fiction, their practice was taken over more by the middle classes. Particularly as these were sometimes published in a cheap form, they may be considered here.

Scenes from the Life of Nickleby Married, 'Edited by "Guess" ', with illustrations by 'Quiz', was published in sixpenny numbers by John Williams (1840). This takes up the story of Nicholas where Dickens left off. The Nickleby family are living happily together; Mrs Squeers keeps a coffee house on the South Bank. After a cold reception back from prison, Wackford Squeers turns to writing begging letters. Mr Mantalini insinuates himself back into his wife's favours, but is again rejected and humiliated by the end of the book. The main plot concerns the theft of over £3,000 from

1. II, 9 February 1839; cf. 'Popular Fiction', *Family Journal*, I, 5 December 1846, p. 15.
2. 'Barnaby Rudge', I, 26 May 1841, p. 75.
3. *Queen's Magazine*, I, 1842, p. 103.

the firm of Nickleby and Cheeryble, when in the possession of
Tom Linkinwater, and the recovery of £2,000 through a fortune
teller operating in a London backstreet. Sir Mulberry Hawk attempts to rid himself of an innocent French wife, Matilda, and to
marry the wealthy heiress Mrs Gambroon. He becomes implicated
with the criminals involved in the robbery from Nickleby. Tom
Brookes, who works for Nickleby, is instrumental in frustrating
his design, and Hawke is killed. Brookes has discovered that
Matilda is no other than his sister. He has been heading for ruin
amid disreputable company: his eyes are opened just in time, and
he reforms and marries Kate Nickelby – Nicholas's eldest daughter. Matilda becomes one of the family. While far short of Dickens,
the writing is lively, and the quite incredible plot is partly compen-
sated for by the vivid pictures of London low life; its music halls,
fortune tellers, thieves, and labyrinths of dirty back streets. It is on
a different plane to *Nickelas Nickelbery*.

Master Timothy's Book-Case (1842), ostensibly a plagiarism by
G. W. M. Reynolds of *Master Humphrey's Clock*, is again a comparatively superior work, although published in penny-issues
(1842, 1847) as well as in volume form. Reynolds criticized
Dickens's work as 'a decided failure', and set about a different
method of unifying the stories. He claimed high motives – the
book was to point the moral that 'we should never trust to appearances', and on the other hand, that to be undeceived is to be unhappy. 'The hero of the work is the same throughout the narrative
parts, and all the tales are told to elucidate these mysteries in
society, or in individual biographies, which cannot be compre-
hended at first sight.'[1] Master Timothy, the guardian spirit of the
Mortimer family, offers the eldest male of each generation whatever gift he desires. Sir Edmund Mortimer chooses 'Universal
Knowledge'. Under the guidance of Timothy, he journeys through
the world, but his curiosity about love leads him to be implicated
in the murder of the husband of the woman he desires: when at
last he retires to meditate on his acquired wisdom, the daughter of
the murdered man enters and stabs him to the heart. This, says
Master Timothy, shows the folly of choosing 'Universal Knowledge', although he did not make the connection between this and
Sir Edmund's fate very clear. It probably did not worry the
readers who had enjoyed a volume of historical adventures. There

1. pp. iii ff.

are other stories in this volume, including the anachronistic 'Pickwick Married', which had already been discussed.

Master Timothy's Book-Case, remotely indebted to Dickens's historical writing, is very much happier than Reynolds's imitation of *Pickwick*. Renton Nicholson, however, was at his best following on Dickens's portrayal of London life, and attempting Dickensian characters. His *Dombey and Daughter* was published in penny parts in 1847, six years after *The Town* with its obscenities had ceased to come out, and when the fat little 'Baron' of the Judge and Jury Club in the Coal Hole Tavern was beginning to show the remorse he evinces in his autobiography. The title-page bears the motto *Solo Nobilitas Virtus*, and an epilogue promises nice tastes that the tale is 'breathing a spirit of morality'. The plot centres around a child, Clara George, born to a homeless girl, and cared for by a working-class family. Mrs Fribble, the landlady of the house, insists that the father be found, and when they learn that the mother had been seen with a Mr Dombey, she sends Shadow, her lodger, to contact him. Shadow finds him at Brighton, and Dombey acknowledges responsibility for the child. He offers to pay for its upkeep if the matter is kept secret. Eventually Cheekey and Fathom, two particularly unpleasant rogues, are hired by Mr Dombey to kidnap the child; she is, however, rescued by Shadow with the help of a regiment of troops that are passing. The captain of the troop turns out to be George Dombey, brother of Daniel Dombey; he has just returned from overseas. A conventional plot is revealed. The mother of Clara was married to George, and the child was heir to a fortune which would go to Daniel if his brother had no heir. George goes abroad, and, as his wife is dead, he allows the London family to bring up Clara until she is of age.

This plot takes up little space in the book, which gives a vivid picture of London slum life. It does not spare the reader the unpleasantness of the slums, with filth flowing down the streets, the disease-bearing vapours, and the prostitutes and young thieves, although social surveys show Nicholson did not exaggerate.

Dirty and slip-shod, improvident wives of improvident mechanics loiter and gossip in gin-shop doorways, with females in figured finery, whose nameless occupation is betokened by the unmistakable evidences of stale carmine and a shameless arrangement of dress, antagonistic to decorum, and in defiance of every known order in the architecture of feminine costume. Children – squalid, in-kneed, bandy, and bow-legged

– fester in the fetid air of leprous exhalations, crying whoop at nightfall from hollow jaws and morbid lungs; and, by day, wayward, wanton, and neglected, playing pitch-and-toss together in nooks, corners, and bye-places, away from the scrutiny of passer and police.

In spite of this, the work is kept from being depressing by Nicholson's fascination with London life and characters. There are the two rival landladies, Fribble and Preen, constantly at war. On one occasion, Mrs Fribble gets drunk and smashes Mrs Preen's windows – but, true-to-life, they at once band together when threatened by trouble from the law. Cleopatra, the urchin kitchen girl at one time dragged down the street by her hair by Mrs Fribble, waits by the pump to get rides on the handle, and chases the small boys of respectable families when she gets a chance. Shadow, the real hero, is 'a batchelor, a wag, and a very good-looking young man'. His character is drawn, not by description, but through the way in which all the other characters, from Cleopatra to a cynical court steward, react to him. All in their way show respect, and when there is trouble, they at once turn to him. Yet he is not a prig. For instance, one of his great delights is to salt his conversation with Fribble, his landlady, with insulting names, and to watch her in her ignorance and middle-aged vanity take them as compliments. Few of the characters remain as caricature. Even Cleopatra grows up and marries Shadow, her first love, and Nicholson comments that she will make a good wife. Nicholson has no class consciousness.

The work has all the faults of Nicholson's exuberance. Words are used, as in the passage quoted above, with careless profusion. His attempts to portray high spirits are sometimes merely silly, as when Shadow dances a polka to celebrate Dombey's acknowledgement of the child, and rides down the stairs on Mrs Fribble's back. He overdraws the affections of the family for the foundling. Yet the book is never dull. It is one of the very few novels reviewed in this chapter which can be re-read today simply for pleasure.

The style of *Dombey and Daughter* is different to that found in Nicholson's journalism: he was evidently trying to write in a 'Dickensian' way. In conclusion, therefore, it must be asked what associations were aroused in the working-class mind by the name of Dickens. The traditional 'Dickens spirit', as Humphry House has suggested, implies Christmas, stage coaches, plentiful good food, and hearty benevolence. All of this is lacking in lower-class plagiarisms. This conception was fostered largely by *A Christmas Carol*, which sold 16,000 copies on the day of publication alone, and attracted many plagiarisms: however, almost none of these were either in price or content aimed at the lower classes. The two exceptions are themselves significant. One has already been mentioned, Henry Hewitt's adaptation, *A Christmas Ghost Story (Parley's Illuminated Library*, 1844). A court injunction prevented the second half of this from appearing, and I have never seen a copy of the first. The lines of the adaptation, however, are indicated by the accounts of the law-suit. Although the characters and incidents followed those of Dickens, 'incongruities in the *Carol*', claimed the defence, 'had been tastefully mended by Mr Hewitt's critical experience of dramatic effect'.[1] *A Christmas Carol* owed a considerable debt to effects popular in the early Victorian playhouse, and Hewitt probably worked on this aspect since he thought it most likely to appeal to his audience. The change of the title from 'Carol' to 'Ghost Story' supports this contention. Although the work was an abbreviation, Hewitt added a song of sixty lines for Tiny Tim, 'admirably suited to the occasion and replete with pathos and poetry'.[2]

The Christmas Log (1846), published by Edward Lloyd at two shillings and sixpence, attempts to recreate the spirit of Christmas, but produces something very different from the Christmas of Dickens. The story is about Uncle Bootle, a benevolent rich man who, in order to test the Jarvises, his relatives, pretends he has died and left them his fortune together with an injunction that they should look after his grand-daughter. Previously he had disowned this girl, for she was the result of his daughter's liaison with an unfaithful soldier. Under the influence of wealth, the Jarvises become caricatures of evil, and the uncle arrives disguised as a deaf old woman to watch their cruelty to his grandchild. Finally they are all called to his house where, in a theatrical tableau, he reveals who he is, the child is shown to be legitimate, and, as the Jarvises leave the house in confusion, her parents enter to receive the blessing of the uncle. A summary cannot convey the lifeless and mechanical way in which the story is told. There is no real expression of the ideal of benevolence.

1. H. Hewitt, *Chancery Affidavit*, January 1844, P.R.O., C. 33/666, pt 2, p.5.
2. Hewitt, op. cit., p. 5.

Dickens was probably associated in the lower-class mind with something more fundamental than a particular theme or atmosphere. Criticisms which compared Dickens and Reynolds, although they were radically dissimilar writers, have already been mentioned. Two comments help to explain them. 'In [Reynolds's] *Pickwick Abroad* we have the same brilliancy of colouring and the same force of feeling which characterises the works of Dickens.'[1] Writing of *Retribution* (1842) another reviewer declared 'there is a terseness about the style which reminds us of "Boz" ',[2] although the modern reader of this murder story will be reminded only of Eugène Sue. Dickens began to write at a time when the large new class of readers who were living in the hard and disillusioned culture of the towns sought something more vital than the outworn conventional fiction of the Gothic and the sentimental novel. For them, Dickens brought a new intimacy and strength into writing, and it was this vitality above all that they associated with him. Therefore, although comparatively few lower-class readers read Dickens direct, he has a central place in the development of cheap popular literature. Working-class fiction was apprenticed to Dickens's plots and characters, and by plagiarisms experimented in the popular taste; it was nurtured by this reflected popularity, and it bore the distorted marks of its first mentor long after it had set out on its own account.

1. Q., W. Miller, art. cit., *Dickensian*, p. 9 (no source given).
2. *Penny Sunday Chronicle*, I, 19 June 1842, p. 1.

5

Further Literary Influences: the Tale of Terror and the Historical Novel

THE term 'Gothic' has been used indiscriminately to describe early Victorian penny-issue fiction ever since Montague Summers published his *Gothic Bibliography* in 1940, and the practice is encouraged today by booksellers who find this raises the price of these novels on the American market. If by 'Gothic' we really mean the tale of terror, in the form established by such writers as Horace Walpole, Mrs Radcliffe, M. G. Lewis, and Maturin, the fashionable usage is misleading. In this popular fiction the genres of the domestic romance, the fashion novel, and stories of criminal life are more common. It is also a mistake to consider the stories of terror which appear in the early Victorian cheap novels, together with the earlier Gothic romances, without noticing the differences which mark them off from the literature on which they drew.

By 1830 the old publishers of the Gothic tale were losing ground. The Minerva Press had turned to producing children's books. The many publishers of the 'blue books' – the chubby, blue-bound novelettes selling at sixpence or a shilling – were closing down, or, like Thomas Tegg, turning to other fields. They could not compete with the new, larger printing presses, which turned out quarto and folio magazines for a penny; and at the great literary watershed of the years 1830–36, the working classes were seeking rather political or 'useful knowledge' literature.

A few periodicals, noted in Chapter 2, did continue to publish fiction over this transitional period, however. Many of their stories are in the old Gothic tradition, as those in *The Calendar of Horrors: a Series of Romantic Legends, Terrific Tales, Awful Narrations and Supernatural Adventures* (London, G. Drake, 1835–6). These Gothic tales are often taken from upper-class magazines or collections. They had an immediate sensational appeal, and are of a convenient type for magazine publication, for they do not require character or plot to be built up; they aim only at providing a situation where the reader feels a quiver of fear. Probability is a positive disadvantage. One story can be taken as a fairly typical example of the rest.

In 'The Bohemian Gardener'[1] a youth, Walter Marloff, is induced to accept the hospitality of a little old man, who gives him food and lodging in a little hut in a small valley. During the night he wakes to see a beautiful lady standing behind a casement. He is infatuated and passes through it into a room: they embrace and exchange rings; then the lady disappears. The next morning Walter realizes that the host and the lady deal with the powers of evil, and so he flees, losing the lady's ring on the way. He comes to a farm, joins in a village festivity, falls in love with the farmer's daughter, and marries her. Soon he has a prosperous business and a happy family. One day a little dog comes up to him from out of the wood. He stoops to stroke its silky ears and falls dead. A long time later his ghost returns to his destitute wife, bringing a bag of gold. His wife sees a beautiful lady standing at the door, her face distorted with hate. The final paragraph resolves in a crude, horrific picture all the questions posed by the story; the identity of the woman, of the dog, of a horse which is stirring at the edge of the wood, and of Walter's death:

> Swift and dark two gigantic steeds rushed almost close to [Walter's wife] amidst the crashing underwood; – a single flaming torch threw a lurid glare as they passed, – 'My God, my God!' once more burst from the miserable woman's lips. An old, withered, one-eyed hag turned upon her one glance of hideous triumph; – the hell-hound bounded high and bellowed loud; – and Walter, the victim, groaned audibly as they plunged into the viewless blackness of wood and night.

Such stories are to be found in cheap periodicals right into the 1840s, but from about 1836 they become progressively rarer, and less in tone with the other fiction. The Gothic novels which appear from 1839 to 1946 – for example, *Love and Crime* (1841), or *The Death Grasp* (1844) – are distinct from the earlier fiction of this sort. These changes are the result of certain changes in popular taste.

One important factor was the Romantic movement, which, particularly between the years 1815 and 1840, was helping to turn the appetite for the strange and the wonderful into new channels.

1. *Penny Novelist*, I, 22, 29 August 1832, pp. 30 ff., 35 ff.

Critics have largely ignored the lower-class audience enjoyed by Byron, Shelley, and Southey, although it is an important element in the relationship of these poets to their age.[1] Romantic poetry was in fact one of the most consistently profitable lines of publication to lower-class publishers at this time, catering as it did for both intellectual and political interests.

Shelley was profusely quoted in radical periodicals, particularly by the Owenites. His poem most popular with this audience is undoubtedly *Queen Mab*, which came out in numerous cheap editions, including at least three from Richard Carlile (1822, 1823, 1826); one from William Clarke (1821), and one as late as 1840 from James Watson. His *Zastrozzi* was serialized in *The Romancist and Novelist's Library* (1839). Byron too was popular; I have noted in the bibliography twenty-five lower-class editions of his various works, and this does not include reprints. Again, his political sentiments were much of his appeal – Cleave issued *A Vision of Judgement* 'enriched with valuable notes by Robert W. Smith, Professor Wilson, etc.' (1837), as a political tract – but his Romantic melodramas also caught the imagination of the lower classes. *Mazeppa* and *The Deformed Transformed* were made into pennyissue novels, and he much influenced the early Gothic works of G. W. M. Reynolds. Wordsworth had less appeal, although he is occasionally quoted in radical journals, and was read by the more intelligent lower-class writers such as Ebenezer Elliott, Spencer T. Hall, and Thomas Miller. He almost certainly helped foster the large volume of pastoral verse put out by lower-class poets.

Robert Southey's popularity among the lower classes comes as a surprise in the light of his later Tory views. His *Joan of Arc* (1796) went through various cheap editions, and was dramatized by Fitzball (1822) – a good indication of popular success. A pennyissue novel of the same name (1841) follows Southey even down to lengthy quotations, although the 'child of nature' aspect of Joan's character is mainly omitted. Most popular of all, however, was *Wat Tyler*, a turgid dramatic poem written 'in three days at Oxford' in 1794 and printed, without his permission, in 1817. It became immediately popular. Richard Carlile alone sold some 25,000 copies in five years, and, when his political literature failed, it kept him in business. It was published also by Fairburn, Hone, Sherwin, and Cleave. The agitated Southey sought a court

1. See Philip Collins, *Thomas Cooper the Chartist*, Nottingham, 1970.

injunction restraining the radical publishers from publishing the work, but Chancellor Eldon, enjoying the discomfiture of his old enemy, refused to issue one.

The popularity of Romantic poetry influenced the verse of radical poets, for writers like Shelley had provided imagery to express the overthrow of evil by the powers of good. Romantic concepts can be recognized beneath the ranting rhythms of many a radical song –

> The time shall come when earth shall be
> A garden of joy from sea to sea –
> When the slaughterous sword is drawn no more,
> And goodness exults from shore to shore.[1]

The biographical romance about a political hero, in the style of Southey's *Wat Tyler*, was also carried on by other writers. J. H. Newton wrote *Hofer; or, the Patriot of the Tyrol* (*c.* 1842), and James Cooke produced *Jack Cade* (1840). William Tell was particularly popular, at least three works were published recounting his exploits (J. Watson, 1836; T. Paine, 1841; H. Such, *c.* 1842), perhaps because Schiller's drama had gone through several translated editions in England. The plot and characterization of Schiller's play is perhaps discernible in these works, although distorted and padded out with stock situation from domestic romance. Newton's *William Tell* (1841) even includes an episode where the heroines are rescued from a blazing building, the almost inevitable cliché of this popular fiction. Schiller's Romantic intensity is completely lost.

In these 'radical' romances written after the first Reform Bill we find the idealism of the Romantics modified. In Pierce Egan, Jun.'s *Wat Tyler* (1841), for instance, Egan remarks of the abortive insurrection:

With discretion and coolness, they might have tumbled the monarchy into the dust, and from the grossest state of slavery and despotism, have sprung into an enlightened and popular form of government.

Without coolness and discretion, the working man could be his own worst enemy. These are also the first of many works to have

1. T. Cooper, 'Chartist Song', *Collected Poems*, 1877, p. 288.

young working men as their heroes, to be followed by many others after 1850 as a juvenile audience became more and more in evidence. In the same year as his *Wat Tyler*, Pierce Egan, Jun., always quick to sound out commercial possibilities, published *Quintin Matsys*. Based remotely on the life of Quinten Matsys of Antwerp (1466–1530), this story offered nineteenth-century English apprentices many a vicarious thrill. Quintin risks death rather than complete a suspicious-looking iron-work apparatus, and quite right too, for it turns out to be a cage for the German Emperor. He leads a band of apprentices successfully against the conspirator von Haalst, who ordered the cage, and wins the hand of the girl he loves by revealing that he has hidden talents as a painter. If we doubt the story, we are invited to inspect iron-work by Matsys in St George's Chapel, Windsor Castle.

If the radicalism of Romantic heroes and Romantic poetry appealed to the lower classes, they also enjoyed its mystery. Southey's *Thalaba the Destroyer* (1801), is a turgid, highly coloured poem that tried to introduce Oriental mythology into the poetic field. It tells how Thalaba destroys Domdaniel, 'a seminary of evil magicians under the sea'. Southey himself doubted the validity of the imagery, but, to unsophisticated tastes, it was indubitably 'poetic'. Fitzball achieved the formidable task of dramatizing it in 1836, and it was performed at the Theatre Royal, the Coburg Theatre, Covent Garden, and, with a full complement of elephants, brahmin bulls, and ostriches, at the Surrey Zoological Gardens. (It might be pointed out to the directors of Hollywood spectaculars.) Two prose versions also appeared, one based on the play (J. Duncombe, 1836), another very well adapted from the original verse by one Thomas Moore (Hetherington, 1841).

In these works the Oriental scenery and the 'miracles' were clearly the main attraction. The appeal of the Oriental and exotic element to the public can be seen also in the reprinting of such works as F. Sheridan's *Solyman and Almena* (Limbird, *c.* 1834); *The Arabian Nights Entertainments* (Limbird, 1830); J. Ridley's *Tales of the Genii* (Limbird, *c.* 1839) and R. M. Bird's colourful South American Romance, *Abdallah the Moor* (Novel Newspaper, 1839; E. Lloyd, *c.* 1850). Fantasy with an element of significance was attempted by H. J. Copson in *The Mountain Field* (1841).

Here the main plot tells how Mythus, the Magician of Sensual Delight, like Milton's Comus, imprisons anyone without sufficient powers of self-denial: this fate leads to 'total ruin, and sometimes even not unaccompanied by sudden death'.

Matilda falls into his power, and can only be released by a Scottish knight, possessed of virtue, strength, unsullied affection, valour, and 'an unlimited confidence in the supreme powers of heaven'. Such a knight is found in Sir Oswald. Coming to the castle where Matilda is imprisoned, he liberates a spirit confined in a cavern, and kills a huge serpent which, expiring, ignites the forest. Nothing daunted, 'as fleeth the eagle in the face of the fierce solar blaze, so advanced the brave, the dauntless lover'. He meets another dragon 'breathing forth sulphur and fire ... the brazen scales of the monster reflected with brilliancy upon the awful scene, and his glaring and bloodshot eyes, added to the terror of his high erected crest, shone forth with terror and dismay'. When, after long battle, the monster fell, 'the forests shook with his ponderous weight, and an ocean of blood, dark as the inmost recesses of the tomb, flowed from his wounds'. Here we have echoes of the popular traditions which Bunyan and Spenser also drew upon. With all its obvious grammatical and stylistic faults, it has some of the spontaneous exuberance of popular art.

The allegory is continued. Sir Oswald, having overcome the dragon is weak in his moment of success, and himself falls a prey to the Mountain Fiend. He is tortured in the Fiend's castle, and sees there an enemy also in torment. He shows pity instead of delight, and after this act of compassion, the castle vanishes. He then defeats Moguilso, a magician who turns himself into a lion (cf. Spenser's *Fairie Queene*, V, ix, xvii–xix). Then he evidently falls a prey to lust, for he has failed to take from before the castle a branch of Amarynth, which symbolizes truth and benevolence, and is defeated by the monster Centrebus. 'Mark well', says the author; 'the fatal consequences of the dominion of youthful passion.' In prison he is nearly overcome by an unnamed 'Giant Dispair'. 'His sable robe was embroidered with human woes, and the tattered margin was fringed with clotted gore.' He offers Sir Oswald a drink from the fatal 'goblet of Oblivion', but, like the Red Cross Knight in Spenser's poem, he is saved by a female spirit. His saviour is called Urganda, who has washed away the stain of an unspecified crime with 'tears of repentance': the name, but not the character, is that of an all-powerful sorceress in Southey's popular translation of *Amadis de Gaul* (1803). Finally,

Sir Oswald is able to overcome the Mountain Fiend, and liberate Matilda. Interwoven with this allegory, to complicate matters further, are four sub-plots intermingling historical and domestic romance, none of them very clearly handled.

The Mountain Fiend is an exception – I have never read another novel of this type making such a thorough, and such a chaotic attempt to write allegory. On one hand such writing is clearly related to the love of arcane rituals shown in friendly society and early trades-union ceremonies. On the other, it shows that some of this popular fiction was written with literary aspirations, and the fact that such novels were published and ran their full course indicates similar interests in many readers. These writers had some glimmerings of past English literature, and tried to air their knowledge: Edward Montague's *The Demon of Sicily* (*c.* 1840), for instance, applied the cosmology and demonology of Milton's *Paradise Lost* (cheap serial issue, eighteen numbers, 1825–6) to Gothic romance, and has verbal echoes of Milton's work.

Such a rehandling of the Gothic type of story was indicative that this genre was no longer a living one, but one of the several traditions of storytelling the hack writers were using as they thought fit. One element of the Gothic story which was adapted and extended to all types of tale was the presence of supernatural powers, protecting the heroine, giving heightened significance to the conflict between the evil villain and the immaculately pure heroine. Earlier heroines, like Richardson's Pamela, defended their virtue with willpower, and chastity, while the major issue, was not a divine principle defended by an invincible Providence. In the new fiction, apart from the work of the realistic deviationists G. W. M. Reynolds and Thomas Frost, the Gothic supernatural is called to the aid of middle-class domestic morality; the Supreme Powers protect the heroine, and the defeat of chastity would destroy the whole pseudo-religious structure against which the drama is played out. In the most impossible situations, Heaven provided a way out. We may take an example from *Love and Crime; or, the Mystery of the Convent* (1841). Hildargo, a villainous monk, has Agnes alone in a castle high on a mountain. The door is locked, and no one coming to help. He may be forgiven a certain confidence as he approached the couch where his unarmed victim lay.

'Vile wretch!' said the horror-struck Agnes, 'think you that the

Omnipotent will permit you to do such an act, and not instantly blast
your detested form? Hark you not how the thunder roars?'

Hildargo continues to approach, and the Omnipotent does not
permit.

. . . one side of the mansion, no longer able to resist the combined
forces of the outrageous elements, fell with a hideous roar on the sands;
and the monk, who, appalled at the tremendous peals, had started away
from Agnes, was precipitated on the ruins below.

Agnes remained safe in bed. It must be noted, however, that
this applies to the main characters only. In the novel *Vileroy*, for
instance, a brigand tells an appalling story of casual rape and
murder in a Venetian gondola, although the heroine herself is
protected. Often this protection is less dramatic than in the case of
Agnes just cited, but hardly less impressive. Another heroine,
imprisoned at the mercy of an unprincipled ruffian, declared: 'Ten
months elapsed in this manner . . . and it is astounding how I
continued to prevent the designs he had upon me.'[1]

If the heroine was surrounded by the powers of the Omnipotent,
the villain is in the power of Hell. As Vicensio in *The Demon of
Sicily* dies:

. . . the attendant fiends of hell, in anxious expectation, stood awaiting
[his soul's] escape from its mortal coil, they seized it in their sharp
talons, grining [*sic*] horribly they darted through the bosom of rifted
earth, and plunged it deep in red oceans of unextinguishable flames.[2]

The inflexible moral structure of these stories need not be taken
to indicate an upright moral code in the readers, although it may
have gained added appeal as an escape from the actual degradation
and licence of town and factory conditions. The struggle of good
against evil and the victory of good is essential to the aesthetic
structure of the popular story. To disintegrate the morals would
be to disintegrate the dynamic form of the plot. I suspect this is
true of even the sophisticated reader who accepts a tragic ending,
for he only fits the tale into a more sophisticated moral structure,
and one which accepts the fitness of tragedy, or even futility.

1. T. P. Prest, *Emily Fitzormond*, p. 279.
2. E. Montague, *The Demon of Sicily*, p. 10.

The heightening of moral issues enhanced the popularity of the Gothic theme of Lewis's *The Monk*, or Maturin's *Melmoth the Wanderer*, that of a soul sold to the devil. Byron followed this in *The Deformed Transformed* (1821), where the crippled Arnold sells his soul to Satan in exchange for a magnificent body. *The Mysteries of the Forest; or, the Deformed Reformed* (c. 1849) takes this basic story, keeping Byron's names, although making certain drastic changes. For instance, Byron's Arnold is born crippled, a significant feature in the light of the author's club foot; in the adaptation he has been wounded in a fight, and sells his soul after killing a brother through jealousy, and later becoming banished. But there were several permutations of the 'bargain with the devil' theme. In Reynolds's *Wagner the Wehr-wolf* (1847) an old German peasant gains from Satan perpetual youth on condition that he becomes a werewolf every seven years. After many horrible happenings he is saved, rather unfairly, by the Rosicrucians.

The seminal work of all these tales is of course the Faust story. Reynolds used it as the basis for a full-length novel, *Faust* (1846), but echoes of it occur in a number of these stories, particularly in the horrific final hours. In both *The Demon Huntsman* (c. 1842) and *Bianca and the Magician* (1841), for instance, a parent begs the hero to repent before it is too late, and the spectacle of devils reaching out for the agonized soul was a medieval terror that had not lost its power over the popular imagination in the nineteenth century. In the last moments of Sforza and Baldacini in *Bianca*:

. . . shapes of portentious and horrible appearance flew around, to the extreme terror of the ecclesiastic, who, hissing terrificly and vomitting flame, sprang forward as if to seize the helpless man . . . The infernal hubbub increased, the planets seemed starting from their spheres; until one tremendous thunderbolt struck the ruined mansion, which, unseated from its foundations by the shock, toppled headlong to the ground, burying its inmates in the ruins.[1]

Even this short extract, however, shows how the story was told on the purely superficial level of effect, and how much it loses in comparison with the human anguish of Marlowe's hero.

Reynolds's *Wagner the Wehr-wolf*, the heroes of 'Wilhelmina Johnson's' *The Ranger of the Tomb* (1847) and *The Demon Huntsman*

1. *Bianca and the Magician*, pp. 129 ff.

4. The Gothic Novel

(a) The female Wizard presenting the Magic Helmet
to Hieronymo

(b) 'A flight of stairs was immediately revealed'

(c) 'Heaven,' said Caroline, 'will not desert the innocent'

(d) 'I am here, then,' sobbed Flora, 'in the lair of the tiger'

(*c.* 1842), besides the characters of many other of these Gothic stories, were German. German fiction and drama enjoyed an immense vogue in England towards the end of the eighteenth century, and took a leading part in the Gothic tradition; two of the 'horrid novels' in Jane Austen's *Northanger Abbey*, *Horrid Mysteries* and *The Necromancer*, are German. However, contrary to the impression given by works such as Montague Summers's *Gothic Quest*, many of these German stories have little to do with the supernatural, but are largely tales of romance. Some of the most popular German tales of terror were short folk tales, brought out in volumes like the frequently reprinted *Popular Tales of the German* (1791) by J. C. A. Musaeus, and *Grimm's Märchen* (1823). We have already examined one, 'The Bohemian Gardener': one of the most popular was Burger's *Leonore*, translated by Walter Scott as 'The Chase' in 1796. Like the latter work, most of these stories illustrated the terrible results of wishing the dead to return.

Some English writers tried their own hand at these legends, with unhappy results. *The Demon Huntsman; or, the Fatal Bullet* (*c.* 1842) is based on the tale of the hunter (cf. Weber's *Der Freischütz*) who is given seven bullets by the devil. Six of them belong to Satan, and do the hunter's will, but the seventh belongs to God, and can do only good. Gaspar, the hunter, uses one bullet to win a girl in a shooting competition from her true lover. Then the plot breaks down, because the writer could not recreate the feel of the supernatural which comes through, in all its crudity, in the translations; the author changed to the more familiar ground of a man selling his soul to the devil in exchange for immortality, on condition he provides Satan with a soul every seven years. He fails, and the book ends in the customary pall of brimstone.

Alongside the German influence we find themes and styles from English Gothic writers. Three penny-issue editions of M. G. Lewis's *The Monk* have been recorded, (although I have only seen two of them). There are certain traces of this extremely popular work in certain penny-issue romances; for example, the heroine's vision in *The Fate of Gaspar* (*c.* 1843) reads very much like that of Antonia in Lewis's work, and there are a crop of lecherous monks in novels such as *Love and Crime*. The resemblances, however, are superficial: these penny novels did not recapture the adolescent sensuality and steamy atmosphere of *The Monk*.

In fact, the 'horrid' element in lower-class literature tended to be a direct attack on the nerves rather than the creation of a frightening mood. Popular ghost stories of a previous age could chill the spine as well and better than any from an upper-class source. The cosmopolitan worker, however, was cynical about the supernatural, and, as the lower-class writers had not enough skill to create through atmosphere a suspension of disbelief, they tried to shout down doubt. In T. P. Prest's *The Death Grasp* (*c.* 1844), for instance, Adolphe de Floriville debauches, then murders, Eugene de Bonison. Eugene dies with the following curse:

'Peace shall henceforth be a stranger to thy breast! In the festive scene – in thy waking hours, and in thy fevered slumbers, my spirit shall ever more be with thee. My ghastly cheek, – my bleeding form, – my filmy eye, – shall be thy constant objects; and, as dying I clutch thee now, so, in life and in death, shall my cold, clammy hands grasp thee.'[1]

Throughout an active life – he commits bigamy, murders the brother of one of his wives, kills his brother and engages in blackmail – he is haunted by the feel of that clammy hand.

Whether he slept, he knew not; but the horrible circumstances that aroused him could never be erased from his memory. A hand, cold as the Winter's ice, and damp and clammy with the moisture of death, clasped him with the vehemence of expiring agony! – Good God! – how can we portray the horror that paralysed his whole frame? It curdled the current of his quivering veins . . .[2]

A skilful narrator presents a subtle balance of the incorporeal and the concrete – we may compare the above passage with the account of the clutching hand in *Wuthering Heights*. The 'death grasp' is as supernatural as wet kid gloves.

One way to purvey tales of terror to readers cynical about the supernatural was to arrange an explanation at the end of how it was all really done. The master, or mistress, of this type of story was Mrs Radcliffe. Her novels were so frequently reprinted in cheap serialized form, and had such an influence on popular fiction at this time, that it is worthwhile outlining their plots here. *The Mysteries of Udolpho* (1794), most popular of all, tells the story of the orphan Emily St Aubert. She is placed under the cruel control

1. T. P. Prest, *The Death Grasp*, p. 14.
2. ibid., p. 23.

of her aunt, Mme Cheron, who denies her access to her lover, Valancourt, and herself marries Montoni, a brigand. They all go to the castle of Udolpho, in the Appenines, then to Château-le-Blanc, in Languedoc. These places are full of unexplored passages, and wandering about Château-le-Blanc Emily discovers part of a mysterious manuscript relating, it turns out, to the fate of a second aunt. There is also a 'picture' so terrible that Emily faints at the sight of it; apparitions appear on the ramparts, strange music is heard, and a mysterious voice rings out when Emily is being importuned by Montoni. Mme Cheron dies, and on the threat that all protection will be withdrawn from her, Emily resigns her claims to the estates that are rightfully hers. In the end all escape, Emily receives Mme Cheron's property, but refuses other possessions from the accomplice of a man who murdered her aunt. Valancourt clears his name from an imputation of being a gambler, leaving the way open for a happy marriage. All the 'mysteries' are explained: the apparitions were the robbers who were using the castle, and a Monsieur Du Pont, who also provided the voice that Emily heard; the mysterious music had been played by a lady driven temporarily insane, and the 'picture' was an image of a corpse rotted with worms, an object used for penitent contemplation by a past inmate of the castle.

In this story Emily has a locket containing a miniature of her aunt. The motif of the locket goes back at least to medieval popular romance, but Mrs Radcliffe gave it new currency. Mysterious lockets appear again and again in novels right down to Dickens's *Oliver Twist*. Valancourt and Emily meet through a road accident: this situation, again, constantly reoccurs in romances – for instance, in T. P. Prest's *The Gipsy Boy* (*c.* 1847). The discovery in a castle of a manuscript bearing on the main plot becomes practically a rule in this type of story. In *Almira's Curse* (1842), to take an example at random, a girl imprisoned by Sir Martin de Lancy finds in the Black Tower of Bransdorf a manuscript written by Almira, Sir Martin's previous mistress, telling how she was seduced, and forced to throw her child down a well.

The Mysteries of Udolpho helped to fix the scene of these Gothic romances in a castle. Other Gothic stories had of course been set in castles, notably Horace Walpole's popular *Castle of Otranto* (1764), another seminal novel. This, however, accepts the supernatural; the usurper Manfred holds a castle full of weird auguries of doom, presided over by the gigantic figure of Alfonso's ghost, who finally pulls the edifice to the ground. The castles of the penny-issue novels are much more isolated places full of secret passages, moveable pictures, and so on, to provide the mechanics for the *apparently* ghostly events. Above all, they were prisons for a long-suffering heroine. They generally had an important role in unifying these stories, which were written from week to week, through the single setting and the common collection of stage properties.

A work by Mrs Radcliffe also helped to provide a stock villain – the monk-cum-brigand. Her novel, *The Italian* (1797), tells how Ellena Rosalba is prevented from seeing Vivaldi, her lover, because Vivaldi's mother fears a *mésalliance*. She has Ellena removed to a nunnery by Schedoni, her confidant, a monk and a bandit. Schedoni, on the point of murdering Ellena, becomes convinced that she is his daughter, so spares her. She is really the daughter of his wife by his elder brother, whom he had murdered. In the end Ellena is freed, receives estates rightfully hers, and is happily married to Vivaldi.

A good example of Mrs Radcliffe's influence is *Angela the Orphan* (1841), which amalgamates the two summarized works. Angela de Montgolfi, on the death of her father, is consigned to a nunnery by her uncle. On the way Bertrand, the monk who is taking her, reveals himself as a bandit, and imprisons her in a castle. She is looked after by a girl who, like Emily St Aubert's servant, is engaged in a love affair. She also finds the inevitable manuscripts. She is then taken overseas to another castle – again like Emily. Finally she is freed, and united to Valerio, her lover. There are various additions, such as a rescue attempt by her lover disguised as a musician, but Mrs Radcliffe's influence is plain.

A summary of plots gives very little idea of the real qualities of her writing, however. Mrs Radcliffe is of the age of sensibility, which exalted the feelings as creating the character, communicating with supra-sensual values, and showing true goodness. While she mistrusted the cult of sensibility that produced Henry Mackenzie's *Man of Feeling* (1771), where the tears dropped are indexed at the back as a catalogue of his hero's goodness, she used the situations of Gothic romance to create pictures of a girl's delicately felt reactions to mood and atmosphere, the dominant tones being terror or picturesque beauty. A few of the early penny-issue novels did try to emulate these qualities of writing.

Further on, a cataract was seen rushing down the steep rock into the valley. Here the view was truly picturesque and sublime; the waters, covered with foam, mingled with the stream below, into which the trees dropped their overhanging branches; the silence was only interrupted by the dashing of the waters and the musical notes of the feathered chanters who built their airy habitations in the trembling summits of the lofty trees.

The beams of the sun glittered on the waters, and diffused a bright glow over the scene which filled the heart of Anna with delight. Orlando observed the pleasure which glistened in her eyes as she surveyed this lovely scene; the glow which only exercise of the exquisite emotions of the heart can call forth, beamed on her downy cheek.[1]

The last sentence is particularly significant. The 'exquisite emotions of the heart' were to be an important attribute of the heroine in works besides those directly indebted to Mrs Radcliffe.

These novels also show a tendency to rationalize the Gothic story by putting it in a historical context. *The Black Monk* (1844), perhaps the most popular of the later Gothic novels, shows just how far the confusion between the various historical and Gothic traditions could go. Alicia Brandon is murdered by Morgatani (the Black Monk), who, as a member of a Jesuit conspiracy, is planning to kill King Richard, oust his followers, and rule England through King John. (The author felt there was nothing odd in having Jesuits in the Middle Ages.) The Jesuits have made a systematic study of English castles, and know many facts that would surprise their owners. Morgatani, a monastic in the tradition of Mrs Radcliffe's Schedoni in *The Italian* and Abellino in M. G. Lewis's *The Bravo of Venice* (1804), is a lonely figure of frightening aspect and strange power. Pressed to reveal his beliefs, he says, 'in a hissing whisper', he believes in 'nothing'. His aim is to dominate mankind. Sir Rupert Brandon, believing his wife Alicia to have died a natural death, goes off to the crusades, leaving behind Agatha Weare, his sister-in-law whose love he has slighted, and her cowardly brother Eldred, whose main interest in life is making love to the cook. They become tools in the hand of Morgatani, who arranges to have Sir Rupert convicted of the murder of Alicia on his return. He is opposed by the Wizard of the Red Cave, whom the Black Monk has driven insane by seducing and causing the death of his sister Beatrice, a nun.

1. Anon., *Love and Crime*, 1841, p. 169.

A knight called Sir Kenneth Hay returns to carry out Sir Rupert's business. Although he is poisoned, defeated in a tournament, and thrown into a dungeon, he emerges safe and sound thanks to the ministrations of a page to one Fitzhugh – this page turns out to be a disguised girl, once seduced by Fitzhugh, and now intent on reparation. King Richard arrives at the castle with visor down, followed later by Sir Rupert and other knights, also disguised, and there follows a trial of strength between them and the traitors. The lack of any historical decorum and the tiresome facetiousness in this work can be seen in this short extract where King Richard (the crusader), dines with his enemies.

'Welcome,' said the crusader, laying his battle-axe on the table with such a crash, that everything shook again.

'Thank yer,' stammered Eldred, 'I am very much obliged to you – how are you? I hope all your family are quite well? Don't you think you'll find that chopper inconvenient?'

'No,' said the knight. 'I like to carry it about with me. And on a feast sometimes comes a fray, and it's useful to be prepared.'

King Richard doubles Eldred up with a slap on the back, and defeats a plot to poison him by using Venetian goblets like those in *Udolpho*, which splinter when containing poison. Morgatani's headquarters in the Gray Tower, blazing with stage fire, are belatedly attacked, and its occupant buried alive in a subterranean passage. Sir Rupert's children, thought to have been murdered, have been safe with the Wizard of the Red Cave, and all ends happily in an England again ruled by King Richard.

This novel is a transitional one, uneasily uniting debts to the Gothic novel with the background of Scott's *Ivanhoe*. James Malcolm Rymer's *Varney the Vampyre* (1847), probably the best-known of these penny-issue novels after *Sweeney Todd*, shows the author in the actual process of shifting his styles and attitudes as he tries to find a more congenial type of fiction, a movement only a long-running serial novel could illustrate.

The model for Sir Francis Varney was clearly that of Polidori's *The Vampyre* (1819; cheap serial version, R.N.L. 1840). Polidori's creature has tusks and metallic eyes: Varney was a 'tall gaunt form – there was the faded, ancient apparel – the lustrous metallic-looking eyes – its half-opened mouth, exhibiting the tusk-like teeth!' Both vampires are doomed to drink human blood or die, and their victims become vampires. They cannot be drowned, and are revived by moonbeams. The Gothic potentialities of the story are exploited to the full – it has some really effective moments. For instance, it opens on a stormy night. Flora is reading by a dim light in the lonely hall, made uneasy by the sounds of the storm outside. An old house is full of strange noises, but a persistent scratching sound makes her look up. Spreadeagled across the casement is the clinging figure of the vampire!

Here comes the first complication. Conscious of the scepticism of his urban readers, Rymer arranges that it can all be explained. Sir Francis Varney tells Charles Holland – the lover of Flora – that he is really only using the tradition of vampires to frighten away the occupants of Bannerworth Hall, so he can search the place for treasure hidden there by an earlier Bannerworth. Flora of course will be all right – she was only frightened. Varney goes to elaborate lengths to be seen 'shot' and 'revived by moonbeams' by one of the villagers.

Some loose ends, however, are not tied up – there is no explanation of how he received, unharmed, a bullet fired in a duel at short range, for example – and when the treasure has been discovered, and the story is ready for completion, Varney is suddenly revealed to be a real vampire; the discovery comes as a shock even to Sir Francis himself. Flora's romance with Charles Holland is forgotten, and the story starts off on a new track for forty further numbers. The immediate cause for the prolongation was no doubt the fact that the publisher requested Rymer to continue a story that was selling well, but the way in which the story developed shows the author continuing to experiment with characterization and type of plot. In the first half, Varney is presented early on as an embittered character with sardonic detachment like that of Schedoni. 'I love no one, I expect no love from anyone, but I will make humanity a slave to me.' He then becomes more humane. He begins to take considerable trouble not to cause undue suffering to the Bannerworth family – he takes risks to assure Flora Bannerworth she need not be anxious, for she has not been harmed. He becomes 'a man of distinguished courtesy and polished manners, [and of] the rare and beautiful gift of eloquence.' Rymer is showing himself ill at ease with the traditional Gothic attitudes, and is turning to a more human type of character. Next, Rymer tries to make him a tragic figure, cast out by society, like Godwin's Caleb

Williams. A plot devised, it is true, by Varney, rebounds on him out of proportion to his fault, as the mob picks up the rumour of his being a vampire. His house is razed to the ground, and he is wounded and hounded across the countryside by an ignorant rabble. Rymer takes this further. At this point Varney realizes he is in fact a vampire, driven to evil by powers beyond his control. He hurls himself into the river to drown himself, but water casts a vampire back. A little later he cries:

'Since death is denied me, I will henceforth shake off all human sympathies . . . no spark of human pity will find a home in this once racked and tortured bosom. Fate, I thee defy!'

The Bannerworths even take pity on him: 'It's in the nature of the beast, and that's all you can say about it.'

Here the story begins to fail, and most of this latter part is left out of the reprint (1853). Instead of becoming truly tragic, Varney becomes merely an animal. The story becomes forced as, to keep the printer supplied, Rymer introduced a vampire from Hungary, and then five others (unaccountably) conducting an orgy on Hampstead Heath. Varney makes a dull succession of attacks on various girls, enlivened by an episode, borrowed from Polidori, where a corpse of one victim is being transfixed with a stake at a crossroads when its eyes open, and it emits a piercing shriek. An ineffectual clergyman begs Varney to repent, but Varney prefers to jump down Vesuvius.

When Varney left England for Italy, he left a manuscript detailing newly remembered past experiences, including adventures with Charles II and Rochester. Again the Gothic is fused with the historical. These writers of course ingurgitated any material to hand, but the historical, with its claims to authenticity which appealed to the cosmopolitan, knowledge-seeking reader, was increasingly ousting the Gothic traditions. History was respectable, and when the carpenter John Overs presented his slender claims to recognition by the upper classes with *Evenings of a Working Man* (1844), prefaced by Dickens, he naturally chose historical fiction.

Besides other historical works, of fact and fiction, popular in Mechanics' Institute libraries, we may note a demand for the *Anglo-Saxon Chronicle*. An enterprising anonymous writer, using the translation by Anne Gurney (1819), from which it quotes, used it as the setting for *The Black Warrior* (*c.* 1842), reissued as *The Red Cross Warrior* (1843). It opens in the eleventh century, with the Danes making raids along the coast. On the Isle of Thanet there is a highly organized resistance led by the mysterious Black Warrior and his band. Herman, a Saxon in the castle, loves Maude, who is being brought up by a priest in the village on the plain below. Two captive Danes have been received into the castle community, Cedric, who is loyal to his captors, and Leonwolf, who secretly aids the enemy and desires the hand of Maude. Herman, wounded in a skirmish with the Danes, is taken to the cliff headquarters of the Black Warrior, and finally initiated into his order by means of a curious allegorical ceremony with a low corridor expressing humility, stones on the ground to express patience, and so on. This order, we are told, was one of 'Benevolence', founded by the Christians in Rome 'during the cruel persecution of the disciples of the Cross'. More surprises are in store for the reader – the Black Knight is the brother of the murdered Edward the Martyr, hiding from a Queen Elfrida and the evil Earl Godwine. Maude is his daughter. It is Godwine, not the Danes, who finally forces the Black Knight and his band to flee to France. The priest uses his exile to convert many heathens, and all return to Thanet when the danger is past.

Clearly there were many gaps in the author's education, but for all its shortcomings, it is very much more worthwhile than the professionally slick production of *Ivanhoe* I watch occasionally on the television over tea. There is more variety of character and interest, but, above all, the novel fails because the author tried to do too much, rather than, as in the television serial, boiling down the historical situation into the lowest common denominator of superficial excitement. The position of Cedric and Leonwolf, and of the Black Warrior caught between foreign and domestic enemies, shows some apprehension of the complexity of England's development.

Scott's *Ivanhoe* (1820) no doubt helped to make this a point of interest, which raises the question of Scott's popularity. Scott's novels were expensive when they appeared; indeed, they were instrumental in raising the cost of novels on the market. Price did not prevent determined lower-class readers from reading them; Thomas Cooper, for instance, managed to gain the use of an upper-class library at a greatly reduced rate, and bore off volumes of *Waverley* as if they were gold. There were a few cheaper issues, *The Beauties of Scott* (J. Limbird, 1829); *The Waverley Novels* (shilling parts, 1836–42); and *Waverley* and possibly others in the series (penny-issues, Edinburgh, R. Cadell, 1842), and extracts from Scott's works sometimes occurred in cheap periodicals. A number of lower-class libraries stocked them in the later 1830s. The impression remains, however, that the main impact of Scott on the lower classes came through the numerous and popular dramatizations of his works, and that even this interest declined in the 1830s. His works were probably too prolix and long for most lower-class tastes. Of the many penny-issue periodicals appearing at the time of his death, only *The Thief* (6 October 1832), to my knowledge, noticed his passing.

This picture excludes *Ivanhoe*. However much it was read – for I have never seen a cheap issue – *Ivanhoe* dominated the field of historical fiction up to the coming of Ainsworth in the 1840s. It made a perfect transition from the old world of fiction to the new. It used the themes of popular romance, and rationalized them. A mysterious knight rides into the lists, but he is an ordinary man bent on reclaiming his rightful possessions. The fairy who lends him a suit of armour when he is in need is a mercenary Jew. Wicked Templars are politicians, and the whole is set firmly against a historical background of England at a particular date. Even the popular hero Robin Hood is brought in, given an 'authentic' name, Locksley, and shown acting in actual historical events.

The incognito knights who appear in *Love and Crime* and *The Black Monk*, and Sir Rupert's journey to the Crusades in the latter work, are but two examples of *Ivanhoe's* omnipresent influence. *Richard of England* (1842), by the dramatist Thomas Archer, is the most thorough plagiarism I have examined. Apart from chapters 13 to 34, this is a mere rewriting of Scott's novel, sometimes even a verbatim transcription. Archer changes only the names – Ivanhoe becomes Sir Eustace de Vere; Isaac, Eleazer; Rebecca, Rachel and so forth. The middle chapters tell of the Crusades with a plot reminiscent of a medieval romance, spiced with the atmosphere of Byron's Mediterranean tales. The savage Malek falls in love with the Christian princess Ada of Cypress: he captures her, and treats her with respect. Agnes, a warrior princess, loves Malek. Eustace de Vere, captured by the Turks, is immediately released when they discover he is not a Templar. The most remarkable incident, however, is perhaps King Richard's prayer before engaging in battle against overwhelming odds, with the infidels.

'Remain thou neutral, Oh, Lord! and victory is ours.'

The Christians win.

In the 'Scott' sections of this work, Archer gave particular attention to the theme of Rebecca and Isaac. Four out of every five of the numerous dramatizations of *Ivanhoe* mention one or both of these characters in their titles. Rebecca's generosity, her aura of mystery, and the pathos of her unrequited love, made her – to use the popular phrase with its contemporary flavour – 'highly interesting'. This was exploited in other penny-issue novels. T. P. Prest's *The Hebrew Maiden* (1841), although it has many other debts to *Ivanhoe*, concentrates on a Rebecca who is recognizably Scott's heroine. In general she has a different role to play than has her original; she spends most of this very long novel passing between a bandit called Black Ivan (a wronged nobleman in disguise), Sir Gaston de Neville, and a Templar. She resists all their importunities, and finally marries her Hebrew lover, Reuben Grenard.

It is interesting to note that Jews and Jewesses were generally portrayed favourably in this lower-class fiction. *The Jew and the Foundling* (*c.* 1846), by Prest, is indeed virtually a pro-Semitic tract. This may have been partly due to the fascination excited by the separate Jewish community – Mrs Gore exploits this in *The Money Lender* (1843) – and partly due to the fact that Lloyd was catering for the Jewish population of Shoreditch and Holywell Street where he had his offices. It is very likely, however, that it also indicates an acceptance of Jewish elements into the working-class communities who read these novels.

The Hebrew Maiden, and most of the penny-issue novels published approximately between 1838 and 1848, have a distinctly stiff and unnatural quality of their own. They are clearly distinguishable from the fiction written even a few years either side of this period. Mr Willson Disher has suggested that this is due to the residual influence of the Gothic novel and chapbooks.[1] This is but half the truth. Quaint and highly mannered as earlier popular literature often was, its style had a certain rightness which came

1. *Pilot Papers*, II, March 1947, pp. 45 ff.

(a) 'The black waters of the Fleet-ditch were clearly visible'

(b) 'The conflict that now ensued was terrific'

(c) 'My liege,' cried Isaac, 'you see before you a broken-hearted father'

from their being written in harmony with their period and their audience. In the fiction under review, we see several traditions of literature cut off from their roots, mixed by literary hacks eager for material, and suspended in a jargon of melodrama. Such an unstable compound could not last, and it gave way before changes in taste that were appearing in the upper as well as the lower classes as the nineteenth century advanced.

In the field of literature, this change of mentality can be seen by comparing, for instance, *The Waverley Novels* with the historical works of G. P. R. James and W. H. Ainsworth. Here we see the romantic appeal of the archaic neglected in favour of a more superficial interest in the spectacular in historical buildings, dress and characters. Interest in the state of early England in *Ivanhoe* is succeeded by delight in the gloom of the Tower of London (Ainsworth's *The Tower of London* [1840]), or in the hysterical terror of the plague and fire in Ainsworth's *Old St Paul's* (1841). Rymer, referring to this emotional exaltation of the historical setting, called Ainsworth a charlatan.[1] The periods chosen by the later historical writers also tend to be more recent, the settings more localized, to give them more direct appeal. Characters tend to be portrayed in a more contemporary manner, with less historical colouring.

Lloyd, as might be expected, was quick to plagiarize this new style of historical writing. Ainsworth's *The Tower of London* was published in shilling parts, January to December 1840. As it came out each number was 'adapted' and issued as *A Legend of the Tower of London*, and issued as the original work of 'W. H. Hainsforth'. The preface declares the work has dispersed 'a host of pirates', and it would be interesting to know how much these statements were a cheeky joke, or whether Lloyd was seriously concerned to convince his readers his versions were the originals.

As Ainsworth's story so suited the popular taste, the plagiarism followed it closely, sometimes with mere changes in the wording. However, the changes are significant. Particular attention is paid to the comedy of the stone kitchen, a type of farce we have noticed expanded in the plagiarisms of Dickens. To give them more familiar interest, the giant Magog is rechristened Hugh, and the dwarf Xit, Christopher Dumps. The love of the 'ordinary' character Cholmondeley for the orphaned heiress Angela, whom he finds

1. *Queen's Magazine*, I, 1842, p. 103.

imprisoned in the Tower, is a theme of domestic romance, and given in full. To take this further, a gypsy sybil is introduced who dogs the footsteps of Angela's gaoler, and murders him.

Ainsworth has a love of elaborate, pseudo-poetic descriptions, and this fitted in exactly with a working-class taste looking backwards to chapbook stories and the costume plays of the Elizabethans, and forward to the cockney pearly kings, and the exotic birds, lions, ferns and improbable ladies that decorate fair-ground amusements. A good example of Ainsworth's purple passages would be:

[Lady Jane's] dress consisted of a gown of cloth of gold raised with pearls, a stomacher blazing with diamonds and other precious stones, and a surcoat of purple velvet likewise furred with ermine, and embroidered with various devices in gold. Her slender, swan-like throat was circled with a carcenet of gold set in rubies . . .[1]

We may compare this with the lower-class writer's equivalent:

[Lady Jane] was apparelled in white cloth of gold of damask, with a mantle of the same, furred with ermine, fastened before her with gold and silk, and rich knobs of gold, tasselled at the ends; her beautiful fair hair hanging down behind her back with a caul of cloth of tinsel, set with pearls and stones, and above it a round circlet of gold, also so richly set with precious stones that the value of it was inestimable.[2]

Here, the lush description of Ainsworth has been made even more elaborate, and words are used for their sound rather than for their sense, of which the author has only the vaguest idea. We hear also in this work of music from 'minstrelsy, among which were the now long explored instruments, called shalms and sackbutts'; in other novels we get such curiosities as 'cruentable falchion', or the query 'Or haps it you are on salliance to a folkmote with the water nymphs?' Absurd as they may be, they have a vigour which later more professional writing was to lack. Many will have enjoyed imagining the music from 'shalms and sackbutts', just as many enjoy music they imagine produced by Coleridge's 'damsel with a dulcimer', although they have never heard a dulcimer.

The same tastes are reflected in many of the woodcuts to the

1. W. Harrison Ainsworth, *The Tower of London*, p. 6.
2. W. H. Hainsforth, *A Legend of the Tower of London*, p. 2.

penny-issue novels, which are crowded with fantastic ornamentation of dress, buildings and furniture. In the closely allied trade of theatrical woodcuts, illustrations were decorated further with coloured cloth and tinsel. They are vigorous and unselfconscious, but certainly not without style. Indeed they are part of a working-class decorated baroque found also in fair-grounds, circuses and cheap pottery figurines to the end of the century, when this began to fail before the inroads of mass production and the beginnings of American influence. Against the dingy town conditions, its brightness had a particular appeal, and investigators found woodcuts and theatrical sheets decorating slum walls.[1]

On the other hand, the squalor had its own fascination, and this too was exploited by popular novelists. Ainsworth drew the darker side of London at the time of the Plague and Great Fire of 1665 in *Old St Paul's*, which was serialized in *The Sunday Times*, a paper popular in public houses and coffee rooms. At the centre of the story is the middle-class merchant Stephen Blount, and his household, in particular his daughter Annabel, who is pursued by Charles II, Rochester, and their entourage of depraved nobility and hired criminals. She is protected by a working-class youth, Lawrence, but Rochester achieves his fell purpose. Besides being serialized in *The Sunday Times*, this work was closely followed in *The Mysteries of Old St Paul's* (1841) (which however preserved the heroine's chastity), and it provided the setting and certain elements for *The Monument; or the Great Fire of London* (1841) by 'Rip Rap'. Lloyd unaccountably withheld his hand, possibly because it did not drape its sexual excitements with the trappings of more conventional romance.

Writers tended to move nearer and nearer to contemporary events. William Leman Rede's *The Royal Rake* deserves mention because it was the first novel to be serialized in a newspaper; it appeared originally in *The Sunday Times* (5 January–27 December 1840). It is also one of a number of works set in the days of George III and the Prince Regent. The early Victorians looked back to this period rather as we look back to the 1920s, as a period of frivolous extravagance, combining the fascination of the past with the interest of things half-remembered, although the early nineteenth-century situation was much the more sordid. These romances tended to give exclusive attention to the darker elements

1. *S.S.L.*, XI, 1848, p. 218.

– the *historical* appeal of the picture of the Prince Regent, surrounded by mirrors, taking a bath with a beautiful girl, while her accomplice robs him, can only be incidental. There are a good many such incidents in G. W. M. Reynolds's *The Mysteries of the Court of London*, that ran from 1849 to 1856, and it was the most popular romance set in this period. These novels are the *Forever Ambers* of early Victorian fiction.

As Reynolds has received a good deal of attention from critics such as Dr Dalziel in *Popular Fiction a Hundred Years Ago*, it is better to end with an examination of a work from the group of novelists J. F. Smith, J. M. Rymer and Pierce Egan, Jun., any of whom could challenge Reynolds on the point of popularity, and whose changing styles of writing are more typical of the trends which popular fiction was following as it moved towards the 1850s.

J. F. Smith was the son of George Smith, the manager of the Norwich Theatre circuit, and in his youth he did some acting as a 'heavy' character. This need not call up shades of Crummles: Smith appears to have had a respectable education – tradition has it from a Jesuit, although he broke away from Roman Catholicism soon afterwards. He spent part of his youth travelling on the continent. The story that he was decorated by the Pope for services rendered as a secret agent can certainly be discounted; nevertheless, his travel broadened his outlook, and gave him experience he could use later in his novels. By 1849, when he emerges into the field of popular literature, he had written two competent middle-class novels, *The Jesuit* (1832) and *The Prelate* (1840), a handful of plays, and some poetry.

Smith published 'Marianne', a short story, in *The London Journal* on 12 May 1849; the next week he commenced the immensely popular *Stanfield Hall* which went into the first of many independent reprints in 1851. This story, perhaps influenced by Horace Smith's *Brambletye House* (1828), traces the fortunes of the Stanfield family from the Middle Ages to the Restoration.

In the first volume the heir to Stanfield is Ulrich. Others possess his rightful estates, and he has been brought up secretly by Father Oswald, a converted druid. He is nearly destroyed by the jealous accusations of one Herman that he has murdered Earl de Bigod, the Danish overlord, but with the help of Oswald he is vindicated. He receives his rights, flees when documents are forged by one

Ralph de Gaul implicating him in treason, finally overcomes his accuser in fight, but dies soon afterwards.

The hand of Scott is still not far away. The contest of Richard Cœur de Lion against the usurping John in *Ivanhoe* finds a parallel in the struggle of Robert of Normandy against his unscrupulous younger brother, William Rufus. Jews come in with the rich father Abram, who gives Ulrich a suit of armour in return for services rendered, and there is a beautiful Jewess, Hester. Here there is a curious aberration from the tradition – Hester becomes converted and marries a Christian hero, although the father almost succeeds in poisoning her by putting strong toxic in the baptismal font. She goes into a trance, for the original poison has been changed by a disguised character who emerges as one Walter Tyrrel. Tyrrel has figured earlier in the book in an attempt to rape another daughter of Abram, Rachel. He is captured by Abram, and has his face entirely changed by means of plastic surgery. An outcast from all who knew him, he spends the rest of the time covered in the book expiating his wrong.

Plastic surgery is not the only curious prophetic touch in the book. In the 'medieval' volume we have also the use of a gas-bomb, in the second volume, electrolysis, in the third, a cinema and although the workings are not explained, it is stressed that they are not magic, but done by science. Inventions like this are quite unlike anything in previous fiction: they are a sign of Victorian inventiveness spilling over into romance, and look forward to the futuristic boys' stories at the end of the century with their flying machines, a Steam Horse and electrical weapons.[1]

In the second book the heirs of Stanfield Hall are Lady Mary Stanfield and her mother, Catherine. The father has been murdered by Sir John de Corby, who now tries to kill the remaining heirs. He is frustrated mainly by the young clerk, Walter, who finally marries Lady Mary and becomes Lord of Stanfield. The story is given much of its interest by the court jester, Patch. He is the son of Perkin Warbeck, whom he believes the rightful heir; deprived of his true rights, he resigns himself to his position, setting up a barrier of cynicism which preserves him throughout the intrigues of the court of Wolsey and Henry VIII, of Edward VI and of Queen Mary. When the last monarch rouses him to loyalty, he is killed saving her from an assassin.

1. See E. S. Turner, *Boys will be Boys*, 1957, pp. 167 ff.

'He hurried with all the precipitation in his power towards
the main road'

Patch at once befriends Walter, and the loyalty between them brings out a certain complexity in the jester, who finds his cynicism disturbed by warmer feelings. Smith is somewhat weak in his love themes, but strong in his portrayal of male comradeship; Ulrich and Mirvan in the first volume, Richard Wilton and Herbert in the third, and Patch and Walter. 'Earth hath many a gem more prized, but none more pure than manly friendship's honest, priceless tear.' After the sensuality of Reynolds, Smith comes like a refreshing wave of cold water.

The dialogue of the work may appear falsely archaic and undistinguished, but in comparison with that of most other similar writers, it positively glitters. Patch brings out intelligent aphorisms like 'whilst I keep a secret I am its master: when I reveal it, I become its slave'. There is an example of effective applied metaphor when, shortly before Wolsey's fall, the King goes hunting. Henry's hawk pursues a heron, and one courtier cries, too loud, 'Fly, Cardinal, rise, King'. After an expectant hush, the King smiles and repeats the cry, and the fates of the King and the cardinal are linked with the birds when, after a pursuit, they kill each other. Moreover Smith keeps his pages well packed with material where others were content to fill out a little matter to make weight. This is all the more surprising when the rapidity with which he wrote is considered: he would do his weekly instalment at one sitting, shut up with his papers, and a bottle of wine above the printing office and claiming his fee when he came down with the text.

In its main lines, the historical background is reasonably accurate. Smith refers to a good many sources, such as Leland, Froissart and 'the Cottonian mss'. He shows a good grasp of court affairs. In certain episodes, however, he allows his imagination some startling flights. For example, in the first book, when King Henry III is crowned, Harold suddenly appears to give the Prince his dying blessing: he had gone into hiding after Hastings, having recovered from a dangerous wound in the eye. No less improbable an event occurs in Book Two, where Wolsey appears disguised as a mendicant monk to inquire into the mystery of the Stanfield inheritance.

One actor in the last volume is none other than Milton. The tale is set in the civil wars, and although the house of Stanfield is traditionally royalist, the rights and wrongs of both Charles and

Cromwell are presented and Herbert Stanfield, the hero, together with the heroine, Mary Keinton, seek to be fair to both parties, nearly being destroyed by both. They are aided by Milton, who is drawn with a character quite different from that suggested by Robert Graves. At one point 'a glorious smile lit the melancholy countenance of the poet, as he listened to the noble sentiment, for he was formed by nature to appreciate all that was beautiful in art and lovely in nature'.

Once this romantic figure has been drawn, it is natural to have him acting Michael to the Satan of the villain Barford. 'And my commission,' replied Milton, drawing his sword, 'is from the King of Kings. It bids me shelter a defenceless woman.'

These flights of the imagination, like the introduction of anachronistic gas-bombs and plastic surgery, may sound curious alongside an essentially sound grasp of historical events: in reading they are surprisingly successful, thanks to the pace of the story and the easy style in which it is written.

Stanfield Hall, in fact, although in many ways it looks back to the earlier fiction that has been discussed, has the professional ease of the new fiction written not only by Smith, but also Rymer, Reynolds, and Pierce Egan, Jun. These writers are significant: they have a middle-class background and a literary ability far beyond that of the authors of *The Mysteries of Oronza* or *The Mountain Fiend*. They were not men of exceptional talent, but rather, good craftsmen able to vary their styles and plots as the popular taste changed – Pierce Egan's *Quintin Matsys* (1841) is very different from *The Flower of the Flock* (1858); Rymer's *The Black Monk* (1844) from *Secret Service* (1861); Reynolds's *Faust* (1845) from *Mary Price* (1851). Prest, who was never able to change from the style of his successful *Ela, the Outcast*, fell from favour, and died a pauper, while Rymer was able to retire rich. Popular fiction for the working classes had grown out of the experimental stage into big business.

6

The Paradox of the Domestic Story

THE 'domestic story' lies at the heart of almost all the penny-issue fiction published during the 1840s. Having said this, it is very hard to define what a 'domestic story' is. The index to *Chambers's London Journal*, under 'Literature – Domestic', listed such diverse items as 'Burns Illustrated and Explained', 'The Experiences of Benjamin Bluesteel' (humorous tales of bachelor life) and a romance of high society, 'A Fashionable Marriage'. The most famous 'domestic' drama of the preceding century was a tale of illicit love, robbery, and murder, George Lillo's *The London Merchant; or, the History of George Barnwell* (1731), which told of the apprentice Barnwell seduced to lust and crime by the courtesan Millwood. Clearly, then, it does not mean a tale of home life, as we would expect today. The term denotes not so much a particular subject, as an approach to the subject. G. D. Pitt defined a domestic romance when he declared 'the events are brought home to the evidence of our senses, as consonant with scenes of real life'.[1]

The movement in fiction towards 'life as it is', to use the tag frequently attached to the titles of these stories was, of course, part of a wider development apparent in all classes of literature. In 1841 we find Mrs E. C. Grey complaining:

> Novel-writing has completely changed its character. From its high-flown, elaborate style, it is now fallen into its opposite extreme; from improbabilities, always impalpable, sometimes gross, now, in their place, we find nothing but the hum-drummeries of reality.[2]

The modern reader will not grudge the changes that produced Thackeray, Jerrold, and Dickens, or the work of writers such as Mary Howitt, whose fiction found its way into cheap periodicals. But let us look closer at lower-class 'domestic' tales.

1. *The Wreck of the Heart*, 1842, p. iii.
2. *The Little Wife*, 1841, p. 93.

In *Jane Brightwell* (1846) Rymer pinpoints the cause for the popularity of 'domestic' themes – the old world of the Minerva Press romance has no appeal for the cosmopolitan reader, for its settings and moral attitudes are out of touch with the experience of the readers. This is particularly true of the mainspring of romance, woman's love.

It is the maudlin, sickly fashion of the present day to call all this [romantic love] 'the devotion of the female heart', 'the singleness of woman's dear affections', 'the love that clings even to an unworthy object provided it has once been enshrined in the heart &c., &c.,' . . . All this clinging affection, about which so much romantic nonsense is continually written by ladies' maids, and lovesick boys, merely arises from habit and a weak intellect.

Rymer will now show how romantic love really works out in real life.

Squire Grantley has a feud against the Brightwell family, because the father had been his successful rival in love. Grantley's son, Edgar, finds favour with Jane Brightwell, the farmer's daughter. He seduces her, ruins the Brightwell family financially, comes into his father's fortune, and enters fashionable life in London, taking the love-sick Jane with him. He does not marry her, but, acting by the novelist's ideals of selfless devotion, she continues faithful to him. But this love is dangerous. She finds her parents are keeping a small bookshop in London, and gives them the only valuable she has on her, a ring given her by Edgar. When they try to sell it, they are convicted of theft, and, true to her overwhelming loyalty to Edgar, she does not dare to risk a breach with him by defending her parents. Her mother goes to prison, Edgar dies, then Jane's father. Jane goes to his death-bed to beg forgiveness.

Jane Brightwell is, by the standards of this fiction, readable and comparatively realistic. In the weak, love-craving heroine he provides a character nearer to flesh and blood than most conventional heroines of romance. Yet he does not prove his chosen case, for if Jane had been consistent to the ideal of 'romantic' love, she would not have parted with the ring Edgar had given her. Even examining her by the standards of truth to life, however, she is not 'real'. She is moved like an automaton by a ruling passion that is not related to other aspects of her character or actions. In the classic

English novel, sexual love becomes the focus of such areas as work, social background, or family relationships. Rymer tried to write of 'life as it is', but did not provide the depth needed to make it meaningful. If the romantic theme is revalued, the conventions within which it is set remain the same. Edgar is the traditional moneyed seducer, and the death-bed scene between Jane and her father is a reconciliation with convention.

The conventions of domestic romance lie within the rise of the novel in the mid-eighteenth century, when it emerged in response to middle-class demands for didactic morality and for human sentiment. Samuel Richardson's *Pamela* (1742) and, to a lesser extent, *Clarissa* (1748), with their prolonged explorations of female 'virtue' under stress, mothered the whole genre. Three lesser novels must also be mentioned.

The Vicar of Wakefield (1766), by Oliver Goldsmith, was reprinted in cheap form right into the 1840s. The benevolent figure of Dr Primrose frequently appears, under various names, in domestic fiction, but in the nineteenth century the focus of interest was the seduction of his daughter Olivia by the villain Thornhill.

'Would that [Goldsmith] were living now to paint the scene so feebly depicted above [declared Leman Rede], and to awaken the sympathies of virtuous woman for her betrayed and degraded sisters.'

The novel gave strong emotional and moral overtones to the theme of chastity betrayed, and Olivia's poem can be found quoted in penny periodicals, taken out of its context in the book, where Olivia is found to have been legally married at the time of her seduction.

> When lovely woman stoops to folly,
>   And finds too late that men betray,
> What charm can soothe her melancholy,
>   What art can wash her guilt away?

Mrs Opie's *Father and Daughter* (1802) reiterated this theme, and brought it nearer to melodrama, for the weakness of the daughter turns the father insane. It was rewritten by T. P. Prest as the popular novel *The Maniac Father* (1844), with Mrs Opie's heroine, Agnes, rechristened Rosabelle. There are other changes to the basic story. As popular fiction cannot allow a sad ending, the seducer Alfred finally marries Rosabelle, as a reformed character. Also, lacking Mrs Opie's more delicate interest in character, Prest exhausts the plot by page eighty-seven. He therefore resurrects Alfred's ex-valet, Adder. This villain, aided by a group of smugglers, continues to pursue Rosabelle; the father goes mad again, and with the help of the two sub-plots, the novel continues for more than 500 pages. After this the father regains his sanity, blesses his daughter and dies. All the villains have been executed, one by one, so Rosabelle is able to look forward to a peaceful married life. *Father and Daughter*, however, was not only plagiarized but also imitated. Other fathers go insane over erring daughters (e.g. in *Vice and Its Victim* [1850]), and madness is given a place in the domestic story. Most important was the way it joined melodramatic effects to the pathos of the suffering heroine; and it is relevant to note that Mrs Opie also wrote plays.

Mrs Inchbald's *Nature and Art* (1796) also saw a revival in the 1840s, adapted by George Dibdin Pitt as a novel and a play both called *The Wreck of the Heart; or, Agnes Primrose* (1842). This name shows that the main interest was again the feelings of the betrayed heroine. The plot was also influential in portraying the two contrasting types of male character: the unfaithful William, who eventually becomes a judge, and sentences to prison the girl he has reduced to penury, and the honest, solid Henry. This contrast was to recur frequently in domestic romance.

Domestic romance is indebted not only to these novels but also to the volumes of the circulating libraries and 'number men'. In particular, these contributed the contrast between country and city life. We may take as an example a novel whose popularity continued, through cheap reprints, into the period of this study. It is Mrs Helme's *The Farmer of Inglewood Forest* (1825).

The story opens in the country, with the family, Emma, Edwin, Reuben, and William, gathered around the father, who is sitting under a tree reading the Bible to them. The scene is described with the traditions of Christianized pastoral. Emma is 'as innocent as the dove, playful as the lamb and as fair as Milton's Eve'. Into this garden of Eden comes Satan in the form of Whitmore, who enters, in the traditional manner, through a coach accident. He is nursed back to health by the farmer's family, and forms designs on Emma. To further these, he takes her brother Edwin back with him to the city and sets him up in fashionable society. Here the town life

7. *The Domestic Story*

(a) 'There was a charm about the mellow glorious voice
of Adeline, which tempted him to linger'

(b) 'Emily trimmed the lamp, and then taking the manuscripts from her bosom, read the contents aloud to Patty'

(c) 'Beauteous damsel, banish your fears'

(d) 'The tall and majestic form of a woman rushed
precipitately in between them'

depraves Edwin with a rapidity that amazes even the rake Whitmore. He marries a rich lady, returns to the country to seduce his
fiancée, Agnes (who dies bearing him a child), and after other mis-
demeanours goes out to Jamaica to estates he has gained by marriage; he murders a negro, sells out his interests, and returns to
England. Meanwhile Emma, who has been seduced by Whitmore
in the city, sinks to prostitution. She finds herself lying beside
Edwin: in the shock she repents and returns home to die of exposure after being found outside her father's door. Edwin finally
commits suicide after attempting to rape Anna, his daughter by
Agnes.

Throughout, the horrors of the story have been played out
against the contrasting background of the good life in the country
where William has been building up his fortunes as an honest
farmer. Now the evil which entered with Whitmore has spent itself. The final scenes show the grafting back of the broken limb.
Anna, the daughter of Edwin by Agnes, marries Reuben, the
youngest of the family, and the group is again gathered around the
farmer to receive his blessing. He gives his name to the book, not
because he does anything in the action, but because he is the representative of the goodness of the family and of country life. This
core of positive belief lends a certain purpose and conviction to
the book through all its appalling events.

The theme of the innocent country girl pursued by the member
of the upper classes appears in the play by Buckstone, *Luke the
Labourer* (Adelphi 1826), which has been noticed as being the first
fully Anglicized melodrama.[1] This play opens with a group of
harvesters singing:

> Our last load of corn is in now, boys.

It tells how Charles, an honest country lad, loves Clara Wakefield.
Clara, however, is pursued by the Squire, who uses Luke (a
labourer with a grudge against Farmer Wakefield), to get possession of the girl. She is saved by her brother, Philip Wakefield, who
earlier had been stolen by Luke, and brought up by gypsies.

The theme of the lower-class girl pursued by an aristocrat runs
through most of the domestic romances examined here; *Gideon
Giles, The Maniac Father*, and *Eliza Grimwood* being a few examples.

1. E. B. Watson, *Sheridan to Robertson*, 1926, p. 70.

This is not fundamentally altered when, as often occurs, the 'poor girl' turns out to be an heiress, or marries eventually the rich, handsome baronet. The heroine always spends part of her life as a member of the lower or lower-middle classes and the villain generally comes from the upper classes, if army officers can be included in this category.

Portrayal of country life and the aristocracy of this fiction requires some comment. For the theme of 'fashionable life', it is curious that this bears little relation to the 'silver fork' type of novel then at the height of its popularity, although extracts from the latter did occasionally appear in lower-class periodicals. Such writers as Mrs Gore, Susan Ferrier, and Lady Blessington delighted in showing the extravagances of fashionable life for their own sake; in the lower-class fiction, if the way aristocrats lived is mentioned at all, it is only with ridicule or condemnation. Prest gives a typical view of a society lady:

> The Honourable Euphemia Bamford was rather pretty, but excessively bold, superlatively vain, and insupportably ignorant.[1]

> Splendour only concealed vice.

> There are greater villains rolling along the city streets in their carriages than are to be found in the sinks of St Giles's or the stews of Petticoat Lane.[2]

The pictures of high society causing suffering really supplies the lack, pointed out in the *Quarterly Review*, of authors who would 'contemplate fashionable society, not only in its own limited sphere, but in its effects upon the other classes and circles on which those of that order immediately act or impinge';[3] their accounts of fashionable life, however, were themselves completely lacking in reality.

The theme of the goodness of country life also became a convention, but it had firmer roots. Mrs Helme writes of the actual pleasures of the countryside before the advent of enclosure and agricultural depression, 'a dance on the green in Summer; or, in the manor-hall in Winter'.[4] It stressed the essential goodness of

1. *Ela*, 1841, p. 164.
2. E. P. Hingston, *Helen Porter*, 1847, p. 138.
3. XLVIII, 1832, pp. 165 ff.
4. *Farmer of Inglewood Forest*, p. 324.

the English yeoman. George Dibdin Pitt describes a figure familiar in this fiction when he portrays the heroine's father as 'an honest, upright farmer, in a small way, at the end of the village. Old Primrose, though fond of his daughter, and a kind-hearted man withal, had all the native pride of an English yeoman – unflinching in principles, and the sworn enemy of vice.'

The titles of these domestic novels sometimes stress the country origin of the heroine – *Mary, the Primrose Girl* (*c.* 1846), *Phoebe; or the Miller's Maid* (1842), or *The Cottage Girl* (penny-issues, *c.* 1845). They are a direct continuation of the number book traditions of earlier days, and sometimes written by the same hands. *Emily Moreland* (1829), *The Pride of the Village* (1830) and *The Curate's Daughter* (1835), all by Hannah Maria Jones, were published in penny-issues. They did not have a continuing success, and in 1854 Mrs Jones died in abject poverty.[1]

The country life shown in these novels was highly formalized. In Mrs Kentish's *The Maid of the Village; or, the Farmer's Daughter* (penny numbers, 1847), the village maid's home is described in full.

The green shades cast a refreshing shadow over the parlour, where everything breathed the pure spirit of the youthful goddess, whose hand had entirely embellished it. It was two small square rooms, thrown into one by folding doors; towards the orchard it opened through a little gothic porch and painted glass door; the front, which looked into the flower garden by a gothic window, [was?] also of exquisite painted glass, which was now thrown open, and shaded by the green Venetian blinds; plants in china flower pots, on little beautiful stands painted by Adela's hand, shells arranged among china vases of flowers, and a little bookcase, containing a few books neatly bound, and elegantly selected, Byron, Shelley, Chateaubriand's Genie de Christianisme, Volney's Ruins, the Corinna of Madame de Stael, Holstein, and Paul and Virginia of St Pierre, were here mingled.

(Adela's reading, particularly *Paul and Virginia*, reminds us that the earlier rural novel had been influenced by the Romantic movement.)

This example is a little extreme. In contrast with the average romance come the works of three novelists who have country backgrounds, and attempt to bring authentic country life into their novels. Thomas Frost's *Emma Mayfield* (1848) and *Paul the*

1. *Gentleman's Magazine*, April 1854, p. 440.

Poacher (1848), try to portray life in the west country. Thomas Cooper, whose interesting inquisition on village life in Lincolnshire at the turn of the century, *Alderman Ralph* (1853), was a middle-class, three-volume publication, and so outside our scope, used Lincolnshire people and scenes for his historical novel, *Captain Cobler* (penny-issues, J. Watson, 1850), and their actuality shows up the weakness in the description of the Pilgrimage of Grace in the sixteenth century. The most popular tale about country life circulating among the lower classes, however, was undoubtedly *Gideon Giles* (1841) by Cooper's friend, Thomas Miller. It was serialized in *The London Journal* (1848), and did well enough for them to follow on with Miller's *Godfrey Malvern* (1842–3). It was praised by *The Athenaeum*,[1] and S. T. Hall recounts meeting a labourer who had undergone a mental awakening through reading it.[2]

The basic story is a conventional one, the pursuit of Ellen Giles by the Lord of the Manor, Sir Edward Lee, and Banes, his steward. There is another romantic plot, equally unimportant to the real qualities of the book. For *Gideon Giles* is a loving recreation of village life in 'Burton-Woodhouse' (West Burton), and the country south-west of Gainsborough. Miller provided readers of *The London Journal* edition, in the correspondence columns, with directions showing how to follow the story on foot over this area. The dialogue abounds in Lincolnshire dialect – potatoes 'done to a wabble', 'kept me wacken', and, allowing for a certain exaggeration, the characters are based on observation. The best are undoubtedly Ben Brust and his wife. Ben Brust is a bulky countryman, completely out of touch with the modern world, with no understanding of money – he prefers to work for his food and drink – at one with the warmth of the sun, the green fields, and dusty roads; living for sleep and food. The character is basically a comic one, and lacks the darker shadows required to give it full realization, but in spite of this, Ben drowses and eats his way through the book as a recognizable and delightful character. The description of how he cooked (and ate) the supper for cousin William is a convincing picture of the power of matter over mind. His complement is a thin, practical, shrewish wife who is constantly quarrelling with him, but never for long, since it takes two to

1. 701, 1841, p. 260.
2. Hall, *Biographical Sketches*, 1873, pp. 321 ff.

make a quarrel and quarrelling is outside Ben's capabilities. Other country folk are deftly sketched – the sluttish Mrs Brown with fashionable pretensions who confides she can wear the latest fashions in shoes because her little toes cross over, and the stubbornly honest Gideon Giles.

Even this summary will have hinted at the overwhelming optimism of the book. Good is shown in all the characters, even the villains, in a way that mars the plausibility of the story. Miller was in any case unhappy when dealing with sordid elements. But whereas popular fiction shows people with 'hearts of gold' usually to assure its audience that human beings – including of course the readers – are basically decent, Miller was clearly writing from an overflowing good humour and delight in the world, which he communicates to the reader. This quality is so rare – if not unique – among these popular writers, that the critic is inclined to forgive many inadequacies.

Throughout *Gideon Giles* runs an account of a tribe of gypsies encamped near the village. Gypsies are one of the most persistent elements in this fiction. They were of course much more common then, both in the country and in the towns, where they periodically descended to sell their wares, and tell fortunes, than they are today. They were also much more accepted in the country community, where vagrancy and dirt were not the stigma they are in the present welfare state. Alexander Somerville wrote of friendly relations with the gypsies, and even a romance with one of the dark-eyed girls. George Borrow's *Zincali; or, an Account of the Gipsies of Spain* (1841), which told of their history from their emergence in the Middle East in the fourteenth century, increased interest in them, and writers such as Susannah Reynolds and Thomas Frost evidently drew on this work in penny-issue novels. The mystery of their origin and their wandering life gave them a fascination similar to that of the Jews, the Wandering Jew in particular. The allure mixed with fear felt for them is well illustrated in the portrait of Dangerfield in Mrs Jones's *The Gipsy Chief* (1840), a description remarkably like that taken from life by Borrow.

[He was] a tall athletic man, whose deep olive complexion, raven locks hanging in wild profusion, and piercing black eyes, would have induced anyone to pronounce him a native of a warmer clime than he now inhabited. His features were particularly handsome, and his whole figure in spite of the meanness of his dress, was imposing; but, there was a look as he raised his eyes to reply to some observation of Mrs Hatherleigh that made her shudder, so strongly was it expressive of vindictiveness and ferocity. The lines too around his mouth were indicative of craft and cunning, and altogether his appearance was so repulsive, as for a few minutes to cause her to waver in her intention of making known to them her vicinity.

Belonging to the realms both of fiction and everyday life, 'a singular union of romance and reality', the gypsies provided a natural bridge between the Gothic and the domestic novel. Dr J. M. S. Tompkins has written that 'the three weird sisters rocked the cradle' of the earlier fiction,[1] and the three weird sisters are still present in a few early penny-issue novels, opening the scene with such chants as:

> Sister, what should all this be?
> Longs he unto thee or me?
> ... The rudder's lost,
> The vessel's lost
> Upon the raging main ...

Their function here, as in *Macbeth*, is to set the story within a frame work of fate, and introduce a sense of foreboding. Their ragged mantles were assumed by the gypsies who appear at the beginning of domestic romances with monotonous regularity. Even the story of Maria Marten is retold, with a gypsy chanting the doom in store, as H. J. Copson's *The Gipsey's Warning* (1841).

These gypsies were often integrally part of the plot, frustrating the plans of the villain, and this was almost certainly suggested to lower-class writers by the popularity on the stage of Meg Merrilies in Scott's *Guy Mannering*, a gypsy who frustrates Glossin's plan to disinherit and murder Bertram Ellangowan. Sometimes they were not gypsies at all. The 'hero' of Prest's *The Gipsy Boy* (1847) turns out to be none other than the Honourable Eugenia Cleveland, abandoned by her wicked father. However, she finally marries back into the nobility, and Sir Lawrence repents and comes to his daughter's wedding.

Frequently, gypsies have a motive of (honourable) revenge for their actions. The most famous gypsy in this fiction was the

1. *The Popular Novel in England, 1770–1800*, 1932, p. 219.

heroine of Thomas Peckett Prest's *Ela, the Outcast* (1839–41), in part a plagiarism of Hanna Maria Jones's *The Gipsy Girl* (1838). A reprint of 1841 claimed that the novel had sold 30,000, a high but not impossible figure for such a popular title. It was still in demand ten years later, and its success may have led Edward Lloyd, who had previously published mainly plagiarisms, to branch out into specially commissioned fiction for the working classes.

The opening is conventional. There is a storm, and during it a child is found abandoned. The complicated and sometimes inconsistent plot can be summarized as follows. The child is Fanny, daughter of the fearsome gypsy Ela, who dogs the footsteps of Edward Wallingford and his family crying:

> A curse shall attend the deceiver's race,
> His reward shall be misery and disgrace,
> On his house shall fall a deadly blight,
> That shall turn his days into dreary night.

Ela, originally the daughter of the aristocrat Angela Beranzio, is saved by Wallingford from a burning house. (If the heroine in one of these romances was saved from a burning house, she was doomed.) Wallingford seduces her, then abandons her to his fellow-libertine Rackett, who completes her ruin. Being a girl of spirit, Ela murders Rackett, and goes to live among the gypsies. Her daughter Fanny is found abandoned by the Wallingfords.

Ela recovers Fanny, and refuses to let the son of the gypsy chief marry her; tensions develop, and there are various attempts to murder Ela. Finally, Ela receives estates left her by her mother, and retires to Spain, where Fanny marries a Lord Helvendon. Returning to England, Ela forgives Wallingford, and when his wife dies, the two old lovers come together as friends. Ela's curse, however, must be fulfilled. The gypsies murder him in mistake for Ela.

There are many other events in the story, and a secondary plot, the romance of Maria Herbert and Edward Wallingford's son, Walter. Maria is pursued by Barnell, a 'coarse, vulgar, mean looking man, with a very large nose ... his person was thick and clumsy, his clothes of the newest cut, but [they] could not hide the excessive vulgarity, for which he was remarkable ...' He finally

8. *Ela* (1839–41)

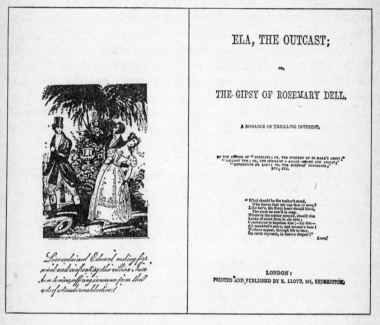

ELA, THE OUTCAST;

or,

THE GIPSY OF ROSEMARY DELL.

A ROMANCE OF THRILLING INTEREST.

BY THE AUTHOR OF "ANGELINA; OR, THE MYSTERY OF ST. MARK'S ABBEY;"
"GALLANT TOM; OR, THE PERILS OF A SAILOR ASHORE AND AFLOAT;"
"ERNESTINE DE LACY; OR, THE ROBBERS' FOUNDLING;"
ETC., ETC.

"What should be the traitor's meed,
Who leaves that fair one thus to weep?
Like her's, his flinty heart should bleed,
The tares he now'd to reap.
Where'er the traitor strayed, should rise
Looks of scorn from flashy eyes
Condemned to hopeless woe ;—his fate—
All mankind's scorn, and women's hate
Without appeal, through life to bear,
On earth reproach, in heaven despair!"

Anon.

LONDON:
PRINTED AND PUBLISHED BY E. LLOYD, 231, SHOREDITCH.

Sear exclaimed Edward rushing forward and confronting the villain Save here he odious suffering innocence from the deadly effects of treacherous blandishments!

dies, and Maria and Walter are united. The last scenes are like those at the end of *The Farmer of Inglewood Forest*, with the evil purged, and Ela sitting happily with Walter and Maria, who themselves have a family and are 'possessed of all those intrinsic qualities that ennoble mankind, and is [*sic*] the only true source of earthly joy'.

At this point it is interesting to compare popular domestic romance with *Oliver Twist*, which is indebted to it on several counts. *Oliver*, like *Ela*, opens with the introduction of a mysterious child. The tradition of the locket, although it does not come into this particular work by Prest, has been mentioned as a common device, given fashion by *Udolpho*, although of course an aboriginal device in story-telling. As Oliver is later protected by the kindly Mr Brownlow, so Fanny is looked after by the benevolent Dr Hartley.

The most important debt, however, is the love of Rose for Harry Maylie. The modern reader finds this romance unreal, and wonders why such a sub-plot should occur beside the realism of

Oliver's career. Such a secondary story, however, was the tradition with domestic novels (including *Ela*), and if Dickens's characters appear unconvincing, it is because this convention had not been successfully absorbed by the more vital writer.

For these conventions go back into the different world of the eighteenth century, and are followed by the early penny-issue novels. In them, love-making is still shown through the 'delicately turned' compliment (if the phrases are by this time somewhat stilted), and physical sex is taboo. Description is highly formal, even when the sensual is close beneath the surface. One heroine is thus described:

Her cheek [was] pure as the spotless marble . . . upon her alabaster forehead lay a profusion of golden ringlets; her nose had a fine Grecian outline, while her mouth resembled two streaks of cord moistened with the May morning dew. Her teeth were even rows of lilies . . . Her neck resembled the ivory's highly polished surface . . .[1]

Most heroines were well educated. We may compare Amanda revelling in the castle library in Mrs Roche's *Children of the Abbey* (1796), with the delight of Prest's heroine Caroline in finding a library in a castle. True, Caroline had her limitations.

[The books] consisted chiefly of the works of the best authors in most languages, but of those she only understood German, French and Italian. Fore-seeing what a fund of entertainment she might have derived from the others, she lamented the want of more learning.[2]

The accomplishments of these heroines are progressively thrust into the background, but it is presumed that even farmers' daughters have good educations, and will be on equal intellectual terms with an aristocrat, should they finally marry one.

These heroines also, more and more, lose the extreme sensibilities of those in earlier romances. Though they may occasionally faint under great stress, most of them show 'woman's high mental fortitude in moments of protracted trial',[3] which in the circumstances is as well. Only Reynolds took this to its farthest lengths. For him, to be the conventional type of heroine was to be lost.

1. *Oronza*, p. 50.
2. *Vileroy*, 1844, p. 10.
3. Prest, *Florence Graham*, 1846, p. 140.

The Days of Hogarth (1848) is a historical romance in which he interweaves the stories behind Hogarth's series *The Rake's Progress*, *Idleness and Industry*, and *The Harlot's Progress*. The 'Harlot' is revealed to be a clergyman's daughter, Kate Hemmings, pious and sensitive. She has no moral equipment for the cruelties of life, and is raped, falls to vice, and ends on the streets. On the other hand we have Ann Hayes, an impudent girl who, on hearing Colonel Charteris has designs on her, sets out to profit from it. When she meets Ruffles, similarly a self-sufficient criminal love matures between them. They are both fallen, but they have strength of personality – when Ruffles is deported, she waits faithfully seven years for his return. They finally settle down happily to married life. Ann is no exception: similar examples occur throughout Reynolds's work, such as Nisida in *Faust*, and Letitia Lade in the first volume of *The Mysteries of London*. True worth of character, he suggests, may express itself through crime, but it will nevertheless find happiness at the end.

Such belief runs exactly contrary to the general trend in the portrayal of heroines. While their sensibility decreased, their immaculate purity became more and more pronounced. This appears to be the delayed arrival of the Romantic 'pure child of nature' conception. The heroine is moved by her soul. Amy's 'gentle loving soul spoke out through her soft blue eyes, while the tenderness and purity of her heart was made known by every word she uttered'. The rose on her clear cheeks varied 'in its depth with each passing emotion of her soul'.[1] The heroine's goodness is shown above all in her capability for love. 'How little do they know of true woman who speak lightly of a woman's love.'[2]

> The love that burns in woman's breast
>   Is a pure and holy thing,
> It is bright as the joys of the blest,
>   'Tis sweet as the anthems they sing.[3]

Because of this, marriage contrary to these affections is 'moral adultery, which, in the eyes of the infinite purity, is a direct infringement of one of the holiest commandments'.[4]

As the heroine became more central to the story, so the theme

1. Hingston, *Amy*, p. 138.   2. Prest, *Florence Graham*, p. 244.
3. *Lloyd's Penny Atlas*, II, 1844, p. 192.   4. *Florence Graham*, p. 155.

of the family became less and less important to lower-class fiction. It is true that we still get tales concerning rival brothers, loving sisters, or fathers and daughters, but there is no longer the overall sense of the family's importance. The most popular theme becomes that of the unprotected heroine, alone in the world, and the model changes from *The Vicar of Wakefield* or *Nature and Art* to the anonymous favourite *Fatherless Fanny* (1819). Fanny is a foundling, and is brought up amid general contempt. Lord Ellencourt visits the establishment where she is confined, seeking a lost pet dog. He falls in love with her and eventually marries her. She is revealed to be the legitimate daughter of the Duke of Albemarle, and enters into a life of prosperity, to the confusion of her previous persecutors. The tale is of course the archetypal one of Cinderellas but the popularity of this romance may well have brought it, potentialities to the notice of novel-writers; it is the theme of many domestic romances, including *Oliver Twist*.

A sociologist may connect this shift away from interest in the family, with the actual breakup of family life in the overcrowded towns, and the preoccupation with the heroine's purity as an escape from the depravities of the social conditions. An interest in unrecognized heiresses would be natural to lower-class girls, particularly if they were doing drab and insignificant jobs; but the theme of the unknown origin may have also appealed to a sense of 'not belonging', the same feeling T. S. Eliot suggests with tangled family connections in *The Confidential Clerk*.

The most famous of penny-issue fiction heroines was probably Ada in J. M. Rymer's *Ada, the Betrayed* (1845). The story opens in a storm. The baby heroine emerges dramatically from a blazing smithy in the arms of the wild-eyed and smoke-blackened villain, Gray. He thrusts Ada into the arms of a bystander and she is brought up by the Seyton family. She has all the attributes of a true heroine. A (presumably male) reader felt moved to poetry.

> A violet, sweet and tender, emblems thee –
> Retiring, modest, yet with much within
> Of Passion breathing of mortality.
> But, ah! Mortality without its sin.[1]

But trouble is gathering. Her father had been murdered in the

1. *Lloyd's Penny Weekly Miscellany*, I, 1843, p. 742 (extract).

9. The Fortunes of Ada

(a) 'A deed of blood!'   (b) 'The child of the dead – save her!'

(c) 'To the wicked can there be a more terrible
apparition than youth, beauty, and innocence?'

smithy by the blacksmith, Andrew Britton; Gray was the witness. The murder had been instigated by her uncle, Learmont, who took over his brother's estates. Now, to gain more power over Learmont, Gray kidnaps Ada and takes her to London, where her purity shows up all the brighter against the criminal underworld. She is sought and rescued by the young Albert Seyton, who loves her. Meanwhile the conspiracy of Britton, Gray, and Learmont begins to crack – the distinct characters of the three and their interaction is one of the points of interest of the book. Gray, a cunning, weak-willed scoundrel, prey to his conscience, is the first to go. He had leagued with Britton to blackmail Learmont, but the forthright workman hates him for his superior intellect, and combines with Learmont to murder him. Gray, however, wily to the last, has left a full confession which is to be given to the police should he disappear: this is read, and Learmont arrested. Finally, the smith also is caught. With the reading of the confession, it is also discovered that Ada is an heiress, and she marries Albert Seyton with unclouded prospects. The whole story moves with a good pace, and the plot and characters are well defined for this type of novel.

Ada succeeds because of the gusto with which Rymer uses his melodramatic conventions. The anonymous *Adeline; or the Grave of the Forsaken* (1842) succeeds in a quieter vein. The plot is traditional. The heroine is rescued from a fire by the future seducer; there is the common contrast between a solid, honest character and a superficial gallant; there is a Gothic scene in a churchyard. The descriptions of the countryside are unreal, and the main interest is the emotion of a girl who dies after losing her virginity ('weak' girls could fall in this fiction but they had to die). And yet it is a story out of its class.

The story opens unpromisingly with Herbert Mandeville seeking out the grave of Adeline, and dying. There is a flash-back of four years. Mrs Mordant and her fatherless daughter, Adeline, move into the village of Bracebridge. They are retiring, and take an uncertain niche in the life of the community, but Adeline receives the attentions of Charles Leslie, a wealthy farmer, who protects them against the village gossip. Herbert Mandeville comes to live with the vicar, Endsleigh. He is an undergraduate who has been rusticated for getting a girl with child. The country-against-town contrast begins to develop, with a new turn. Herbert

meets Adeline, and genuinely thinks he is in love with her. There
are various reasons for this, which all build up a recognizable
character. He is essentially a good person, with the attractiveness
of potential goodness. 'He had many virtues, he worshipped truth
in his heart.' But he is unsure of himself. 'The great fault of his
character consisted in that easy ductility of mind which made him
the slave of anyone who would take the trouble to assume a command over him by flattery or satire.' This failing was aggravated
by an education which put great emphasis on success. 'It was a
vicious course of education which had engendered those feelings
of jealousy and personal anxiety.' He lived by proving himself,
and showing himself successful. 'Herbert was one of those who
needed the constant stimulus of difficulty to be overcome, and
something to be conquered.' This leads naturally to a moral weakness. As Endsleigh tells him, 'You love fame more than you love
virtue'.

These aspects of character are well worked out in his actions.
Adeline is a challenge, particularly as she is receiving the attentions
of a strong, good character who has everything he lacks in moral
qualities. He uses all his natural charm and the experience gained
from town life to win her. Adeline is not easily won. 'Beneath the
charming innocence of manner which so won upon all hearts,
there was likewise a strength of character, and a firmness of disposition, that [Herbert] would do well not to arouse.' When at last
she falls to him, after a painful struggle with herself, she is truly
and deeply in love. Once he is in possession, his affections, which
he felt to be genuine, suddenly dissolve. His alienation comes not
only because his love was purely possessive, and he becomes
frightened of the love he has aroused in Adeline, but also because
he is shocked to hear Adeline's brother is a criminal. He breaks off
relationships with the seduced girl.

Yet he has become a victim to his own act. He no longer loves
her, but the realization of what he has done reveals his own character to himself, and shatters his self-respect. He returns to London,
and plunges into debauchery. He loses his inheritance.

Here the story falls prey to sensationalism. Adeline, like Clarissa,
loses the will to live and, after a prolonged death-bed scene, she
dies. When she has been buried, Herbert returns in the hope of
recovering his peace of mind with the girl whose purity had once
so attracted him. He finds her grave, and dies on it from sorrow,

hunger, and the effects of dissipation. The sentimental ending does not invalidate the fact that the author has shown some grasp of the psychological springs of action. Most of the book's characters have some individuality, and the passages of action, however conventional in subject, are well done. The whole work sustains the reader's interest.

Unfortunately this is not true for most of this domestic romance. Usually the conventions stifle any spark of creativity. Nevertheless the genre became the dominant form of popular fiction after the decline of the Gothic, through the interminable tales of periodicals like *The Family Herald*, to the women's magazine romances of to-day. Almost any magazine stall will be found crowded with 'true stories' nearly as true as *Ada, the Betrayed*. It is a logical form of fiction for a 'democratic' age. Its stories tell of people one can recognize. The reader can feel at home with it, place him (or more usually her) self in the picture. At the same time the realism is illusory. The situations are romanticized, the people less complicated, the horizon always, finally, bright. So Ada is truly betrayed.

7

The Contribution of the Upper Classes: Religious, Moral, and Instructive

No picture of the reading of the lower classes would be complete without a consideration of the massive flood of printed matter poured out upon them by those anxious to improve their minds and souls. By far the greatest category of their literature was religious tracts. Tracts were a ubiquitous part of Victorian life. One tract, *The Soldier* (*c.* 1823) shows a benevolent gentleman riding his horse through the country on an autumnal evening. He 'blithely carolled' a hymn.

> A pair of saddlebags were thrown across his saddle; and every now and then he pulled from his coat-pocket a bundle of tracts and scattered two or three in the road.[1]

The analogy between this figure and the Biblical sower of the Word is too close to be unintentional, and some of the seed does fall on fertile ground. A returning soldier takes a tract from him, reads, and is converted.

The gentleman was the Victorian tract-distributor's ideal self-image. Tracts were sown broadcast, thrown out of carriage windows, distributed at political meetings, thrown inside public houses, systematically delivered at every house week after week throughout whole districts. The picture of the tract received, however, is somewhat over-optimistic. There is abundant evidence that the working classes, even when they could read tracts (and Mayhew's informant was told that barely one out of fifty coster-mongers receiving tracts could read),[2] were often resentful and contemptuous of the efforts of the upper classes to improve those they considered their inferiors. This was particularly so during the Radical agitation, when tracts were patently used to uphold the

1. *Houlston's Tracts*, no. 60, pp. 2–3.
2. H. Mayhew, *London Labour and the London Poor*, 1861, I, p. 23.

established order in the name of Christian piety. The Wesleyan–Methodist, *The Patriot*, for instance, recounts the confessions of one Thomas Maxwell, who fell in with a group of 'such miserable-looking fellows, that I am sure, if I had met them sober, I should have shunned them – who called themselves "reformers and friends of the people"'. They read Paine, Carlile, Cobbett's *Register* and *The Black Dwarf*, and met on Sunday night until past midnight, getting thoroughly drunk. Lucky indeed was Maxwell to be reconvinced of the sanctity of King and Government, and rescued from Radicalism and the Devil.

During industrial distress, the lower classes were also angered by the way in which tracts were distributed to save souls to the neglect of the more pressing needs of food, clothing, and sanitation. In Paisley the starving unemployed in 1837 were assiduously supplied with Bibles.[1] This indignation can be seen in popular fiction. In *The White Slave* (1844), the starving Millicent is given a tract, and Rymer can think of no better way of illustrating Sweeny Todd's demonic hypocrisy than having him distribute tracts to the orphans of the man he had murdered. The tract distributor made an easy target of fun for Dickens with his character Mrs Pardiggle, Thackeray with Lady Emily Sheepshanks, and Wilkie Collins with Drusilla Clack.

While their enemies scorned the efforts of the tract distributors, religious magazines and biographies are full of accounts of tracts avidly read and conversions made. A typical tract-distributor wrote from Bristol:

I do not remember one instance in which my tracts have not been respectfully and gratefully received, the people frequently expressing themselves as being interested in reading them . . .[2]

In such a case one suspects that the writer, if honest, was certainly gullible; but not all accounts were by enthusiastic distributors. The anonymous 'Working Man' who wrote *Scenes from my Life* (1858), for instance, gives the impression of being an independent and intelligent witness. The first part of the book is a lively account of his tough life in Spitalfields. When, struggling to keep his wife and family on ten shillings a week, the tract distributor re-

1. Q., Altick, p. 108.
2. *Wesleyan Tract Reporter*, N.S. XXIX, 1850, p. 116.

proved him for working on Sundays, he gave the answer one would expect. But the gradual persistence of the tract distributor brought an atmosphere of peace in which the author was able to win through to order and prosperity as a Wesleyan Methodist. He was also, we note, turned from Radicalism.

> The domestic jangle ceased, the repining spirit became more hopeful, the fierce democratic hatred of the rich was softened.

Supporting evidence also varies. Mayhew reported tracts distributed to costermongers who could not read them, or in lodging-houses where they were used to light pipes, 'at the lodging-houses they're laughed at'. On the other hand the Religious Tract Society were told of a hawker who, decades after Hannah More challenged chapbooks with Cheap Repository Tracts, still sold some £1,300 worth of tracts in three years.[1] The truth of the tract movement lies in between failure and success. It is important to realize that religious reading was the most popular form of literature well into the century. In the towns, tracts were generally treated with contempt by the workers, with variations according to the type of tract and the personality of the tract distributor. Many more nonconformist tracts found acceptance than those presented by the Anglican Church, with its associations with tithes and the aristocracy. Many were read not for their content but because they were presented where reading matter was scarce or expensive. In the country, where the remains of the feudal system softened the hatred of 'charity', and literature was much scarcer, tracts were more favourably received. A report to the Friends Tract Association from Lincolnshire, for instance, tells of tracts read by from ten to fifty persons per copy.[2] It is against this complex background that we can turn to the movement itself.

The tract movement grew up as a product of the religious and educational movements of the eighteenth century already noticed, with their reverence for education and the written word. John Wesley was one pioneer of cheap literature, establishing a publishing house in 1745 which was to grow rapidly, and to provide the poor with booklets at a penny, or, if they could not afford this,[3]

1. Henry Mayhew, *London Labour*, I, p. 23 and p. 458; see Altick, pp. 99–108; William Jones, *The Jubilee Volume*, 1850, pp. 215, 219.
2. *Friends Tract Assn Report*, 1832, p. 2.
3. John Wesley, *Letters*, 1931, IV, p. 262.

free. In 1698 the Anglican Church had started the Society for the Promotion of Christian Knowledge, although it lost its vigour in the ensuing century, and in 1750, the Society for the Diffusion of Religious Knowledge among the Poor. A new development came in 1794, when Hannah More began publishing the Cheap Repository Tracts, for these religious booklets with their woodcuts, vigorous style, homely settings, and such devices as serialization, were designed to look like, and to compete with, secular chapbooks. By offering them at a lower price, she was able to have them sold by hawkers, and their immense circulation made them a commercial success.[1] Her methods were followed by the Religious Tract Society (1799), which also used the chapbook format, and in 1812 formed the Hawkers Tract Society to supplement their other means of distribution. The Religious Tract Society became the largest source of religious tracts, and served all Christian denominations, including the Anglican Church. The other denominations, however, formed their own organizations as well; the Christian Tract Society (Unitarian, founded 1819), The Wesleyan Methodist Tract Society (founded 1822), The Friends Tract Association (founded 1828), the Baptist Tract Society (founded 1841), The Baptist Evangelical Society (founded 1845), the Catholic Institute (founded 1838). The Congregational Church appears to have held back until 1852 before starting the Congregational Tract Society. The British and Foreign Bible Society (founded 1804), The London Bible Society (founded *c.* 1804), and the Trinitarian Bible Society (founded 1831), issued cheap or free copies of the scriptures, and the Primitive Methodists issued Bibles and hymn books. There were also a number of Temperance Tract Societies, such as the British Temperance League (founded 1834). These central agencies were backed by the host of tract societies that flourished outside London. These were to be found in every major town, and in many small towns and villages. Sometimes these were denominational, sometimes united efforts: the Liverpool Tract Society, the Derby Wesleyan Tract Society, the Bristol Society for the Promotion of Christian Knowledge, and many others. These were frequently supplied from the London societies, but the major ones also produced their own tracts.

The trade in tracts, however, was not entirely for religious or philanthropic motives. From the time that Hazard and Marshall

1. M. G. Jones, *Hannah More*, Cambridge, 1952, pp. 139–41.

continued to publish Cheap Repository Tracts, against Hannah More's wishes, for their own gain, tracts had become a growing part of the bookselling business. Charles Manby Smith gives an amusing but fair picture of Paternoster Row on 'Magazine Day', when the immense trade was 'of a peculiar kind, being mostly in publications of a low price, and of a religious character'.[1]

'Come, it's my turn,' bawls one; 'am I to wait here all day? Pots of manna, six; and phials of wrath, thirteen as twelve. Look alive, will you?'[2]

The most important of a number of purely secular publishers of tracts was F. Houlston and Son of Wellington, Salop, and Paternoster Row, London. Houlston and similar publishers generally paid for tracts, the price varying between three guineas for a tract, to 'eight guineas a sheet, presumably of sixteen pages'. Here we may note that the fashion of tract reading led William and Robert Chambers to enter the field with a series *Miscellany of Useful and Entertaining Tracts* (1844–7). These did not contain religious matter but otherwise took the form of a normal tract. The success was immense: in 1846, 4,000 copies of each issue were being sold in Leeds, and this was claimed to be more than any other cheap periodical sold there at the time.[3]

The number of tracts published by this host of organizations was huge. The Religious Tract Society issued 14,339,197 in 1834; four years later this number had risen to 18,042,539, but in 1844 the number was reduced to 15,367,676 (a decline which probably mirrors a reaction from the literary ferment of the 1830s and the emergence of the new penny-issue fiction), then in 1849 issues rose again to 18,223,955.[4] Some Anglican disquiet at the success of an interdenominational society, which we see in episcopal charges,[5] helped to stimulate the S.P.C.K., under the leadership of the Bishops of London and Chichester, to make new efforts. In 1830, the Society formed the Committee for General Literature and

---

1. C. M. Smith, *The Little World of London*, 1857, p. 45.
2. ibid., p. 45.
3. *Churchman's Monthly Penny Magazine*, I, June 1846, p. 57.
4. S. G. Green, *The Story of the Religious Tract Society*, 1899, p. 57.
5. e.g. 'The Bishop of Lincoln's Charge', *Stamford Mercury*, 29 June 1825, p. 4.

Education which undertook to 'counteract the effect of infidel and other mischievous publications now circulated with more than usual activity'.[1] Besides tracts, the Committee produced its greatest success, *The Saturday Magazine*, which after ten months of its inception had a steady circulation of 80,000 a week.[2] In 1834, part of its burden was eased by the formation of a Tract Committee. In 1835, the S.P.C.K. was issuing 1,955,580 tracts,[3] in 1844, 2,795,153,[4] and in 1850, 3,446,038.[5]

Next in size came the Wesleyan Methodist Tract Society. Here again the twenty years between 1830 and 1850 show an increase in output, and we find the small, roughly written minute book changed for a large ledger with business-like entries. The success was partly due to the vigorous backing of their publisher (John Mason, Methodist Book-room Steward, 1827–74). 427,354 tracts were published by the Society in 1830–31 (the accounts running from July to July);[6] by 1840–41, this number had risen to 870,093 (1,326,049 including handbills and printed covers issued with other works).[7] After this, the number remains fairly steady, the 1849–50 number being 848,299 (1,349,463 with handbills and covers).[8] Another typical smaller society was the Friends Tract Association, which, in 1832, published 69,108 tracts;[9] in 1839 985,556,[10] and in 1851 123,648.[11]

It must be pointed out that all the national tract and Bible societies sent a certain number of these religious works abroad; indeed, they brought out tracts translated particularly for this purpose, and these are another indication of the religious and literary links between England and the continent at this time. Yet the export of tracts did not have a serious effect on the immense distribution at home; typical comparisons of tract figures for home and abroad reading are, for the Friends Tract Association, in 1830 1,896 exported out of 59,528;[12] for the S.P.C.K. in 1844 51,153 exported out of 3,268,659;[13] in 1850 31,283 out of 3,446,038.[14]

1. *S.P.C.K.*, MS. minutes, XL, 1829–34, p. 41. 2. ibid., p. 382.
3. *Report of the S.P.C.K. for 1835*, p. 41. 4. ibid., 1844, p. 11.
5. ibid., 1850, p. 5.
6. *Wesleyan M. Tract Soc., MS. minutes*, 16 July 1831, n.p.
7. ibid., July 1841, n.p. 8. ibid., July 1850, n.p.
9. *Annual Report*, 1832, p. 1. 10. ibid., 1839, p. 1.
11. ibid., 1851, p. 1. 12. ibid., 1830, p. 1.
13. S.P.C.K., *Report*, 1844, p. 79. 14. *Report*, 1850, pp. 104–6.

An indication has been given of the size of the output of tracts, but even this has not taken into account the larger number of religious magazines of a low price and attractive appearance – in effect, serial tracts – which were being circulated. *The Saturday Magazine*, already discussed, was only one of these. The latter periodical had a cheaper rival in the half-penny *The Weekly Visitor* (1834–5), which was also modelled on the 'useful knowledge' magazines: as well as this, the R.T.S. published *The Tract Magazine* (1824–6). Many other similar periodicals followed such as *The Baptist Tract Magazine* (1835–7), or *The Churchman's Monthly Penny Magazine* (1846–80). In 1858, eight years outside our period, yet dealing with a situation which had not radically changed, Brougham selected eighteen 'religious works of a wholly popular nature' from the large number in circulation, and estimated their combined circulation came to 90,000 per issue.[1]

The tracts themselves would require an extended study if they were to be considered adequately. They were aimed at many types of lower-class reader; at servants (e.g. anon., *A Sunday Evening's Present to a Female Servant* [*c.* 1830]); sailors (e.g. Rev. John Shipman, *A Sailor's Struggle for Eternal Life* [1848]); railway workers (e.g. anon., *To the Railway Excavators* [*c.* 1848]); railway travellers (e.g. – an ominous one this – anon., *The Importance of Constant Preparation for Death. A Railway Tract* [*c.* 1840]); drunkards (e.g. S. Johnson, *The Witch of Endor and the Dram Shop* [1837]); prostitutes (e.g. anon., *Mercy for the Outcasts* [*c.* 1832]); Radicals (e.g. anon., *The Patriot* [1831]); theatre-goers (e.g. Valentine Ward, *The Stage, a Dangerous and Irreconcilable Enemy to Christianity* [*c.* 1830]); dancers (e.g. anon., *Death's Visit to a Ballroom* [*c.* 1831]); and many others. There were tracts also within the churches themselves airing differences of opinion (e.g. anon., *David and Nathan* [Huddersfield, 1830]). Above all, as educational movements among the lower classes advanced, bringing the need for more reading matter and small prizes, more and more were aimed at children. Nevertheless, in spite of this diversity, certain critical judgements can be made. One point which must be noticed is the general mistrust of fiction. Hannah More had made use of fiction in her tracts, slight though the story often was. In the early nineteenth century, a little group of religious writers, notably Mrs Sherwood, Mrs Cameron, and Mrs Tonna, continued to produce fiction. A typical example

1. *Address on Popular Literature delivered . . . at Liverpool,* 1858, p. 31.

of this type of story is Mrs Sherwood's *Joan: or, Trustworthy* (*c.* 1830). This tells how Mrs Timmins, housekeeper to Lady Oak-wood, weary of petty thefts in her establishment, takes into her service Joan, a mere rustic, who has neither education, nor talents, in the hope that she will, at least, prove honest, Mrs Timmins acts as a severe guardian to the girl, who is kept from mixing with her fellow-servants for fear that she will be contaminated. The day comes when Mrs Timmins falls ill, and Joan is left with the charge of controlling the provisions for the whole household. The rest of the servants unite against her, and the story effectively portrays the fear and the shy stubborn courage of a girl suddenly faced with unimagined responsibility. This part of the work shows how, by dealing with acute moral dilemma, the narrative tract could touch on a fruitful branch of story-telling. The effect is soon marred, however, by a didactic and conventional ending. The maids try to have Joan convicted of theft by placing a stolen purse in her box, but a thread from a riband which belongs to the real culprit is found on it: Joan is vindicated and the reader is told to make the (false) conclusion that honesty is always rewarded.

These stories were generally issued by secular religious publishers such as F. Houlston and Son, rather than by the main tract societies. These shared the evangelical mistrust of fiction on the inexorable logic that fiction was not true, and what was not true was a lie, and a lie was a sin. The Religious Tract Society laid down as one of their rules:

The tract should contain pure truth, flowing from the fountain of the New Testament, uncontaminated with error, undisturbed with human systems; clear as crystal, like the fountain of life.[1]

On the precedence of *Pilgrim's Progress*, however, allegory was admitted. Weak imitations of Bunyan can be found in such tracts as *The Mysterious Traveller* (*c.* 1831), and *The Picture-Room at Benevolent Hall* (*c.* 1830).

In 1830 the Bishop of Chichester made the important decision to advise the S.P.C.K. to provide literature that was not directly religious, and beside the *Saturday Magazine* other secular matter was published. The other tract societies slowly followed. By 1850 the R.T.S. was publishing such stories as 'The Golden Napoleon'[2]

1. Green, p. 3.   2. *Tract Magazine*, I, 1850, pp. 6–15.

a highly improbable, but quite exciting, story of the Napoleonic wars, telling how Willy, a small boy, tried to go fishing, was captured by the French; but, because of his anxiety about his mother, Napoleon presented him with money and let him return.

The great majority of religious tracts published during the years 1830–50, however, were either didactic treatises or narratives of the lives and deaths of pious individuals who had actually existed. These religious biographies could be handled in various ways, according to the writer. Comparatively few appear to have been written by upper-class writers such as Thackeray's Lady Emily Sheepshanks, author of 'those sweet tracts, "The Sailor's True Binnacle" and "The Applewoman of Finchley Common"',[1] although a number were attributed to 'a Lady'.[2] Many nonconformist tracts were written by clergymen or lay Christians about people they knew. The majority, however, were written by authors with experience in writing tracts, like George Stokes, who during his twenty-nine years with the R.T.S. saw 5,325,850 copies of his tracts published, and many more copies of his contributions to tract periodicals.[3] A writer like the Reverend Legh Richmond showed how a very slight basis of a factual conversion and death could be built into an effective sermon by means of dialogue, incidental description, and a careful control of the story as it rises towards the climax of death, then opens out into joy at the prospect of salvation, which the reader is invited to make his own. *The Dairyman's Daughter* was probably the most successful tract ever published: it had sold over 2,000,000 copies in English alone during the first eighteen years of publication, and continued to be in demand until well beyond 1850. By reports, it was productive of remarkable conversions. It was translated into most continental languages, and was particularly successful among the French. Its very title invites amused condescension from the modern reader, and it is certainly emotional, written in the style of the sentimental novel. Nevertheless, it is one of the best works of its kind, told with sincerity and a skilful combination of narrative, description, reflection, and unforced appeals to the reader. It avoids the morbidity which marks most 'holy death' accounts, particularly those of the nonconformists. We may look at his description of the girl's patient suffering:

1. *Vanity Fair*, 1848, p. 75.
2. e.g. *The Man that Killed His Neighbours*, 1838.   3. Grimshawe, p. 279.

> I left the house an hour after she had ceased to speak, I pressed her hand as I was taking leave, and said, 'Christ is the resurrection and the life'. She gently returned the pressure, but could neither open her eyes, nor utter a reply.[1]

This may be compared with the appalling incitement to dwell on death and corruption inculcated by many other death-bed accounts:

> She could not but anticipate the change that would take place in her mortal part, when her happy spirit should leave its earthly tabernacle; but she had a particular desire that there should be nothing unpleasing to the sight of her survivors; and therefore she employed great pains and care upon her dying body, collected the different articles of clothing in which she desired to be buried, and made other arrangements, which are too tender for recital, in preparation for her approaching funeral . . . she had been accustomed to contemplate the state of the pious dead, under the beautiful Christian simile of sleeping in Christ.[2]

Besides morbidity, religious tracts of this time abound with sensationalism, and heavy moralizing which can have appealed only to those who were converted, and so were not their intended audience. Yet it is also true that the various tract societies were on constant guard against shortcomings; the Religious Tract Society laid down as its fifth rule that all its tracts must be *Entertaining*,[3] and committee minutes of other bodies show a constant concern that the works should be specially designed for the tastes and mental attitudes of the readers, expressed in plain language. It is easy to underestimate their success in this. Death-bed scenes appealed to the same interests that brought crowds to public executions, even if the former were on a more laudable plane, and they had a grim relevance at a time when in some towns half the population died by the age of seven. The intense earnestness of most narrative tracts gave them an edge lacking in much popular fiction, and their preoccupation with the realities of life and death opened up a spiritual dimension related to the Gothic.

> Horror struck into the soul of D—. What had become of his unhappy friend? What would become of himself? *There is* (he remembered and

1. R.T.S. Ed., 16 mo., *c.* 1830, p. 136.
2. Rev. James Jones, *The History of Susan Clarke*, 1837, p. 23.
3. Green, p. 6.

repeated the exclamations of his dying friend) *there is another world – I have a soul that can never die – there is a world of endless misery.*[1]

M. G. Lewis's Ambrosio, faced with the consequences of his evil, gave a similar cry. The Brontës were brought up with 'mad Methodist magazines' introduced into the Haworth rectory by Aunt Branwell, and in spite of Emily's denunciation of them, they probably helped in the formation of their imaginations.[2]

Care in making the tracts of interest to the lower classes was backed by an impressive thoroughness of distribution. After a successful experiment in Liverpool in 1818,[3] the various tract societies divided up all the larger towns and many of the smaller ones and villages into areas that were made the responsibility of one or two visitors. The task of these visitors was to see that every family was supplied with a tract every week or fortnight, preferably on a Sunday morning when the workers of the family would be free. To make sure that these were not thrown away on receipt, borrowers were lent tracts, and asked to return them against the loan of the next issue. Sometimes a small charge was also made.

'You hits upon the plan of giving 'em what costs nothing – a little religion, a tract – which is to be kept clean and *guved* up again'

grumbled a character in Rymer's *The White Slave* (1844), but the scheme was successful enough to make tract distribution a fashionable benevolent activity, with its own magazines, such as *The Wesleyan Tract Reporter* (1841–9), and thousands of devoted workers throughout the country. Many, even most, of the tracts were probably used for lighting pipes, wrapping groceries and certain unmentionable purposes. Nevertheless, it is hardly credible that a movement of such size and perseverance failed to have some impact on those at whom it was aimed.

Secular literature, aimed at instruction and moral improvement, has been noticed appearing alongside the *Penny* and *Saturday* magazines at the beginning of the 1830s. It was ten years, however, before the middle class as a whole turned its interest to this field. Thomas Carlyle's *Chartism* (1839), which sold out an edition of

1. *Domestic Visitor*, March 1831, p. 31.
2. Grace E. Harrison, *The Clue to the Brontës*, 1949, pp. 73–5.
3. William Jones, *The Jubilee Volume*, 1850, pp. 215–19.

1,000 immediately on publication, was one factor behind this interest; the group of men gathering around F. D. Maurice, including Charles Kingsley, calling themselves the 'Christian Socialists', were another. Their own venture into popular literature *Politics for the People* (1844), edited by Maurice and J. M. Ludlow, failed, but they influenced others. Camilla Toulmin, who was to turn her facile pen to write pleasant tales for the working classes, wrote:

I was under the spell of the age, when the majority of even thoughtful people believed that we had only to educate the people to make them good, wise and happy; when Pope's warning about a 'little' was altogether eschewed, and when to be 'the heir of all the ages, in the foremost files of time', was believed to be the earnest of never falling back from the onward course.[1]

In 1846, William Howitt, an associate of Maurice and an active worker for lower-class education, started *The People's Journal*, with help from the journalist John Saunders. It sought 'in the spirit of T. Carlyle . . . to aid in the solution of the mightiest of all problems – How Shall We Emancipate Labour'. Like Leigh Hunt before them, the editors saw the solution in culture, and they aimed 'to "vivify, elevate and spiritualize" life, in a word, to make it happy, in the highest sense of happiness, by the study and enjoyment of Art, Music, Poetry and Literature'.[2] They would have been pleased with the Parliamentary Report that mentioned their reproductions as helping to improve industrial design.[3] The magazine also included lectures by the influential Unitarian Radical, W. J. Fox, and some sketches called 'Scenes from Society', which were ably illustrated by Kenny Meadows. It contained fiction by Camilla Toulmin, Margaret Gillies, Mary Howitt, and others.

At the end of the year, William Howitt and John Saunders quarrelled. According to Mary Howitt,[4] this was over financial management, but the real quarrel was over leadership, for it involved a petty but bitter controversy as to whose idea the *Journal* had been.[5] The Howitts withdrew and, in January 1847, started

1. N. Crosland, *Landmarks in a Literary Life*, 1893, p. 160.
2. 'Preface', I, 1846, p. 1.
3. *P.P.L.*, sec. 1280.
4. M. Howitt, *Autobiography*, 1889, II, p. 39.
5. S. T. Hall, p. 314.

Howitt's Journal. Their publisher was William Lovett, who, broken in health by his imprisonments for Radical activity, had turned bookseller. In addition to the Howitts, contributors included Eliza Meteyard ('Silverpen'), Edward Youl, and, with the pseudonym, 'Mather Cotton Mills', Mrs Gaskell, making her first literary appearance. It started off well with a circulation of 25,000,[1] but neither it nor *The People's Journal* could prosper in competition with each other. In 1849 *Howitt's Journal* disappeared, and Saunders continued his magazine as *The People's and Howitt's Journal*.

The fiction of both periodicals generally had a didactic purpose. 'We like always that some principle should be illustrated if possible,' wrote Mary Howitt to William Carleton, 'this, we think, gives an aim and purpose to the writer beyond mere amusement.'[2] In Mary Howitt we see how didactic purpose helped a moderate writer to compose stories that made very good reading. 'The Beginning and End of Mrs Muggeridge's Wedding Dinner'[3] is a fair example. It tells how Mrs Muggeridge, a poor but respectable country wife, seeks to provide a particular treat for her wedding anniversary. She inquires the price of hare, a delicacy she particularly loved in childhood, from her butcher, but finds that it is too expensive. The butcher's boy comes after her, and promises to sell her one cheap. She expends her savings to buy it. The anniversary comes. The children do not like the hare very much, but otherwise the evening's celebrations go well. A few days later, she is prosecuted for buying hare illegally. The magistrates will not accept her genuine plea of ignorance of the laws. She is fined five pounds, and as she has no money, all her belongings, including the furniture, are seized. So far Mary Howitt has been following Harriet Martineau in writing a tract against the game laws, but she is not only making a social protest. Left destitute, Mrs Muggeridge is forced to do sewing for money, and Mr Muggeridge has to look for a job with more pay. The end of the story, which carries the moral, shows the couple in a far better situation than before because of their positive reaction to suffering. This is frequently a theme in Mary Howitt's stories.

Mary Howitt gives the impression that she knows the poor she is writing about. The same knowledge is shown in Mrs Gaskell's

1. J. W. Dodds, *The Age of Paradox*, 1953, p. 113.
2. J. D. O'Donoghue, *Life of William Carleton*, 1896, I, pp. 100 ff.
3. *Howitt's Journal*, 1847, p. 25.

first published story, *Life in Manchester, Libbie Marsh's Three Eras*,[1] even though this does contain stock situations of sentimental domestic stories and of the temperance tract. Libbie is an orphan with a terrifying background. Her father, drunk with gin, murdered her baby brother, drank himself to death, and left his wife dying of grief. Libbie gives her heart to a consumptive child, Frankie, who is as sweet as his name suggests. She gives him a canary as an anonymous valentine. She is contrasted against the worldliness of her friend, Ann Dixon, who married a reckless fellow full of the enjoyment of life. Libbie suffers in comparison. In the last of the three 'eras', however, where Frankie dies, Mrs Gaskell manages to bring the reader's feelings for Libbie round to respect. She manages to convey the fact that Libbie is not a prig; she is ugly, lonely, and unprotected, sincerely doing the best she can in her situation. She chooses to live with Frankie's mother, who is generally disliked as a termagant, but who is desperately lonely. Together they find happiness. 'It is better to remain a spinster, if it means one can get a purpose in life.' Mrs Gaskell clearly liked the people, uninhibited by feelings of class; she describes with pleasure the friendly jeers of the workboys returning home when they pass her. The story has passages of sympathetic description, as that of a working man's holiday in Dunham woods, or of a workman who is an expert on caged birds. There is genuine Lancashire idiom, for example, 'Sooner than not have a quarrel, she'd fight right hand against left'. With all its many faults, the story is sincere and fresh.

This story also indicates another almost invariable feature of this middle-class fiction for the lower classes: it is vigorously anti-romantic. 'Oh Ned,' says Mary Leslie in a story[2] by Mrs Vincent Novello, 'you would not praise my arms if you saw them in the morning, with my sleeves up, and my elbows red as a piony [*sic*], with scrubbing and brushing up the house; nor talk of my glossy hair if you saw it tucked up under a plain linen mob cap, which keeps me cool when baking or brewing.' To which Ned makes the correct response, 'Indeed I should, dearest Mary, and I should also remember your cheerful industry and right disposition.'

As this example suggests, many of these stories make their middle-class origins and designs to produce well-mannered ser-

1. ibid., I, 1847, pp. 310, 334, 345.
2. *The People's Journal*, I, 1847, p. 247.

vants painfully clear, although it is true to say they generally also advocate fair and genuinely helpful attitudes in the upper classes. To quote Sarah Hale on the writing of the prolific Eliza Meteyard ('Silverpen'), they try 'to improve the habits and minds of the poor, as an effective means of bettering their physical condition'.[1] Even Eliza Cook, chiefly remembered for her platitudinous morality and nostalgia in poems like 'The Old Arm-Chair', did not escape from the genuine issues of the day, as does her modern counterpart, Patience Strong.[2] In *Eliza Cook's Journal* (circulation 50,000–60,000 copies a week) she hoped to give 'her feeble aid to the gigantic struggle for intellectual improvement going on'.[3] She wrote poems about such subjects as the suffering of the poor, and the Lancashire cotton famine.

Throughout the 1840s, styles of cheap fiction for the lower classes continued to change. In January 1850 the Chartist poet Thomas Cooper tried to resurrect styles of the previous decade in *Cooper's Journal*, published by his old radical ally, James Watson. It failed after six months. A newcomer to the field, however, made a highly successful bid for the audience of educated working men Cooper had hoped to reach. John Cassell, a prosperous coffee and general grocery merchant living next to the Howitts in St John's Wood, launched into publishing with *The Tee-total Times, and Monthly Temperance Messenger* (1846–51). In 1848 he also issued a stamped weekly newspaper advocating free trade, which included fiction, and in 1850 he commenced publishing *The Working Man's Friend, and Family Instructor*. It was good value for a penny, even when its thirty-two octavo pages were reduced to twenty-four by the end of the first year. In a sprightly, optimistic tone which presaged the increased prosperity of the 1850s, it claimed that work brought 'health, comfort, and happiness' and was ennobling; nevertheless, doors always opened before enterprise. In 'The Carpenter's Boy'[4] Albert, a carpenter's apprentice, falls in love with the nobly born Lelia, who believes mechanics are 'a presuming set of blockheads'. Albert, however, works his way up, and gains not only Lelia's admission she was wrong, but also her hand. Readers probably did not ponder the fact that Lelia recanted only when Albert had left the working classes. It is also interesting

1. *Woman's Record*, New York, 1853, p. 848.
2. *Woman's Own*, 12 April 1958, p. 3.
3. *Cook's Journal*, I, 1849, p. 1.   4. I, 1850, pp. 364 et seqq.

to note that Cassell himself had started life as a carpenter's apprentice.

Other fiction, often of a good standard, was provided by Mary Howitt, Eliza Meteyard, and Miss Rathbone. Cassell evidently knew his public, for by the end of the first year circulation was 100,000 per issue.[1] In view of this success, it is interesting to note the prominence given in it to such educational features as a course in French, a 'Technical Expositor', and articles on law, gardening, and cookery. Even more remarkable was a supplement of articles by working men and women published from March 1850. Typical contributions were 'The Deism of Skilled Workmen' and 'The Mother's Mission' (by a shoemaker's wife). Contributors chose books as prizes: a list of those chosen are of the calibre of *Locke on the Human Understanding* and Bacon's *Novum Organum* in the original Latin.

Reading these essays one feels one is back where this study started, with the popularity of *The Penny Magazine* and the inauguration of the Mechanics' Institutes. But although the overall proportion of lower-class workers interested in cultural subjects was probably much smaller than in 1832, *The Penny Magazine* would rarely have published articles *by* working-class men. From the working-class side, attitudes towards education and culture were becoming more progressive.

1. S. Nowell-Smith, *The House of Cassell*, 1958, p. 23.

8

Fiction from America and France

Up to about 1834 the main foreign influence on lower-class literature had been Germany. As this declined, and as no outstanding
writers appeared in England to supply the new demand for popular fiction, the way was left open for a flood of literature from
America and France. French and American authors expressed a
democratic culture, and brought the work of vivid imaginations
to a reading public seeking novelty and sensation. The great
fashion for American literature came a few years before that for
the French, and can conveniently be considered first.

The traditional picture of the American to both upper and lower
classes was of colonial barbarity. Charles Mathews portrayed a
typical Englishman in his popular 'At Home'. This character,
touring America, was amazed to find the 'Yankees' ate with
knives and forks, and sat in chairs.

'... had heard of squatters; thought you all squatted, and chewed
tobacco, and spit in each others' faces.' 'My dear Sir, why did you think
so?' – 'Don't know, but I fancied it. What do you do with your
prisoners, eh! do you eat them? you know you do; there's a great
picture of it done by West, one of your own people; so it must be true;
besides, I saw a great many of you come out two years ago at the
English Opera'. 'Do you recollect their names, Sir?' – 'Yes; there was
Silver-top, *Blue-mountain*, *Grey-squirrel*, and I don't know what all; all
drest in fur, feathers, and tomahawks.'

The picture of rough country life was further developed by the
humour of such South-West Frontier journalists as T. B. Thorpe
(whose Arkansaw bears lard the lean earth and explode like boilers
when shot), J. S. Robb, and Robert Thomas. *Sketches and Eccentricities of Davy Crockett*, wonderful tales of frontier life ostensibly
told by their larger-than-life hero, was issued in penny numbers by

J. Limbird (1834), and appeared, in extract, as 'Davy Crockett's Exploits' in *Cleave's Penny Gazette* (14 July 1836 et seqq).

Drama also played an important part in building up the popular image of Americans. Morris Barnett's *The Yankee Pedlar* (1836) enabled the American actor George G. Hill, to introduce English audiences to 'the side-splitting possibilities of "down-east" eccentricities and dialect'.[1] The hero of W. T. Moncreiff's popular *Tarnation Strange* (1838) was the American Johnathon Goliah Bang, who is vain, boasting, rough-mannered, but with the charm of uninhibited self-confidence. He is modelled in part on Davy Crockett, whose words he quotes in a song:

> I'm half-alligator, half horse,
> Half a snapping turtle too . . .[2]

He lets fall a stream of witticisms of the type defined by the critic in *The London and Westminster Review* as 'The man who put his umbrella into bed and himself stood up in the corner, and the man who was so tall that he had to go up a ladder to shave himself, with all their brethren . . .'[3] The public found these so funny that the front page of *Cleave's Penny Police Gazette* (14 July 1836) blossomed with illustrated 'Johnathonisms', and Moncreiff provided the text of the play with two sets of jokes, so that those who came back to see it a second night would be regaled with a fresh supply.

While exaggeration continued to be the dominant type of American humour, a more subtle genre was being introduced by Washington Irving, Seba Smith, and T. C. Haliburton, with the knowing observations of Sam Slick, hero of *The Clockmaker* (1835). All these three were quoted in lower-class periodicals as well as appearing in more expensive volume form in England. I quote at random a passage from *The Clockmaker*.

Anyone, he replied, that understands horses, has a pretty considerable fair knowledge of women, for they are just alike in temper, and require the very identical same treatment. *Encourage the timid ones, be gentle and steady with the fractious, but lather the sulky ones like blazes.*

1. V. C. O. Chittick, *T. C. Haliburton*, New York, 1942, p. 363.
2. J. Dicks, n.d., p. 7; *Crockett*, 1834, p. 164.
3. XXXII, 1839, p. 140.

'[It] affects us by its quiet truth and force,' commented the critic in *Bentley's*, 'and the piquant satire with which it is flavoured. In a word, *it is the sunny side of good sense*.'[1] The lower-class anthology, *American Broad Grins* (1838), did not limit itself to either kind of humour.

Not all pictures of Americans were (in design) comic. On the one hand, intellectuals from the United States, notably Benjamin Franklin and Elihu Burritt, who made a powerful impression on the lower classes during his visit in 1846, provided a different image. In 1845 *Lloyd's Penny Atlas* quoted *The Eclectic Review*, with apparent approval, that 'The great body of the [American] people are, as regards knowledge, far in advance of the English.'[2] On the other, slavery and the aristocratic society of the deep south called up the deepest dislike.

Lucy Neale (E. Lloyd, 1847), starts with a negro dance inspired by the American performer T. D. Rice with his impersonation of 'Jim Crow', a shuffling negro hosteller (Surrey Theatre, 1838).

'Now ladies and gentlemen, hi! hi! hi! all ob you will see what all ob you will see, hi! hi! hi! Dis is de great-est ob curiosities ob de fancy ball. Get out ob de way ob de master ob ceremonies, you black fellow, will you? Now ladies for de grand cocoa dance.'

After this comic start, the writer turns to give 'a true and living picture of what slavery is in the United States of America, a country where there is more real pride, aristocratic feeling, and the oppression of class upon class, than in any spot on the inhabited globe.' He does this by transposing a domestic romance from England to the deep south of America. Lucy Neale, a negress, is pursued by Adolphus Deal, son of the plantation owner, the over-seer John Grubson, and (a knock at the missionaries), the Reverend Tobias Slankey. There is even a Gothic element – a ghostly giant of the plains called 'di Mangoni'. Attempts to have Lucy's lover Caesar Bob convicted of theft fail, for he escapes, and returns to lead a bloody and successful insurrection against the plantation owners. But Lucy has died of fever, and Bob shows himself a true son of Oroonoko by paddling his canoe to his death over a cataract.

The story tries incompetently to exploit the current interest in

1. XIV, 1843, p. 87.   2. III, 1845, p. 380.

America that produced a flood of traveller's tales, and caused the elder Weller to plan to remove Mr Pickwick from the Fleet prison in a 'pianner forty'. 'Have a passage ready taken for "Merriker" . . . Let the gov'ner stop there till Mrs Bardell's dead, or Mr Dodson and Fogg's hung . . . and then let him come back and write a book about the "Merrikins" as'll pay all his expenses and more, if he blows 'em up enough.'[1] This interest added greatly to the popularity of original American fiction in England. *The Monthly Magazine* reviewer liked Washington Irving's *Astoria* (1836), because 'The scenery is new, the state of society is altogether different from that to which we are accustomed: there is all that can stimulate curiosity and nothing that can offend the most scrupulous regard for truth and probability.'[2]

A good deal of American fiction was published in cheap periodicals. These were often published anonymously, and are only recognizable because they have American settings and assume an American reader. In 1847, however, it was claimed that the work of thirty-seven American authors had been published in *Lloyd's Miscellany*.[3] This fiction was generally of a poor quality, but there were exceptions, such as Poe's 'The Cask of Amontillado', published by *The People's Periodical* (6 February 1847). A typical selection from the good many American stories published in *The Family Herald* during 1847 would be 'The Courtship of Dombey and Daughter', by Seba Smith; J. H. Ingraham's 'The Silver Ship of Mexico'; a slight, anonymous romance 'The Lives of Grace and Isabel' about Isabel who was good and Grace who was not, and 'Settlement Fun', a bawdy account of how a shoemaker becomes the hero of a squatter village by giving his wife twins.

Many full-length American novels also were published in cheap form. The first volume (1838–9) alone of the *Novel Newspaper* contained R. M. Bird's *Peter Pilgrim* and *Nick of the Woods*, J. F. Cooper's *The Spy* and J. H. Ingraham's *The Pirate*. The most popular American novelist at this time was undoubtedly James Fenimore Cooper. His work *The Pilot* was chosen to launch *The Novel Newspaper* (1836); it appeared in the first volume of *The Novelist* (1838), besides starting the more expensive *Bentley's Stand-*

1. *Pickwick Papers*, Oxford University Press, 1948, p. 438.
2. XXII, December 1836, p. 560.
3. *Lloyd's Miscellany*, I, 1847, p. 838.

ard Novels (1831) and *Parlour Library* (1846). This novel had been popularized by the immense success of Fitzball's play which, starring T. P. Cooke, had run for over a hundred nights at the Adelphi Theatre in 1825, and had been frequently revived. The play turns the book upside down. Instead of telling the story of Americans outwitting the British, and saving two maidens from a house on the shores of Northumberland, the play is set in North America with the Pilot, Griffiths, and Barnstable transformed into British tars outwitting the Americans. It ended with the song 'Rule Britannia', much waving of the Union Jack, and was cheered to the roof by the sailors at Portsmouth. Nevertheless, the book had no such adaptation, and was very successful. It was followed by cheap serializations in 1838 of *The Spy*, *The Prairie*, *The Pioneers*, *The Red Rover*, *The Water Witch*, *Lionel Lincoln*, and *The Last of the Mohicans*. *The Borderers* was successfully dramatized under its American title *The Wept of Wish-ton-Wish* (Adelphi 1831), with Madame Celeste as the 'Wept'. Cooper became the touchstone of American writers. The publisher commended *Guy Rivers* by W. G. Simms to the public as 'an American novel equal to some of Cooper's'.[1]

In spite of the transformation of the dramatized version of *The Pilot*, the English public appears to have accepted the anti-British sentiments of many of these works, perhaps because they were taken as anti-imperialist, rather than against the British people as such. In *The Patriot's Bride* (*c.* 1846), which is set in Boston at the time of the passing of the Stamp Act, 'Barred doors were the only safeguard against the insolence of the British soldiers'. Lieutenant Cleverling gets his head covered with pitch, and a very good job too, because he had persecuted the sister of a colonist. Her brother shows magnanimity by saving the Governor of Boston's life in the rioting, and goes to England where he persuades Pitt to repeal the Stamp Act.

Some of these stories use the American War of Independence as an indistinct backcloth. *The Black Vulture* (1847) is a sea story of this era. The hero, an American privateer, and the villain, a mere pirate, desire the same girl. In a particularly remarkable passage where the villain has the heroine on his ship and is about to subject her to a fate worse than death, the privateer is able to come up unseen across the open sea, silently board the ship, and enter the

1. *Odd Fellow*, III, 1841, p. 44.

cabin to 'hurl him with superhuman force across the apartment'. The situations in these American stories are often even less probable than those in comparable English tales, and the fight scenes more lurid. In this it may be possible to foreshadow the mentality that produced Hollywood. An English story about the American privateer, *Paul Jones* (1847), by Pierce Egan, Jun., is very staid in comparison.

Second-rate American stories became available in greater numbers as the industry of popular fiction grew in the United States. American editions to be found in English collections of Victoriana particularly with the imprint of W. Colyer, New York, suggest that American editions may have been on sale in England, although I have not found any evidence of extensive importation. Instead, English publishers pirated these works. The writers who suffered most in this way, apart from Cooper, were E. Z. C. Judson, and J. H. Ingraham, the American counterparts of J. M. Rymer and T. P. Prest.

Judson had had an exciting life. He had run away to sea at the age of fourteen to join the American navy, and for his courage was soon promoted to the rank of an officer. In order to become accepted by his mess-mates, he fought and defeated eight of them in succession, the rest refusing to fight. His travels in the navy helped him in his adventure stories, for although his plots are conventional and often highly improbable, his description and narrative are above the average.

The King of the Sea (1848) is an example of the type of story he told. Mr and Mrs Edmiston flee to America to escape Lord Hawkhurst's attentions to the wife. While her husband is away as captain of an American ship, pirates in the pay of Hawkhurst seize Mrs Edmiston: she is rescued, but a son grows up among the pirates, finally becoming their chief, 'the King of the Sea'. He meets his parents when he captures a ship they are on, and finally defeats Hawkhurst. He goes to England, where he exchanges a captive ship and seventy to eighty passengers for an amnesty and the extensive estates which were his by inheritance.

Such a compromise with England would not have been accepted by J. H. Ingraham who, perhaps because of his extreme radical views, and because he was also one of the most prolific writers of his time, comes second only to Cooper in the number of lower-class editions of his works. His views about the English aristocracy are expressed by Morris Graeme, the Harvard graduate turned pirate in *The Freebooters* (*c.* 1848).

> 'I am leagued with men who get their subsistence by their wits. Men of bold spirits and ready hands. Men who, like you have been victims of a false system of society; gently reared, partially educated, taught to look towards gentility, and taught nothing else; who, having no trades when ill fortune laid her iron grip upon them, and the world scorned them, flew to crime to save life, and avenge the wrongs society had done them . . . You should have been a mechanic with your father's means. Now you must needs be a villain.'

Ingraham weighted his adventure with instruction. We get long reflections on such subjects as reverence for the female spirit,[1] or religious experience,[2] and in *The Gipsy of the Highlands* (J. Pratt, 1847) – nothing to do with Scotland – a Jewish gypsy is won round, after ten pages of intense debate, to belief in the Nicene creed. He also goes to great lengths to describe minutiae of action and appearance, a habit disliked by Poe.[3] When, in 1851, Ingraham forsook popular fiction to become a Deacon in the Episcopal Church, he no doubt gave his congregation in Nachez, Mississippi, good measure.

The high moral tone of Ingraham's fiction does not occur in all American works. A few of these stories are licentious in the extreme. One example of this is *The Unhappy Bride; or, The grave of the Forsaken* (1847). Frederick has a devoted wife, Catherine, but is making love to Julia, a loose woman who sees nothing wrong with adultery.

> 'The cattle will go where they can find the greenest pastures, the most refreshing brooks, and the coolest shade. And it would be strange if a woman were not as wise as a dumb beast.'

She tells Frederick to murder her husband. Before he can commit this crime, Frederick's father, who has heard he is living in vice, cuts him off from his inheritance. At once Julia leaves him, and turns her attentions to another victim, Charles Medford. Frederick secretly borrows a large sum of money, and appears in society in a glitter of wealth. As he expected, Julia at once returns to him, and invites him to her bedroom. He enters, draws out a

---

1. *The Cruiser*, p. 25.   2. *Morris Graeme*, p. 107.
3. *Southern Literary Messenger*, II, 1836, p. 595.

knife, and cuts her throat. He is given into the hands of justice, while Charles Medford drinks himself to death. The horrors of the story are told in an emotional way which makes them appear worse than equally unpleasant events in English stories.

Yet if some American fiction was crudely sensational, the better writers such as J. F. Cooper and R. M. Bird brought a breath of fresh air to the stuffy world of English popular fiction. This can be seen, partly via the work of the French writer, Gustave Aimard, in Percy B. St John's tales of prairie life, which began to appear in lower-class periodicals from about 1848.¹ Other fresh adventure stories include the later works of J. M. Rymer and J. F. Smith. In previous romances narrative action tended to be secondary to description and dialogue; now it became fluent, and important for its own sake.

American writers, in particular Cooper, also brought new interest into characterization. When the eighteenth-century hero of sensibility had become discredited, and the solitaries such as Caleb Williams and Melmoth the Wanderer had gone with the passing of the romantic impulse that created them, the hero in popular romance had become singularly colourless. Cooper's Pilot, as portrayed by T. P. Cooke in 1825, made a sensation with his air of brooding mystery, and readers will have enjoyed Cooper's other tragic figures, separated from their fellows by some mysterious frustration or suffering such as Birch in *The Spy*, or the 'Skimmer of the Seas' who at the end of *The Water Witch* disappears over the horizon of the sea with his bride. Other American novels have similar characters. *The King of the Sea*, for instance, opens with the appearance of a man with:

... a face which once seen could never be forgotten ... He seemed a being born to command, with full comprehension of his birthright; yet without the power to ensure its dues, for his face was marked with the furrows of care and vexation.

English styles of popular fiction were in any case changing, but it is probable that American heroes played their part in producing a more vivid and complex figure, a man of action, such as Patch in *Stanfield Hall*, or J. M. Rymer's later heroes.

1. e.g. 'The Raven of the Reynards', *Lloyd's Weekly Volume*, n.s. I, 1847, pp. 112–17.

American fiction continued to be popular, but from about 1844 the main outside influence on English lower-class fiction was from France. Here again, political and cultural ties played an important part. Contrary to the generally held opinion, the English public did have a considerable interest in French affairs at this time that the Napoleonic wars had done surprisingly little to affect. As early as 1816, some 15,000 Englishmen were visiting France and, during the depression that followed the war, workmen like Charles Manby Smith crossed to France to find employment. They no doubt returned with an interest in French ways, and it is significant that a group of 'coffee, public, and eating houses' in a lower-class area in 1838 were found to contain almost as many French newspapers as they did those of the English provinces.[1] English radicals kept in touch with French working-class movements and, during the 1848 revolution, sent them messages of support. In popular fiction, there are French villains as there are English villains, but characters are never viewed unfavourably for being French.

In 1836, the French newspaper *Le Siècle* started a feature that was to have an important effect on the development of English popular fiction, *le roman feuilleton*, or novel specifically written to be serialized in a newspaper. The feature was taken up by other French papers, and recruited such writers as Eugène Sue, Dumas *père*, Paul Feval, Frédéric Soulié, Honoré de Balzac, Eugène Scribe, Jules Janin, and George Sand. This stream of fiction appearing across the channel, specifically written for issue in instalments – that is, with plenty of sensation, and a situation left in suspense at the end of each part – was the answer to many lower-class publishers pressed to provide material for the rapidly growing volume of cheap publications. Many of these may have echoed Crummles's advice to Nicholas Nickleby about playwriting; 'Invention! What the devil has that go to do with it! . . . Just turn that [French work] into English, and put your name on the title page.' French fiction formed the backbone of *The London Journal, The London Pioneer*, and *The Family Herald* between 1845 and 1849, and appeared liberally elsewhere: not a single issue of *The London Journal* between these years was without some French literature in translation.

Often the English serial ran parallel with the French *feuilleton*. Thus, while *Les Sept Péchés Capitaux* by Eugène Sue was running in *Le Constitutionnel* (9 November 1847–14 May 1848), *The Seven*

1. *S.S.L.*, I, 1838, p. 486.

Deadly Sins was running in *The London Journal* (27 November 1847–
12 May 1849), *The Family Herald* (11 December 1847–5 May 1849),
and, from 'Anger' to 'Voluptuousness' only, in *The London
Pioneer* (23 September 1848–9 December 1848). Differences in
timing were partly due to the French issues being daily, the English weekly. When the original was discontinued, the translator was
in an embarrassing position. Thus a note appears in the index to
The Family Herald (1848), with regards to 'Gregorio Matiphous' –
'This tale is translated from the French, and the sequel has not yet
been published.'

Not all the translated French fiction appeared in periodicals.
Whole series of novels appeared devoted exclusively to French
fiction; *The Mirror of French Romance* (*c.* 1846–8), *The French Novelist*
(*c.* 1840–43), *Roscoe's Library Editions* (*c.* 1846–8), and *The Library
of French Romance*, edited by J. C. James (*c.* 1846–7). Other novels
appeared separately. Many of these have not survived. Some can
be traced through advertisements, such as 1842 penny-issue editions of George Sand's *Georgette* and *Indiana*;[1] others, like earlier
translations of Balzac's works referred to by W. Hazlitt in the
preface to his translation of *La Marana* (1842), appear not to have
left even these signs of existence.

Not all this French fiction, on the other hand, came from *feuille-
tons*. In 1836, before the *feuilleton* industry got under way, a list[2]
of the French writers most popular in England gave pride of place
to the 'volume' novelist Paul de Kock. Although Thackeray
commented, 'The English certainly gave Mons. Paul a hearty
welcome,'[3] it appears he was most read, at least in English editions,
by the working classes. His novels were serialized in *The Romancist
and Novelist's Library*, in *The Novelist*, and (eight of them), in *The
French Novelist* of William Dugdale, but very few upper-class
editions of his works appear. No doubt this was because he was
considered too coarse; 'a gross and indecent caricaturist',[4] was a
typical comment. Indeed, he is coarse by any standards. The short
tale *Jean*, for instance, tells how a young husband runs crying for
'*La garde*' (the midwife). He is misunderstood, however, and the
girl in labour finds herself surrounded by soldiers. Even lower-
class publishers expurgated his works.

It was probably not so much his sexual licence that offended

1. *Bell's Penny Dispatch*, I, 3 April 1842, p. 4.   2. *Q.R.*, LVI, 1836, p. 65.
3. *Fraser's Magazine*, XXVII, 1843, p. 349.   4. ibid., p. 194.

nineteenth-century readers, for they accepted equally titillating situations from other writers with much less protest, but his failure to dress up his romantic elements with the trappings of sentiment and feigned protest. He offers an irreverent mockery of all life in the tradition of Rabelais, if on an inferior level. *The Three Students of Paris* is a comedy of poverty, the adventures of three students in search of clothes, food, and money and the way they lose them. Money is a theme considered indecent to popular-fiction writers, unless as a cause of dire tragedy when lacking, and immeasurable bliss when vaguely and vastly present. It is this earthiness that makes de Kock enjoyable today. He has remarkable inventiveness in character and situation, particularly as he claimed to have written 400 books. His exuberance never flags, even if often on the level of Bouchenot, in *The Three Students*, appearing drenched and naked before his inamorata, claiming a right to her attentions because he says he has swum the Hellespont.

His later writing, however, shows the influence of the new romantic fiction of Victor Hugo and Dumas *père*. *The Barber of Paris* (1840), for instance, ends with the Hugoesque situation of a noble ascending a tower to tell the girl he has been persecuting that he has discovered he is her father. Before he can break the news, the girl throws herself off the tower to escape him, and is drawn dead from the lake by both her father and her lover. In spite of offering such excitements, however, de Kock could not hold his own against his new rivals. Hugo's *Hans of Iceland*, whose hideous dwarf exploits the two Romantic themes of folklore and a man pitted against society, was serialized in *The Mirror of French Romance* (*c.* 1843), which continued with his novel *The Noble Rival* (*c.* 1844). Dumas was even more popular. *The Mirror* series published no less than eight of his novels. Some other English versions, in cheap form, of these writers' novels will be found in the additional notes to this chapter.

Great as the popularity of Dumas and Hugo was, it was eclipsed in the 1840s by that of Eugène Sue, whom the critic of *Reynolds's Miscellany* bravely declared to be 'far more talented than A. Dumas'.[1] Sue was the son of a naval physician, and himself began work as a naval doctor. Under the influence of James Fenimore Cooper he turned his hand to naval romances which were only translated into English later, when his reputation had been

1. I, 1848, p. 48.

established. These earlier tales only interweave naval episodes into stories that have little to do with the sea, and they are also marred by a repulsive sadism. *Brulart* (J. Clements, 1846), for instance, abounds with such atrocities as a sailor being flogged and cast adrift lashed to two dead negresses.

Later, sadism became exchanged for extravagance and fantasy. A readable short romance by him, *The Female Bluebeard* (W. Strange, 1845), tells how Polyphemus de Castillac seeks out on a remote island, for her wealth, a woman who reputedly has killed her three previous husbands, and is now living with a hunter, a cannibal, and a pirate. The three husbands turn out to be disguises of the Duke of Monmouth, the Bluebeard is his Duchess, and the pair are hiding from the Flemish, who wish to execute them for treason, while the French want them to lead an insurrection on England. Polyphemus risks his life to save them from their enemies, before setting out for new adventures.

This spirited nonsense shows the imaginative extravagance that made it immediately appealing even to middle-class readers. One reviewer declared:

'Read we must, and in spite of ourselves; and the critic, (for truth must out, that critics are mortal), though compelled for conscience-sake to abuse this book, is obliged honestly to confess that he read every word of it, and with the greatest interest too.'[1]

For all its absurdities, this fantasy was part of the French Romantic movement, and could put on pretensions to poetic truth. These pretensions lay behind Sue's long and curious work, *The Wandering Jew*,[2] for which the most elaborate allegorical interpretations were offered.[3] This novel could almost have been called *The Wandering Sue*, for Sue himself declared he did not know where he was going. The theme is the efforts of the Jesuits to keep an inheritance worth eight million francs from the six remaining members of the Renneport family. They are to receive the money on 13 February 1832, so the Jesuits, through their international organization, plan ruthlessly to prevent any of them being there. The six characters are assorted and bizarre, from two small children in the charge of Dagobert, an old soldier, to an Indian Prince

1. *Foreign Quarterly Review*, XXXI, 1843, p. 233.
2. *Le Juif Errant, Constitutionnel*, 25 June 1844–12 July 1845.
3. V, *Family Herald*, II, 1844, p. 574.

and a fine society lady. The ways the priests act are equally curious. A strange 'prophet', Morok, with a menagerie of wild beasts, is set on Dagobert and the children. The society lady is betrayed into a madhouse. A mob is incited to burn down the house and factory of another Renneport. Through all this stalks the mysterious figure of the Wandering Jew, unable to rest, and working out his salvation by combating the Jesuit anti-Christ. At the apparent climax, when no one appears for the money, a Wandering Jewess enters, declaring the money will be given out at a later date.

The Jesuits appear to triumph. When they finally come to get the money, the room is crowded with the coffins of the six Renneports. But as they reach out for the inheritance, the Wandering Jew throws the notes in the fire: the head of the Jesuits grasps a branch of hyssop, but it has been poisoned by one of his own agents, so he dies.

This work was immensely popular in England. During 1844 and 1845 no fewer than nine English publishers were issuing it in some form or other.[1] One was a plagiarism by Edward Lloyd, a weak affair, as might be expected, concentrating on the theme of Dagobert and the two girls. It left Sue altogether to conclude the book with the father of the children returning to Paris, and leading a successful revolution against the Republic. E. Appleyard also brought out *The Parody of the Wandering Jew* (1845) with 300 'humorous' engravings, and *A Key to M. Sue's Romance of the Wandering Jew* (1845).

The popularity of *The Wandering Jew* was rivalled by that of *The Mysteries of Paris*.[2] Curiously, this novel appears to have been prompted by Pierce Egan's *Life in London*, although two works less similar in spirit would be hard to find. Superficially, Sue was part of the movement of socialist thinking in France which included Lammenais, Fourier, Proudhon, and Louis Blanc. He declared:

Notre unique espoir est d'appeler l'attention des penseurs et des gens de bien sur de grandes misères sociales, dont on peut déplorer, mais non contester la réalité.[3]

1. V, Appendix III (b).
2. *Les Mystères de Paris, Le Journal des Débats*, 19 June 1842–15 October 1843.
3. *Journal des Débats*, 8 February 1843.

His main character in *Les Mystères* was Rodolphe, Grand Duke of Gerolstein. He is a radical, intent on doing good, who has already established a model farm outside Paris and now, protected by Murphy, a phlegmatic 'Englishman', possibly a metamorphosis of Egan's Corinthian Tom, he extends his benevolent work to the slums of Paris. With his fists he defeats the toughest and most feared thugs, and they become reformed and his faithful servants. But there are other elements to the story. Rodolphe had been married to a scheming English girl, Sarah Seyton. When he discovers that she married him only for his possessions he quickly divorces her, but she and her brother pursue him into the Paris underworld, and Rodolphe has to adopt desperate measures to evade them. In the slums the Duke also rescues La Goualeuse, a gamine who turns out to be his own daughter. She reforms, and becomes loved by her cousin Prince Henry. She has, however, turned from a prostitute into a girl too pure to allow her lover to touch a body once defiled, and she goes to a nunnery to die of a broken heart. Many other strange and wonderful things happen which need not be mentioned here.

In spite of the sordid setting of the book, some better-class English critics were approving. One of them wrote:

> It is a great satisfaction that a man like Eugène Sue has arisen to vindicate the literature of his country from the reproach which the Paul de Kock school has thrown upon it . . . The object of Paul de Kock is, at best, to prove that society is nothing more than a set of men and women employed in seeking how best to amuse themselves and gratify their vicious inclinations. Sue looks on man in a higher light – a creature of mingled instincts; capable of being raised to the highest point of virtue, or degraded to the lowest abyss of crime, and this by the operations of the laws to which he is exposed.[1]

On its own level, this is true. In these his later works Sue has a certain moral purpose, and is more concerned with telling an imaginative story than with sensuality. Even the prostitute La Goualeuse is as likely to tempt young girls to vice as is Nancy in *Oliver Twist*.

The Mysteries of Paris evoked a flood of 'Mysteries' in France and elsewhere. In London E. Appleyard published a translation of Vidocq's *Les Vrais Mystères de Paris*, which were indebted to Sue's

1. *Brighton Herald*, 11 January 1845, p. 4.

work, as *Life in Paris; or, the Adventures of a Marquis* (1847). From America came *The Mysteries and Miseries of New York* (1848) by E. Z. C. Judson, from Germany, *The Mysteries of Berlin* (1845), translated by C. B. Burkhardt from an anonymous work. Reynolds, Miller, and E. L. Blanchard were the authors of *The Mysteries of London* (1846–50), which will be discussed later. J. S. Pratt, of Stokesley, published a second *Mysteries of London* (1847), by Paul Féval.

Féval's work had been commissioned by Antenor Joly of *Le Courier Français* to counter the attraction of Sue's work in *Le Journal des Débats*, and, as Dickens noted,[1] it made a huge sensation. It had been begun before Féval had been out of France, and the reader of this highly imaginative work will find it incredible that Féval, coming to London, expressed satisfaction that the place was exactly as he described it. The novel is immensely long, but the underlying story is that the Marquis de Rio Santo, once a Scottish laird, rules over the upper and lower worlds of London. During the book he tries to murder his brother, who is also in London, and to get his nephew and niece into his power. Like Sue's *The Mysteries of London*, it used a central aristocratic figure as a focus for all the activities and social levels of the city, which is shown as a fascinating microcosm. It exploited the filth of the slums to create a setting with a macabre fascination of its own, and linked to this the interest of up-to-date criminal fiction. It was strong stuff:

Upon this straw was to be seen, lying down, a hideous population – dirty, squalid and miserable, of all ages and of both sexes. Among them were young women, whose features, correctly drawn by the hand of nature, had assumed, under the influence of vice in some degree hereditary, a most revolting expression; there were the small girls who, like poor Loo, were singing half naked, reclining on their filthy straw, near some pitcher containing doubtless some inebriating liquor; there were old women, of whom no known terms are sufficient to depict the disgusting hideousness.

The French writers did not deal only of vice in the cities. Féval's *La Quittance de Minuit*,[2] published by George Pierce as *The Midnight Reckoning*, for example, ostensibly deals with the Molly Maguire in Ireland, although the Irish scenery almost certainly

1. *Letters of Charles Dickens*, Nonesuch Press, 1938, I, p. 810.
2. *Le Journal des Débats*, 23 January–17 May 1846.

comes from Sir Walter Scott's novels of the Scottish lowlands. Morris MacDiarmid is one of the patriot band of the Midnight Reckoners, but also a pacifist. When a Lord Monteith seizes his fiancée, Jessie O'Brien, Morris captures him and contents himself with making him marry Jessie. Monteith sets about starving his new bride to death, but she is finally rescued and her persecutor commits suicide. The Midnight Reckoners have been destroyed and Morris, who has survived, marries Jessie, and they emigrate to America. If the scenery or the characters are not particularly Irish, the story sustains the interest, and gives an imaginative picture of the underground resistance movement among the peasants.

Such a novel, however, was an exception to the more usual type, which dealt with vice in high society and among criminals, such as Paul Féval's *The Loves of Paris* (1846), or Soulié's *The She-tiger of Paris* (1850).

What a strange opinion the world will have of the French society of today! [declared Thackeray] Did all married people, we imagine they will ask, break a certain commandment? They all do in the novels. Was French society composed of murderers, of forgers, of children without parents, of men subsequently running daily risks of marrying grand-mothers by mistake? of disguised princes, who lived in the friendship of amiable cut-throats and spotless prostitutes; who gave up the sceptre for the savante, and the stars and pigtails of the court for the chains and wooden shoes of the galleys? All these characters are quite common in French novels.[1]

Other critics were much more severe. French novels were seen to 'demoralize those weak minds who have little depths of experience',[2] and even to cause 'half the existing infanticides'.[3] The actual evil effect of these was probably small. Recent studies of the effects of television on children suggest that elements such as violence have little effect when in a patently unreal situation; cowboy or gangster films, for instance. They only begin to influence the viewer when set in a situation like his own. Even the more sordid of these stories were always kept 'distanced' by touches of fantasy – for example, a scene of night-club debauchery in *The*

1. *Fraser's Magazine*, XXVIII, 1843, p. 349.
2. Anon., *Jerry Abershaw*, n.d., p. 135.
3. Cyrus Redding, *Yesterday and Today*, 1863, III, pp. 168 ff.

Loves of Paris has the startling entry of a group dressed as an owl, a bear, a turkey-cock, and a melon. The result of this extravagance has been well expressed by the critic in the *Daily News*:

> The French novelists seem to set about such pictures [of vice] in a kind of jocular, half-credulous vein, which they communicate to their readers, and which inspires a feeling of half-reality, very consoling in horrors, and leaving full enjoyment of the comic in the gayer scenes. No Englishman could at all attempt that light *charlatanerie* of the French, and for us to rival it by taking such stories more *au serieux* is equally hopeless.[1]

The last caution is particularly true. Some English writers, in particular G. W. M. Reynolds and Thomas Frost, tried to model their styles on the French. Their 'lighter' touches fell flat, and their salacious descriptions of sadism and vice may well have had a disturbing effect on minds already open to the temptations of city and factory life.

The influence of French fiction on the English went much wider than this. The appearance of periodicals such as *Figaro in London* and *Punch, or the London Charivari* points to the close relations between English and French journalism, and the evolution of the *feuilleton*, besides leading to the serialized novels appearing in *The Sunday Times*, or to the 'Feuilleton of French Literature' incorporated in *The Mirror* (1842), affected the whole evolution of cheap fiction. When the English writers came to produce periodical literature, they had the model of the French stories, 'like Peter Pindar's razor, really not made to shave, but to sell; not written to present life as it really is, but to present it as a series of startling incidents and surprising contrasts'.[2] A critic in *The Morning Chronicle* remarked that penny-issue novels formed 'the English reflection, exaggerated in all its most objectionable features, of the French feuilleton'.[3]

The influence extended to the style. The writing of such fiction as *The Mysteries of London* was condemned as being 'a vile imitation of Sue; every page being cut up into a number of disjointed paragraphs, like so many aphorisms, instead of presenting a continuous flow of thought'.[4]

1. 'Lucretia' (review), 12 December 1846, p. 5.
2. *Brit. Quart. Rev.* III, 1846, p. 507.
3. 'Labour and the Poor', 5 November 1845, p. 5.
4. *Literary Annual Register*, 1845, p. 8.

The effect of spasmodic speech to heighten effect had long been used in popular fiction and drama:

'You weep, my father; but what do I say? I have no father, – no brother, – I am alone, cursed even in existence.'[1]

What Sue, Reynolds, and those who followed them, did, however, was to split up all the prose, making it rough and febrile. We may compare typical passages from *Les Mystères de Paris* and *The Mysteries of London*.

Au risque de se blesser en tirant contre la poste à brûle-bourre, il espérait peut-être l'ébranler . . . il chercha cette arme, il ne la trouva pas, elle avait glissé de sa poche lors de sa lutte avec le Maître d'École . . . sans ses craintes pour Murph, Rodolphe eût attendu la mort avec sérénité . . . s'il avait commis des actes reprochables . . . il avait fait du bien, il aurait voulu en faire d'avantage. Dieu le savait!

Even while he reflected upon other things – amidst the perils which enveloped his career, and the reminiscences of the dread deeds of which he had been guilty, – amongst the reasons which he had assembled together to convince himself that the hideous countenances at the gate did not exist in reality, – there was one idea – unmixed – definite – standing boldly out from the rest in his imagination, – *that he might be left to die of starvation*!

This disjointed style shows, in Reynolds, the beginning of the evolution towards cutting the story into small separate paragraphs.

> A week contains a hundred and sixty-eight hours.
> And he worked a hundred and nineteen hours each week!
> And earned eight shillings!!
> A decimal more than three farthings an hour!!![2]

Later, this style was to become extreme, and whole pages were taken up with independent phrases, separated by double spacing.

By this time, however, the great popularity of French literature among the working classes had passed, and an attempt to revive it in the 1850s by republishing works by Dumas, Hugo, and Sue completely failed.[3] In the next decades the most popular French

1. Mrs Helme, *The Farmer of Inglewood Forest*, 1825, p. 269.
2. *Mysteries of London*, 1845, I, p. 170.
3. W. Wilkie Collins, *My Miscellanies*, 1863, I, pp. 187–8.

writers, George Sand, Émile Zola, and Balzac, were read by a better class of reader. In spite of the popularity of Hugo and Dumas, the pre-eminence of Eugène Sue suggests that lower-class appreciation of French literature had been largely uncritical, enjoying mainly the sensational content and its flights of imagination. Nevertheless, these works had provided entertainment at a time when the native English popular authors were particularly lacking in originality. Many readers, as later they turned to other books, must have looked back with pleasure to the penny-issue translations of Sue and Féval.

9

The Impact of the Towns

In *The Farmer of Inglewood Forest*, Reuben, a country boy, goes to London and looks into a lower-class quarter. He sees it 'full of the most ill-looking, gloomy beings I ever saw, many of whom were silent, and apparently lost in thought, their eyes fixed on the ground, their foreheads knit, and their eye-brows scowling; others were talking fast and loud, and, seemingly, by the little my ear could catch, enumerating'. Trade was a meaningless muddle – 'enumerating'. The city had become Hell.

This vision must have been that of many country people looking at the dark towns of Manchester and Birmingham, or the slums of Whitechapel. Yet through the years of the early nineteenth century the workers drawn into the cities were being superseded by generations that had known nothing but urban life. Resilient human nature was forming new ways of life and interests amid the sprawling jungles of back-to-backs and crowded tenements. For these people town life had its own fascination, which they betrayed even in their protests against its squalor. Their literature became informed by new outlooks and the new idiom of urban drama, song, newspapers, and criminal slang.

Towns had no monopoly of the drama. Theatrical companies toured the country circuits, and villagers had 'barnstormers' and amateur theatricals. But in the towns it had a more intensified appeal. Theatrical companies were resident longer, the 'star' system was built up, and inter-theatre rivalries stimulated interest. With mass audiences, the theatres had a communal appeal fostered by local theatrical magazines; in towns such as Birmingham these played a leading part in the development of local journalism. These were supplemented by London magazines such as *The Theatrical Times* (1846–7), and by drama columns in national newspapers such as *The Age*.

It is not surprising, therefore, that drama had an important influence on popular fiction. Long series of stories were based on plays, such as Duncombe's *Dramatic Tales* (c. 1836–44), or Lloyd's

Tales of the Drama (*c*. 1836–7) drawing on the publicity of the stage versions just as novels today advertise themselves as 'the book of the film'. Today, if films have no original novel, one is written afterwards – I have even seen a paperback 'book of the film' called *Look Back in Anger*. Similarly, early Victorian stage successes such as Isaac Pocock's *The Miller and His Men*, or J. B. Buckstone's *The Green Bushes*, became penny-issue fiction (*c*. 1848 and 1851 respectively). Movement was in both directions. Successful penny-issue novels were thought worthy of dramatization – *Ela, the Outcast*, for instance, was presented on the boards of the Royal Pavilion Theatre by Mrs Denvil (*c*. 1839) – and the relationship could at times become complicated. 'Emily Fitzormond' was presented to readers of *Lloyd's Companion to the Penny Sunday Times* as 'Founded on the Popular Drama of that name, now Performing at the Royal Pavilion Theatre ... This eminently Successful Drama, is founded on the celebrated work now publishing in penny numbers at the Office of this Journal.'[1]

Most writers moved easily between the two fields. We know T. P. Prest, James Cooke, Thomas Archer, E. P. Hingston, and J. F. Smith were both novelists and dramatists, but there were almost certainly others, concealed behind anonymity. On one hand, this shows a lack of distinct artistic traditions. At this period hack writers were turning their hands to whatever employment they could get. James Cooke's description of the dramatist would fit a popular novelist almost equally as well.

Like a provident husbandman our friend has provided himself with a goodly stock in trade, having, for the last six weeks, been hard at work both night and day, the result of which has been the putting together of about a dozen dramas. One or two have their foundation in a nautical novel, another in a fashionable tale that has appeared either in the 'Keepsake' or other annual, two are taken from the work of 'Boz', while the suggestions for the remainder have been derived from the 'Newgate Calendar' or 'Record of Horrors'.[2]

On the other hand, both drama and fiction have the same approach to style, plot, moral outlook, and character portrayal – that of melodrama. Melodrama has traditionally been traced back to Rousseau's *Pygmalion* (1775), where the effect of Pygmalion's

1. I, 26 September 1841, p. 1.
2. 'Theatrical Etchings', *Odd Fellow*, I, 1839, p. 2.

dramatic monologue to the statue of Galatea is heightened by violin music. It developed into an intensely emotional and stylized form, employing the full resources of background music, and tending towards a climax where speech was dumb before the rising crescendo from the orchestra pit. These dramas, with their conventions of heavy villains, wilting heroines, dumb men and maidens and performing animals, came to England mainly with the plays of René-Charles Guilbert de Pixerécourt, writer for Le Théâtre de l'Ambigu Comique in Paris, whose works were translated and acted across the Channel as soon as they came out, often without acknowledgement. Their popularity in England was enhanced by the fact that they did not count as 'legitimate drama', so could be produced outside of the two theatres which alone were licensed to present plays, but even the 'legitimate' theatres gave them production.

The conventions passed directly into popular fiction. We find dumb boys in *The White Slave* and *Amy; or, Love and Madness*, and as a dog defeats the villain in Pixerécourt's famous *Hound of Montargis*, a hound points suspicion at Sweeney Todd. Stage pyrotechnics appear with little disguise in the red and yellow flames bursting from the Gray Tower in *The Black Monk*, and a banger exploding in *Varney the Vampyre*. More important, melodrama provided fiction with an approach to the story in which the aim is emotion, emotion for its own sake rather than as an effect incidental to human situations. Characters become reduced to easily recognizable stock figures, very good or very bad, and the plot only serves to lead up to the 'strong' scene where, in stylized ritual, the hero confronts the villain, or the villain confronts the heroine. (This ritual ending is of course also endemic to popular drama, from that of the Elizabethans to cowboy films and Perry Mason today.)

These styles of plot, climax, and formalized speech and character, all appear in penny-issue novels. For instance, taken apart, neither the play nor the novel of *The Miser of Shoreditch* (1854) would be distinguishable from a host of dramas and romances written over the previous decade. Yet the differences between the versions are minimal. In the play Jasper Scrupe, a miser, murders his brother-in-law William Wilmot for his money. Evelyn and Oliver, good and bad nephews of Jasper, respectively, both love Constance, but Evelyn is loved by the gypsy Mabel. Oliver tries to

10. The Theatre and the Novel

(a) Madame Celeste as the Dumb Arab Boy

(b) 'Shock not mine ears with thine odious vows, in
every one of which is pollution'

rob and murder Jasper, but the uncle is rescued from the blazing house by one Samson Brayling, who gets Jasper to confess he has murdered Wilmot. He also exposes Oliver for setting fire to Jasper's house: Oliver fires at Evelyn, but kills poor Mabel, who reveals herself his brother. He expires in a fit of remorse, and Evelyn marries Constance.

A summary of the novel would be precisely the same, except that a scene in a Gothic house, and incidents with the accomplices of Oliver and Jasper, pad out the story. At the end, Jasper escapes for further adventures.

The dialogue needed even less change. We may compare the handling of a scene by the two versions. First, the play.[1]

JASPER. All's safe: No one observes me; my wealth is all secure as when I last beheld it. Now, go ye there, and rest with thy glittering companions, [*taking two bags out of pouch and counting them*]. One – two – three – four! Ha, ha, ha! Oh, how my wealth increases! How little doth the eye of suspicion penetrate the golden treasury this ancient tree conceals. But I must be quick; [*Music – deposits the money in the hollow of a tree – Oliver watching him – Jasper approaches, L., raises his lantern, the light falls upon Oliver, and discovers him – chord.*]

JASPER [*wildly*]. Ah! I am betrayed! Wretch! – Villain! – prying sycophant! Thou shalt not have my treasure. [*imploringly*] Good sir, do not – oh do not rob the old man of his gold! [*wildly*] but thou shalt not rob me of my money! My arm is strong enough to resist thee – miscreant! Robber! [*grasping Oliver by the collar – hurried music*].

OLIVER [*fiercely*]. Rash old idiot! – let go thy hold! I am a desperate man! Yield up thy money!

Now the novel.[2]

'All's safe', he muttered to himself, 'no one observes me – now to my secret hoard. Oh, how little doth the eye of suspicion penetrate the golden treasure this ancient tree conceals. But I must be quick.'

He parted the brushwood that cloaked the opening in the trunk, and then taking from under his cloak a little dark lantern which he had brought with him, he put his head to the hollow, and groped and looked anxiously about.

'My wealth is all secure as when I last beheld it,' he said, with a chuckle of satisfaction, 'now go ye there, and rest with thy golden companions'.

1. Lacey's ed., I, scene V, p. 17.   2. R. Beard, 1855, p. 19.

As he uttered these words he took the same bags of gold he had brought with him from his pockets, and gazed on them eagerly.

'One – two – three – four!' he ejaculated; 'all is safe! Ha! Ha! Ha! – oh, how my wealth increases. But now to conceal it!'

He was about to deposit the bags of money in the trunk of the tree, when Oliver Dalton accidentally coughed; the old man started round and discovering him, in a frantic voice, exclaimed:

'Ah! I am betrayed! – discovered – wretch! . . . villain! prying syco-phant! Thou shalt not have my gold! My arm is yet strong enough to resist thee. Miscreant! Robber!'

'Rash old idiot!' cried Oliver, fiercely, 'let go thy hold! – I am a desperate man! Yield up thy money!'

These rhetorical speeches could have come from almost any penny-issue novel. J. F. Smith, however, tended to write in Shake-spearean blank verse. In this speech of Wolsey in *Stanfield Hall* I have omitted only narrative, and arranged it in verse form.

> 'Dead! . . . Oh Power! how empty is thy greatness.
> My word can clothe the naked wretch with ermine;
> deal war or peace, as to my will seems meet;
> say to my foe, thou shalt not live an hour;
> yet cannot bid my friend exist one minute.
> The crozier, like the sceptre, smells of earth.
> I am sick of greatness . . .'

The speech continues without breaking the metre. Shakespearean influence in these novels is rare, apart from the inherited structure of *Macbeth*. *Macbeth* and *Hamlet* are fairly frequently quoted – or misquoted – but there is no sign of intelligent appreciation of his plays. Melodrama ruled supreme, and the most popular Shake-spearean drama was Edmund Kean's intensely melodramatic per-formance of *Richard III*. Kean, with his flashing eyes and electric gestures, made his own contribution to the conception of the villain in drama and fiction.

Kean and other actors were the subject of popular woodcuts that were sold to be hung on people's walls. Factories producing these woodcuts existed before the arrival of penny-issue fiction, and the periodical publishers took over their styles and conven-tions. Albert Smith noted in *Christopher Tadpole* that the illustra-tions to penny-issue novels had theatre curtains down the side: not only is this common, but we even get, in an illustration designed for the novel, footlights included.[1]

These woodcuts and the stories perfectly supplement each other. The outstretched hands point to the power of destiny, the falling curve of the heroine's body illustrates her helpless innocence, the villain's enormous eyes – Sala as a woodcutter was told to make them larger[2] – show devouring lust. They convey the conventional poses of both actor and stock characters, designed to evoke a crude but precise response from the back of the 'gods', or a semi-literate reader struggling to understand the story. The illustrations were more than ornament. Today, when we are deluged with pictorial art, it requires an effort of imagination to see the impact of pictures on early nineteenth-century readers. The appreciative Wilkie watched in tears a stage representation of his picture 'The Rent Day', and Cruikshank's series of etchings, 'The Bottle', was made into a novel, and often dramatized. It is well known what detailed care Dickens demanded of his illustrators.

Another element in popular culture that contributed to the fiction was the ballad. Ballads were popular in the towns, particularly in the years following Waterloo. They were printed by at least thirty publishers in London and the provinces, crudely, on flimsy yellowy paper, but with a bold appearance that appealed to their readers. They were sold in sweet shops, tobacconists, general stores, and by itinerant salesmen such as the 'chanter' (singer, like Autolycus), or 'pinner-up' (who stood in front of his fluttering boards of leaflets, reciting his wares). Broadsheets, with their transitional offspring the ballad magazines, and crude pamphlet-periodicals like *Cleave's Penny Police Gazette*, were the ground from which periodical fiction grew.

Ballads can also be linked with drama and fiction in other ways. Ballad sellers often dressed up and acted characters in their songs, and comedians did the same in the profusion of 'music halls' in the towns which had grown out of the 'Free-and-Easies' and 'Cock-and-Bull' social gatherings of the earlier years of the nineteenth century. These were of an endless variety, from mere public houses providing entertainment to the superior 'Evans's' frequented by Dickens, Jerrold, and Sala: 'White Conduit Gardens' 'elysium of milliners' girls and larking apprentices',[3] or dubious

1. *Varney*, 1846, p. 441.   2. G. A. Sala, *Life and Adventures*, 1895, p. 109.
3. Guess, *Nickleby Married*, pp. 290 ff.

places like the 'Royal Harmonic Saloon' described in *Nickleby Married*, where one could hear flighty songs by ladies in the briefest of muslin dresses. Besides sentimental songs ('The Rose that Blooms for Ever'), drinking choruses ('Give me Wine, Rosy Wine'), many were character songs like 'The Literary Dustman', from Pierce Egan's *Life in London*. These were important in that they preserved intimate character drawing and close rapport with the audience when these qualities were being lost on the stage with melodrama.

These songs were frequently inserted in penny-issue novels as drinking songs in a robbers' carousal, or the song of a minstrel. (This practice of course goes back in English popular fiction at least as far as Deloney's *Jack of Newbury* [1598], and was used by Bulwer Lytton in *Paul Clifford*, and Ainsworth in *Jack Sheppard*.) Popular songs and ballads were also transformed into penny-issue novels, such as Prest's *My Poll and My Partner Joe* (*c.* 1849), or *The Blind Beggar of Bethnal Green* (1848). This was not usually very successful, since the chief virtue of a ballad is concision, and they were soon exhausted by the novelist. *Lloyd's Penny Atlas* did better with a series of short stories based on popular songs.[1] Usually, too, ballads – 'Willikins and his Dinah' and 'Billy Barlow' are good examples – have a colloquial vigour and realism lacking in the fiction. No hero in fiction would have cut his throat with a piece of glass as did the disappointed lover in 'The Ratcatcher's Daughter'.

Many popular songs, and several novels based on them, are about the sea. Popularity of naval romance was stimulated by receding memories of the Napoleonic wars, and their living relics retailing tall stories in exchange for drinks in public houses. As we, some ten years after the end of the Second World War, had a welter of war stories published, so, when Trafalgar was beginning to sink into the past, a spate of naval romances appeared including works by Captain Walter Glascock, Basil Hall, Frederick Chamier, Edward Howard, W. Johnson Neale, Michael Scott, and above all, Marryat. In general, these stories look back to the great progenitor of sea novels, Tobias Smollett, although his crudity was purged. We get reproductions of his naval characters such as Commodore Trunnion and Tom Pipes, and people speak in the naval jargon by which running becomes 'clapping on sails', marriage, 'being

1. I, 1843, p. 225, et seqq.

spliced', and God Almighty, 'the Lord High Admiral Aloft'.

This school of fiction could not but have some impact on the lower-class writers. Characters and situations from Marryat appear occasionally in their novels, and *The Odd Fellow* reviewer dismissed one penny-issue novel *Jack Trench* (1841) as 'one of the many small craft following in the wake of Marryat's "Poor Jack"; and, we may add, at no very remarkable distance'.[1]

On the whole, however, lower-class writers felt these novels too complex to express popular notions of sailors and the sea. About the sailor's position there was no doubt. He had saved England from Napoleon, and he was the successor to the English yeoman farmer as the symbol of courage, honesty, and a feeling heart.

> The sailor you see, was Dame Nature's designing,
> And match him no power on earth ever can,
> In his heart love and honour's with courage entwining,
> A sailor's the chap – aye, a sailor's the man![2]

His figure was established on the stage by T. P. Cooke, who had himself seen service at the age of ten in *The Raven* at the siege of Toulon, and had later taken part in the siege of Brest. This point is worth making, for the legend of the honest British sailor was built up, not by romanticizing laymen, but by ex-sailors such as Cooper, Dibdin, and Jerrold, who had seen the navy at first hand. Cooke's most famous part was William, the sailor hero of Douglas Jerrold's *Black-eye'd Susan* (1829). Court-martialled and sentenced to death for striking his drunk captain in defence of his sweetheart, William receives tearful tributes to his manly virtues from all ranks and, nautical to his last phrase, mounts to meet his death as a sailor should, when the captain rushes in with a pre-dated discharge proving William had left the Service when the offence was committed. Cooke cut such a figure in the part that the play ran for over a hundred nights at the Surrey Theatre, Cooke hurrying across London in a cab after the performance to re-enact the part as an afterpiece at Covent Garden.

The tar in the fiction had all the admirable attributes of William. (*Black-eye'd Susan* itself was made into a novel by 'E. F. Marriott'

1. III, 1841, p. 67.
2. Edward Lancaster, 'The Origin of Sailors', *London Singer's Magazine*, I, 1839, p. 214.

[1845]). *Poor Tom Bowling* by W. T. T(ownsend?) was a romance suggested by the song of that name by the most popular and prolific of nautical song-writers, Charles Dibdin. At the end of the book Tom marries, and at the wedding his captain and mates all turn up to reward him for his 'good conduct, integrity of purpose, manly courage and sobriety'. Tom shows the other essential of a sailor by weeping.

'Better than all the speeches in the world, Tom [said Captain Hamilton] tears speak a language not to be mistaken; I have never known a man fight the worse for having a feeling heart...'

The popular image of the sailor was, however, soon absorbed into the conventions of domestic romance. When Tom Clewline, the hero of T. P. Prest's *Gallant Tom* (1841), goes to sea, he is followed by a sailor who is none other than the disguised Rosina, the lovely ward of Earl Fitzosbert, driven by love. The disguise is effective enough to protect her secret amid the crowded life between decks, until those dressing a wound she receives in the Battle of the Nile make a sensational discovery. It also emerges that both Tom and Rosina are children of the elder Fitzosbert, believed murdered by his brother the present earl. Their parent, however, miraculously appears, and they are all taken into captivity by Saib, the black servant of the usurper. They escape, the younger brother is confronted, forgiven, and promptly dies of a broken blood vessel. Tom marries his rural sweetheart, and they live happily ever after. Tom's aristocratic qualifications do not prevent him being in the best conventions of the manly British tar, or finally merging into the manly British yeoman, although such convolutions show the final decadence of these literary traditions.

In connection with this it is interesting to note that in *Lady Hamilton* (1849), Nelson, usually a subject for reverent biographies, is shown as a conventional seducer, even down to rescuing Lady Hamilton from a fire. In the end she is deserted and dies in poverty without even Nelson's legacy to her, which the government withholds. By the end of the 1840s, a suffering woman knocked down the beam when weighed against a sailor on the scales of popular sentiment.

If the sea came into popular fiction mainly from the drama and popular song, other elements in these stories were influenced by a third feature of the urban scene, journalists. 'Penny-a-liners', so called because they were paid a penny a line for their work, were a familiar sight in the towns, sitting in coffee shops, public houses, or even riding a fire engine to be first on the scene at the latest 'dreadful conflagration'. They carried boards to which were clipped a number of carbon interleaved sheets, and whenever they found a piece of news they would produce several copies of an article and take it round to as many newspaper offices as they could. Items accepted were paid for at a penny a line.

It is again difficult to ascertain how many 'penny-a-liners' wrote penny-issue fiction, although both industries drew on the same group of literary hacks and the proportion will have been fairly high. Sala notes meeting one worker in both fields.[1] This may account for writers in both liking certain themes, such as a fire or a trial. (One reporter was Charles Dickens, who drew on this experience to portray the trial of Bardell v. Pickwick.) There is also a common stiffness of style in descriptions, abounding with prolixity and polysyllabic phrases such as 'devouring element'. Both were concerned to get as much script out of as little material as possible, and shared techniques.

Journalists with specialities also tended to extend their experience into their fiction. Renton Nicholson, practised in racy accounts of pubs, brothels, theatres, and their inmates, was well placed to portray London people and places in *Cockney Adventures* (1837), and *Dombey and Daughter* (1847). Pierce Egan, Sen., sports reporter for *Bell's Sunday Times*, and H. D. Miles, sporting correspondent on *The Constitutional*, brought professional accounts of boxing, wrestling, and horse-riding into their novels. Turpin's horse, in Miles's *Dick Turpin* (4th ed., 1845), is described as follows:

Her head – and in no part is blood so strikingly developed – was little and angular; from the little white star on her ample forehead, her finely chiselled face tapered towards the muzzle, then suddenly swelled out to form the widely-dilated cartelaginous nostril, so essential not only to beauty, but to free respiration. Her lips were thin, firm and well supported. Full, large and expressive eyes bespoke her intelligence and docility, while her little and spirited ears, placed wide apart, gave by their constant and live action, token of spirit, temper and endurance.

One awaits an announcement of the odds on her race to York.

1. G. A. Sala, *London Up-to-Date*, 1894, pp. 287–8.

Another element in popular journalism had regrettably little effect on serial fiction, but it is important enough to be considered as popular fiction in its own right. This was the 'comic crime reporting' appearing in such papers as *The Morning Chronicle* from about 1820, and in some penny 'newspapers' of the 1830s and 1840s to avoid the tax on news. In the former case basing themselves on an actual indictment, these reports created an imaginative sketch around the incident. In this item from *The Morning Chronicle*, a cabby is being charged with asking an excessive fare:

Vy your Honor, I vas giving von of my hintimate friends a lift past the Duke of Devonshire's, ven this here gentleman plies me, and accordinglye ven I draws up he claps that there young lady into my wehicle. Arter that ere he shoves a shilling into my fist, and tells me to drive her to South Audley-Street. Ven I had druv'd the lady there, I gets down, and werry civilly, ax'd her if that vos the place. The lady makes arnser in these werry words: – 'Coachman, I vonts to go to Green-street, vich you nose, and I insist on being set down at that there place'. Werry well, marm, says I: but, says I, marm, as its a werry rainy night mar, and my fare aint more an a shilling, marm, I hopes you take my sitivation under your pertection. Ven I draws up in Green-street the young lady takes out a sixpence, quite wollunteer without me axin for nothin.[1]

This cockney coachman appears in the paper for which Dickens was writing, before the appearance of the elder Weller. Although these sketches, some of which are well known and collected in James Wight's *Mornings at Bow Street* (1824), have not the humanity of the creations of Dickens, the claims of W. H. Watts, another reporter, bear consideration.

Forty years ago, until about twenty years from the present day, the humorous delineation of *real* life was mainly confined to one or two newspapers. The writers of that day – the Purcells, the Hayneses, the Wights, the Conways, kind reader, will you add your humble servant, and some half-dozen others, whose very names have gone out of recollection – undoubtedly laid the foundation of that peculiarly English kind of literature which Messrs Thackeray, Dickens, and their legion imitators have for the last twenty years rendered so popular. How far clever writers of this school have been indebted to the genius and style

1. 'Police Intelligence: Marlborough Street', 17 March 1835, p. 4.

of humour of their less known predecessors might be a curious enquiry. It will not, however, be going too far to assert that forgotten police delineations of character have furnished the 'idea' of some of the most original and believed-to-be-original characters in some of the most popular works of our most popular comic writers.[1]

'Serious' crime reporting had a much larger effect on penny-issue fiction. Accounts of the careers and dreadful ends of criminals, although apparent in Elizabethan prose and drama (e.g. *Arden of Faversham*), came to their peak of popularity in the realism of the eighteenth century. Besides 'biographies' like those of Defoe, Paul Lorraine's account of his experiences as chaplain to the condemned as 'The Ordinary of Newgate' (*Numerical Account of All Malefactors*, 1712), leads to a host of works containing potted biographies of many criminals, the most famous of which was *The Newgate Calendar* (*c.* 1774, and frequently reprinted in various versions). Today, crime reports make the *News of the World* the most popular English Sunday newspaper, although semi-naked girls have displaced portraits of famous criminals on lower-class walls, and the curtailment of the death sentence and the enclosing of executions has denied the malefactors of today the unequalled publicity of a public hanging. Perhaps, too, the psychiatrist and the social worker, with their talk of maladjustment and mental factors, have dealt an irreparable blow to the old conception of the criminal, who dared to live dangerously and defy all the constraints of society. We can still, however, see elements in public interest in criminals going beyond the central aspect of morbid curiosity and sadism. We have elements of crime in us, and in different circumstances might be in the dock. In reading of violence, larceny, and murder we are vicariously exploring the dark corners of our own personality.

In the early Victorian era the popularity of Jack Sheppard, Dick Turpin, Claude Duval and other highwaymen shows the appeal of the criminal mainly as the successor to Robin Hood and the companion of Schiller's romantic apotheosis of villainy, Karl von Moor. They symbolize human freedom opposed to organization, and spirit in the face of dull respectability. Like Robin Hood, they accreted an immense cycle of stories around them, and became the nineteenth-century equivalent of the popular epic. The progres-

1. W. H. Watts, *My Private Note-Book*, 1862, p. 16.

sion from fact to fiction can be illustrated in the life of Dick Turpin.

Richard Turpin, common highwayman, was hanged in 1739. His career became publicized by the account of *The Trial of the Notorious Highwayman, Richard Turpin at York Assizes . . . taken down in Court by Mr Thomas Kyll* (c. 1738). Tales of his ride from London to York caught the public imagination, and his reputation was kept alive by criminal biographies and extended through accounts in chapbooks and broadsheets. Broadsheets were an extremely important section of the criminal literature trade – in executions they were able to 'scoop' the newspapers because they were printed *before* the execution. The moment the drop fell their cries would advertise the criminal's last dying words, but sad was the procession of sellers returning to the Seven Dials printing offices in London when there was a reprieve. As they 'celebrated' their subject, with due monitory verses to the readers, rather than giving a strictly factual account, they were an important factor in the romanticizing of criminals' lives.

In 1834 the Turpin legend, and criminal biography generally, was given a great stimulus by the popularity of W. H. Ainsworth's *Rookwood*. Ainsworth, with a skill and thoroughness beyond the capabilities of broadsheet writers, showed Turpin to be an essentially good character driven to crime by causes outside himself. It was published before plagiarisms got under way, but it appeared on the stage in such dramatic versions as W. S. Sutter's *The Adventures of Dick Turpin and Tom King* (c. 1835), and later Book Four was twice republished (unacknowledged) as *Turpin's Ride to York* (Glover, 1839), and *Dick Turpin's Celebrated Ride to York* (Purkess, 1841).

H. D. Miles's *Dick Turpin* (1839), was extremely popular: Miles looked back to *Tom Jones* rather than *Rookwood*. Besides echoes of Fielding's minor characters, Turpin is an attempt to recreate his hero.

Unused to control, and courageous even to a fault, ready to resent injury, yet easily satisfied, he possessed the requirements of a great villain or a great hero, characters which have a closer affinity than the flatterers of conquerors, and such like enemies of their species, are likely to admit.

Miles failed to bring this character alive, partly because he did

11. Nautical Novel and Criminal Romance

(a) 'Nothing but death surrounded us on every side'

(b) Marian is seized by Clarrington

not show in action the positive side of Turpin's impulsiveness, and partly because anything complex was outside his range. Tom King, a good-natured villain, and Thurtell, an ill-natured one, are uncomplicated and much more successful. The long story is told without repetition or slackening of interest, and Miles reveals his fair knowledge of literature, history, music and painting without pedantry. It should be noticed that in this story Turpin kills his friend Tom King by mistake, and shows his manly self-control by not flinching a muscle. When, however, his horse Black Bess dies, he collapses in tears. The love of Turpin and Bess formed the basis of all Turpin stories, it was acted out in equestrian dramas such as H. D. Milner's *Turpin's Ride to York* (*c.* 1836), and was prominent in the ride which was pirated separately from Ainsworth's novel. Today, cowboy films, for all their gun-slinging, have the same basic appeal – the love of man and horse.

This aspect featured highly in the popular romances that marked the final stage in the romanticizing of criminals. In these, even the semblances of realism preserved by Ainsworth and Miles disappeared. Jack Rann, another criminal, was portrayed in W. Jackson's *The New Newgate Calendar* (1796) as 'a bold, ignorant fellow . . . fond of boasting . . . exceedingly apt to be quarrelsome when in liquor'. James Lindridge's *Jack Rann* (1845) portrayed this eighteenth-century Teddy boy thus:

Dark-chestnut locks, falling in graceful curls (after the fashion of the time) down his back, served only partly to hide a brow, which, save for summer labour in the fields, would have been one of snowy whiteness. In addition, and to his adornation, he possessed a nose perfectly aqueline [*sic*] – none too long – none to short – . . . eyes, black as jet, and dark as midnight, shot forth such lightning in their angry glances, in indignation or in quarrel, that many a spirited man, although possessing double age and double strength, succumbed, ere they would chance a conflict with BOLD AND BRAVE JACK RANN.

Jack Rann and *Gentleman Jack* (1852), were the first of a number of romances about criminals, including *Black Bess* (1863), *Blueskin* (1867), and *The Blue Dwarf* (*c.* 1870). These were marathon novels – *Gentleman Jack* and *Black Bess* ran for four years. They become communal affairs. For instance, in the former, Dick Turpin (1706–39) is saved from the gallows by Claude Duval (1643–70), and Jack Rann (1749–74). During the immense length of the story all three are killed – Jack Rann twice – the last to go being Dick Turpin. Passages of Gothic and fashionable romance are included – Duval descends the vaults of an English convent through horrors which 'transcend [his] imagination', to save a lovely girl from the wicked Monk, Father Garvey. The criminals are all 'as much public characters as Members of Parliament are now'. When the Secretary of State for Home Affairs (a Lord Abingdon), gives an order for Claude Duval's arrest, Duval goes in disguise to see the Secretary. Disclosing himself, he makes Lord Abingdon revoke the order, and ask his pardon. These romances reflect a changeover from adult to juvenile audiences, immature and enjoying adventure, however improbable. They provided a complete escape from the realities of life, and stress the criminal as a rebel.

The most popular criminal in the 1830s and 1840s, however, was not a dashing highwayman like Turpin or Duval, but a London apprentice, who fell in with bad company, and committed a series of thefts that today would have earned him a moderate prison sentence – his first theft was a bale of cloth – but in 1724 earned the lad, scarcely twenty-two, a sentence of death. Then followed three almost incredible escapes from prison and he became a public figure, with crowds paying three-and-six to see him in gaol. He hoped to escape at the last by having his friends resuscitate him at a surgeon's house directly after the execution, but rioting around the scaffold prevented this faint hope from being realized. He was the subject of a number of pamphlets by Defoe and others: in 1839, however, his career suddenly caught the imagination of the lower classes, and in ten years following at least seven separate works about him appeared in cheap form. The immediate cause for this was undoubtedly Ainsworth's *Jack Sheppard* which was serialized in *Bentley's* (1839), and the ensuing dramatic versions. But he was able to hold the popular imagination because of the other attraction of criminal biography – the readers felt the story might have happened to them.

The various novels based on his life show an amazing range of interpretations. *The Life and Adventures of Jack Sheppard* (G. Purkess, 1849), is a plagiarism of Ainsworth. *The History of Jack Sheppard* (John Williams, 1839) shows Jack forced into crime to get Edgeworth Bess (in life his favourite doxy, here a pure and persecuted heroine) her rightful inheritance. *The Eventful Life and Unparalleled Exploits of the Notorious Jack Sheppard* (T. White, 1840), on the other hand, is centred on the Jacobite intrigues of Sheppard's master, Kneebone; an affair between his wife and a Major Hamilton, and the attempts of Francis Esdaile to recover his inheritance from Sir Luke Gascoine. Jack Sheppard's career is huddled into an unassimilated summary at the end of the book.

This work was one of a number of novels that are only ostensibly about a particular criminal, but use their subject merely as a 'selling line', while writing about something else. The outstanding book of this genre is *Eliza Grimwood. A Domestic Legend of the Waterloo Road* (B. D. Cousins, *c.* 1838). A bare outline of the plot gives little indication of the qualities of the novel. Eliza is born in Spain of a young English soldier and a Spanish girl, but the girl's former lover assassinates the couple, leaving the child to be brought up in an English country house with three girls, Ellen Langdale, Kate Elmore, and Betsy Barry. The theme usual to domestic romance appears – they are pursued by the Lord of the Manor – but the characters are freshly conceived. The avaricious bailiff of Lord Rakemore, for instance, is described as:

One of the old, long-necked, long-jawed breed of cattle, one of those lanky, lean animals that never get fat, but with a neck long enough to reach to the further side of the fence for anything that grows there.

The feelings of the girls are also described with originality. Betsy, for example, is knocked down by the hounds in a hunt.

Darkness – a heavy quivering darkness – smothered her, and crushed some voices which she heard, as if the voices had been glass broken in her ears.

This effectively conveys the painful harshness of sounds heard when semi-conscious. Her reaction to the men around her appears to be excessively naïve, but Betsy is in fact being ingenuous: her innate desires are arguing with her strict schooling.

Her ideas of temptation and evil were derived from the instruction she had received; which made her believe that temptation and evil came from the devil in person. Seeing *men* standing around her, she considered herself safe from all evil as the spiritual tempter would not dare to come where there were so many men and dogs, and especially *guns*.[1]

1. p. 12.

First of all Betsy, then Kate Elmore, is abducted. In a vivid piece of action, Kate, cornered in a hunting lodge, murders Mrs Bruin, Lord Rakemore's procuress, and is rushed off to London. Kate's brother, coming to rescue her, discovers Mrs Bruin and is convicted of her murder.

In the meantime, a fortune falls to Eliza, but this is contested by a relative, and lawyers deprive her not only of her inheritance but of her own savings. She finds employment with the Langdale family; the son, George Langdale, falls in love with her, but his natural reticence holds him back. When he does ask her to marry him, it is too late, she has already been ruined by Rakemore, and driven against her reason by passion, she flees to London with her seducer. Rakemore uses her, then has her drugged, and set loose in the streets. She finds employment, but Rakemore, jealous of her returning prosperity, entices her away (in a way similar to that in which Oliver Twist is taken from Mr Brownlow), placing her disappearance in the worst possible light with her employers.

This part of the book contains many vivid and curious pictures of London life. Of particular interest are the activities of a group of penny-a-liners, Brookes, Grey, Donovan, Whittle, and George Augustus Crowe, 'a tall, hungry-looking man', pock-marked, the son of a Scottish farmer. I have not been able to identify these and the many other vividly sketched characters that appear, but a description he gives of the 'Lushington' club, held at the Harp tavern, Little Russell Street, Covent Garden, where members seated themselves according to their financial condition, and those in 'suicide' ward received charity, exactly tallies with a description of it in *The Town*.[1] This and the gratuitous details he gives of various people suggests he was drawing a highly libellous picture of the London he knew. 'Lushington' is officiated over by 'the Rt Hon. (John or George, or some Christian name I forget) Hucklebridge'. Licentious publications were issued with the imprint ' J. Hucklebridge', and it is quite likely in this short, sharp-eyed heavily whiskered man we see this publisher. This would show another link between cheap publications and the world of London entertainment, for Renton Nicholson ran 'The Judge and Jury Club', a similar affair, at the Coal Hole, Covent Garden.

In his portrayal of the seamier side of London life, the author of *Eliza Grimwood* himself resembles Nicholson, but he is far from

1. *Eliza*, pp. 61 ff.; *Town*, I, 1837, p. 21.

the sly prurience of *The Town*. A brothel is described, but only to provide broad comedy. A country lad is inveigled in, and quickly relieved of all his money: his uncle, the pastor of a nonconformist chapel, enters the brothel to try to extricate his nephew. The brothel catches fire, and a squire, long the enemy of the sect, also in the house, finds the pastor there, and accuses him of stealing his money. Using the threat of prosecution as blackmail, he forces the chapel to provide money for another establishment to replace the destroyed establishment.

There was a house-warming, to which all the religious contributors were invited. But they held a solemn fast in their chapel, to counterbalance the iniquity they had done. The establishment took the name of the 'New Jerusalem Joint Stock Company of Love and Liberty!' But it was commonly known in the Waterloo Road, where it was situated, as THE JEROO.

The burning down of the old brothel was itself a notable piece of narrative, far removed from the descriptions that generally appear in newspapers and romances. The old keeper of the house drowses off, and the corner of *Bell's Weekly Dispatch*, which she has been reading, catches flame from the candle.

In an amazingly short time 'Robert Bell' was burnt, and also the black paragraph on the outside, yet the flame was a small, very small blue one with a yellow edge, not altogether more than half an inch high.

Then for four and a half pages the author traces the flames' progress over the paper, skilfully interweaving this with a minute description of the still room, the drowsing of the woman, and her nightmare of a huge cat. In this way the atmosphere of the place is created and the tension is keyed up for the description of the actual fire.

Eliza Grimwood eventually finds herself in the 'Jeroo'. Meanwhile, George and Ellen Daleford, with whom she had originally stayed, have their possessions taken away from them by Lord Rakemore, and the main story is now how they regain their inheritance. Eliza recognizes Davidson, Rakemore's agent, when he is fleeing from the law and, in a quick tying together of the story, he murders her. Here the author appears to have lost interest. The murder is briefly described, partly through newspaper reports, and the trial is not concluded in the book.

The untidy structure of the story – only the main plots have been given in this summary – gives the same feeling of disappointment as do parts of the writing. The author clearly has considerable potentialities: his narrative is good, his character portrayal is original, and if it does not always succeed, it shows the author reaching after something fresh and perceptive. He also has a lively if ribald, sense of humour. Yet he writes carelessly, never troubling to bring his powers to fruition. One wishes one could find a sequel to this book, showing that the writer progressed to a better sphere of literature: although his uninhibited approach to London life, which is his happiest field, would not have been acceptable to the readers of Dickens, Thackeray, and Jerrold.

From novels which took a factual crime as their pretext, it was not far to the story of purely imaginary crime. The origins of Sweeney Todd are said to lie in a French crime recorded in *Les Rues de Paris*. The version known in England may have originated when Thomas Peckett Prest was looking through back numbers of *The Tell-Tale* for usable material. Here, in the only known written English account of the affair,[1] he would have found the main outlines of the plot – the murders, the tunnel connecting the barber's shop with the patisserie where the bodies were made into pies, and the obstinacy of the dog after his master had disappeared. Sawney Beane, the man-eater of Midlothian, is probably somewhere in the background – even the names Sawney and Sweeney are similar. There was also a case in 1818 of James Catnach being imprisoned for a broadsheet that intimated that Mr Pizzey of Drury Lane made sausages from human flesh, a charge taken seriously enough to cause a riot outside the unfortunate butcher's shop. An ingenious critic might say Todd was living by capitalist principles, that eating people is right: there are parallels with George Cruikshank's famous etching of work-girls being fed into a mincing machine that turns them into bags of gold. But whatever the source of the story, the idea was in the air, for in 1843 Tom Pinch in *Martin Chuzzlewit* was hoping that no one would think he had been made into meat pies.

On 21 November 1846 an innocuous-looking story appeared as a second feature in *The People's Periodical*, called *The String of Pearls*.[2]

1. 1825, cols. 509–12.
2. Dramatized by G. D. Pitt as *The String of Pearls (Sweeney Todd)* at the Britannia, Hoxton, 1847.

Readers soon found it, to use the right phrase, 'strong meat', with Sweeney Todd swinging a regular supply of customers down the trapdoor, by means of double reversible chairs, on to spiked rocks below. The string of pearls in the title were a gift from the sailor hero to his sweetheart, but an interesting process of association of ideas is suggested by the fact that the London Directories record an 'S. Todd, pearl-stringer', who lived in Clerkenwell at this time. The writer is unknown, but Prest is traditionally the author, and this is likely on stylistic grounds.

The story is well known. While Todd was doing good business selling valuables taken from his victims, he also did the basic dissection of the bodies which were then duly processed into pies by a captive never allowed out of the cellar-kitchen below the shop. The sales side was the province of Mrs Lovett. She is strictly on a business relationship with Todd. Ignoring the metaphysical problems raised, she cries 'I have sold my soul to you, but I have not bartered myself.'

The net closes round the pair so quickly that the author has his ingenuity strained to keep the story open. The dog belonging to Northill, a sailor bringing Joanna pearls from her sweetheart, tries to attract attention when his master does not return. Tobias, Todd's servant, understandably begins to suspect the truth; he is sent to Peckham Rye madhouse to be disposed of, escapes, but for some reason does not bring his old master to justice at once. The police, Sir Richard Blount and Mr Crockett even investigate Todd's premises, but arrest is delayed. For good measure Mrs Lovett is seen sleepwalking like Lady Macbeth, and the worshippers in St Dunstan's are disturbed in their devotions by the stench of rotting human offal. In the first version the climax comes when the pies brought up to the shop are flung into the air, and the cook stands up from under them to proclaim 'truth is beautiful at all times, and I have to state that Mrs Lovett's pies are made of *human flesh*!'

Todd tries to drown Mrs Lovett, unsuccessfully, poisons her, successfully, and is shot escaping from prison. The cook reveals himself as the missing sweetheart of Joanna, and the two are happily united. In the second version, however, Todd is not shot escaping from prison, but he gets away, and the story continues for a considerable time with his adventures and those of the Reverend Lupin, a particularly unpleasant character who philanders under the guise of religion and murders his two wives.

The author made the most of his material, providing gruesome murders, and such refinements as children consoling themselves in their tearful grief for the loss of their father by nibbling Mrs Lovett's pies. Such examples raise the perennial question of whether or not the moral tone of popular literature has degenerated in the modern age. Frederic Wertham (in *Seduction of the Innocent* [New York, 1954]) has described American juvenile literature telling of a baseball match played with the parts of a dismembered body – the entrails forming the boundary, and so on; but this is an extreme example, while *The String of Pearls*, admittedly unusually 'strong', was running in a popular family magazine. Superficially the face of modern mass literature is the more respectable. Nevertheless, *The String of Pearls* does not evoke its horror for sensationalism alone: in its crude way it builds its horrific theme into an imaginative whole. Todd becomes a grotesque monster with its own puppet-like animation, when alone looking into the mirror 'making the most hideous face, just for the fun of the thing'. With delight in the refinements of hypocrisy, he goes out distributing tracts among the poor. Mrs Lovett is equally bizarre with her cold villainy and strange love of a Major Bounce – 'The love of one cockroach for another.'

Apart from its horrific theme, the story sustains the reader's interest, and is occasionally relieved with gentler passages of description, as where Tobias emerges from the madhouse into the cool of a garden at night, with 'one of those beautiful mountain-ash trees, which bend over into such graceful foliage'. The author added to the interest by setting the story recognizably in London: Londoners were invited to think, as they passed St Dunstan's Church, of the congregation convulsed with the rising stench from Todd's abattoir, or imagine Mrs Lovett's shop in Bell Yard. This is true of other novels set in the towns. An old reader of nineteenth-century popular fiction wrote to the *Bootle Times*:

> To my mind, the most fascinating part of the old stories was the fact that they often treated of places you knew ... I can remember first reading the story of 'Jack Sheppard' and spending much spare time in exploring Wych-Street, and Clare Market...[1]

Many penny novels were written to exploit just this interest,

1. 'Old Boys' Periodicals', *Bootle Times*, 30 June 1916, p. 8.

for instance, James Malcolm Rymer's *The Lady in Black* (1847), which purported to tell the story of Sarah Whitehead, a mentally deranged woman who gained fame wandering outside the Bank looking for her brother, who had been executed for forgery in 1812; or *The Old House of West Street* (1846), by Prest, which tried to exploit the interest aroused that year by the demolition of a famous thieves' den down Chick Lane in London. Rymer did not even get Sarah's name right, and high sales kept Prest's story going after he had shown the police cleaning up the hideout; but the intentions were there.

Interest in the towns on a wider plane was exploited by the far more numerous 'Mysteries' which, following Sue's *Mysteries of Paris*, tried to show city life, with all its activities and classes of society, as an organic whole. The picture is held together by a central character moving among all classes – in Sue's work, Duke Rodolphe; in the first two volumes of *The Mysteries of London*, the Prince of Alteroni and Eugene of Montoni.

The Mysteries of London was one of the most successful penny-issue works of its time. By the second series it was claiming a circulation of 40,000 and it was dramatized at the Pavilion, Marylebone, and Victoria theatres.[1] It was translated, and exported as far away as Russia, where it may have had an effect on the Russian image of English society.[2]

A brief survey of the first section is sufficient to give a taste of the whole. It opens with Eliza Sydney masquerading as a man through the streets of London. She is seized by a gang of criminals and thrown down that trapdoor into the Fleet river without which no criminal hideout was complete. She miraculously escapes, and her story becomes known to the reader. Prompted by a Mr Stephens, who stands to profit heavily, she has been disguised as her brother, who is presumed dead, for the purpose of getting a legacy due to him. The plan falls through, and she spends a period in prison: then she emigrates and while abroad marries the Grand Duke of Montoni. Another story involves Richard Markham, a rich young man who is introduced to the world of gambling by a Mr Chichester. Mr Chichester cheats him, and he finds himself falsely imprisoned for forgery. In prison he meets a resurrection man, the head of the gang of criminals employed by Montague Greenwood, financier and politician, who is to be his enemy.

1. *Reynolds's Miscellany*, I, 1846, p. 125.   2. ibid., p. 259.

Coming out, he finds his sentence has ruined his life (the iniquity of society towards those who have been in prison is one of the moral themes of the book). After various adventures, which serve to bring the central characters into contact with as many spheres of London life as possible, Markham becomes the Prince of Montoni, while Greenwood is seen to be his long-lost brother. Reynolds wrote as a Chartist[1] and in *The Mysteries of London* we see the emergence in fiction of the radicalism of the Chartist press. The portrayal of rich and poor is used to stress the social injustices of town life. We are given the average annual incomes of the various classes.

The Sovereign	£500,000
The member of the Aristocracy	£30,000
The Priest	£7,500
The member of the middle classes	£300
The member of the industrious classes	£20

Is this reasonable? Is this just? Is this even consistent with common sense?.

The capitalist system is seen in action in the person of Greenwood, the refined successor to Cleave's 'Bloody Bludgeon-man, Bloody Red Slave-mark, Bloody Poor-grinding Aristocracy'. He mercilessly ruins all who come into his hands, taking the honour of the ladies and the money of the men. He stands in Parliament to declare:

'... there was too much of what was called *freedom*. He would punish all malcontents with a little wholesome exercise upon the tread-mill ... it was coolly alleged that in entire districts [the poor] wanted bread. Well – why did they not live upon potatoes? ... There was a worthy alderman at his right hand, who could no doubt prove to the House that bread spoilt the taste of turtle ...'

This speech drew from Sir Robert Peel 'a patronising nod of most gracious approval'.

The book attacks many other abuses; the conduct of the courts, prison conditions (with a dietary chart for Clerkenwell gaol),

1. For the Brighton bookseller who told Thackeray Reynolds was popular because 'he lashes the aristocracy', see W. M. Thackeray: 'Charity and Humour', *Collected Works*, Smith, Elder, 1898, VII, p. 772.

12. The Rich and the Poor: The Mysteries of London

(a) Richard Markham becomes Regent of Castelcicala

(b) Woman in a workhouse, refused permission to see her dying husband

(c) The public executioner initiates his deformed son into his trade

(d) Two luxurious beauties talk of love as they disrobe

letter-opening by the Post Office, the economic pressures that lead to crime and prostitution, to name but a few. In a rather gauche chapter he even suggests the reigning monarch has been forced by the expediency of money and politics to marry against her inclinations, for such were the inevitable evils of aristocracy. Reynolds's radical attitudes do give him a point of reference amid all the scrambling diversity of the book, and they show a social conscience lacking in almost all other popular fiction at this time. This also gave him a deeper understanding of the way environment and society condition human action. Reynolds was a talented writer, and could have made a real contribution to the popular culture of his time. However, his writing shows the mixed qualities one might expect from the engraved portrait he appended to his works whenever possible. This shows a young man in fashionable, rather dandified dress, with effeminate curls, intelligent eyes and forehead, and sensual and indecisive chin. His abilities fell to the lure of sensation and easy popularity. His radicalism serves a dramatic rather than a genuinely social purpose, and is finally subject to the conventions of romance. Markham, the hero in *The Mysteries of London* must finally become a Prince; Isabella, the girl he loves, a Princess. The upper classes are caricatured, and are either idealized royalty in disguise, or soul-less monsters. The middle classes are hardly represented at all. The lower classes are made up of thugs, resurrection men, fences, prostitutes, or starving paupers. The best of the working classes as they really existed – the courageous artisan overcoming his difficulties by hard work and determination – is never shown. Reynolds's social criticism is overbalanced by his sensationalism, as when he shows Poverty in Ellen Munroe selling her face to a painter and her virtue to a capitalist.

Popular fiction of this time generally failed to use town life creatively in the manner of, say, Dickens. At times its vitality breaks in, as when in *Ada the Betrayed* Bond the butcher runs into Learmont's stately ball playing the tune on marrow-bone and cleaver of the Smithfield apprentices. The use of town slang, 'lumbered' for caught, 'panea and caslan' for bread and cheese, and the like, is also not a literary affectation as it is in the novels of Ainsworth and Bulwer, but related to the popular idiom. But town life is mainly drawn upon for the sensational effect of gloom and crime – which is perhaps the way the tenement dweller would see

it. Nunnery vaults are exchanged for slum basements, and charnel
houses for town refuse.

Poverty frequently compels the unhappy relatives to keep the body
for days – aye, and weeks. Rapid decomposition takes place; animal life
generates quickly, and in four-and-twenty hours myriads of loathsome
animaculae are seen crawling about. The very undertaker's men fall sick
at these disgusting – these revolting spectacles.[1]

Resurrection men – traders in dead bodies – were a stock-in-trade
for the novelist – Herbert Thornley in *Life in London* even tells of
the one who gave his son a skeleton as a doll to introduce it to the
trade early.

The urban context of this literature probably had more interesting indirect effects. Some penny-issue novels continued the conventions of the fainting, pure heroine, but others, as I have suggested, found ways of reconciling the heroine's goodness with the
tougher sensibilities engendered by urban life. Some, like Ela or
the heroines of Reynolds, could be 'fallen' women. They took on
other persona. Ela became a gypsy prophet for the period of the
story, dropping the role at the end. Ada spent part of her adventures dressed like a boy, and acting with male decision. Prest's
Susan Hopley (1842) had two heroines, the passive, conventional
Miss Wentford, and the resourceful Susan, referred to as '*our*
heroine' (my italics). This line cannot be pursued too far, as in
middle-class fiction Charlotte Brontë's *Jane Eyre* (1847) was changing the image of the heroine, too. The hero also took on various,
more active, guises. One of the most popular was the good-hearted
sailor of Prest's *Jack Junk* (1849) or *My Poll and My Partner Joe* (*c.*
1849). We also see the development of the anti-hero, monsters like
Varney the Vampyre or Sweeney Todd, or criminals like Jack
Sheppard. Popular aspirations were expressed through figures
opposed to the established order. These tendencies were to become more extreme in the decades that followed, forming, as we
will notice, an even less respectable sub-literature.

As the Lloyd-type penny-issue novel faded out, the situation
became more complicated. The better type of periodical, *The
London Journal*, *The Family Herald*, and *Reynolds's Miscellany* (later,
Bow Bells), sailed on, joined by others such as *The Working Man's
Friend*, *Eliza Cook's Journal*, *The Home Companion*, and *The English-*

1. Reynolds, *Mysteries*, I, p. 43.

woman's Domestic Magazine, which frequently had a family or feminine audience in mind. An improvement in the social and economic position of the workers was reflected in more polished and 'respectable' cheap periodicals, and many who had bought penny-issue novels probably turned to the cheap half-crown reprints of the 'Parlour' and 'Railway' libraries which were started in 1847 and 1849 respectively.

Dr Margaret Dalziel, in *Popular Fiction a Hundred Years Ago*, has called this ensuing periodical literature 'The Purified Penny Press' but this was the literature that branched out upwards. A considerable portion branched downwards, to produce a popular penny press that was far lower than the publications of Lloyd and White. The curious feature of this is that it is ostensibly a juvenile fiction, although no doubt many adults read it, just as many juveniles read *Ada* or *Varney*. This reflects a genuine change in the wide working-class readership formed by the radical and educational movements – it was laudable to read *The Poor Man's Guardian*, and this attitude lingered on, but in the 1850s reading was 'children's stuff', unless you were the type of reader not interested in penny-issue fiction anyway. But more adults probably read juvenile fiction than would have done if it had not been ostensibly for children. The B.B.C. finds more adults watch educational programmes when they are 'for schools', because watching an 'adult' educational programme is 'highbrow', and 'highbrow' is a dirty word. In the opposite direction, reading trashy 'adult' fiction implies you accept its extravagant nonsense – 'looking in', from a superior position, on 'kid's stuff', leaves you free to enjoy it.

The volume of juvenile literature produced was immense, and a good deal of it, such as Brett's *Boys of England* (1866–99), was stirring, sometimes sadistic stuff, but with some pretensions to respectability. Another type, however – and it is the direct successor to the penny-issue fiction about criminal and town life – was a different case. These bore colourful titles such as *The Wild Boys of London* (1863), *The Skeleton Horseman* (c. 1859), *The Outsiders of Society; or, the Wild Beauties of London* (c. 1863). Not only, as we have seen in *Gentleman Jack*, were the vestiges of probability and consistency thrown away, all moral inhibitions went too, and violence, rape, and sexual indulgence were accepted.

There is also a relative sophistication in exploiting sex and violence that was lacking in even the worst types of the earlier fiction. Here, in a scene from *The Outsiders of Society* (*c.* 1863), Mrs Chetwynd goes to confession.

'I do not understand your meaning, Father Wilkinson,' Mrs Cherwynd resumed, 'in speaking about temptation being too great.'

And the fair woman rose, and looked around the small room. There was a frightful amount of carnal longing in that woman's eye.

Her nostrils dilated, and her lip quivered, and she attempted to breathe!

If the following comparison may not be considered too strong, would it not suggest to one the picture of a beast of prey, gloating upon his victim.

For the fair woman knew she was irresistible.

She soon felt that, by the wild stare of her confessor.

A smile of triumph appeared again upon her lip.

'If one sin by thought, or by deed,' she asked, 'which is worse?'

Several steamy columns later comes the orgasm. 'She had conquered Father Wilkinson.' Today this heavily overdone scene appears comic: it is doubtful whether it would have done so to the semi-literate Victorian. Notice, for all its faults, the development in technique beyond the cheerful lechery of *Fanny Hill's New Friskey Chanter*. There is the use of comparatively sophisticated words such as 'carnal desire', and a prurient play on the 'sin' of the action – 'sin' does not appear in all *Fanny Hill*. There is the use of pseudo-logic, 'what is worse, thought or deed?' There is a certain development in the art of exploitation, however crude this may be.

Looking at the general picture of popular literature in the early nineteenth century and today, there is no doubt that it has become professionally more sophisticated. It has also become more expert in the art of manipulating its readers. One of the attractions of the earlier period is its open-ended variety. Popular tastes and traditions emerged and disappeared to some extent free from the dead hand of editorial formulae. Readers also had a more open mind. Many educators of the 1830s thought universal education would introduce a utopian age of reason. They did not see that it would bring what R. P. Blackmur has called 'the New Illiteracy',[1] unless accompanied by a total education in ways of reading, seeing and living.

1. *The Lion and the Honeycomb*, 1956, p. 6.

APPENDIX I

Some Minor Poets and Poetry

JOHN POOLE, in his description of a meeting of the Little Peddlington Useful Knowledge Society, tells how Mr Jubb rose to quote from his work 'META-PHYSIC-IANA, a Philosophical Poem in twenty books, of three hundred stanzas each . . .'[1] In providing his village with a local poet, Poole would have been acting on his own actual observation, for amateur poets were appearing in town, village, and countryside at this time. This was partly a continuation of the old traditions of local poets some of whom, like Stephen Duck, Ann Yearsley, Clare, and Bloomfield, had been lifted to public notice, but the movement was made much wider by the increasing standard of literacy among the lower classes, and such organizations as the Mechanics' Institute. At least one such body – the Blackburn Independent Order of Mechanics – brought out a volume of poetry written by its members. Many lower-class poets left only a few anonymous contributions to local periodicals to fame, but even so a large number produced volumes of verse, or left behind other records of their activity. Among these better-remembered writers are John Nicholson of Derbyshire, Richard Furness of Derbyshire, and Thomas Brown of Normanton Wood-house. The new towns gave rise to their own literary cultures – Manchester poets with a working-class background include Elija Ridings, F. Dyer, James Kenworthy, and John Critchely Prince. Blackburn had William Gaspey and Richard Dugdale. The best-known of the Sheffield poets were Ebenezer Elliott and James Montgomery. Nottingham had a particularly well-integrated group centred on the bookshop of William Howitt, where Charles Danby, Robert Millhouse, Samuel Plumb, Thomas Miller, Sydney Giles, and Frederick Enoch (later connected with the *Pall Mall Gazette*) used to discuss and read poetry. Their leader and biographer was Spencer T. Hall, who became known as the 'Sher-wood Forester' for his insipid rhymes describing the beauties of

1. *Little Peddlington*, II, p. 262.

Sherwood, and his smooth-running versification of the Robin Hood stories.

These poets vary enormously in style and quality. Richard Furness appears to be unique in clinging obstinately to the model of Pope, perhaps because of his isolation in Derbyshire.

> See, Man! the butt of envy or of pride,
> If rich, – how flatter'd! poor – how all deride!
> Prudent – mistrusted! just – at once despised:
> By wisdom shunn'd, by folly well advised.[1]

Generally they can be placed at the tail-end of the Romantic movement, having the conception of the poet writing in an 'exalted' mood, using emotionally charged words and sentiments. In some cases this led to long pseudo-philosophic poems after the fashion of the works of William Sotheby, John Abraham Heraud, and Edward Atherstone, or the later 'spasmodic' poetry: this type of poem was satirized by Poole in his description of META-PHYSIC-IANA. Examples would be Robert Millhouse's *The Destinies of Man* (1832–4), or Thomas Cooper's *The Purgatory of Suicides* (1845). Nevertheless, this type of work is essentially middle class – the 'spasmodic' poets Ebenezer and Ernest Jones, although they were Chartists, are not truly lower-class poets, and the examples just quoted have a moral purpose lacking in the poems of the main tradition. Lower-class poets wrote more typically in the minor key of Mrs Hemans. Above all they wrote about nature, using nature as an escape from the realities of the towns.

> Leave the town, leave the town, come,
>   To the quiet, green woods we will be bound,
>   Like true friends, like true friends roam
> Where there's health, if not wealth to be found!
>   In happy fancy we can raise
>   An altar there,
>   Or sylvan temple, and breathe praise,
>   And whisper prayer.[2]

If we turn to these poems hoping to find the fresh observation of talents unspoilt by learning, we will be disappointed – these

---

1. 'The Rag-Bag', 1832, II, ll. 27–31, *Poetical Works*, 1858, p. 105.
2. Elija Ridings, 'An Invitation', v. 3., *The Village Muse*, Macclesfield, 1854, p. 247.

poets were all the more anxious to show that though working class they had had a full poetic education.

> But softer scenes on Malham water view,
> When its smooth breast reflects the azure blue;
> Or when the skiffs, departing from its shore,
> Convey the lovely nymphs of Craven o'er,
> The still lake ruffled by each rower's stroke,
> And its smooth surface into surges broke, –
> The circling woods return their cheerful song,
> As nymphs and swains harmonious glide along.[1]

Of these poets John Critchely Prince stands out for the vigour of his imagination. Today, his boldest strokes appear pretentious:

> Sabbath! thou art my Ararat of life,
> Smiling above the deluge of my cares, . . .[2]

> Then Milton rose, like a rocket of fire,
> When the nation was buried in gloom, . . .[3]

Yet his poetry retains a little of the enthusiasm which led to comments such as 'This is true Poetry; it is the breathing forth of "that music of the soul"', which tunes the harsh dissonance of the world . . .'[4]

> Man cannot stand beneath a loftier dome
> Than this cerulean canopy of light –
> The ETERNAL'S vast, immeasurable home,
> Lovely by day, and wonderful by night!
> Than this enamelled floor so greenly bright,
> A richer pavement man hath never trod,
> He cannot gaze upon a holier sight
> Than fleecy cloud, fresh wave, and fruitful sod –
> Leaves of that boundless Book, writ by the hand of God![5]

1. 'Airedaile in Ancient Time', v. 2, *Poetical Works of John Nicholson*, 1876, p. 2.
2. J. C. Prince, 'The Poet's Sabbath', ll. 1–2, *Hours with the Muses*, 1850, p. 31.
3. 'Let us drink to the Bards', v. 3, *Hours*, p. 195.
4. 'Neglect of Literary Men', *Manchester Courier*, 9 September 1846.
5. 'Poet's Sabbath', v. 27, *Hours*, p. 38.

Today we see the weaknesses of this verse – the use of clichés, for instance, but there is no question that Prince wrote sincerely, often powerfully, and was on the mental wavelength of his readers. At times, too, he could use his experience of suffering and poverty – he and his wife watched one of their children starving to death – to bring something fresh into the conventional themes of poetry. This is a comparison of an early primrose with a poor man's child.

> Welcome thou art, though like a poor man's child,
> Brought without joy into a home of gloom;
> Mid mournful sounds and tearful tempests wild,
> Thou camest forth, fresh, fair and undefiled
>   From Nature's womb . . .[1]

This leads us to regret that these poets, apart from Ebenezer Elliott, who will be discussed later, did not turn more often to the life in which they found themselves, and, on the occasions that they did, that the results are so trite and conventional.

> Sweet child! departed day-star of my soul!
> The light is gone, I'm lonely on my way,
> Like ship on ocean when the storm doth roll,
> A compass lost, the barque can go astray:
> And thou sleepest sound beneath a load of clay
> Which brings affliction's tear drop from the heart.
> No light is left to guide me on my way
> Save the light that illumines thy immortal part.[2]

This non-political part of lower-class poetry was generally a form of intellectual escapism. Nevertheless, it had serious aspirations, and enjoyed a certain amount of interest from upper-class sources. Robert Southey published his *Lives of Uneducated Poets* (1835), and gave his advice to all who asked for it, notably Ebenezer Elliott, whom he helped to turn from turgid Gothic romances to his truer *métier* as 'The Corn-Law Rhymer'. One wishes all lower-class poets had received and taken to heart his advice to Elliott – '. . . it is to truth and nature that we must come

1. Prince, 'To an Early Primrose', *Hours*, p. 54.
2. R. Dugdale, 'On the Death of a little Grand-daughter', v. I; George Hull, *Poets and Poetry of Blackburn*, Blackburn, 1902, p. 34.

at last. Trust to them, and they will bear you through'.[1] Wordsworth visited William Howitt's Nottingham group,[2] and gave
Thomas Cooper a magnanimous welcome at Rydal Mount.[3] Lady
Blessington interested herself in Thomas Miller when he came as
a basket-maker to London,[4] and Dickens introduced the carpenter
John Overs to the public, giving a generous amount of his time in
trying to develop the would-be poet's meagre talent.[5]

In some cases, this patronage was an important factor in the
success of the lower-class writers. Without enthusiastic notices
from Bulwer Lytton in *The New Monthly Magazine*[6] and from Carlyle in *The Edinburgh Review*,[7] Ebenezer Elliott's fame would have
been very much less. Southey's introduction to the pleasant but
slight talents of the servant John Jones alone brought Jones to
public view. Indeed, upper-class patronage was as much for the
fact that the idea of a 'working-class poet' was a novelty as for any
intrinsic merits. Thomas Miller cannily affixed the title 'basket-
maker' to his name when publishing. Ebenezer Elliott, however,
while signing himself 'C.L.R.' (Corn-Law Rhymer), violently
resented any suspicion of the fact that he was being lionized mainly
because of his background. 'Must I then conclude,' he snapped,
'that I owe the notice which has been taken of the *Corn-Law
Rhymes*, to the supposition that they are the work of a mechanic?'[8]
He continued with the hint that if the upper-class critics really
understood what he was saying, they would not be so glib with
their praise.

This leads to the second side of lower-class poetry – radical
verse. This was an important part of the radical and the Corn-law
movements as an emotional stimulus, and as a means for communal expression of ideals, for most of them were primarily meant
to be sung, and the tunes were frequently appended to the titles.
They are strongly emotional. Today much of the sentiment appears brash and blindly over-confident, but they were written at a

1. *Life and Correspondence of Robert Southey*, ed. C. C. Southey, 1849–50, IV,
p. 336.

2. S. T. Hall, *Sketches*, p. 308.

3. T. Cooper, *Life*, p. 292.   4. Hall, p. 321.

5. John Overs, *Evenings of a Working Man*, 1844; Edgar Johnson, *Charles
Dickens*, 1953, I, pp. 309–10.

6. XXXI, April 1831, pp. 289 ff.   7. LV, 1832, pp. 338–61.

8. Preface, 'The Ranter', *Poetical Works of Ebenezer Elliott*, Edinburgh,
1840, p. 100.

time when high hopes appeared real; they are sincere, with little or none of the cynical vindictiveness Kingsley portrays in the Chartist poetry of Alton Locke and his friends. If they have no high rating by the normal standards of poetry, they are versified rhetoric admirably suited to their real political purpose. Sometimes they achieve a strength of their own.

The type of political song varied immensely. Sometimes they were modelled on traditional songs, such as 'The Canadian Boat Song' (T. Cooper, 'Chartist Song'). Others have the rollicking metre of a street or public-house song:

> There's a grim one-horse hearse in a jolly round trot;
> To the churchyard a pauper is going, I wot:
> The road it is rough, and the hearse has no springs,
> And hark to the dirge that the sad driver sings:
> 'Rattle his bones over the stones
> He's only a pauper whom nobody owns'.[1]

Another important influence was hymnology, a fact that stresses the relationship between certain elements in the nonconformist religious movement and political activity. Radical hymn books were issued, such as Robert Owen's *Social Hymns* (1840), or *Democratic Hymns and Songs* (1849). Many borrow the metre, style, and even the imagery of Christian hymnology.

> Crucified! crucified every morn
> Beaten, and scourged and crowned with thorn!
> Scorned, and spat on, and drenched with gall:
> Brothers, how shall we bear that thrall?
> *Chorus*: Mary and Magdalen! Peter and John!
> Answer the question, and bear it on.[2]

Scriptural imagery also fitted easily into the Radical themes of evil-doers overcome, and the apocalyptic hope of the new world on earth. In the more reflective poetry this is seen in the importance of religious themes: Robert Millhouse's *The Destinies of Man* (1832–4), for instance, traces the origins of the world's social evils to the Biblical Fall. (These adaptations of course treated evil as synonymous with political oppression, thus drastically limiting the significance of the Christian originals.)

1. 'The Pauper's Drive', *Northern Star*, 5 February 1842, p. 3.
2. Ernest Jones, 'Chartist Hymn', *Red Republican*, I, 1850, p. 56.

Another important influence was the Romantic movement. We have already noted the popularity of Shelley, Byron, and the early works of Southey: poems such as *Queen Mab*, or *A Vision of Judgement* provided precedents for expressing the class struggle in visionary terms.

> Shall Freedom's dawn be never
>   On Labour's heaving sea:
> Shall Love and Truth and Beauty
> In toiling hearts ne'er be?
>   Shall God-like Action veil its eyes
>   Before Wealth's idle mockeries,
>   The weak bow to the strong?
>   Oh, when shall slaves like gods arise,
>   How long, O God! how long?[1]

The longest and probably the best of this type of verse work was Thomas Cooper's *The Purgatory of Suicides*, one of a number of Chartist poems written by Cooper and others to cheer times of imprisonment for political agitation. Cooper selects the crime of suicide because he sees evil as in itself self-destructive. He portrays a gathering of men of all ages who took their own lives, and who are in a huge cavern being purged in readiness for the Paradise that is to come on earth. A poem in ten books, written with Miltonic phraseology in Spenserian stanzas, and jumbling together Cooper's omnivorous reading in the Greek and Roman literature, American and European histories, Voltaire, Gibbon, Mozart, travel books, and much else, arouses the reader's worst anticipations. Cooper's very limitations stood him in good stead, however, since as the reading was not assimilated at a deep level he was able to unify all his diverse elements on his own imaginative plane. His strong sincerity and moderate imaginative powers carry the reader along in spite of frequently irritating attempts at Miltonic style. In content it expresses the very best of Radical ideals – after the overcoming of evil he sees the triumphant powers as those of forgiving love and intellectual self-development – true heroes attain

> lofty purpose, patient power to treat
> Their foes with gentleness; what height they gained
> Of mental grandeur . . .[2]

1. Sheldon Chadwick, 'Labourer's Anthem', ibid., I, 1850, p. 120.
2. X, v. 62, Cooper, *Works*, 1886, p. 262.

Cooper's radicalism was unusually thoughtful and intellectual – although he was willing to suffer imprisonment for it – and the type of vision seen by Enoch Wray in Ebenezer Elliott's *The Village Patriarch*[1] will have been more germane to working-class minds. In the latter hysterical picture, reminiscent of the early work of Shelley, the workers are seen as frozen in attitudes of servility around a gigantic corpse – 'undying death', the sterile principle of exploitation.

Ebenezer Elliott claims an interest beyond that which is owing to the slender merits of his verse. With his early Gothic verse, his desire to return to the simplicity of nature, his concern with passion and his protests against social injustice, he is a particularly clear instance of the way in which radical poetry was linked with the Romantic movement. Yet he also stands on his own. He frequently describes nature, but never with real vision. He himself declared with appealing honesty, 'A primrose is to me a primrose, and nothing more – I love it because it is nothing more.'[2] A quotation from 'Win-Hill' is a fair specimen of his descriptive verse.

> High on the topmost jewel of thy crown
> Win-Hill! I sit bareheaded, ankle-deep
> In tufts of rose-cupp'd bilberries; and look down
> On towns that smoke below, and homes that creep
> Into their silvery clouds, which far-off keep
> Their sultry state! and many a mountain stream
> And many a mountain vale, 'and ridgy steep'...[3]

'Rose-cupp'd bilberries' is fresh, and the impression of the distant buildings 'creeping' into the whispy clouds is well observed. Yet this is immediately spoilt by the word 'homes', which suggests closeness, warmth, and affectionate associations, while he is trying to describe buildings, dwarfed and insignificant through distance. The 'stream', 'vale', and 'ridgy steep' are merely catalogued, with the effect of poetic exhaustion, while the use of inverted commas for the last phrase emphasizes a false striving after poetic effect. His nature poetry carries a little more power when,

1. VII, vv. iv–vii, *Works*, 1840, pp. 72–3.
2. *MSS, Autobiography*, Sheffield Public Library, p. 22.
3. 'Win-Hill', v. 21, *Works*, 1840, p. 131.

as occurs elsewhere in lower-class poetry,[1] the beauty of nature is used to point the contrast of this to the ugliness and cruelty of man.

> As when the fells, fresh bath'd in azure air,
> Wide as the summer day's all golden wing,
> Shall blush to heaven, that Nature is so fair,
> And man, condemn'd to labour and despair.[2]

As a political writer, Elliott shows no outstanding originality or strength of thought and he concentrated his vehemence against the Corn Laws, often without keeping them in perspective with the many other problems that lay behind social distress. His main asset was his personal irascibility, probably springing from a certain feeling of insecurity bred in him by the trials and vicissitudes of his early life; one may suspect this vehemence when we see for example how an imagined slight from Byron made him hurry away to compose a bitter satire on his quondam hero, and annul the praise of his earlier poems with vicious notes.[3] Yet it did give his political verse a powerful edge. This is particularly apparent when, for example, we compare the *Corn-Law Rhymes* with William Gaspey's *Poor Law Melodies* (1841). There is acid in the poems of Elliott.

> Child, is thy father dead?
> Father is gone!
> Why did they tax his bread?
> God's will be done.[4]

Yet Elliott deserves attention for more even than his mordant political verse, or his importance as the figure who brought working-class intellectual and social aspirations and the very existence of a working-class culture to the notice of the upper classes. Sitting in his little iron-dealer's office, surrounded incongruously by busts of Shakespeare, Ajax, Achilles, and Napoleon, writing ideas for poems among the orders in the day book,[5] he provides an

---

1. e.g. R. Peddie, Title Poem, *The Dungeon Harp*, Edinburgh, 1844, p. 47.
2. 'Village Patriarch', X, xvi, ll. 62–5, *Works*, 1840, p. 80.
3. E. Elliott, 'The Giaour', 1823, e.g. 'Village Patriarch', IV, note (d).
4. Song. Tune – 'Robin Adair', v. i. *Works*, 1840, p. 106.
5. A. A. Eaglestone, *Ebenezer Elliott . . . 1781–1859*, Sheffield, 1959, p. 3.

image of the worker in the transition into the industrial age. He expresses a confused fascination with the world of knowledge and of writing, and deep spiritual dissatisfaction with the results of the industrial revolution. He expressed these themes in poems, which although uneven like almost all his work, contain much of his best verse – 'The Village Patriarch', 'The Ranter', and 'The Splendid Village'. Here he justifies his claim to be 'an unfortunate follower of Crabbe',[1] and the ambiguity of 'unfortunate' does not need to be stressed. Here, the tragedy of the passing of rural England, and the spiritual poverty of lives lived for commercial gain alone, touch him to passages which have the strength, sincerity, and feeling of poetry. Here are a few selections. Referring to country allusions in Sheffield street names he writes:

> Scenes, rural once! ye still retain sweet names . . .[2]

> But, mourning better days, the widow here
> Still tries to make her little garden bloom –
> For she was country-born . . .[3]

> New streets invade the country; and he strays
> Lost in strange paths, still seeking, and in vain
> For ancient landmarks, or the lonely lane
> Where once he played at Crusoe, when a boy.
> Fire vomits darkness, where the lime trees grew . . .[4]

The reference to Crusoe in the last extract compares the happy self-companionship of a boy alone in the country with his imagination, against the new loneliness of a man in the midst of a bustling city. But the most striking line is the last. Here there is a strong contrast between the lime trees – which have the lightest of leaves – and the forceful, menacing darkness of the smoke. Fire itself had previously been productive of warmth and light – now it is a worker of evil, vomiting the darkness that blights the life of the workers.

In 'Steam at Sheffield', Elliott was to go beyond all working-

1. Preface, 'The Village Patriarch', *Works*, 1840, p. 55.
2. 'Village Patriarch', I, xv, l. I, *Works*, 1840, p. 58.
3. ibid., I, xvi, ll. 1–3, p. 58.
4. ibid., I, xii, ll. 3–8, p. 57.

class political contemporary poets to see not only the evils of industrialization, but also the prosperity it was bringing. Andrew's

> sightless eyes
> Brighten with generous pride that man hath found
> Redemption from the manacles that bound
> His powers for many an age . . .

Yet even in his poetic delight at the 'glorious harmony in this Tempestuous music of the giant, Steam', a sense of its inhumanity remains to balance the picture.

> But thou canst hear the unwearied crash and roar
> Of iron powers, that, urg'd by restless fire,
> Toil ceaseless, day and night, yet never tire,
> Or say to greedy man, 'thou dost amiss'.

Here we find the qualities that make certain lower-class poetry worth reading. It was written by men of strong convictions, and when they were not led astray by false conceptions of the poetic, they can turn out passages of verse which still pulse with the excitements and aspirations which called them, however imperfect in form, into being. Even the lower-class verse which strikes us as commonplace and imitative must be seen in its setting, where it provided intellectual stimulus for the writers and for many readers, who, as S. T. Hall remarks,[1] could appreciate the vision of a minor writer with a similar mental background better than they could the much better work of upper-class writers. For all its faults, working-class poetry was a vital and exciting part of the best of the working-class culture of this period.

1. *Sketches*, p. 331.

APPENDIX II

London Publishers of Penny-issue Fiction 1830—50

THIS list has been compiled from the title-pages of books actually examined, and from advertisements -- though not from advance notices. Additional information has been gained from the Censuses of 1841 and 1851, the London Directories for 1832, 1838, and 1844, *Cowie's Printer's Handbook* (1834–5), Mr A. E. Hextall's manuscript lists, and the other sources listed. Although the information has been made as full as possible, it gives dates when publishers were known to be functioning, and not necessarily the first and last years they were in business.

Many of these ninety publishers were small, and either stationers, printers, or newsagents as well. I have, however, tried to limit the list to people in the book distribution trade; journalists, writers, or editors whose names appear occasionally on the publisher's imprint, have been generally excluded. I have also omitted the offices of periodicals, the well-known publishers Charles Knight, Robert and William Chambers, and the publishers of religious works.

E. Appleyard	86 Farringdon St	1845–51
H. Barth	4 Brydges St, Covent Gdn	1849–51
W. Bennett	*address unknown*	1841
G. Berger	42 Holywell St, Strand	1832–8?
,,	19–20 Holywell St, Strand	1838–64
George Biggs	421 Strand	1843–50
W. Brittain	11 Paternoster Row	1841
Norman Bruce	84 Farringdon St	1844–51
(*as* Bruce & Wyld)	84 Farringdon St	1845–7
Mrs W. Caffyn	31 Oxford St, Mile End	1848–51
J. Caton	11 Catherine St, Strand	1845
S. Chauntler	Amen Corner, Paternoster Row	1847
J. Chidley	123 Aldersgate St	*c.* 1848

W. M. Clarke (Printing Office)	8 Warwick Sq.	1834–5
,,	16–17 Warwick Lane, Paternoster Row	1838–51
(Printing Office)	10 Red Lion Ct, Fleet St	1848
J. Cleave	1 Shoe Lane, Fleet St	1832–45
,,	61 Wardour St, Strand	1832
,,	1 Pearl Row, Blackfriars St	1835
J. Clements	21–2 Little Pulteney St	1832–51
J. Crisp	Ivy Lane, Paternoster Row	1833
J. Cochrane	108 Strand	1840–44
Samuel Y. Collins	113 Fleet St	1850–51
B. D. Cousins	18 Duke St, Lincoln's Inn Fields	1832–48
G. Cowie	312 Strand	1832–45
G. Cowie	Stone Cutter St	1838
J. Cumberland	Cumberland Terr, Camden Town	1834
John Cunningham	Peterboro' Ct, Fleet St	1839
,,	Crown Ct, Fleet St	1839–44
J. W. Cuthbert & Co.	40 Chichester Place, King's Cross	1841
J. Day	Needsby Ct, Fashion St, Spitalfields	1844
J. Dicks	7 Wellington St, Strand	1845–68
Edwin Dipple	42 Holywell St, Strand	1844–51
G. Drake	12 Houghton St, Clare Market	1836
W. Dugdale	3 Wych St	1832–40?
,,	37 Holywell St	1841–50
,,	16 Holywell St	1851
J. Duncombe	1 Vinegar Yd, Brydges St, Covent Gdn	1822–3
,,	19 Little Queen St	1832–42?
,,	Middle Row, Holborn	1842–8?
G. Edwards	12 Russell Ct, Brydges St	1849–50
E. Elliott	14 Holywell St	1841–50?
Mrs Mary Elliott (widow?)	14 Holywell St	1851
William H. Elliott	475 Oxford St	1851
W. Emans	43 Aldersgate St	1841–8?
(probably only 6d. and 1s. parts)	10 Red Lion St	1848
Ebenezer Farringdon	16 Bath St, Newgate St	1845–51
T. Farris	340 Strand	1848
A. Forrester	310 Strand	1838
Foster and Hextall	268 Strand	1838–9
S. Gilbert	26 Paternoster Row	1841
F. Glover	Water Lane, Fleet St	1839
G. Goodger	169 Strand	1831
S. Graves	30 Curtain Rd	1839
R. Groombridge	Paternoster Row	1836–48
S. Haddon	18 Pickett St, Strand	1843
W. Hall	18 Upper Cleveland St, New Rd	1843

J. Haydon	30 Curtain Rd, Shoreditch	1839
George Henderson	2 Old Bailey, Ludgate Hill	1839–41
H. Hetherington	13 Kingsgate St, Holborn	1831–7?
,,	126 Strand	1838–41
,,	13 Wine Office Ct	1841–9
F. Hextall	Catherine Ct, Strand	1839–41
,,	83 Farringdon St	1841
,,	12 Wellington St, Strand	1841
,,	11½ Catherine St, Strand	1842
,,	113a Strand	1843
(Joined with Wall, 1842) Hextall & Wall	11½ Catherine St, Strand	1842–5
Orlando Hodgeson	111 Fleet St	1841
Hodgeson & Co. (ibid. ?)	10 Newgate St	1850
T. L. Holt	266 Strand	1837?–9
W. Howden	194 Strand	1832
J. Hucklebridge	2 Charles St, Hatton Gdn	c. 1840
Joseph Last	113 Strand	1833
F. Lawrence	113 Strand	1851
H. Lea	22 Warwick St	1851
J. Limbird	143 Strand	1822–59
Edward Lloyd	8 Hayes Ct, Greek St, Soho	1832–5?
Edward Lloyd	44 Wych St	1835–8?
,,	62 Broad St	1840–41
,,	30 Curtain Rd, Shoreditch	1840–41
(Lloyd sometimes	44 Holywell St, High St, Shoreditch	1840–42
published from more	231 High St, Shoreditch	1841–2
than one address at	12 Salisbury Sq.	1842–52?
one time)	12 Salisbury Sq. (Office of *Lloyd's Weekly Newspaper*)	1845
,,	12 Salisbury Sq. (Office of *Illustrated Editions of Standard Works*)	1846–7
J. Lofts	262 Strand	1838–50
Robert Macdonald	30 Gt Sutton St, Clerkenwell	1841
George Mansell	3 King St, Boro'	1838–51
,,	21 Warwick St, Paternoster Row	1851
Renton Nicholson	310 Strand	1841
Joseph Onwhyn	3–4 Catherine St, Strand	1830–51
A. Park	Leonard St, Finsbury	1842
J. Pattie	4 Brydges St, Strand	1834–40
T. Paine	12 Bride Lane, Fleet St	1840–41
,,	20 Holywell St, Strand	1842
George Peirce	310 Strand	1844–50
(*as* Peirce & Hyde)	310 Strand	1848
R. Percival	59 Fleet St	1832
George Purkess (Sen.)	61 Wardour St	1832–40?
,,	60 Dean St, Soho	1841
,,	60 Old Compton St, Soho	1842–58

G. W. M. Reynolds	7 Wellington St North, Strand	1851
John Robins	3 Bride St, Fleet St	1832
S. (or J?) Robins	17 Barbican	1836
John Robins	2 Tooks Ct, Chancery La.	1841
,,	57–8 Tooley St	1845
R. Seton	26 Brydges St, Covent Gdn	1830–32
Chas. Smith	6 Hart St, Mark La.	1836
H. Smith (agent for Dugdale?)	37 Holywell St	1840
B. Steill	20 Paternoster Row	1831–44
William Strange	49 Holywell St	1832
,,	21 Paternoster Row	1832–46
H. Such	177 Union St, Boro'	1842?
R. S. Swift	6 Little New St, Shoe La.	1850?
T. Tegg	73 (and 111) Cheapside	1822–50
R. Thompson	James St, Gray's Inn Rd	1841
J. Viar	Holywell St	1833
George Vickers	28 Holywell St	1841–8
,,	3 Catherine St, Strand	1846
Anne Vickers (widow)	28 Holywell St, Strand	1849–51
George Vickers (son)	28–9 Holywell St	1851
J. Watson	15 City Road, Finsbury	1835–40
W. Wakelin	1 Shoe La.	1836–7
T. White	59 Wych St, Strand	1841–2
W. J. White	79 Gt Queen St, Lincoln's Inn Fields	1844
John Williams	44 Paternoster Row	
,,	43 Aldersgate St	1839–48
Willoughby & Co.	22 Warwick La.	1838–50
W. Wynn	34 Holywell St, Strand	1850–51

Check-list of Penny-issue Novels

Partially Listed in or Omitted from Montague Summers's
Gothic Bibliography

Abbreviations used

A.	Information from advertisement: date not necessarily that of first publication. Advance announcements *not* made use of.	H.W.	Hextall and Wall, London.
		J.	Frank Jay, *Peeps into the Past*, London, 1918.
		Ja.	Collection of W. L. G. James.
Ap.	E. Appleyard, London.	L.	Edward Lloyd, London.
Be.	G. Berger, London.	La.	Collection of late A. W. Lawson.
Bod.	Bodleian Library, Oxford.		
B.M.	British Museum, London.	Li.	J. Limbird, London.
B.	N. Bruce, London	M.	G. Mansell, London.
B.W.	Bruce and Wyld, London.	Med.	Notes of late J. Medcraft in *Collector's Miscellany.*
C.	W. M. Clarke, London.		
Ca.	W. Caffyn, London.	N.N.	*Novel Newspaper.*
Cl.	J. Clements, London.	Ono.	Barry Ono Collection, British Museum, London.
Cle.	J. Cleave, London.		
Co.	B. D. Cousins, London	P.	George Peirce, London.
Cu.	John Cunningham, London.	Pa.	T. Paine, London.
D.	William Dugdale, London.	Pe.	Collection of F. Pettingell, Esq.
Di.	Edwin Dipple, London.		
Du.	John Duncombe, London	Pu.	G. Purkess, London.
F.H.	Foster and Hextall, London.	R.N.L.	*Romancist and Novelist's Library*
H.	Collection of J.V.B.S. Hunter, Esq.	Ro.	Collection of R. E. J. Rouse, Esq.
		S.	William Strange, London.
He.	F. Hextall, London.	V.	George Vickers, London.
Hex.	MS. notes of A. E. Hextall, Esq.	V.A.	Anne Vickers, London.
		W.	Willoughby and Co., London.
Ho.	T. L. Holt, London.	Wh.	T. White, London.

The works in the *Novel Newspaper* were 2d. a number: all other items listed came out in 1d. numbers unless stated otherwise.

I have omitted to list the 2d. issues of the *Romancist and Novelist's Library* as complete series of this are available in the Bodleian and British Museum Libraries. The main purpose of this check-list has been to supplement information ordinarily available.

Check List of Penny-issue Novels

Short Title	Author	Publisher	Date	Source of Information
Adventures of a Vagabond	Anon.	L.	1847	Hex.
Agnes Primrose	G. Dibdin Pitt	L.	1842	Ono.
Almira's Curse	T. P. Prest	L.	1842	Ono.
Angela the Orphan	Anon.	Paine	1840	La. Pe.
Arabian Nights' Entertainment	Anon. (from Transl. of M. Galland) 39 nos.	L.	1847	Ono.
Assassin of the Stone Cross	Anon.	L.	n.d.	Pe.
Banshee (short stories)	Anon.	Du.	c. 1845	A.
Barnaby Budge	'Bos'	L.	1841	W. Miller
Belisarius	Anon.	Li.	c. 1836	A.
Bellgrove Castle	Anon.	V.	c. 1842	Pe.
Ben Bolt	T. P. Prest	P.	c. 1842	Ono.
Bianca and the Magician	Anon.	Wh.	1840	L.
Black Forest	Anon.	Pa.	c. 1841	L.
Black Warrior	Anon.	H.	c. 1841	R. Brimmell
Black-eye'd Susan	E. F. Marriott	L.	1845	La.
Blind Beggar of Bethnal Green	Anon.	P.	c. 1846	L.
Blueskin's Life of Jack Sheppard	Anon.	Glover	1839	A.
Bravo of Venice	M. G. Lewis	Be.	1839	A.
Brigands and Banditti	Anon.	C?	1842	H.
British Logbook	Anon.	C.	1838	H.
"	"	Cle.	1839	A.
Cain	Lord Byron	Watson	1839	A.
Canterbury Tales	G. Chaucer	Cumberland	1834	A.
Castle	Anon.	S.	1841	M.
Castle Spectre	Anon.	He.	1841	M.
Castles of Athlin and Dunbayne	A. Radcliffe	Li.	c. 1836	A.
Castle Fiend	Anon.	L.	1847	B.M.
Catherine Hayes	S. Hunt	L.	1840	Ro.
Child of Fate	Anon.	Wh.	c. 1841	A.
Chronicles of the Sea	Anon.	C.	1838	Pe.
Christmas Log (2/6d.)	Anon.	L.	1846	Ono.
Clarence	Anon.	F.H.	1838-9	Hex.

Short Title	Author	Publisher	Date	Source of Information
Claude Duval	Anon.	Wh.	c. 1841	A.
Cleveland	W. T. Haley	Co.	1841	A.
Coarston the Pirate	W. T. Haley	Cle.	c. 1841	A.
Cockney Tales	R. Nicholson	C.	1838	Ono.
Constance	Anon.	Pu.	1848	Ono.
Corsican Brothers	T. Frost	Pu.	c. 1852	Ono.
Cottage Girl	E. Bennett	W. Wynn	1850	La.
Curate's Daughters	H. M. Jones	L.	1853	Ono.
De Lisle	Anon.	Ca.	c. 1849	La.
Demon Dwarf	Anon.	Brittain	1841	A.
Demon Huntsman	Anon.	C.	c. 1848	La.
Demon of Sicily	E. Montague	D.	1841	Pe.
Destroyer (from Southey's *Thalaba the Destroyer*)	'Thomas Moore'	Hetherington	1842	B.M.
Deveril the Cracksman	'Old Bailey Barrister'	C.	(c. 1842)	La.
Doings in London	G. Smeeton	Hodson	1850	Ono.
Don Sebastian	A. M. Porter	Cu. (N.N.)	1839	Pe.
Don Juan	Lord Byron	Co.	1846	A.
Doomed Ship	W. Hurton	W.	c. 1849?	Pe.
Dora Livingstone	G. Lippard	Pu., L.	c. 1850?	Ono.
Double Man	Anon.	Lofts	c. 1840?	Ono.
Dramatic Tales (over 40 personally examined)		Du.	c. 1843–6	Pe.
Dream of Life	Anon. (*not* E. C. Grey)	L.	1843	Ono.
Eccentric Tales	A. Crowquill	Du.	c. 1843	A.
Emma Mayfield	T. Frost	Caffyn	1848	La.
Emmeline, the Orphan of the Castle	C. Smith	Lofts	c. 1850	La.
Evelina	T. P. Prest	L.	1842	Ono.
Farmer of Inglewood Forest	E. Helme	Li.	c. 1836	A.
Family Secrets	J. M. Rymer	L.	1846	Ono.
Fate of Gaspar	Anon.	S.	1842	La.
Flying Dutchman	Anon.	He.	1841?	Hex.
Gambler's Wife	Anon.	L.	c. 1846	Ono.
Gentleman Jack	Anon.	L.	1848–52	Ono.
George Barnwell) (Life of George Barnwell)	E. L. Blanchard	Wh.	c. 1841	Ono.

Short Title	Author	Publisher	Date	Source of Information
George Barnwell, The City Apprentice (another edition, no title-page).				Ono.
Gilbert Copley	T. P. Prest	L.	1844	Ono.
Gipsy Sibyl	Anon.	Cle.	1841	La.
Green Bushes	Anon.	L.	1847	Ono.
			1851	La.
Grimm's Goblins	Anon.	V.	n.d.	Ono.
Hampstead Murder	Anon.	L.	1845	Ono.
Hangman's Daughter	E. P. Hingston	L.	1851	B.M.
Heiress (Brandon Castle)	Anon.	A. Park	1842	Ro.
Helen Porter	E. P. Hingston	L.	1847	B.M.
History and Lives of the Most Notorious Highwaymen . . .		L.	1836–7	Ono.
Hungarian Brothers	A. M. Porter	Ho. (N.N.)	1839	Pe.
Illustrated Garden of Romance (short stories)		W. Hall	1843	Ono.
Illustrated London Life	R. Nicholson	Nicholson	1843	Hex.
I'm Afloat, I'm Afloat	Anon.	L.	1847	Ono.
Indian Chief	Anon.	H.W.	1843	Pe.
Life of Jack Rann	Anon.	Hodgeson & Co.	c. 1850?	Ono.
Jack Sheppard	'Barrister'	M.	1847	Ono.
History of Jack Sheppard	Founded on Ainsworth	John Williams	1840	Ono.
Life and Adventures of Jack Sheppard	Anon.	Pu.	c. 1849	Ono.
Life and Surprising Adventures of Jack Shepperd	'Obediah Throttle'	J. Caton	c. 1850?	La.
Life and Adventures of Jack Sheppard	Lincoln Fortescue	Jas. Cochrane	1845	Ono.
Eventful Life and Unparalleled Exploits of Jack Sheppard	Anon.	Wh.	1840	Ono.
Life of Jack Sheppard	Anon.	Glover	1840	Ono.
Jack Tench	Anon.	W. Brittain	1841	A.
Jane Shore	J. M. Rymer	L.	1846	Ono.

Short Title	Address	Publisher	Date	Source of Information
Jem Bunt	'Old Sailor'	W.	1835	La.
(1st ed., 39s. 6d. or 1s. nos., 2nd 35s. 1d. nos.)			1849	
Julia de Roubigné	H. Mackenzie	Hodgson	1841	La.
Kenilworth	W. Scott?	Caffyn	1847	Med.
Lady Godiva	Anon.	L.	1849	La.
Lady in Black	J. M. Rymer	L.	1847	Ono.
Lady Jane Grey	Anon.	F.H.	1840	Pe.
Library of Romance (some listed separately)		Cle.	1839–45	La.
Life in London	H. Thornley	Di.	1846	Ono.
Lloyd's Family Portfolio (illustrated tales)		L.	Lond. *c.* 1845	La.
Logan, the Negro Chief	C. Smith	Ho. (N.N.)	1844	A.
Louisa	C. Smith	Cu. (N.N.)	1840	Pe.
Love and Crime	Anon.	Pa.	1841	Pe.
Love Child	J. M. Rymer	L.	1847	Ono.
Lucy Neal	Anon.	L.	1847	Ono.
Luke Somerton	Anon.	L.	1845	Ono.
Mabel	Anon.	L.	1846	Ono.
			1851	Ono.
Magdalena	Anon.	Cle.	*c.* 1843	A.
Maid of the Village	Mrs Kentish	L.	1847	La.
Manfrone	A. Radcliffe	Cu. (N.N.)	1840	A.
Manuscripts from the Diary of a Physician	J. M. Rymer	L.	1844, Vol. 1, 1847; Vol. 2, 1848?; New Series.	Pe.
Marianne the Child of Charity	T. P. Prest	L.	1845	Ono.
Mariette	T. P. Prest	L.	1844	A.
Mary Bateman	Anon.	L.	1850	Ro.
Memoirs of Hariette Wilson	By herself	D.	*c.* 1840	La.
Memoirs of Serjeant Paul Swanston	By himself	Co.	*c.* 1840	Bod.
Mendicants of London	'One who has carried a wallet'	V.A.	1849	Ono.
Mildred Winnerley	E. P. Hingston	L.	1848	Ono.
Miser's Son	R. Bedingfield	R. Thompson	1844	Pe.

Short Title	Address	Publisher	Date	Source of Information
Moll Cutpurse	R. Bedingfield	S.	1846	Pe.
Monk	M. G. Lewis	D.	1841	A.
		L.	*c.* 1841	Pe.
		Pu.	*c.* 1848	Pe.
Murder Castle	Anon.	L.	1847	B.M.
Mysteries of Old Father Thames	T. Frost	Caffyn	1848	Ono.
Mysteries of the Madhouse	'Discharged Officer'	Chauntler	1847?	Ono.
Mysteries of Udolpho	A. Radcliffe	Li.	1836	La.
Mysterious Dagger	Anon.	He.	1840	Med.
Mysterious Freebooter	F. Lathom	W. J. White	1844	Pe.
Nell Gwynne	Anon.	Barth	*c.* 1849	Pe.
Life of . . . Nelson	Anon.	FH.	*c.* 1842	La.
Night Adventurer	'Author of Newgate'	L.	1846	Ono.
Nourjahad	F. Sheridan	Li.	1836	A.
Oath (13 nos. only seen)	Anon.	D.	*c.* 1849	Pe.
Obi	Anon.	L.	*c.* 1846	La.
Ocean Child	Anon.	L.	1846	Ono.
Old English Baron	C. Reeve	Li.	1836	A.
Old London Bridge	H. G. Rodwell	W.	*c.* 1848?	La.
Ordeal by Touch	Anon. (not E. C. Grey)	L.	1846	La.
Peer and the Beggar	Anon.	Wh.	*c.* 1840	Ono.
Percy Anecdotes	T. Percy	Cumberland	1834	A.
Peter Wilkins	R. Paltock	J. Limbird	1846	A.
Phoebe: or The Miller's Maid (Summers gives inaccurate title)	Prest?	L.	1842	Ono.
Pilgrims of the Thames	P. Egan Sen.	S.	1838	B.M.
Pirate Queen	Anon.	Pu., L.	*c.* 1848	Pe.
Poetical Works (2d. nos.)	Lord Byron	C.	1836	A.
Poor Little Jack	E. F. Marriott	Li.	1840	Pe.
Popular Stories about Genii, Fairies and Magicians	Anon.	(No title page)		Ono.
Posthumous Papers of the Cadger's Club	Anon.	L.	1838	Ono.
Pride of the Valley	H. M. Jones	Lea	1851?	La.

Short Title	Address	Publisher	Date	Source of Information
Queen Mab	P. B. Shelley	Watson	1839	A.
Queenhoo Hall	J. Strutt	Ho. (N.N.)	c. 1841	A.
Ranger of the Tomb	Wilhelmina Johnson	L.	1847	Ono.
Rankley Grange	Anon.	E. H. Bennett	c. 1850	Ono.
Recess	Sophia Lee	B. (N.N.)	c. 1841	A.
Red Cross Warrior	Anon.	H. W.	1843 (a reissue of *The Black Warrior*)	Pe.
The Rivals	J. M. Rymer	L.	1847	La.
Revenge	R. Bedingfield	B. Thompson	c. 1842	La.
Reward of Crime	Anon.	Wh.	1842	A.
Richard of England	T. Archer	He.	1842	B.M.
Robinson Crusoe	D. Defoe	Li.	c. 1836	A.
Robert of Artois	T. Archer	Farringdon	c. 1843	La.
Rochester Castle	G. Viner	H. Elliott	1851	La.
Roderick Dhu	T. Archer	He.	c. 1845	La.
Roderick Random	T. Smollett	Li.	c. 1836	A.
Romance of the Pyrenees	C. Smith	Ho. (N.N.)	c. 1840	A.
Royal Twins	T. P. Prest	Pu.	1848	Ono.
Saint Clair of the Isles	Mrs Helme	Li.	1836	A.
		Cu. (N.N.)	c. 1840	Pe.
Sam Hall the Burglar	Anon.	W. Barth	c. 1849	Pe.
Sea-fiend	G. D. Pitt	L.	1846	Ono.
Secrets of the Harem	Anon.	Office, 18 Pickett St	c. 1841	A.
Seduction	Anon.	L.	1846	Pe.
Seventy-Six	C. Smith	Cu. (N.N.)	c. 1840	A.
Life of Simon Smike, a Factory Lad	Anon.	Wh.	c. 1841	A.
Sir Walter Tyrrell	Thos. Wilson	Brittain	c. 1844	La.
Smuggler's Daughter (about Eugene Aram)	Anon.	J. Day	1844	La.
Solyman and Almena	J. Langhorne	Limbird	c. 1844	A.
Spanish Gipsy	Anon.	W. S. Johnson	1851?	Ono.
Stranger's Grave	H. Villiers	W. J. White	1842	Hex.
		P.	c. 1846	A.
Stuart Sharpe	Paul Eaton	Be.	1839	La.
Susan Hopley (6d. nos. ?)	Mrs Crowe	W. Tait	1848	La.
Tales of the Drama	Prest?	L.	c. 1837; a later series n.d.	Ono. Algar.

Short Title	Author	Publisher	Date	Source of Information
Tales of Travellers	Anon.	Clarke	1836–8	Pe.
Vicar of Wakefield	O. Goldsmith	Li.	*c.* 1836	A.
Victoria; or the Mysterious Stranger	Anon.	L.	1839	A.
Vileroy	Anon.	L.	*c.* 1850	Ono.
Vision of Judgement (v. Bibliog.)	Lord Byron	Wakelin	1836	A.
Waverley	Sir W. Scott	Edinburgh Robert Cadell	1842	H.
Wild Witch of the Heath	'Wizard'	Wh.	1841	Ro.
Will Watch	Anon.	C.	1841 ?	La.
Witches' Cliff	Anon.	H.W.	*c.* 1843	Ono.
Wolf of the Black Forest	J. W. James	L.	1850	Pe.
Wreck of the Heart	G. D. Pitt	L.	1842	Ono.

LIST B:

FRENCH WORKS IN TRANSLATION (EXCLUDING THOSE IN PERIODICALS) AND ATTRIBUTED AUTHORS

Short Title	Author	Publisher	Date	Source of Information
Arthur	E. Sue	Cle.	*c.* 1844	A.
"	E. Sue	C.	*c.* 1846	J.
Agib	Marie Aycard	P.	*c.* 1846	A.
Asmodeus	A. R. le Sage	S.	1840	Ja.
Attar-Gull	E. Sue	Ap.	1847	P.
Barber of Paris	C. P. de Kock	D.	1839	A.
Basque Smuggler	E. Lemoine	P.	1848	A.
Bastard of Mauleon	A. Dumas	P.	1848	La.
Belisarius	J. F. Marmontel	Cu. (N.N.)	*c.* 1841	La.
Black Mendicant	P. Féval	Pierce & Hyde	1848	Bod.
Brother Jacques	C. P. de Kock	H. Smith	1842	B.M.
Brother James	C. P. de Kock	D.	1842	A.
Brulart (Attar-Gull)	E. Sue	Co.	*c.* 1845	A.
Cartouche	A. L.	P.	*c.* 1848	A.
Celebrated Crimes	A. Dumas	P.	*c.* 1847	A.
Commander of Malta	E. Sue	Ap.	1847	Pe.
Constable of Bourbon	B. M. Royer	P.	*c.* 1848	A.
The Convent	M. Gonzales	Co.	1846	A.
Crime of Vengeance	F. Soulié	Co.	1846	A.
Cross Roads	J. Janin	C.	1841	La.

Short Title	Author	Publisher	Date	Source of Information
Curé Buonaparte	Marie Aycard	P.	*c.* 1845	A.
Devil on Two Sticks	A. R. Le Sage	S.	1839	Ja.
Dream of Love	F. Soulié	Co.	1846	A.
Fascination	?	B.W. (N.N.)	1846	H.
Female Bluebeard	E. Sue	S.	1845	L.
Ferragus	H. de Balzac	D.	1842	A.
The Frozen Nose	A. Dumas (attrib.)	P.	*c.* 1846	A.
Galley Slave	A. Dumas	P.	*c.* 1848	A.
Georgette	G. Sand	D.	1842	A.
Gil Blas	A. R. Le Sage	S.	1840	A.
Godolphin the Arabian	E. Sue	B.W.	1846	J.
Gustavus	P. de Kock	D.	1839	A.
Hans of Iceland	V. Hugo	P.	*c.* 1846	A.
Henry of Montmerency	'W.N.'	P.	*c.* 1848	A.
Indiana	G. Sand	D.	*c.* 1842	A.
Jane of Naples	Anon.	P.	*c.* 1848	A.
Kardiki	E. Sue	B.W.	1846	H.
La Esmeralda	V. Hugo	F.H.	1838–9	A.
,,	V. Hugo	P.	*c.* 1846	Ja.
La Marana	H. de Balzac	Co.	*c.* 1842	Bod.
,,	H. de Balzac	Cl.	*c.* 1842	Bod.
Labyrinth of Love	E. Sue	H. Lofts	*c.* 1849	L.
Library of French Romance	ed. J. C. James	B.W.	1846	B.M.
Life in Paris	E. F. Vidocq	Ap.	1848	Ono.
Loves of Paris	P. Féval	V.	1846	La.
Lucretia Borgia	V. Hugo	Co.	1842	A.
Marie Antoinette	A. Dumas	P.	*c.* 1845	L.
Margaret of Navarre	A. Dumas	P.	*c.* 1848	A.
Martin the Foundling	E. Sue	V.	1847	A., J.
,,	E. Sue	Co.	1846	A.
Mary Stuart	A. Dumas	P.	*c.* 1847	A.
Matilda	E. Sue	Co.	1846	A.
,,	E. Sue	C.	*c.* 1846	J.
Masaniello	E. Scribe	P.	*c.* 1845	A.
Memoirs of a Physician	A. Dumas	Ap.	1849	L.
Midnight Mass	'W.N.'	P.	*c.* 1846	A.
Midnight Reckoning	P. Féval	P.	1846	L.
Mirror of French Romance	(entered separately)	P.	*c.* 1844–8	La.

Short Title	Author	Publisher	Date	Source of Information
Moustache	P. de Kock	H. Smith = D.	*c.* 1840	La.
	P. de Kock	F.H.	1840	B.M.
My Wife's Child	P. de Kock	D.	1839	A.
Mysteries of Paris	E. Sue	V.	1845	A.
,,	E. Sue	Ap.	1845	A., J.
,,	E. Sue	C.	1845	B.M.
Mysteries of the Heaths	F. Soulié	B.W.	1845	Ja.
Mysterious Mansion	H. de Balzac	P.	*c.* 1846	A.
Noble Rival	V. Hugo	P.	*c.* 1848	A.
Paul and Virginia	B. de St Pierre	B.W. (N.N.)	1842	A.
Paula Monti	E. Sue	Ap.	1847	Pe.
,,	E. Sue	Cle.	*c.* 1845	A.
Pearl Fishers of St Domingo	E. Gonzales	P.	*c.* 1848	A.
Piquillo Alliago	E. Scribe	P.	*c.* 1848	A.
Popery	P. Féval	P.	*c.* 1845	B.M.
Portrait	'Aiph. Brot.'?	P.	*c.* 1846	A.
Prisoner of If	A. Dumas	P.	*c.* 1847	La.
Prosper Chavigni	J. Janin	Cl.	*c.* 1842	La.
Road to Marriage	Amédée Aycard	P.	*c.* 1846	A.
Salamander	E. Sue	B.W.	1845	A.
Salamander	E. Sue	Cle.	*c.* 1844	A.
Seven Capital Sins	E. Sue	Ap.	1847	La.
She-Tiger of Paris	F. Soulié	J. Sinnett	*c.* 1850	La.
Sicilian Bandit	A. Dumas	P.	*c.* 1848	A.
Sin of M. Antoine	G. Sand	Ap.	*c.* 1847	La.
Smuggler Without Knowing It	A. Dumas	P.	*c.* 1847	A.
Temptation	E. Sue	V.	1845	La.
Theresa Dunover	E. Sue	Cle.	1845	La.
Thérèse	E. Sue	V.	1845	La.
Three Musketeers	A. Dumas	V.	1846	La.
Touroulou	P. de Kock	D.	*c.* 1842	A.
Victims of Etiquette	'W.N.'	P.	*c.* 1848	A.
Vidocq (Life and Adventures of Vidocq, written by himself)		Chidley	*c.* 1848	La.
Wandering Jew	E. Sue	Ap.	1845	La.
,, (Abbrev.)	E. Sue	L.	1845	Ono.
,,	E. Sue	J. S. Pratt	1845	A.
,,	E. Sue	Cle.	1844–5	A.
,,	E. Sue	B.W.	1845	A.
,, (1½d. pts.)	E. Sue	C.	*c.* 1846	B.M.

LIST C: AMERICAN WORKS IN ENGLISH EDITIONS

Short Title	Author	Publisher	Date	Source of Information
Wandering Jew	E. Sue	The Mirror, n.s. VI	(1844)	B.M.
,,	E. Sue	The Mirror, n.s. VII	(1845)	B.M.
,,	E. Sue	New Parley Library I	(1844)	La.
,,	E. Sue	New Parley Library II	(1845)	La.
,,	E. Sue	D.	1844–5	A.
Key to . . . 'Wandering Jew'	Anon.	Ap.	c. 1844	A.A.
Parody of 'The Wandering Jew'	Charles Philipon, Louis Huart	Ap.	c. 1846	A.A.
Well of Murder	Vincompte D'Arlingcourt?	P.	c. 1846	A.
Widow's Walk	C. Rabou	Ap.	c. 1848	La.

GERMAN WORKS IN TRANSLATION

Short Title	Author	Publisher	Date	Source of Information
Undine	De la Motte Fouqué (tr. T. Tracy)	Cu. (N.N.)	1840	La.
Abdallah the Moor	R. M. Bird	Cu. (N.N.)	1839	A.
,,	R. M. Bird	L.	c. 1849	Ono.
Black Vulture	Anon.	L.	c. 1848	La.
Captain Kyd	J. H. Ingraham	Cu. (N.N.)	1839	Pe.
,,	J. H. Ingraham	L.	c. 1846	H.
Corsair	Harry Hazel (J. Jones)	L.	c. 1846	Ono.
Cruiser	J. H. Ingraham	L?	c. 1847?	La.
Diary of a Hackney Coachman	J. H. Ingraham	L?	c. 1847?	La.
Freebooters	J. H. Ingraham	P.	1848?	La.
Governess	J. F. Cooper	S.	1845	A.
Green Mountain Boy	D. P. Thompson	Ho. (N.N.)	1840	A.
Hawks of Hawks Hollow	R. M. Bird	Cu. (N.N.)	1838	A.
Horseshoe Robinson	J. P. Kennedy	Cu. (N.N.)	1838	Pe.
Imagination	J. F. Cooper	Cl.	1841	A.
Infidel's Doom	R. M. Bird	Cu. (N.N.)	c. 1840	A.

Short Title	Author	Publisher	Date	Source of Information
King of the Sea	E. Z. C. Judson	P.	1848	Ono.
King's Daughter	W. Hurton	P.	1847	La.
Last of the Mohicans	J. F. Cooper	F.H.	1838	A.
"	J. F. Cooper	Cu. (N.N.)	1839	Pe.
Linwoods	Mrs C. M. Sedgwick	Cu. (N.N.)	c. 1840	A.
Lionel Lincoln	J. F. Cooper	Ho. (N.N.)	c. 1840	A.
"	J. F. Cooper	F.H.	1838	Pe.
Morris Graeme	J. H. Ingraham	P.	c. 1848	La.
New Home, – Who'll Follow?	C. M. Kirkland	Cu. (N.N.)	c. 1840	A.
Nick of the Woods	R. M. Bird	Cu. (N.N.)	1838	Pe.
Ormond	C. Brockden Brown	Cu. (N.N.)	c. 1839	A.
Peter Pilgrim	R. M. Bird	Cu. (N.N.)	1838	Pe.
Pilot	J. F. Cooper	Ho. (N.N.)	c. 1840	Pe.
"	J. F. Cooper	He.	1839	B.M.
Pioneers	J. F. Cooper	Cu. (N.N.)	1839	Pe.
Pirate; or Lafitte	J. H. Ingraham	Cu. (N.N.)	1839	Pe.
Pirate's Doom	'Trysail'	H.W.	1843	Hex.
Poor Mary	Anon.	L.	c. 1846	La.
Prairie	J. F. Cooper	Cu. (N.N.)	1838	A.
Professor	J. H. Ingraham	Cu. (N.N.)	1839	A.
Red Rover	J. F. Cooper	Cu. (N.N.)	1839	Pe.
Rob of the Bowl	J. P. Kennedy	Cu. (N.N.)	1839	Pe.
Robin Day	R. M. Bird	Cu. (N.N.)	1839	A.
Rosebud	Lieutenant Murray	Pu.	1847	La.
Slave King	J. H. Ingraham	Ap.	c. 1845	La.
Spy	J. F. Cooper	Ho. (N.N.,	1839	Pe.
Unhappy Bride	Anon.	L.	c. 1846	La.
Water Witch	J. F. Cooper	Cu.	1839	Pe.
Wieland	C. Brockden Brown	Cu. (N.N.)	c. 1840	A.

Supplementary Notes

Page

3. Sunday Schools: F. Hill, *National Education*, 1836, p. 101; E. G. E. L. Bulwer-Lytton, *England and the English*, 1833, I, p. 398.

4. Manchester schools: T. S. Ashton, *Economic and Social Investigations in Manchester*, 1934. Adult Education: J. W. Hudson, *A History of Adult Education*, 1851, pp. 2–3, 23.

5. Parish libraries: *P.P.L.*, sec. 2052.

8. Coffee houses: 'London Coffee Houses', Anon., *Tegg's Magazine*, I, 1843, pp. 61 f.

8. Public readings of newspapers: R. Altick, *English Common Reader*, Chicago, 1957, p. 330.

12. Routledge: F. A. Mumby, *The House of Routledge (1834–1934)*, pp. 25 ff. et passim.

12. Limbird: 'The Pioneer of Cheap Literature', Anon., *Bookseller*, 1859, p. 1326.

19. Founding a periodical cheaply: *Mr Punch*, Anon., 1870, pp. 38 f.; J. F. Wilson, *A Few Personal Recollections*, 1896, p. 24.

21. Cheap periodicals fail: *Christian Reformer*, I, 1832, p. 310.

22–3. J. S. Pratt, catalogue: bound in B.M. copy of J. H. Ingraham, *Captain Kyd*, 1846. Abel Heywood: G. B. Heywood, *Abel Heywood*, Manchester, 1932; *Clever Boys of Our Time*, J. Johnson, 1893; Holyoake, p. 102; W. J. Linton, *Memories*, 1895, p. 27; *I.L.N.*, 26 August 1893, p. 246; 'Alderman Heywood', *Manchester Faces and Places* (various), 1890, pp. 121–4.

27–8. Other novel series include: *The Library of Foreign Romance*, 1846–?; W. Strange's *Illustrated Standard Works*, 1841–?; *The Humorist; and Entertaining Companion*, 1839–?; *Penny Novelist and Library of Romance*, *c*. 1845–?.

28. Edward Lloyd: J. Hatton, *Journalistic London*, 1882, pp. 188 f.; Wilson, pp. 35 f.; 'The Founder of Lloyd's', *Lloyd's Weekly News*, 30 November 1902, p. 20; 'Edward Lloyd', *Graphic*, XLI, 1890, p. 444; T. H. S. Escott, *Masters of British Journalism*, 1911, p. 279; J. Medcraft, *A Bibliography of Bloods*, Dundee, privately printed, 1945, passim; Boase; *D.N.B.*

35–6. Printing costs: particular mention should be made of Cowie's *Printer's Pocket Book*, 1833/4, 1836/7, and G. P. Harrison, 'Cheap Literature Past and Present', *Companion to the British Almanack*, 1873, pp. 60 f.

37 f. Publishing periodical fiction: Frost, *Reminiscences*, pp. 31, 49 f.; T. Catling, *My Life's Pilgrimage*, 1911, pp. 39 f.; W. Tinsley, *Random Recollections*, 1900, II, 179–80; Harrison, p. 71.

38. T. P. Prest: *Register of Deaths* (S.H.), June 1859, col. 116.

40. H. Ingram: Boase; Bourne, p. 119.

41. Lloyd's Illustrated London News: J. Hatton, *Journalistic London*, 1882, pp. 188–94; W. Jerrold, *Douglas Jerrold*, 1915, p. 579.

41. J. M. Rymer: A. Johanssen, *House of Beadle and Adams*, Oklahoma 1950, II, pp. 250–55; F. Jay, *Peeps into the Past*, 1918, p. 21; Catling, *Pilgrimage*, pp. 38 f.; Rymer, 'Early Recollections', *Scrapbooks*, II, p. 14; Scottish Record Society, *Register of Marriages, Edinburgh 1751–1800*, Edinburgh, 1922, p. 685; *Index of Patentees*, P.R.O., 1846, p. 496; Rymer, *Varney*, p. 315 ff.; Rymer, 'Popular Writing', *Queen's Magazine*, I, 1842, pp. 99 f.; *Principal Probate Register* (S.H.), 1884, p. 734.

44. Family reading: E. E. Kellett in *Early Victorian England*, 1934, I, pp. 49 f.

45–6. G. W. M. Reynolds: J. J. Wilson, 'Old Penny Romances', *Bootle Times*, 28 January 1916, p. 2; J. V. B. Stewart Hunter, 'Reynolds', *Book Handbook*, IV, 1947, pp. 225 f.; Montague Summers, *Gothic Bibliography*, 1940, pp. 146–59; *Bookseller*, July 1868, p. 447; ibid., July 1879, pp. 660 f.; *L.J.*, II, 1845, p. 191; *N. & Q.*, 12th Ser., X, 1922, p. 333; Blanchard, *Life*, pp. 55, 487; material in archives of *Sunday Citizen*; information from A. Reynolds, Esq.; Boase; *D.N.B.*

47. J. F. Smith: p. 93 n.

49. Surveys of lower-class literature, *c.* 1850, include: 'Literature of the Lower Orders', *Daily News*, 29 October, 7 November, 9 November, 1847; F. Mayne, *Perilous Nature of the Penny Press*, 1850, 'Labour and the Poor', *Morning Chronicle*, 5 November 1849, p. 5; 'The Public Press', *Churchman's Monthly Penny Magazine*, I, 1846, pp. 57–8; 'A Letter', 'Penny Press', *Englishwoman's Magazine* n.s. V, 1850, pp. 619 ff., 721 ff.; T. C. Worsley, *Juvenile Depravity*, 1850, pp. 113 ff.; H. Dunckley, *The Glory and Shame of Britain*, 1851; pp. 5 f.; P.P., *Stamp Duties*, 1850 (249), passim; *Ragged School Magazine*, II, 1850, pp. 193 ff.

51. Periodicals publishing quotations for advertisement: W. O. Oliphant, *William Blackwood and Sons*, Edinburgh, 1897, I, p. 502.

52. Dickens plagiarisms: (1) *Penny Pickwick*: E. T. Jaques, *Dickens in Chancery*, 1914, pp. 40 ff.; 'Dickens v. Berger', *Times*, 12 January, 1844, pp. 6 f.; 'Founder of Lloyd's', *Lloyd's News*, 30 November 1902, p. 8; (2) 'A Christmas Ghost Story': Jaques, passim; F. G. Kitton, *Dickensiana*, 1886, p. xii; *Chancery Affidavits*, P.R.O., 9, 10, 11 January 1844, press-marks C. 31/666/7.7, 13.14, 15.14, 20.19, 9.9, 9.8, 6.7, 8.8; J. Forster, *Life of Dickens*, 1927, p. 291.

54. Dickens and the Drama: E. R. Davis, 'Dickens and the Evolution of Caricature', *P.M.L.A.*, LV, 1940, p. 231; S. J. A. Fitzgerald, *Dickens and the Drama*, 1910, pp. 76 ff.; R. C. Churchill, '*Dickens, Drama and Tradition*', *Scrutiny*, X, 1942, pp. 358 ff.; *The Origin of Sam Weller* (Anon.) 1883.

55. 'Pickwick Club', *The Town*, I, 1837, p. 117.

55. 'Bos': A. de Ternant, *N. & Q.*, 12th Ser., X, 1922, p. 373 (completely unreliable); J. F. Dexter, *Dickens Momento*, 1855, p. 19; Prest is traditionally the author.

59. Pickwick Abroad: identical editions, save for title-page, by Sherwood and Co., 1839; Gilbert and Piper, 1839; T. Tegg, 1839; W. Emans, 1842. H. G. Bohn reissued it, 1864.

87. Thalaba (drama): J. Fitzball, *Thirty-five Years*, 1859, p. 81.

89. Paradise Lost, Demon of Sicily: v., e.g. *D.S.*, p. 80, *P.L.*, I, l. 215, *D.S.*, p. 114, and Milton's Satan; *D.S.*, p. 151 and Milton's cosmology.

102. Scott and the lower classes: libraries, *S.S.L.*, I, 1838, p. 485; Cooper, *Life*, p. 65; periodicals, e.g. *Olio*, V, 1829, p. 185; stage: Fitzball, *Thirty-five Years*, p. 92; H. A. White, *Scott's Novels on the Stage*, Yale, 1927, passim; lower-class criticism, *Cleave's Penny Gazette*, I, 28 July, 4 August 1838.

109. J. F. Smith: *Q.R.*, clxxi, 1890, p. 162; *Cassell's Family Paper*, II, 1858, p. 385; *Speaker*, I, 1890, pp. 254 ff.; *Saturday Rev.*, LXII, 1886, pp. 659 f.; *Macmillan's Mag.*, LXXX, 1866, pp. 96 f.; Jay, *Peeps*, 1919, pp. 8 f.; *N. & Q.*, 7 Ser.; v, 1900, pp. 277, 459; vi, 1900, pp. 14, 75; 11th, Ser.; vii, 1913, pp. 221, 276; vii, 1913, pp. 121, 142; x, 1914, pp. 102, 183, 223, 262, 292, 301; 12th. Ser., i, 1916, pp. 156, 159; Boase.

124. Gypsies: A. Somerville, *Autobiography*, pp. 55 f.; Frost, *Emma Mayfield*, 1848, pp. 1, 7; Susannah Reynolds, *Gretna Green*, 1847, p. 26; T. Archer, *Roderick Dhu*, 1843, p. 466.

139. Religious tracts: C. Williams, *George Mogridge*, 1856, p. 279; W. K. Lowther Clarke, *History of the S.P.C.K.*, 1959, p. 187.

144. Tracts 'entertaining': *Wesleyan Methodist Tract Soc. Minutes*, Feb. 1832; *S.P.C.K.* Ms. Minutes, XL, 1834, p. 485; *Friends Tract Assn. Rep.*, 1832, p. 1.

152. American humorous articles in cheap periodicals: 'An American Hotel Dinner', *Lloyd's Weekly Volume*, I, 1845, p. 53; W. Irving, 'The Broken Heart', *L.J.*, XI, 1850, p. 93; 'Sam Slick', aphorism, *L.J.*, I, 1845, p. 349.

159. English emigration to France, 1816: M. Moraud, 'French Drama in England', *Rice Inst. Pamph.*, XV, 1928, p. 113.

Anglo-French radical contacts: *Adresses Amicales du Peuple Anglais*, ed. E. Burritt, Paris, 1848; R. S. Gammage, *History of the Chartist Movement*, Newcastle, 1894, p. 293.

161. A. Dumas *père*, cheap versions in England: see Bibliography; Appendix III (b), under *Bastard, Celebrated Crimes, Frozen Nose, Galley*

Slave, Marie Antoinette, Margaret, Mary Stewart, Memoirs, Prisoners, Sicilian, Smuggler, Three Musketeers.

V. Hugo: v. 'Bibliography': Appendix III (b), under *Hans, La Esmeralda, Lucretia, Noble Rival, Pascal Bruno.*

The Family Herald (1846–9) also published several novels by Hugo and Dumas.

163. *The Mysteries of Paris* and *Life in London*: see N. Atkinson, *Eugène Sue et le Roman-feuilleton*, Nemours, 1929, p. 122.

170. Theatrical periodicals in Birmingham: As Briggs, 'Press and Public in Nineteenth Century Birmingham', *Dugdale Society Occasional Papers*, 1950, pp. 21 f.

172. Pixerécourt: A. Lacey, *Pixerécourt and the French Romantic Drama*, Toronto, 1929.

182. Jack Sheppard in literature: see 'Sheppard' in 'Bibliography'.

Bibliographies

BIBLIOGRAPHY OF SOURCES USED

1. LIBRARIES AND PRIVATE COLLECTIONS

A. Algar Esq. (deceased) – private collection.

Bodleian Library, Oxford.

British Museum Library and Students' Room, London.

Cambridge University Library.

Dickens House Library, London.

Epworth Press Archives, City Road, London.

Friends House Library, Marylebone Road, London.

J. V. B. Stewart Hunter Esq. – private collection.

A. W. Lawson, Esq. (deceased) – private collection. (This collection has now been dispersed: the most important works are in the Library of the University of California.)

London University Library – Goldsmith Collection.

Manchester Public Library.

Nottingham University Library – Collection of Broadsheets.

F. Pettingell Esq. – private collection.

Sunday Citizen Archives, London.

Rochester Public Library – Fitzgerald Collection.

Public Record Office, London.

St Bride's Library, London.

Sheffield Public Library – Ebenezer Elliott Collection.

S.P.C.K. Archives, S.P.C.K. House, London.

Somerset House, London – Register of Deaths, Principal Probate Register.

University College Library, London – S.D.U.K. Collection.

Victoria and Albert Museum, London – Forster Collection.

2. MANUSCRIPTS AND TYPESCRIPTS

Affidavits, Dickens v. Lee v. Haddock v. Haddock v. Hewitt (P.R.O., v. 'Supplementary Notes' to p. 47).

Dalziel, M., *A Study of Popular Fiction, 1840–60, and the Moral Attitudes Reflected in It* (D. Phil. thesis, English, Oxford University, 1952. Bodleian Library pressmark MS. Phil. d. 1181).

Elliott, Ebenezer, *Autobiography* (holograph manuscript, Sheffield Public Library, pressmark B. El. 58 SF.).

Grobel, Monica, *The Society for the Diffusion of Useful Knowledge 1826–46* (M.A. thesis, History, University of London, 1933. Senate House Library).

Hextall, A. E. *Catalogue of Collection with Notes* (manuscript notebook).

Home Office Reports, Census of London, 1851 (P.R.O., pressmark H.O. 107.1511/2/4; (7); H.O. 107.1512/1/6).

James, W. L. G., *Catalogue of the Barry Ono Collection* (Cards, 1958) (The collection has now been recatalogued).

Place, F., *Place Papers* (B.M., pressmark Place Add. MSS. 27, 289; 27, 791; 27, 796; 27, 825).

Principal Probate Register, 1884, (S.H.).

Register of Deaths, 1859 (S.H.).

Register of Patentees, 1846 (P.R.O.).

Rymer, J. M., personal collection of contributions to periodicals (scrapbook, two volumes, in possession of W. L. G. James).

S.D.U.K. Papers (University College Library, separate uncatalogued collection).

S.P.C.K. Minutes, 1829–50 (bound MS. volumes, S.P.C.K. House, London). *Wesleyan Methodist Tract Society Minutes*, 1822–50 (Bound MSS., Epworth Press Library, London).

3. PARLIAMENTARY PAPERS

Select Committee Reports –

into the Sale of Beer	1833 (416) xv
on Laws affecting Dramatic Literature	1831–2 (679) vii
on the State of Education in England and Wales	1834 (572) vii
on Education in England and Wales	1835 (465) vii
on Fourdrinier's Patent	1837 (351) xx
on Import Duties	1840 (601) v
on Mr Koop's Invention for Remaking Paper	1801 (55) iii
on Public Libraries	1849 (548) xvii
"	1850 (655) xviii
on Stamp Duties	1851 (558) xvii

4. PRIMARY SOURCES, COMPRISING: AUTOBIOGRAPHIES, FICTION, PERIODICALS, POETRY, TRACTS

(In giving dates of penny-issue fiction, the year of the *completion* is given. Penny-issue novels are marked 'P', other periodical literature, 'Per'.)

Actors by Daylight, 1838, Per.
Actors by Gaslight, 1838, Per.
Adeline; or, the Grave of the Forsaken, 1842, anon., P.
Ainsworth, W. H., *Jack Sheppard*, 1839.
    Old St Paul's, 1841.
    Rookwood, 1834.
    The Tower of London, 1840.
'An American Hotel Dinner', *Lloyd's Weekly Volume*, I, 1845, p. 53.
American Broad Grins, 1838, various.
Angela the Orphan, 1841, anon., P.
Anglo-Saxon Chronicle, ed. A. Gurney, 1819.
Anne of Swansea, *Conviction*, 1814.
Archer, T., *Richard Cœur de Lion*, 1842, P.
    Robert of Artois, c. 1845, P.
    Roderick Dhu, 1843, P.
Austen, Jane, *Northanger Abbey*, 1818.
Balzac, Honoré de, *La Marana*, 1842, P.
Bamford S., *Passages in the Life of a Radical*, ed. H. Dunckley, 1893.
Baptist Tract Magazine, 1835–7.
Barnett, M., *The Yankee Pedlar*, 1836.
'Barrister of the Middle Temple', *Jack Sheppard; or, Crime in the Last Century*, 1837, P.
Bell's Life in London, 1822–36, Per.
Bell's Penny Dispatch and Newspaper of Romance, 1841, Per.
Bertram, James, *Glimpses of Real Life*, Edinb., 1864.
    Some Memories, 1893.
Bianca and the Magician, 1841, anon. ,P.
Bird, R. M., *Abdallah the Moor*, 1837, P.
    Nick of the Woods, 1838, P.
    Peter Pilgrim, 1838, P.
Blanchard, Edward Litt Leman, *Life and Reminiscences*, ed. C. Scott and G. Howard, 1891.
    Life of George Barnwell, 1841, P.
    The Mysteries of London, 4th. Ser. 1848, P.
The Blind Beggar of Bethnal Green, 1848, anon., P.
The Blue Dwarf, c. 1870, anon., P.
Blueskin, c. 1866–7, anon., P.
'The Bohemian Gardener', anon., *Penny Novelist*, I, 1832, pp. 30, 35.

Borrow, G., *Zincali; an Account of the Gipsies of Spain*, 1841.

'Bos' (pseud.), *Master Humphries' Clock* [*sic*.], 1840, P.

'Bos' (pseud. – another writer – T. P. Prest ?)
  Nicholas Nicklebery, 1837, P.
  Oliver Twiss, 1838–9, P.
  Pickwick in America! 1840, P.
  Posthumous Notes of the Pickwick Club (*The Penny Pickwick*), 1837, P.
  The Sketch Book by 'Bos', 1837, P.

'Brush' (pseud.), *Sketches of Characters, from Master Humphrey's Clock*, *c.* 1840.

Buckstone, E. B., *Luke the Labourer*, Adelphi, 1826.

Bulwer-Lytton, E. G. E. L. *Paul Clifford*, 1830.

Burger (tr. Sir W. Scott), *The Chase* ('*Leonore*'), 1796.

Burn, J. D., *Autobiography of a Beggar Boy*, 1855.

'Buz' (pseud.), *Current American Notes*, *c.* 1842.

Byron, Lord George G. N. (First recorded, though not necessarily the first, editions from lower-class publishers: many of these went through several reissues. Dugdale's works circulated among lower middle as well as lower class, but they can properly be placed here.)
  Cain, R. Carlile, 1822; Benbow, 1824; W. Dugdale, 1826; J. Watson, 1832; Wakelin, *c.* 1836; chapbook version, *c.* 1832.
  Childe Harold, W. Dugdale, 1825; J. Duncombe, 1831.
  Corsair, W. Dugdale, 1825, (Cantos I–IV, W. Dugdale, 1825).
  Don Juan, cantos I–XVI, W. Benbow, 1822; W. Clark, 1826; B. D. Cousins, *c.* 1836.
  The Giaour, Dugdale, 1821; W. Clarke, 1844.
  Lara, W. Dugdale, 1842.
  Manfred, W. Dugdale, 1817.
  Miscellaneous Poems, Benbow, 1825.
  Poems, W. M. Clarke, *Magnet British Poets*, vol. XI.
  Poems on his Domestic Circumstances, W. Hone, 1816; J. Limbird, 1832; W. Wakelin, *c.* 1836.
  A Vision of Judgement, J. Cleave, 1837; W. Dugdale, 1824; W. Wakelin, *c.* 1836; W. T. Sherwin, 1841.

Carpenter's Political Magazine, 1831–2, Per.

Casket and Penny Novelist, 1835–8, Per.

Catling, T. *My Life's Pilgrimage*, 1911.

Chambers's Edinburgh Journal, 1831 – in progress, Per.

Chambers's Miscellany of Useful and Entertaining Tracts, 1844–7, Per.

Chambers's London Journal, 1841–3, Per.

Chambers, William, *The Story of a Long and Busy Life*, Edinburgh, 1882.

Christian Corrector, 1831, Per.

Cleave's Weekly Police Gazette, (*Cleave's Penny Police Gazette; Cleave's London Satirist; Cleave's Penny Gazette of Variety*), 1833–44, Per.

Cleave's Picture Gallery of Grant's Comicalities, 1836.

The Comic Magazine, 1832, Per.

Cooke, James, *The Actor's Notebook*, 1841, Per.
    'The Bachelor's Club', *Odd Fellow*, II, 1840, p. 13; II, 1840, p. 77.
    Jack Cade, c. 1840.
    'Theatrical Etchings', no. III, *Odd Fellow*, I, 1839, p. 236.
    'The World we live in', *Odd Fellow*, I, 1839, p.93–III, 1841, p. 81.

Cooper, James F. (Dates of publication in England in penny parts.)
    The Last of the Mohicans, c. 1838, P.
    Lionel Lincoln, c. 1836, P.
    Pilot, 1836, P.
    Pioneers, 1838, P.
    Prairie, 1838, P.
    Red Rover, 1838, P.
    The Spy, c. 1838, P.
    The Water Witch, c. 1838, P.

Cooper, Thomas, *Alderman Ralph*, 1853.
    Captain Cobler, 1850, P.
    Collected Poems, 1877.
    Life of Thomas Cooper, 1872.
    The Purgatory of Suicides, 1845.
    Cooper's Journal, 1850, Per.

Copson, H. J., *The Gipsey's Warning*, 1841, P.
    Moll Cutpurse, 1845, P.
    The Mountain Fiend, 1841, P.

Crockett, D., *Sketches and Eccentricities of Davy Crockett*, 1843.

Crosland, N., *Landmarks of a Literary Life*, 1893.

Cruikshank, G., *A Slap at the Church*, 1832, Per.

David and Jonathan, Huddersfield, 1830, anon.

Death's Visit to a Ballroom, c. 1831, anon.

Deloney, T., *Jack of Newbery*, 1598.

Democratic Hymns and Songs, 1849, various.

The Demon Huntsman; or, the Fatal Bullet, c. 1842, anon., P.

The Demon of Destruction, c. 1830, anon.

Dickens, Charles H., *Christmas Carol*, 1843.
    Dealings with the Firm of Dombey and Son, 1848.
    Letters of Charles Dickens, Nonesuch, 1938.
    Martin Chuzzlewit, 1843–4.
    Master Humphrey's Clock, 1840.
    Nicholas Nickleby, 1838–9.
    Oliver Twist, 1837–8. *Posthumous Papers of the Pickwick Club*, 1836–7.
    Sketches by 'Boz', 1836–7.

The Dodger (*The Sunday Chronicle*), 1841, Per.

Dramatic Tales, E. Duncombe, *c.* 1836–44, P. (twopence).

Dumas, A., *père*, *Count of Monte Cristo*: *London Journal*, III, 1846, p. 116; VI, 1847, p. 250.

    Margot of Valois: *London Pioneer*, III, 1848, pp. 1–493.

    A Thousand and One Phantoms: *London Journal*, IX, 1849, p. 181; X, 1850, p. 300.

Egan, Pierce (Sen.), *Life in London*, 1820.

    Pilgrims of the Thames, 1838.

Egan, Pierce (Jun.), *Paul Jones*, 1847, P.

Quintin Matsys, 1841, P.

    The Thirteenth; or, the Fatal Number, 1849, P.

    Wat Tyler, 1841, P.

Eliza Cook's Journal, 1849–54, Per.

Eliza Grimwood, *c.* 1838, anon., P.

Elliott, Ebenezer, *Corn Law Rhymes*, 1832.

    The Giaour, 1823.

    The Poetical Works of Ebenezer Elliott, Edinburgh, 1840.

Enoch, Ebenezer, *Songs of Universal Brotherhood*, 1849.

The Family Economist, 1846–60, Per.

The Family Friend, 1849–1921, Per.

The Family Herald, 1845–1939, Per.

Family Portfolio, *c.* 1846, Per.

Fanny Hill's New Friskey Chanter, *c.* 1836.

The Farthing Journal, 1841, Per.

The Fate of Gaspar; or, the Mysterious Caverns, *c.* 1843, anon., P.

Fatherless Fanny, 1819, anon.

'The Feuilleton of French Literature', *The Mirror*, n.s. I, 1842, pp. 5–404, Per.

Féval, Paul, *The Loves of Paris*, 1846, P.

    The Midnight Reckoners, 1846, P.

    The Mysteries of London, Stokesley, 1847; New York, *c.* 1845.

    The Mystery of the Inquisition, *London Journal*, I, 1845, p. 113; II, 1845, p. 58.

Figaro in Liverpool, 1832, Per.

Figaro in London, 1832, Per.

Figaro in Sheffield, 1832, Per.

Fitzball, Edward (previously Ball), *Joan of Arc*, 1822 (not published) (drama).

    The Pilot, 1825 (drama).

    Thalaba the Destroyer, 1836 (not published) (drama).

    Thirty-Five years of a Dramatic Author's Life, 1859.

Fortescue, L. (pseud. ?), *Life and Adventures of Jack Sheppard*, 1845, P. – enlarged version of *The History of Jack Sheppard*, 1840.

The French Novelist, *c.* 1840–43, P.

Frost, Thomas, *The Black Mask*, 1848, P.

    Emma Mayfield, 1848, P.

    Forty Years' Recollections, 1880.

    The Mysteries of Old Father Thames, *c.* 1854, P.

    Paul the Poacher, 1848, P.

    Reminiscences of a Country Journalist, 1886.

Fun for the Million (anthology), 1838.

Furness, R., *Poetical Works*, 1856.

'G. C.', 'Woman's Love', *Lloyd's Penny Atlas*, II, 1844, p. 192.

Gallery of Comicalities, 1831, anon.

The Gambler's Wife: or, Murder will Out, 1850, anon., P.

Gaskell, E. C., 'Libbie Marsh's Three Eras', *Howitt's Journal*, I, 1847, pp. 310, 334, 345.

    Mary Barton, 1848.

Gaspey, William, *Poor Law Melodies*, 1841.

General and True History of the Most Notorious Highwaymen ..., 1742, Anon.

Gentleman Jack, 1852, anon., P.

Goldsmith, O., *The Vicar of Wakefield*, 1766 (Limbird, *c.* 1838).

Gore, Catherine, G. F., *The Money Lender*, 1843.

The Green Bushes, 1851, anon., P.

Grosse, C. F. A., *Horrid Mysteries*, ed. Montague Summers, 1927.

'Guess' (pseud.), *Scenes from the Life of Nickleby Married*, 1840.

Hainsforth, W. H. (pseud.), *A Legend of the Tower of London*, 1840, P.

The Half-Penny Magazine, 1832, Per.

Haliburton, T. C., 'Sam Slick', *London Journal*, I, 1845, pp. 349 ff.

    The Clockmaker, 1836.

Harris, Rev. Wm, *Grounds of Hope for the Salvation of all Dying in Infancy*, 1821.

Helme, Elizabeth, *The Farmer of Inglewood Forest*, 1825.

Hewitt, H. (from Dickens's *Christmas Carol*), *A Christmas Ghost Story*, 1844, P.

Hingston, E. P., *Amy: or, Love and Madness*, 1848, P.

    Helen Porter, 1847, P.

A History of Pirates, Smugglers &c. of all Nations, 1835, anon., P.

A History of and Lives of the most Notorious Highwaymen, Footpads ... *and Robbers of every Description*, 1836–7, anon.

Hodder, S., *Memories of My Time*, 1870.

Holcroft, T., *The Road to Ruin*, 1792.

    (Translation and introduction), *Tales from the German*, 1826.

Holyoake, G. J. *Sixty Years of an Agitator's Life*, 1892.

Home Circle, 1849–54, Per.

Household Words, 1850–59, Per.

'How to get on in the world', *Family Economist*, I, 1848, pp. 2, 33, 48, 83, 97.

Howitt, Mary, *Autobiography*, 1889.

'The Beginning and End of Mrs Muggeridge's Wedding Dinner', *Howitt's Journal*, I, 1847, p. 25.

The Hoxton Sausage, c. 1832, Per.

Huart, L. and Renepon, C., *A Parody of the Wandering Jew*, 1845.

Hue and Cry and Police Gazette, 1818–34, Per.

Hunt, Leigh, *Autobiography*, 1860.

Hugo, Victor, *Hans of Iceland*, c. 1843, P.

The King's Daughter, c. 1845.

The King's Fool, 1842.

La Esmeralda, c. 1844, P.

Illustrated London News, 1842 – in progress, Per.

The Importance of a Constant Preparation for Death, c. 1840, anon.

Inchbald, Elizabeth, *Nature and Art*, 1796.

Ingraham, J. H., *Captain Kyd; or the Wizard of the Sea*, 1846, P.

The Cruiser; or, 'Tis Thirty Years Ago, c. 1847, P.

The Freebooters, c. 1848, P.

The Gipsy of the Highlands, 1847.

Morris Graeme, c. 1842, P.

The Pirate, 1838, P.

'The Silver Ship of Mexico', *Family Herald*, V, 1847, pp. 193–249.

Irving, Washington, 'The Broken Heart', *London Journal*, XI, 1850, p. 93.

Salmagundi, Limbird, c. 1835, P.

Jackson, W., *The New and Complete Newgate Calendar*, 1796.

James, G. P. R., *Richard Cœur de Lion*, 1842.

Jerrold, Douglas, W., *Black-eye'd Susan* (drama), Surrey, 1829; Duncombe, 1829?.

Joan of Arc, 1841, anon., P.

'Johnathonisms', *Cleave's Penny Gazette*, I, 14 July 1836, p. 1.

Jones, Ernest, 'Chartist Hymn', *Red Republican*, I, 1850, p. 56.

Jones, Hannah Maria, *The Curate's Daughters*, 1835.

Emily Moreland, 1829.

The Gipsy Chief, 1840.

The Gipsy Girl, 1836.

The Pride of the Village, 1830.

Jones, Rev. J., *The History of Susan Clarke*, 1837.

Judson, E. Z. C., *The King of the Sea*, 1848, P.

Mysteries of New York, New York, 1848, P.

Kentish, Mrs, *The Gipsy Daughter*, 1839, P.

The Maid of the Village, 1847, P.

Kock, C. P. de, *The Barber of Paris*, 1840, P.

    Brother James, 1839, P.

    Sister Anne (tr. G. W. M. Reynolds), 1840.

    The Three Students of Paris, 1839, P.

Lady Godiva, 1849, anon., P.

Lady Hamilton; or, Nelson's Legacy, 1848, anon., P.

Lancaster, Edward, 'The Origins of Sailors', *London Singer's Magazine*, II, 1839, p. 214.

The Lancashire Beacon, 1849, Per.

Leigh Hunt's London Journal, 1834–5, Per.

Lewis M. G., *The Bravo of Venice*, 1804.

    The Monk, ed. E. A. Baker, 1926.

Library of Foreign Romance, 1846, P.

Library of French Romance, ed. J. C. James, *c.* 1846–7, P.

Library of Romance, ed. Leitch Ritchie, 1833–6.

Library of Romance, J. Cleave, *c.* 1839–48, P.

Lillo, George, *The London Merchant*, 1731 (drama).

Lindridge, J., *Jack Rann*, 1845, P.

Linton, W. J., *Memories*, 1895.

Literature of the Working Classes, 1850, Per.

Lives and Adventures of Notorious Pirates . . ., *c.* 1836, P.

'Lives of Grace and Isobel', *Family Herald*, V, 1847, pp. 1–152.

Lloyd's Companion to the Penny Sunday Times, 1841–?, Per.

Lloyd's Entertaining Journal, 1843–6, Per.

Lloyd's Illustrated London Newspaper – (continued under various titles) 1842–1931.

Lloyd's Monthly Volume, 1845–7, Per.

Lloyd's Penny Atlas, and Weekly Register of Novel Entertainment, 1843–5, Per.

Lloyd's Penny Sunday Times, 1841–?, Per.

Lloyd's Penny Weekly Miscellany, 1843–5, Per.

Lloyd's Pickwickian Songster, *c.* 1837.

The London Journal, 1845–1912, Per.

London Satirist (Penny Satirist, London Pioneer, Literary Pioneer), 1837–48, Per.

London Singer's Magazine, *c.* 1838–40, Per.

Lorraine, Paul, *The Ordinary of Newgate*, 1712.

Love and Crime; or, the Mystery of the Convent, 1840, anon., P.

Lovett, William, *Life and Struggles of William Lovett*, 1876.

Lucy Neale, 1847, anon., P.

Marriott, E. F. (pseud. ?), *Black-eye'd Susan*, 1845, P.

Marryat, Frederick, *Jacob Faithful* (abbrev.) *The Casket* I, 1835, pp. 9–11.

    Naval Officer; or, . . . Frank Mildmay, 1829.

    Percival Keene, 1842.

Martin's Annals of Crime, 1837, P.

Mary, the Primrose Girl, c. 1846, anon., P.

Mathews, Charles, *Account of Mr Mathews at Home . . . Trip to America*,
    2nd ed. J. Duncombe, 1826.

Maturin, Charles R., *Melmoth the Wanderer*, 1820.

'Maude Marsden', *New Parley Library*, II, 1844, pp. 1 ff.

Maurice, F. D. and Ludlow, J. M., *Politics for the People*, 1844, Per.

Mazeppa, 1849, anon.

Meadows, Kenny, and others, *Heads of the People*, 1840.

Memoirs of a Working Man, 1845, anon.

Mercy for Outcasts, c. 1832, anon.

Miles, Henry D., *Claude Duval*, 1850, P.
    Dick Turpin, 4th ed., 1845, P.

The Miller and His Men, 1848, anon., P.

Miller, Thomas, *Gideon Giles*, 1841.
    The Mysteries of London, 3rd ser., 1847, P.

Millhouse, Robert, *The Destinies of Man*, 1832–4.
    Songs of the Patriot, 1828.

Milner, H. M., *Turpin's Ride to York*, c. 1836.

Milton, John, *Paradise Lost*, 18 nos., 1825–6.

The Mirror of French Romance, c. 1846–8, P.

Moncreiff, W. T., *Tarnation Strange*, 1838 (drama).

Montague, E. (pseud. ?), *The Demon of Sicily*, c. 1840, P.

Moore, T. (pseud. ?) (from Southey's poem), *Thalaba the Destroyer*, 1842,
    P.

More, Hannah, *The Shepherd of Salisbury Plain*, 1796.

Mr Pickwick's Collection of Songs, c. 1838.

The Mysteries of Berlin, anon., tr. C. B. Burckhardt, 1845, P.

The Mysteries of Oronza, c. 1841, anon., P.

The Mysteries of the Forest; or, the Deformed Transformed, c. 1849, anon., P.

The Mysterious Traveller, c. 1831, anon.

The National, ed. W. J. Linton, 1839, Per.

The National Library, 1831–2 ?, Per.

Naubert, C. B. E. (Professor Kramer), *Herman of Unna*, 1794.

Nell Gwynne; or, the Court of Charles II, 1849, anon., P.

The New Casket, 1831–4, Per.

The Newgate Calendar, 1774, Per.

Newton, J. R., *Hofer, the Patriot of the Tyrol*, c. 1842, P.
    William Tell, 1841, P.

Nicholson, Renton, *Autobiography of a Fast Man*, 1860.
    Cockney Adventures, 1837, P.
    Dombey and Daughter, 1847, P.
    (ed.) *The Town*, 1837–40, Per.

Northern Star, 1837–44, Per.

'Notices to Correspondents', *Reynolds's Miscellany*, I, 1846, pp. 125, 259.
Novel Newspaper, 1838–48 ?, Per.
The Novelist, 1838–9, Per.
Novello, Mrs V., 'Fortunes of Mary Leslie', *People's Journal*, I, 1848, pp. 247 f., 264, 270.
Odd Fellow, 1839–42, Per.
The Olio, 1839–42, Per.
Opie, Amelia, *Father and Daughter*, 1801.
Outsiders of Society, c. 1863.
Overs, John, *Evenings of a Working Man*, 1844.
Owen, R., *Life of Owen . . . by Himself*, 1820.
'P. G.', 'The Miscellany in 1843', *Lloyd's Penny Miscellany*, I, 1843, p. 559.
The Patriot's Bride, c. 1848, anon., P.
Peddie, R., *The Dungeon Harp*, Edinburgh, 1844.
Penny Magazine, 1832–45, Per.
Penny Punch, 1849, Per.
Penny Story-Teller, 1832–7 ?, Per.
Penny Sunday Times and People's Police Gazette, 1840–49, Per.
'Penny Wise and Pound Foolish', anon., *Fool's Cap*, 13 October 1831, p. 1.
People's Journal, 1846–9, Per.
People's and Howitt's Journal, 1849–51, Per.
People's Periodical and Family Library, 1846–7, Per.
The Pickwickian Songster, 1839.
The Pickwickian Treasury of Wit, or Joe Miller's Jest Book, 1846.
The Picture Room at Benevolent Hall, 1830, anon.
Pitt, G. D., *Agnes Primrose; or, the Wreck of the Heart* (both novel and drama), 1842.
Pocock, Isaac, *The Miller and His Men*, drama 1813; Cumberland, c. 1831,
Poe, Edgar A., 'The Cask of Amontillado', *People's Periodical*, I, 1847. pp. 283 ff.
'Police Intelligence, Marlborough St', *Morning Chronicle*, 17 March 1835, p. 4.
Polidori, G., *The Vampyre*, 1819.
Poor Man's Guardian, 1831–5, Per.
Poole, John, *Little Peddlington*, 1839.
Portraits of Pickwick Characters, 1837.
Posthumous Papers of the Cadger's Club, 1837–8, anon., P.
'Poz', *Oliver Twiss*, 1838.
'Poz', *Posthumous Papers of the Wonderful Discovery Club*, 1838, P.
Prest, Thomas Peckett, *Almira's Curse*, c. 1842, P.
   The Calendar of Horrors, 1835, P.
   The Death Grasp, 1844, P.

Ela, the Outcast, 1839–40, P.
Emily Fitzormond, 1842, P.
Florence Graham, 1846, P.
Gallant Tom, 1841, P.
The Gipsy Boy, 1847, P.
The Hebrew Maiden, 1841, P.
I'm Afloat, I'm Afloat, 1849, P.
Jack Junk, 1849, P.
The Jew and the Foundling, 1847, P.
Lucy Wentworth (drama), 1857.
The Maniac Father, 1844, P.
The Miser of Shoreditch, 1854, P.
My Poll and my Partner Joe, *c.* 1849, P.
The Old House of West Street, 1846, P.
Tales of the Drama, *c.* 1836–7, P.
There's Nothing Like a Friend at Court (drama) (not published), *c.* 1834.
Vice and its Victim, 1850, P.
Prince, John C., *Hours with the Muses*, 1850.
Punchinello, 1832, Per.
Radcliffe, A., *The Italian*, 1797.
The Mysteries of Udolpho, 1794.
The Ragged School Magazine, 1850, Per.
The Reasoner (ed. G. J. Holyoake), 1846–61, Per.
Red Cross Warrior, 1843, anon., P.
Redding, C., *Yesterday and Today*, 1865.
Rede, Leman, *History of a Royal Rake*, 1842.
Reynolds's Miscellany, 1846–9, Per.
Reynolds's Political Instructor, 1849, Per.
Reynolds, G. W. M., *Days of Hogarth*, 1848, P.
Faust, 1846, P.
Grace Darling, 1839.
Master Timothy's Bookcase, 1842, P.
Mysteries of London, 1846–8, P.
Mysteries of the Court of London, 1849–56, P.
Pickwick Abroad, 1839.
Wagner the Wehr-wolf – *Reynolds's Miscellany*, I, 1846, p. 1 – II, 1847, p. 33.
Reynolds, Susannah F., *Gretna Green*, 1847, P.
Richard Parker; or, the Mutiny on the Nore, 1851, anon., P.
Richardson, Samuel, *Clarissa*, 1747–8.
Pamela, 1740 (penny-issues 1840).
Richmond, Rev. Legh, *Annals of the Poor*, 1814 (contains final version of *The Dairyman's Daughter*).
Riding, E., *The Village Muse*, Macclesfield, 1854.

Ridley, James, *Tales of the Genii*, 1764 (Limbird, 1839), P.

'Rip Rap', *The Monument; or, the Great Fire of London*, 1841, P.

The Rival Apprentices, *c.* 1860, anon., P.

Rousseau, J. J., *Pygmalion*, 1775.

Rymer, James M., *Ada, the Betrayed*, 1845, P.

 Jane Brightwell, 1846, P.

 'Leaves from the Notebooks of a Queen's Messenger', *Lloyd's Penny Weekly Miscellany*, VIII, 1848, passim.

 The Rivals, 1847, P.

 Varney the Vampyre, 1846, P.

 The White Slave, 1844, P. (For other works by Rymer, see Appendix III.)

St-John, Percy B., 'The Raven of the Reynards', *Lloyd's Weekly Volume*, I, 1847, pp. 112–17.

Sala, G. A., *The Life and Adventures of G. A. Sala*, 1895.

Sam Weller, A Journal of Wit and Humour, 1837.

Sam Weller's Favourite Song Book, *c.* 1838.

Sam Weller's Scrap Sheet, *c.* 1837.

'Sam Weller's Sentiments on the Poor Law', *Cleave's London Satirist*, I, 16 December 1837, p. 1.

The Satirist, 1836–?, Per.

Schiller, J. C. F. von, *Die Räuber*, 1781.

 William Tell (drama), tr. R. L. Pearsall, (E. Bull, 1829).

Scott, J., *Arabian Nights' Entertainments*, Limbird, 1834, P.

Scott, Sir Walter, *The Beauties of Scott*, 1829 (anthology).

 Ivanhoe, 1820.

 Waverley, Edinburgh, 1814; Edinburgh, 1842, P.

Seymour, Robert, *Humorous Sketches*, 1833–6, P.

Shelley, P. B., *Queen Mab*, W. Clarke, 1821; R. Carlile, 1822; H. Hetherington, 1839?, J. Watson, 1840.

 Zastrozzi, Clements, 1839, P.

Sheppard, John, *The History of Jack Sheppard*, 1839, anon., P.

 Life and Adventures of Jack Sheppard, Manchester, 1840, anon.

 Life and Exploits of Jack Sheppard, Derby, 1840, anon.

 Life and Adventures of Jack Sheppard, Purkess, 1849, anon., P.

 Eventful Life and Unparallelled Exploits of the Notorious Jack Sheppard, 1840, anon., P.

 v. also W. H. Ainsworth, 'Barrister,' 'Blueskin', L. Fortescue, H. D. Miles.

Sheridan, F., *Nourjahad*, Limbird, 1839, P.

Sherwood, M. M., *Joan; or, the Trustworthy*, *c.* 1830.

Shipman, Rev. John (pseud.), *A Sailor's Struggle for Eternal Life*, 1848.

The Skeleton Horseman, *c.* 1859.

Smeeton, G., *The Flash Dictionary*, *c.* 1838.

Smith, Albert, *Christopher Tadpole*, 1848.

Smith, C. M., *A Working Man's Way in the World*, 1853.

Smith, Horace, *Brambletye House*, 1828.

Smith, John F., *The Jesuit*, 1832.
   Minnigrey, 1851, P.
   The Prelate, 1840.
   Stanfield Hall, 1849–50, P.

Smith, Seba, 'The Courtship of Dombey and Daughter', *Family Herald*,
   IV, 1847, p. 769.
   Life and Writings of Jack Downing, 1833.

Smollett, T., *Lancelot Greaves*, 1760–62.

Somerville, A., *Autobiography of a Working Man*, 1846.

Soulié, Frédéric, *The She-Tiger of Paris*, 1850, P.

Southey, R., *Amadis de Gaul*, 1803.
   Joan of Arc, 1796 (R. Carlile, *c.* 1817; Hone, 1817; Sherwin, 1817;
      Cleave, 1835).
   Life and Correspondence of R. Southey, ed. C. C. Southey, 1848–50.
   Thalaba, the Destroyer, 1830 (drama, Fitzball, 1823, not pubd.; prose,
      Dramatic Tales, ser. 2, no. 3, 1836. Adapted 'T. Moore', 1841).
   Wat Tyler, Fairburn, 1817; Hone, 1817; Sherwin, 1817; Carlile, 1825;
      Cleave, 1835.

The String of Pearls, anon., *People's Periodical*, I, 1846, p. 97; II, 1847,
   p. 383.
– as *Sweeney Todd*, 1848.

Sue, Eugène, *Brulart*, 1846, P.
   The Female Bluebeard, 1847, P.
   The Seven Cardinal Sins, *London Journal*, VI, 1847, p. 202; IX, 1849,
      p. 787.
   Les Mystères de Paris, Paris, 1843, P.
   The Mysteries of Paris, 1845, (v. Appendix B), P.
   The Wandering Jew, 1844 (v. Appendix B), P.
   The Wandering Jew, abbrev. and alt., Lloyd, 1845, P.

Sutter, W. E., *The Adventures of Dick Turpin and Tom King* (drama, n.d.).

T., W. T. (W. T. Townsend ?), *Poor Tom Bowling*, *c.* 1846, P.

Tales of Shipwrecks, and Adventures at Sea, 1846–7.

'Tales of the Minstrelsy', anon., *Lloyd's Penny Atlas*, I, 1844, p. 225.

The Teetotaller, ed. G. W. M. Reynolds, 1839–40, Per.

Theatrical Times, 1846–7, Per.

Thornley, Herbert, *Life in London*, 1846.

The Thief (London . . . *Weekly Magazine*), 1832–3, Per.

Thompson, Christopher, *Autobiography of an Artisan*, 1847.

Tinsley, W., *Random Recollections of an Old Publisher*, 1900.

The Tract Magazine, 1824–6, Per.

The Twist and Nickelby Scrap Sheet, *c.* 1839.

The Unhappy Bride; or, the Grave of the Forsaken, 1847, P.

Vidocq, François, E., *Life and Extraordinary Adventures, c.* 1850, P.
   Life in Paris, 1847, P.
Vileroy; or, the Horrors of Zindorf Castle, 1844, anon., P.
Viles, Edward, *Marmaduke Midge, the Pickwickian Legatee, c.* 1852, P.
Vizetelly, H., *Glances Back through Seventy Years,* 1893.
The Wag, 1837, P.
Walpole, *The Castle of Otranto,* 1764.
Watts, W. H., *My Private Notebook,* 1862.
The Weekly Visitor, 1833–5, Per.
Wesleyan Tract Reporter, 1841–9, Per.
West, William, *Fifty Years' Recollections,* 1835.
Wild Boys of London, 1863.
Will Watch, 1848, anon., P.
Wilson, H., *The Memories of Harriet Wilson,* Dugdale, *c.* 1838, P.
Wilson, J. F., *A Few Personal Recollections* (n.d.).
The Witch's Cliff; or, the Fatal Gulf, c. 1843, anon., P.
The Young Apprentices, c. 1860, anon., P.

5. SECONDARY SOURCES, COMPRISING: BIOGRAPHIES; CRITICAL, HISTORICAL, AND BACKGROUND MATERIAL

A'Beckett, A. W., *The A'Becketts of Punch,* 1903.
A'Beckett, Gilbert, 'Penny-a-Line's Phrase Book', *Almanack of the Month,*
   II, 1846, p. 42.
Adamson, J. W., *An Outline of English Education 1760–1902,* Cambridge,
   1925.
'*Address to the Society for the Suppression of Vice*', 1825.
Algar, F., 'T. P. Prest', *Reckless Ralph's Dime Novel Roundup,* 18 January
   1950, no. 208.
Altick, R., *The English Common Reader,* 1957.
Andrewes, A., *A Short History of English Journalism,* 1856.
Ashton, T. S., *Economic and Social Investigations in Manchester,* 1934.
Aspinall, A., *Politics and the Press,* 1949.
'Astoria', (by Washington Irving), anon. rev., *Monthly Magazine,* XXII,
   1836, pp. 560 ff.
Atkinson, N., *Eugène Sue et le Roman-Feuilleton,* Nemours, 1929.
Auster, D., 'A Content Analysis of "Little Orphan Annie"', *Social
   Problems,* II, 1954, pp. 26–33.
Bamford, S., *Passages in the Life of a Radical,* ed. H. Dunckley, 1893.
Bertram, J., *Glimpses of Real Life,* Edinburgh, 1864.
Birchenough, C., *A History of Elementary Education,* 1939.
'Bishop of Lincoln's Charge', *Stamford Mercury,* 29 June 1825, p. 4.
Bleakley, H.; Ellis, S. M., *Jack Sheppard in Literature and Drama,* 1933.

Block, A., *The English Novel, 1740–1850*, 1939.

Boase, F., *Modern English Biography*, 1892–1921.

Bourne, H. R. Fox, *English Newspapers*, 1887.

Briggs, Asa, 'Press and Public in Nineteenth Century Birmingham', *Dugdale Society Occasional Papers*, no. 8, 1950, pp. 21 ff.

Brougham, Henry P.; Baron Brougham and Vaux, *Address in Popular Literature Delivered at . . . Liverpool*, 1858.

Practical Observations on the Education of the People, 1825.

Buday, G., *A History of the Christmas Card*, 1954.

Bulwer-Lytton, E. G. E. L., 'Letter', *New Monthly Magazine*, XXI, 1831, pp. 289–95.

Burn, J. D., *The Language of the Walls*, 1855.

Burritt, E., *Adresses Amicales du Peuple Anglais*, Paris, 1848.

Buss, R. W., *English Graphic Satire*, 1894.

Carlyle, T., 'Corn-Law Rhymes', *Edinburgh Review*, LV, July 1832, pp. 338–61.

Chartism, 1839.

Catling, T., 'The Founder of Lloyds', *Lloyd's News*, 30 November 1902, p. 8.

Chambers, W., *A Memoir of Robert Chambers*, 2nd ed., Edinburgh, 1872.

Chittick, V. C. O., *T. C. Haliburton*, New York, 1924.

Churchill, R. C., 'Dickens, Drama and Tradition', *Scrutiny*, X, 1942, pp. 358–75.

Clarke, G. Lowther, *A History of the S.P.C.K.*, 1959.

'Clericus Londinensis', 'The Public Press', *The Churchman's Monthly Penny Magazine*, I, 1846, pp. 57–8.

Clowes, A., *Charles Knight*, 1892.

Cole, G. D. H., *The Life of William Cobbett*, 1947.

A Short History of the British Working Classes, 1948.

Collett, C. D., *A History of the Taxes on Knowledge*, 1899.

Collins, A. S., *The Profession of Letters*, 1928.

Collins, Philip, *Thomas Cooper the Chartist*: *Byron and the Poets of the Poor*, Nottingham, 1970.

Collins, W. Wilkie, *My Miscellanies*, 1863.

Constable, T., *Archibald Constable and his Literary Correspondents*, 1873.

Cooke, James (collector), *A Bibliography of Dickens*, 1873.

Cooper, Thomas, *The Life of Henry Hetherington*, 1889.

'Corn-Law Rhymes' (by E. Elliott), anon. rev., *London Review*, 1220, 19 June 1831, pp. 385 ff.

Cruse, A., *The Englishman and his Books in the Early 19th Century*, 1930.

The Victorians and their Books, 1935.

Dalziel, M., *Popular Fiction a Hundred Years Ago*, 1958.

Darton, J. F., 'Dickens the Beginner 1833–6', *Q.R.*, CCLXII, 1934, pp. 52–69

Davis, E. R., 'Dickens and the Evolution of Caricature', *P.M.L.A.*, LV, 1940, pp. 231–40.

de Ternant, A., 'Early Victorian Literature', *N. & Q.*, 12 Ser. X, 1922, pp. 372–4; p. 458.

'Dickens v. Berger', *The Times*, 12 January 1844, p. 6.

Dickson, S. A., 'The Arents Collection', *Bulletin of New York Public Library*, 61, June 1957, pp. 270 ff.

'John Dicks', anon., *Bookseller*, 1881, p. 231.

Diprose, J., *Some Account of the Parish of St Clement Dane's*, 1868.

Disher, R. W., *Blood and Thunder*, 1945.

'Penny Dreadfuls', *Pilot Papers*, II, March 1947, pp. 44–50.

Victorian Song, 1955.

Dixon, J. Hepworth, 'Literature of the Lower Orders', *Daily News*, 26 October, 7 November, 9 November 1847.

Dobbs, A. E., *Education and Social Movements*, 1919.

(Dugdale, W.), 'Mischievous Literature', *Bookseller*, 1868, pp. 448–9.

Dunckley, H., *The Glory and Shame of Britain*, 1851.

Engels, F., *The Condition of the Working Class in England in 1844*, 1892.

Escott, T. H. S., *Masters of British Journalism*, 1911.

Evans, John, *Manchester Authors and Orators*, Manchester, 1850.

Everett, G., *English Caricaturists and Graphic Humorists of the Nineteenth Century*, 1886.

Fell, R. C., *Life of Alderman Kelly*, 1856.

Fergusson, A., *A Bibliography of Australia 1846–50*, 1955.

Fitzgerald, S. Adair, *Dickens and the Drama*, 1920.

Ford, G. H., *Dickens and His Readers*, Cincinnati, 1955.

Forster, J., *Life of Charles Dickens*, ed. J. W. T. Ley, 1927.

Franklyn, J., *The Cockney*, 1953.

Friends Tract Association, *Annual Report (1830)*, 1832.

'French Romances', *Fraser's Magazine*, XXVII, 1843, pp. 184–94.

'G. C.', 'Cheap Periodicals', *Christian Reformer*, XVIII, 1832, pp. 310–12; 369–73; 424–7.

Gammage, R. G., *History of the Chartist Movement*, Newcastle, 1894.

Grant, James, *Portraits of Public Characters*, 1841.

Grego, J., *Pictorial Pickwickiana*, 1899.

Green, S. G., *The Story of the Religious Tract Society*, 1899.

Grimshawe, T. S., *A Memoir of the Reverend Legh Richmond*, 10th ed., 1840.

Guest, James, *Birmingham*, 1835.

Hackwood, F. W., *William Hone*, 1912.

Hale, Sarah, *Woman's Record*, 1853.

Hall, S. T., *Biographical Sketches of Remarkable People*, 1873.

Hammond, J. L. and B., *The Town Labourer, 1760–1832,* 1936.

Harrison, C. P., 'Cheap Literature Past and Present', *Companion to The British Almanack,* 1873, pp. 60 ff.

Harrison, Grace, E., *The Clue to the Brontës,* 1949.

Hatton, J., *Journalistic London,* 1882.

Henderson, W., *Victorian Street Ballads,* 1937.

(Heywood), 'Abel Heywood', anon., *I.L.N.,* CIII, 1893, p. 246; *Boase,* Suppt. II, col. 647.

Heywood, Abel (Jun.), 'Newspapers and Periodicals – their Circulation in Manchester', *Papers of the Manchester Literary Club,* I, 1876, pp. 39–58.

Hill, F., *National Education,* 1836.

Hill, G., *Life and Recollections,* New York, 1850.

Hindley, C., *The Life and Times of James Catnach,* 1876.

(Hingston), 'The Late Mr E. P. Hingston', *Era,* XXXVIII, 18 June 1876, p. 10.

Hoare, Archdeacon C. J., 'A Letter', *The Englishwoman's Magazine*; no. V, 1850, p. 497.
 'The Penny Press', ibid., pp. 619–22.

Hollingsworth, Keith, *The Newgate Novel 1830–1847,* Detroit, 1963.

Hollis, Patricia, *The Pauper Press,* 1971.

Hopson, W. F., *Sidelights on W. J. Linton,* New York, 1933.

Hudson, J. W., *A Short History of Adult Education,* 1851.

Hull, Geo., *The Poets and Poetry of Blackburn,* Blackburn, 1902.

Hunter, J. V. B. Stewart, 'George Reynolds', *Book Handbook,* IV, 1947, pp. 225–36.

Jay, Frank, *Peeps into the Past* (suppt. to *Spare Moments*), 1918–19.

'J. F. Smith, Novelist', *N. & Q.,* 12th Ser., X, 1922, p. 276.

Jaques, E. T. (pseud.), *Dickens in Chancery,* 1914.

Jerrold, Walter, *Douglas Jerrold,* 1915.

Johanssen, A., *The House of Beadle and Adams,* Oklahoma, 1950.

Johnson, Edgar, *Charles Dickens,* 1953.

Jones, M. G., *The Charity School Movement,* Cambridge, 1938.
 Hannah More, Cambridge, 1952.

Jones, William, *The Jubilee Volume,* 1850.

'Journalism in France', *British Quarterly Review,* III, 1846, pp. 507 ff.

Keating, P. J., *The Working Classes in Victorian Fiction,* 1971.

Kellett, E. E., 'The Press' in *Early Victorian England,* ed. G. M. Young, 1934.

Kelly, S., ed., *Life of Mrs Sherwood,* 1854.

Kelly's Post Office Directory of Yorkshire, 1850.

'Kingswood District', anon., *Wesleyan Tract Reporter,* 25 November 1850, p. 22.

Kitton, F. G., *Dickensiana,* 1886.

Knight, Charles, *Old Printer and Modern Press*, 1854.
 Passages of a Working Life, 1864.
 Struggles of a Book Against Excessive Taxation, 1850.
Kovalev, Y. V., *The Literature of Chartism*, Moscow, 1956.
Lacey, A., *Pixerécourt and the French Romantic Drama*, Toronto, 1928.
'Labour and the Poor: Manchester', anon., *Morning Chronicle*, 5
 November 1849, p. 5.
Lanarch, S., 'Edward Lloyd', *The Story-Paper Collector*, III, January
 1957, p. 22.
Leavis, Q. D., *Fiction and the Reading Public*, 1932.
(Limbird) 'The Pioneer of Cheap Literature', *Bookseller*, XXXII, 1859,
 p. 1326.
Linton, W. J., *James Watson*, 1879.
Livesey, J., 'The Licentiousness of the Press', *Moral Reformer*, III, 1833,
 p. 63.
'London Coffee Houses', anon., *Teggs Magazine*, I, 1843, pp. 61 ff.
'London Printing Offices', *Typographical Gazette*, no. 4, 1846, pp. 62–4.
'Lucretia' Anon., *Daily News*, 12 December 1846, p. 5.
Ludlow, D. M.; Jones H., *The Progress of the Working Classes*, 1867.
Lurine, M., *Les Rues de Paris*, Paris, 1844.
Lloyd, E., 'To the Public', *Lloyds' Penny Sunday Times*, I, 19 March 1843,
 p. 4.
(Lloyd) 'Edward Lloyd', anon. art., *The Graphic*, XLI, 1890, p. 440.
'Lloyds' Weekly Newspaper', anon. art., *London Journal*, I, 1845, p. 348.
Macabe, J., *The Life and Letters of G. J. Holyoake*, 1908.
Maccoby, S., *English Radicalism 1786–1832*, 1955, ibid., *1832–1852*,
 1935.
Macree, C. W., *G. W. Macree. A Memoir*, 1893.
Malthus, T. R., *An Essay on Population*, 1798.
Manchester Statistical Society, *Report on the State of Education . . . in Bury*,
 1835.
 Report on the State of Education . . . in the Borough of Liverpool, 1835.
Mathews, H. F., *Methodism and the Education of the People*, 1949.
Matz, B. W., 'Plagiarisms of Dickens', *T.P.'s Weekly*, 1907, pp. 265, 302
 333.
Mayne, Fanny, 'The Literature of the Working Classes', *Englishwoman's
 Magazine*, N.S., V, October 1850, pp. 619–22.
 'The Perilous Nature of the Penny Press', privately printed, 1850.
 'Preface', *True Briton*, I, 1851, p. iii.
Medcraft, J., *A Bibliography of Bloods*, Dundee, privately printed, 1945.
 'Crimes that inspired Penny Bloods', *Collector's Miscellany*, 5 ser. 12,
 May 1949, pp. 183–5.
Medcraft, J., 'The Gothic Novel in Penny Number Fiction', ibid., 5 ser.
 9, June 1947, pp. 135–7.

'The Lure of the Fearsome Title', ibid., 5 ser. 16, September 1949, pp. 247–50.

Miller, W., *The Dickens Student and Collector*, 1946.

'G. W. M. Reynolds and Pickwick', *Dickensian*, XIII, January 1917, pp. 8 et seqq.

'Mischievous Literature', *Bookseller*, CXXVI, pp. 445–9.

'Moral Statistics', rep. *S.S.L.*, I, December 1938, pp. 486 ff.

Moraud, M., 'French Drama in England', *Rice Inst. Pamph.*, XV, April 1928, pp. 113 ff.

   Le Romanticisme Française en Angleterre, Paris, 1933.

Morley, J. Cooper, *The Newspaper Press and Periodical Literature of Liverpool*, Liverpool, 1887.

Morison, S., *The English Newspaper*, 1932.

Mr Punch. His Origins and Career, 1870, anon., (Mark Lemon).

Muddiman, J. G., '*The Times' Tercentenary Handlist of English and Welsh Newspapers, Magazines and Reviews*, 1920.

Mumby, F., *The House of Routledge 1834–1934*, 1934.

Mumford, Lewis, *The Culture of Cities*, 1938.

'The Mysteries of London', anon., *Literary Annual Register*, 1845, p. 8.

Neale, W. B., *Juvenile Delinquency in Manchester*, Manchester, 1840.

'The Neglect of Literary Men', *Manchester Courier*, 5 September 1846.

'*Nicholas Nickleby, Part XI*', anon., *Actors by Daylight*, II, 1839, pp. 116–17.

Nicoll, H. J., *Great Movements and Those Who Achieved Them*, 1881.

(Nicholson) 'John Nicholson', anon., *Mirror*, VI, 1844, pp. iii–x.

'Notions of Sam Slick', *Bentley's Miscellany*, XIV, 1843, pp. 81–94.

'Novels of Fashionable Life', anon., *Quarterly Review*, XLVIII, 1832, pp. 165–201.

Nowell-Smith, S., *The House of Cassell*, 1958.

'The Odd Fellow's Review', anon. (W. J. Linton?), *Odd Fellow*, III, 1841, p. 107.

O'Donoghue, D. J., *The Life of William Carleton*, 1896.

'The Old Year and its Doings', anon., *Odd Fellow*, I, 1839, p. 2.

Poe, E. A., 'Lafitte', *Southern Literary Messenger*, II, 1836, pp. 593–6.

'The Poetry of the Poor', anon., *London Review*, I, 1835, pp. 187–201.

Pollard, Graham, Introduction to John Pendred's *The Earliest Dictionary of the Book Trade 1795*, 1955.

   'Serial Fiction' in *New Paths in Book Collecting*, 1934, ed. J. Carter.

'Popular Fiction', anon., E. Dipple's *Family Journal*, I, 5 December 1846, p. 15.

'Popular Literature', anon., *British and Foreign Review*, X, 1840, pp. 223–46.

'The Present Taste in Cheap Literature', anon., *The Bee*, II, March 1833, pp. 9 ff.

'The Press', anon., *Herald to the Trade's Advocate*, I, 1830, pp. 193–6.

P(rest?), T. P., *The Life of Douglas Jerrold*, 1857.

Prothero, R. E., *The Light Reading of our Ancestors*, 1927.

'The Provincial Newspaper Press', anon., *Westminster Review*, XXII, 1829, pp. 69–103.

Quaine, J. P., 'A Bibliography', *Story Paper Collector*, III, April 1956, no. 58.

Quinlan, M. J., *Victorian Prelude*, New York, 1941.

Reach, Angus B., 'The Coffee Houses of London', *New Parley Library*, II, 1844, pp. 293 ff.

Redding, C., *Yesterday and Today*, 1863.

Reid, J. C., *Bucks and Bruisers*, 1971.

'Retribution', anon., *Penny Sunday Chronicle*, I, 19 June 1842, p. 1.

Reynolds, G. W. M., *Modern Literature of France*, 2nd ed., 1841.

   'Master Humphrey's Clock', *Teetotaller*, 4 July 1840 (destroyed, but q. *Dickensian*, XIII, January 1917, p. 10).

'G. W. M. Reynolds', anon., *Reynolds's Miscellany*, II, 1845, p. 191.

   Anon., *Bookseller*, 3 July 1879, pp. 600–601.

   also v. 'Mischievous Literature' supra.

Ritchie, J. Ewing, *Here and There in London*, 1859.

Roberts, W., 'Claude Duval in Literature', *National Review*, LXXXV, 1925, pp. 582–91.

   'Dick Turpin in Literature', ibid., LXXXI, 1923, pp. 883–94.

   'Dumas and Sue in England', *Nineteenth Century*, XCII, 1922, pp. 760–66.

   'Jack Sheppard in Literature', *National Review*, LXXXIII, 1924, pp. 432–40.

   'Lloyd's Penny Bloods', *Book Collector's Quarterly*, XVII, 1935, pp. 2 ff.

Roe, F. C., 'The Penny Pickwick', *Dickensian*, XXII, 1926, pp. 153 ff.

   'Pickwick in America!', *Connoisseur*, CVII, 1941, p. 111 ff.

Rollington, R., *A History of Boys' Periodicals*, Leicester, 1913.

Rosa, M. W., *The Silver Fork School*, New York, 1936.

Ross, J. W., 'The Influence of Cheap Literature', *L.J.*, I, 1847, p. 115.

Rowell, G., *The Victorian Theatre*, 1956.

Rymer, J. M., 'Popular Writing', *Queen's Magazine*, I, 1842, pp. 99–103.

Sadleir, M., *Bentley's Standard Novel Series*, Edinburgh, 1932.

Sala, G. A., *Charles Dickens*, 1870.

   'Answers to Correspondents', *Sala's Journal*, I, 1892, p. 525.

   London up to Date, c. 1894.

'The Schoolmaster', anon., *Blackwood's Magazine*, XXV, 1834, pp. 242 ff.

Scottish Record Society, *Register of Marriages of Edinburgh 1751–1800*, Edinburgh, 1922.

Shannon, L. W., 'The Opinions of Little Orphan Annie', *Public Opinion Quarterly*, XVIII, 1954, pp. 169 ff.

Sheffield Public Library, *Ebenezer Elliott 1781–1859*, Manchester, 1959.

Symons, A., *The Romantic Movement in English Poetry*, 1909.

Simmons, C. H., 'Peter Parley and Dickens', *Dickensian*, XIX, 1923, pp. 129 ff.

Simons, J., *Robert Southey*, New Haven, 1948.

Sketches of Obscure Poets, anon., 1833.

Smith, Adam, *The Wealth of Nations*, 1776.

Smith, C. M., *Curiosities of London Life*, 1853.

    The Little World of London, 1857.

S.P.C.K., *Annual Report* 1835, 1844, 1850.

Royal Statistical Society of London, 'Fourth Ordinary Meeting', *S.S.L.*, III, February 1840, p. 106.

    'Report from a Committee', ibid., XI, 1848, pp. 216–17.

Southey, R., *Lives of the Uneducated Poets*, 1835.

Spinney, G. H., 'Cheap Repository Tracts: Hazard and Marshall Edition', *The Library*, 4th S., XX, 1940, pp. 295–340.

Stephen, Leslie, *English Literature and Society in the Eighteenth Century*, 1904.

Stevenson, R. L., 'Popular Authors', *Works*, Tusitala ed., 1923, pp. 20 ff.

Stevas, N. St-John, *Obscenity and the Law*, 1959.

Summers, Montague, *A Gothic Bibliography*, 1940.

    The Gothic Quest, 1941.

    The Vampyre, 1928.

'The Taste of the Public', anon., *Odd Fellow*, I, 1839, p. 6.

Thackeray, W. M., 'Charity and Humour', *Collected Works*, 1896, vol. VII.

    'Half-a-crown's worth of Cheap Knowledge', *Fraser's Magazine*, XVII, 1838, pp. 279–90.

    'Jerome Paturot', *Fraser's Magazine*, XXVIII, 1843, pp. 349–62.

'The Thieves' Literature of France', anon. rev., *Foreign Quarterly Review*, XXI, 1843, pp. 231–49.

Timperley, C. H., *Encyclopaedia of Literary and Typographical Anecdote*, 1842.

Tinsley, W., *Random Recollections of an Old Publisher*, 1900.

Tompkins, J. M. S., *The Popular Novel in England 1770–1800*, 1932.

Turner, E. S., *Boys will be Boys*, 1957.

Tuckerman, H. T., *America and Her Commentators*, New York, 1864.

Vizetelly, H., *Glances Back through Seventy Years*, 1893.

von Raumer, F., *England in 1841*, 1842.

Waite, Arthur B., 'Byways of Periodical Literature', *Walford's Antiquarian Magazine*, XXII, 1887, pp. 65 ff.

Warner, O., *Captain Marryat*, 1953.

Watson, E. B., *Sheridan to Robertson*, 1926.

Watson, J., *Life of Henry Hetherington*, 1849.

Watt, W. W., *Shilling Shockers of the Gothic School*, Cambridge, Mass., 1932.

Watts, W. H., *My Private Notebook*, 1862.

Webb, R. K., *British Working Class Reader 1790–1848*, 1955.

  'The Victorian Reading Public', *Universities Quarterly*, II, November 1957, pp. 24 ff.

'Weekly Newspapers' (Gibbons Merle), *Westminster Review*, X, 1829, pp. 216–37.

Weiner, Joel H., *Unstamped British Periodicals 1830–1836*, 1970.

  The War of the Unstamped, Ithaca, 1969.

Weld, C. R., 'Conditions of the Working Classes', S.S.L., VI, February 1843, pp. 17 ff.

  'On the Penny Literature of the Day', *Athenaeum*, no. 636, 1840, p. 157.

Wesley, John, *Letters*, 1931.

Wesleyan Methodist Tract Society, *Annual Report* 1830, 1832, 1839, 1851.

West, Julius, *A History of the Working Class Movement*, 1920.

West, William, *Fifty Years' Recollections*, 1837.

Wheeler, J. M., *Biographical Dictionary of Freethinkers*, 1889.

White, H. A., *Sir Walter Scott's Novels on the Stage*, Yale, 1927.

Whittock, N., *The Complete Book of Trades*, 1837.

Wickwar, W., *Struggle for the Freedom of the Press*, 1928.

Wight, James, *Mornings at Bow Street*, 1824.

Wiles, R. M., *Serial Publications in England before 1750*, New York, 1957.

Williams, Rev. C., *George Mogridge*, 1858.

Wilson, John, ('Christopher North'), 'Noctes Ambrosianae', *Blackwood's*, XXXII, 1832, pp. 845 ff.

Wilson, J. F., *A Few Personal Recollections*, 1896.

Wilson, J. J., 'Old Penny Romances', *Bootle Times*, 28 January 1916, p. 2.

  'New Light on an Old Subject', *Collector's Miscellany*, 5th S., 7, September 1930, p. 3.

Winskill, B., 'Old Boy's Periodicals', *Bootle Times*, 30 June 1916, p. 8.

Wirth, Louis, 'Urbanism as a Way of Life', *American Journal of Sociology*, XLIV, July 1938, pp. 1 ff.

Worsley, T. C., *Juvenile Depravity*, 1850.

'Yankeeana', anon., *London and West Review*, XXII, 1839, pp. 137 ff.

Index

A'Beckett, G. A., 19
Actors by Gaslight, 30
Adeline, 132–4
Advertising, 36, 40, 51, 229
Age, 61, 170
Aimard, G., 158
Ainsworth, W. H., 106–8; *Jack Sheppard*, 177, 186–7; *Old St Paul's*, 33, 106–8; *Rookwood*, 183, 198; *Tower of London*, 106
Almira's Curse, 96
America, 151–9, passim; anti-British, 158; boorish, 151; and Dickens, 62–4; humour, 151–2, 230; influence, 158
Angela the Orphan, 33, 97
Anglo-Saxon Chronicle, 101
Arabian Nights, 87
Archer, T., *Richard*, 103–4
Austen, J., 94

Baines, T., 11
Ballads, 176–7
Balzac, H. de, 159–60
Barnard, G., 21
Barnett, M., 152
Bayley, F. W. N., 40
Beazely, S., Jun., 54
Bell, A., 3
Bell's Life in London, 24
Bell's Penny Dispatch, 40
Bell's Weekly Dispatch, 40
Benbow, W., 26
Bentley's Miscellany, 8, 46
Berger, G., 22, 47, 52
Bertram, J., 47
Bianca, 91
Bibles, 9–10, 136
Biggs, G., 44

Bird, R. M., 158; *Abdallah*, 87; *Nick*, 154; *Pilgrim*, 154
Birmingham, 23, 231
Black Bess, 185
Black Vulture, 155
Blanchard, E. L., 37; *Mysteries*, 165
Blessington, Lady M. P., 49, 121, 205
'Blue Books', 83
Blueskin, 185
Bohn, H., 12
Bonner, J., 62
Book auctions, 11
Borrow, G., 124
'Bos', 230 (*see also* Dickens, plagiarisms)
British Novelist, 10, 28
British and Foreign Bible Society, 138
British Temperance League, 138
Broadsheets, 176, 183
Brontë sisters, 145
Brougham, H. P., 141
Brown, T., 201
Bruce, Vice-Chancellor K., 51
Bunyan, J., 142
Buckstone, E. B., 120, 171
Burn, J. D., 11, 32
Burritt, E., 153
Byron, 85, 91, 235

Calendar of Horrors, 8, 83
Cameron, W. A., 141
Carlile, R., 16, 29, 85, 136
Carlyle, T., 48, 205
Carpenter, W., 15
Cassell, J., 149
Chambers, W. & R., 16, 23, 139; *Chambers's Edinburgh Journal*, 16–17; *Chambers's Tracts*, 139
Chambers's London Journal, 47, 114

Chartism, 25, 48, 194 (*see also* Radicalism)

Chastity, 89–90

Chaucer, G., 32

Chamier, F., 177

Cheap Repository Tracts, 138

Christian Socialists, 146

Church of England, 137, 139 (*see also* S.P.C.K.*)

Clarke, W. M., 30, 33, 49, 85

Cleave, J., 8, 24, 30, 37, 72, 85

Cleave's Weekly Gazette (contd under various titles), 24, 48, 51, 61

Cleland, J., *Fanny Hill*, 26

Cobbett, W., 15, 136

Coffee houses, 8–9, 159

Collins, W., 136

'Comic crime reporting', 181–2

Cook, E., 149–50

Cook, J. (dramatist), 30, 53, 68, 171; *Barnaby Rudge*, 77; *Jack Cade*, 86

Cook, T. P., 158, 178

Cooper, J. F., 154, 158, 161; *Pilot*, 154

Cooper, T., 3, 10, 48, 102, 205; *Alderman Ralph*, 123; *Cobler*, 123; *Chambers's Journal*, 149; *Purgatory*, 202, 207–8

Copson, R. J., *Gipsey's Warning*, 125; *Mountain Fiend*, 87–9

Country life, 117–25

Cousins, B. D., 35, 48

Crime, 71, 182–90

Crisp, J., 22

Critical standards, 51

Crockett, D., 151

Danby, C., 201

De Kock, C. P., 160–61, 164; *Barber of Paris*, 161; *Jean*, 160; *Students*, 161

Demon Huntsman, 91

Devil in London, 20

Dibdin, C., 179

Dickens, C., characterization, 53, 77; Christmas, 80–81; drama, 54, 229; illustrators, 176; influence, 82; intimacy, 58; Overs, 101, 205; reporter, 180; *Thief*, 20; works: *American Notes*, 63–4; *Barnaby Rudge*, 77; *Christmas Carol*, 52, 81; *Martin Chuzzlewit*, 190; *Master Humphrey's Clock*, 76; *Nicholas Nickleby*, 73, 75–6, 159; *Old Curiosity Shop*, 76; *Oliver Twist*, 69–70, 127–8, 130; *Pickwick Papers*, 8, 29, 52–4, 69, 153; *Sketches*, 51; plagiarisms: 51–82 passim, 171, 229; *Cadger's Club*, 65; *Christmas Ghost Story*, 52, 81; *Christmas Log*, 81; *Current American News*, 63–4; *Master Humphrey's Clock*, 75–6; *Scenes from the Life of Nickleby Married*, 77–8; *Nicholas Nickleby*, 59, 75–5; *Old Curiosity Shop*, 55, 76; *Twiss* ('Bos'), 34, 59, 70–72; *Twiss* ('Poz'), 72; *Penny Pickwick*, 34, 51–2, 55, 59, 73; *Mr Pickwick in America*, 62–3; *Wonderful Discovery Club*, 68; (*see also* Egan, Sen., Rede, Reynolds)

Dicks, J., 47, 49

Dixon, J. H., 49

Dodger, 34

Domestic story, 114–134, passim

Doyle, J., 24

Drama, equestrian, 183; magazines, 170–71; melodrama, 171–2; and novels, 171–5; urban, 170; woodcuts, 175–6

Duck, S., 201

Dugdale, R., 201

Dugdale, W., 26–7

Dumas, A., *père*, 48, 159, 161, 169, 230

Duval, C., 185

Dyer, F., 201

Edinburgh, 16, 23, 47

Education, adult, 2–5, 200; British and Foreign Schools Society, 3; Charity Schools, 2–3; National Society, 3; private, 3, 228; Ragged Schools, 3; Sunday Schools, 3, 228 (*see also* Mechanics' Institutes, Methodism)

Egan, P., Sen., reporter, 180; *Life in London*, 68–9, 163; *Pilgrims*, 54, 68
Egan, P., Jun., 113; *Paul Jones*, 156; *Matsys*, 87; *Wat Tyler*, 86
Eliza Cook's Journal, 149, 198
Eliza Grimwood, 120, 187–9
Elliott, E., 48, 85, 204–5, 208–11
Emans, W., 10
Enoch, E., 49, 201
Evangelical Movement, 2

Family Economist, 44
Family Herald, 44–5, 159, 198
Family relationships, 120, 129–30
Fanny Hill's New Friskey Chanter, 26–7, 200
Farthing Journal, 35
Fate of Gaspar, 94
Fatherless Fanny, 130
Faust, 91
Ferrier, S., 121
Féval, P., 159, 165–6
Figaro in London, 20, 22–3, 30, 34, 167
Fitzball, J., 85; *Thalaba*, 87
Forrester, A., 35
France, 62, 159, 230; literature, 159–69, passim; fantasy, 166–7; *feuilleton*, 159; style, 167–8
Friends Tract Association, 137–8, 140
Frost, T., 21, 37, 50, 89, 124, 167; *Emma Mayfield*, 122; *Paul the Poacher*, 34, 122
Furness, R., 201

Gamble, J., 12
Gaskell, E., 147; *Libbie Marsh*, 147–8; *Mary Barton*, 5
Gaspey, W., 201, 209
Germany, literature, 91, 94
Gentleman Jack, 185
Gilbert, J., 47
Giles, S., 201
Godwin, W., 100–101, 158
Glascock, W., 177
Goldsmith, O., 116–17, 130
Gore, Mrs, 104, 121
Grant, C. J., 24, 59

Graves, J., 34
Grey, E. C., 114
Grimm, Brothers, 94
'Guess', *Nickleby Married*, 77–8
Guest, J., 22
Gypsies, 71–2, 124–6, 230

Haddock, J., 52
Hainsforth, W. H., 106–7
Haliburton, T. C., *Clockmaker*, 152
Hall, B., 177
Hall, Spencer T., 85, 201, 211
Harrison, J., 10, 28
Haydon, W., 34
Hazard and Marshall, 138–9
Hazlitt, W., 28
Helme, Mrs, *Farmer of Inglewood Forest*, 117, 120–21, 170
Hero, changing, 198; popular, 53
Heroine, changing, 198; class, 121; description, 128; education, 128; protected, 90; rural, 122; sensibility, 128–9
Hetherington, H., 15, 23, 25, 30, 36
Hewitt, H., 81
Heywood, A., 23, 49, 228
Hill, G. G., 152
Hingston, E. P., 38
Historical fiction, 101–13 passim
Hobson, J., 22
Hodder, G., 62
Hogarth, W., 129
Holcroft, T., 54
Holt, T. L., 34
Holyoake, G. J., 18
Houston, F., 139, 142
Household Words, 44, 49
Howard, E., 177
Howden, W., 22
Howitt, M., 17, 146–7, 150; *Mrs Muggeridge*, 147
Howitt, W., 146, 201, 205
Howitt's Journal, 146–7
Hoxton Sausage, 21
Hucklebridge, J., 26, 34, 188
Hugo, V., 161, 168–9
Hunt, Leigh, 16

Illustrated London News, 41

Inchbald, Mrs, *Nature and Art*, 117, 130

'Infidel press', 16–17, 47

Ingraham, J., 154, 156

Ingram, H., 40, 229

Insanity, 116

Jack Tench, 178

James, G. P. R., 106

Janin, J., 159

Jerrold, D., 62, 178; *Black-eye'd Susan*, 178

Jews, 104, 124

Johnson, W., 91

Jones, H. M., 11, 122; *Gipsy Chief*, 124

Judson, E. Z. C., 156; *King of the Sea*, 156–8; *Mysteries*, 165

Kean, E., 175

Kelly, T., 10

Kentish, Mrs, *Maid*, 122

Kenworthy, J., 201

Kildare Place Tract Society, 6

Kingsley, C., 48, 146, 206

Knight, C., 11, 35–6

Lackington, J., 11–12

Lady Hamilton, 179

Lancashire Beacon, 48

Lancaster, J., 3

Last, J., 35

Lee, E., 52

Lewes, G. H., 4, 52

Lewis, M. G., *Bravo*, 98; *Monk*, 91, 94

Libraries, church, 5, 228; circulating (middle class), 6; circulating (lower class), 6; coffee house, 8–9, 228; contents, 5–8; factory, 5; Mechanics' Institute, 5; public houses, 8; school, 5–6; shop, 6–7

Lillo, G., *London Merchant*, 114

Limbird, J., 12, 228

Lindridge, J., *Jack Rann*, 185

Linton, W. J., 30, 75–6

Little Orphan Annie, 51

Lloyd, E., 28, 30, 34, 37, 41, 49, 51, 228

Lloyd's Illustrated London Newspaper, 41, 229

Lloyd's Penny Sunday Times, 39, 41

Lloyd's Penny Weekly Miscellany, 37, 41–3

Locke, J., 2

London, publishing centre, 21–2

London Journal, 45–8, 159, 198

London Pioneer, 48, 159

Lorraine, P., 'Ordinary of Newgate', 27, 182

Love in fiction, 115–16

Love and Crime, 84, 89, 94, 97, 103

Lovett, W., 5, 147

Lucy Neale, 153

Lytton, E. G. E. L., 177, 205

MacGowan, G., 10

Mackenzie, H., 97

Macree, G. W., 8, 49

Manchester, periodicals, 22, 49

Mann, publisher, 22

Mansell, G., 37

Marriott, E. F., *Black-eye'd Susan*, 178

Marryat, F., 177

Marten, Maria, 125

Mason, J., 140

Mathews, C., 54, 151

Maturin, 91, 158

Maurice, F. D., 146

Mayhew, H., 19–20; *London Labour*, 71, 135

Mechanics' Institutes, 25, 68, 101, 201

Meteyard, E., 147, 149–50

Methodism, 3, 137–40, 145 (*see also* Wesleyan Tract Assn)

Miles, H. D., *Dick Turpin*, 180, 182–3; journalist, 19, 180

Miller, T., 49, 85, 201, 205; *Giles*, 120, 123–4; *Malvern*, 123; *Mysteries*, 165

Millhouse, R., 201–2, 206

Milton, J., 89, 112–13, 230

Minerva Press, 83, 115

Moncreiff, W. T., 152

Montague, E., *Demon of Sicily*, 89–90

Montgomery, J., 201

Morality in popular fiction, 90–91, 108–9, 134, 161, 199–200
More, H., 137–8, 141
'Moore, T.', 87
Music halls, 55–6, 176–7, 188–9
Mysteries of the Forest, 91
Mysteries of Old St Paul's, 33

Napier, W. F., 27
National Omnibus, 20, 23–4
Naval romances, 177–9 passim
Neale, J. W., 177
Nell Gwynne, 34
Nelson, T., 11
Newgate Calendar, 182
Newton, J. H., 86
Nicholson, J., 201–2
Nicholson, R., 35, 188–9; *Cockney Adventures*, 26, 180; *Dombey*, 11, 79–80, 180; *Town*, 26
North, C., 2, 4
Northern Star, 48
Novel Newspaper, 28, 30
Novelist, 28
Novelist's Magazine 10, 28
Novelist's and Romancist Library, 28
Novello, Mrs V., 148
Number books, 9–10 (*see also* periodicals)

Odd Fellow, 21, 30, 51
Olio, 13
Opie, Mrs, *Father and Daughter*, 116–17
Orr, W. S., 17
Outsiders of Society, 199
Overs, J., 101, 205
Owen, R., 206

Paine, T. (publisher), 30, 33
Paine, T. (Radical), 136
Paper, 12, 35–6
Parley's Penny Library, 76
Parlour Library, 199
Paternoster Row, 21, 139
Patriot, 135–6
Patriot Bride, 155
Penny Magazine, 17–18, 150

Penny Punch, 20
Penny Satirist, 48
Penny Storyteller, 39
Penny-a-liners, 180
People's Journal, 146–7
Percy Anecdotes, 32
Periodicals, circulation, 22–3, 30–31, 36, 229; correspondence columns, 37, 46; early, 9, 12–13, 28; economics, 9–10, 12–13, 19–21, 33, 35, 37, 45, 214; editing, 19; escapism, 72–3; *feuilleton*, 159; juvenile, 50, 199; number books, 9–11; payment to authors, 37–8; readership, 23, 42, 49–50, 199; style, 38, 104, 106, 167–8, 180–81; Sunday, 39
Pitt, G. D., *Todd*, 190; *Wreck of the Heart*, 114, 117, 122
Pixerécourt, R.-C. G. de, 172, 231
Place, F., 27
Plumb, S., 201
Poe, E. A., 154, 157
Pocock, I., *Miller*, 171
Politics for the People, 146
Poole, T., *Little Peddlington*, 4, 201
Poor Man's Guardian, 15, 24, 199
Pornography, 26–7, 33–4, 199–200
Pratt, J. S., 22, 228
Prest, T. P., 29, 38, 229; *Death Grasp*, 84, 95; *Ela*, 29, 75, 113, 121, 125–6 (drama), 171; *Emily Fitzormond*, 90 (drama), 171; *Gallant Tom*, 179; *Gipsy Boy*, 96, 125; *Hebrew Maiden*, 104; *Jew and Foundling*, 104; *Maniac Father*, 116–17, 120; *Miser of Shoreditch* (novel, drama), 172, 174–5; *Old House*, 193; *Sweeney Todd*, 191; *Vice and Victim*, 117; (*see also* 'Bos')
Prince, J. C., 201–4
Printing, 12, 19, 33, 36
Prompter, 16
Publishing, 21–2, 25, 33–6 (*see also* Periodicals)
Punch, 20, 23–4, 167
Purkess, G., Sen., 22

Queen's Magazine, 42

Radcliffe, Mrs A., *Italian*, 97–8; *Udolpho*, 90–91, 127
Radicals, 14–15, 48, 57–8, 64, 85, 159, 205–6, 230 (*see also* Chartism)
Raikes, R., 3
Rathbone, Mrs, 150
Raumer, F. von, 12
Reading rooms, 9
Red Cross Warrior, 102
Rede, W. Leman, *Pickwick*, 54; *Royal Rake*, 39, 108
Religious Tract Society, 6, 138–9, 142–3
Republican, 48
Retribution, 82
Reynolds, G. W. M., 45–6, 49, 85, 89, 113, 167, 229, 231, 243; *Days of Hogarth*, 129; Dickens, 82; *Faust*, 91; *Grace Darling*, 46; heroines, 128–9; *Master Timothy's Book-Case*, 61, 64, 78–9; *Mysteries of the Court of London*, 47, 109; *Mysteries of London*, 46, 165, 167–8, 193–4; *Noctes Pickwickianae*, 64; *Pickwick Abroad*, 59–62, 230; *Pickwick Married*, 64; *Political Instructor*, 48; *Reynolds's Miscellany*, 46–7, 198; *Tee-totaller*, 64; *Wagner*, 46, 91
Reynolds, S., 124
Richardson, S., 29, 89, 116
Richmond, Rev. Legh, 143–4
Ridley, J., 87
Riding, E., 201–2
'Rip Rap', *Monument*, 108
Robinson, H., 23
Roche, Mrs, *Children of Abbey*, 128
Romancist and Novelist's Library, 28
Ross, J. W., 47
Rousseau, J. J., *Emile*, 2; *Pygmalion*, 171
Routledge, G., 12, 228
Rymer, J. M., 38, 41–2, 77, 113, 158, 229; *Ada*, 43, 130, 132, 198; *Black Monk*, 98–9, 103, 113, 172; *Jane Brightwell*, 115; *Lady in Black*, 193–4; *Mystery in Scarlet*, 42;

Varney, 42, 99–101, 172; *White Slave*, 8, 136, 145, 158

Sala, G. A., 176
Sand, G., 159–60, 169
St-Pierre, B. de, 122
St-John, P. B., 158
Saturday Magazine, 18, 140
Saunders, J., 146–7
Schiller, F., 182
Scribe, E., 159
Scott, M., 177
Scott, W., 102–3; *Beauties of Scott*, 102; *Chase*, 94; dramatizations, 103–4; *Guy Mannering*, 125; *Ivanhoe*, 99, 102–4, 110
Seymour, R., 20, 29, 53
Shakespeare, W., 125, 175
Shelley, P. B., 85–6, 207, 224
Sheppard, J., 186–7, 244
Shepherd (publisher), 22, 49
Sheridan, F., 87
Sherwood, Mrs, 141
Le Siècle, 159
Silver Fork Novels, 121
Sinnett, W., 33–4
Slang, 198
Smith, Albert, 7
Smith, Charles, 20
Smith, C. M., 19, 39, 139
Smith, Horace, 109
Smith, J. F., 39, 47, 109, 230; *Minnigrey*, 47; *Stanfield Hall*, 47, 109–13, 175
Smith, Seba, 152, 154
Smith, J. G., 22
Smollett, T., 177
S.D.U.K., 18
S.P.C.K., 6, 18, 138–9, 142
S.S.V., 27
Soldier, 135
Soulié, F., 159; *She-Tiger*, 34, 166
Southey, R., 85; *Amadis*, 88; Elliott, 204–5; *Joan*, 85; *Thalaba* (incl. plagiarisms, etc.), 30, 87, 230; *Uneducated Poets*, 204; *Wat Tyler*, 85, 87
Spenser, E., 88

Steill, B., 22
Stevenson, R. L., 42
Stiff, G., 45, 49
Stockdale, J. J., 26
Stokes, G., 143
Stokes, T., 3
Strange, W., 21-2, 30, 39, 47, 52
Sue, E., 48, 161, 169; *Brulart*, 162; *Female Bluebeard*, 162; *Martin*, 48; *Mysteries*, 164, 167, 193, 231; *Seven Sins*, 159-60; *Wandering Jew*, 162-3
Summers, M., 83
Sunday Times, 39, 167
Sweeney Todd, 190-91

Tales of the Drama, 171
Thackeray, W. M., 1, 24-5, 27, 39; tracts, 136, 143
Tee-Total Times, 149
Tegg, T., 11, 83
Tell-Tale, 13
Theatrical Times, 170
Thief, 20-21, 98
Thomas, J., 55
Thompson, C., 5, 17
Thornley, H., 198
Tompkins, J. M. S., 125
Tonna, Mrs, 141
Toulmin, C., 146
Town, 26
T(ownsend?), W. T., 179
Tracts, 135-45, 231; circulation, 140-41; death-bed, 144; distribution, 135, 145; entertaining, 142-3, 144, 230; morbidity, 144; readership, 135-6, 140-41, 145; societies (various), 138
Tract Magazine, 141

Turpin, R. (Dick), 183, 185

Unhappy Bride, 157-8
Urban culture, decoration, 107-8; humour, 24; in literature, 192-4, 197-8; industrial, 1-2, 32; intimacy, 21; morals, 90, 117, 120; poetry, 210; prospects, 200; reading, 14-15, 25, 29, 32; supernatural, 94-5
Utilitarians, 4-5

Viar, J., 22
Vickers, A., 47
Vickers, G., Sen., 33, 45-7
Vickers, G., Jun., 49
Vidocq, 164
Viles, E., *Midge*, 64-5
Virtue, G., 10

Walpole, H., *Otranto*, 96
Watson, J., 16, 22-3, 30, 36, 85, 149
Watts, J., 22
Watts, W. H., 181
Weld, C. R., 30
Wertham, F., 192
West, W., 53
Wesley, J., 137
Wesleyan Methodist Tract Society, 138, 140, 145
White, T., 36
Wilson, H., 26
Wight, J., 181
Wilkie, W., 176
Wirth, L., 32
Woodcuts, 24, 53, 107-8, 176
Wordsworth, W., 85, 205
Working Man's Friend, 25, 149, 198

More about Penguins and Pelicans

Penguinews, which appears every month, contains details of all the new books issued by Penguins as they are published. From time to time it is supplemented by *Penguins in Print*, which is a complete list of all available books published by Penguins. (There are well over four thousand of these.)

A specimen copy of *Penguinews* will be sent to you free on request. For a year's issues (including the complete lists) please send 30p if you live in the United Kingdom, or 60p if you live elsewhere. Just write to Dept EP, Penguin Books Ltd, Harmondsworth, Middlesex, enclosing a cheque or postal order, and your name will be added to the mailing list.

Note: *Penguinews* and *Penguins in Print* are not available in the U.S.A. or Canada

Victorian Cities

ASA BRIGGS

'Our age is pre-eminently the age of great cities' – Robert Vaughan (1843)

In 1837 England and Wales boasted only five provincial cities of more than 100,000 inhabitants: by 1891 there were twenty-three and they housed nearly a third of the nation. Meantime London had expanded two and a third times.

Neither were these Victorian cities 'insensate' ant-heaps, as Lewis Mumford has called them. As this century progresses we can better appreciate the energy and civic purpose which created the cities of the nineteenth century.

In this revised and augmented edition of his companion to *Victorian People*, Professor Asa Briggs concentrates his inquiry on Manchester, Leeds, Birmingham, Middlesbrough, Melbourne (representing Victorian communities overseas), and London, the world city. Between these cities of the age of railways, trams, drains, and gas there are superficial resemblances in their problems of housing and sanitation, location of suburbs, schools, town halls, and churches: but Professor Briggs points up the differences too, and he provides us with a fascinating contrast between Manchester and Birmingham, as their civic courses diverged economically, socially, and politically.

Not for sale in the U.S.A.

Victorian People

ASA BRIGGS

'With this book Asa Briggs makes good his right to be regarded and respected as one of the leading historians of the Victorian Age' – G. M. Young, author of *Victorian England*

That 'Victorian' need no longer be considered a derogatory word is made very plain by Professor Brigg's reassessments of people, ideas, and events between the Great Exhibition of 1851 and the Second Reform Act of 1967.

A few of his chapter headings indicate the type of personality on whom the author has based a fresh viewpoint of the period: 'John Arthur Roebuck and the Crimean War', 'Samuel Smiles and the Gospel of Work', 'Thomas Hughes and the Public Schools', 'Robert Applegarth and the Trade Unions', 'John Bright and the Creed of Reform', 'Benjamin Disraeli and the Leap in the Dark'.

Recounted with unusual clarity and humour, the story of their achievements conjures up an enviable picture of progress and independence and adds substantially to the ordinary reader's knowledge of the last century.

'A warm and vivid book, as readable as it is well informed' – *New York Herald Tribune*

Not for sale in the U.S.A.

THE PENGUIN ENGLISH LIBRARY

Charles Dickens

BARNABY RUDGE

Edited by Gordon Spence

Barnaby Rudge was Dickens's first attempt at an historical novel – *A Tale of Two Cities* being the only other – and was strongly influenced by the work of Sir Walter Scott. Written in times of Chartist unrest and set in the period of the Gordon riots, it allowed Dickens to work out imaginatively two of his major preoccupations, private murder and public violence, and the scenes in which an infuriated mob storms through the streets of London and burns down Newgate prison are among the most vivid he ever wrote. But many other strands are woven into the narrative and the strength of the book lies in the variety of interests that it offers and the diversity and vividness of its characters.

THE PICKWICK PAPERS

Edited by Robert L. Patten

G. K. Chesterton described *The Pickwick Papers* as 'something nobler than a novel', which emitted 'that sense of everlasting youth – a sense as of the gods gone wandering in England', and it has been said of the book's reception: 'It is doubtful if any other single work of letters before or since has ever aroused such wild and widespread enthusiasm.' This was the book which carried the 24-year-old Dickens to fame, introduced him to his illustrator, 'Phiz' (Hablot K. Browne), and created, in Mr Pickwick and Sam Weller, characters who have become part of the English mythology. This journey from innocence to experience by the portly middle-aged hero and his guide and mentor, though it contains darker hints, is essentially a young man's book – buoyant, cheerful and ultimately optimistic about human nature.

Charles Dickens

LITTLE DORRIT

Edited by John Holloway

Little Dorrit (1856/7) is one of that handful of masterpieces of Dickens's maturity in which his imaginative genius embraces the whole fabric of a changing society. The Marshalsea, Bleeding Heart Yard, and the Circumlocution Office are only the principal features of a landscape drawn with all his awareness of and delight in the multitudinously refracted surfaces of life. Embedded though it is in the social and political preoccupations of the time, *Little Dorrit* goes far beyond the political. With little hope for change in society itself, Dickens's vision in this novel is of a world of hypocrisy and sham, of exploiters and parasites – a world of prisons, real and metaphysical, in which reality itself is imprisoned by appearances.

HARD TIMES

Edited by David Craig

Hard Times, which has never achieved the popularity and seldom the recognition of Dickens's other novels, is his withering portrait of a Lancashire milltown in the 1840s. In the persons of Gradgrind and Bounderby he powerfully stigmatized the prevalent philosophy of Utilitarianism which, whether in school or factory, allowed human beings to be caged in a dreary scenery of brick terraces and foul chimneys, to be enslaved to machines, and reduced to numbers.

'It has a kind of perfection as a work of art that we don't associate with Dickens – a perfection that is one with the sustained and complete seriousness for which among his productions it is unique . . . The prose is that of one of the greatest masters of English, and the dialogue – very much a test in such an undertaking – is consummate; beautifully natural in its stylization' – F. R. Leavis in *The Great Tradition*

Charles Dickens

THE OLD CURIOSITY SHOP

With an introduction by Malcolm Andrews

In its day the death of 'Boz's Little Nelly' drew tears from the thousands who read it. Nearer our own time, it prompted Oscar Wilde to remark that one must have a heart of stone to read it without laughing. Wilde's judgement has prevailed, so far as Nell is concerned, yet it has given the book a reputation for morbid sentimentality that represents only a small part of the truth.

The Old Curiosity Shop very often shows Dickens at his best, particularly in his handling of the grotesque, the bizarre and the comic. If Nell attracted from her creator an admiration that we can no longer share, Quilp, Dick Swiveller and the others in the great gallery of rogues and eccentrics attracted his genius and his daemonic energy. In this novel of light and darkness, it is the creatures who lurk in the shade that give it its immense vitality.